A CUBAN FROM KANSAS

A Mosaic

Armando Simon

I0561651

© 2008, 2014
Published by Lulu Publishers
Morrisville, North Carolina

ISBN: 978-0-6152-1791-8

I

He was holding on to a record, staring at it. Just staring at it. His mind had been wandering all day and it continued to do so. It was not just any record but his only---his last---48 rpm record. It was inside its khaki green rough cardboard cover. The record was unique, unlike any of his other 200-plus LP records. LP stood for long playing: they went at the slower velocity of 33 1/3 rpm and could play for a much longer time. They were lighter, flexible, and unbreakable. Better. The 48s were heavier, rigid and easily breakable. He had had many others in the past, a present from his aunt---from her younger years, she had said to him---but, unavoidably, they had accidentally broken, one by one, until he now had the last fragile one out of a dozen or so. Before receiving this present from his aunt in his later years, he had wondered as a child why the old cartoons had at times shown records being thrown at a cartoon character, shattering. None of the records that the boy was acquainted with could break (no matter how much he tried). At best, they warped and became wavy when a couple had been forgotten and left inside the car on a hot summer day. Then, after he received the collection of 48-rpm records and one broke in his hand when he jammed it down on the phonograph, he understood.

Anyway, they did not sell records in record stores any more. They sold metallic CDs, compact discs, which were better than regular records. Just like the LP records had been better than the 48s.

He came to with a start, as he had done several times that day. He gingerly put the record down on its rack next to the other records and sighed. He realized that he had unconsciously picked up the record because of the struggle that was going on with him.

His aunt had died. In dying, she had left him her huge Victorian home. Its furnishings and savings she left to a cousin of his, her aunt having been childless. The cousin had already come and gone.

And now he was torn apart, because a developer wanted to buy the property in order to tear it down and build something or other and had offered him a very nice sum.

Evans was in his forties and had a year ago gone through a messy divorce, from which he was just recovering. He wanted a fresh start, away from this worthless, backwaters state. New York, maybe, or California. Maybe Oregon. Somewhere where it was bustling. This money would easily realize his goal.

Except . . . that he was not sure. It seemed wrong, somehow.

Part of it was that he had such good memories of that old house.

Both he and some of his friends had, at different times, remarked that the old saying was really true that, anymore, "you can't go back." Old schools, old dance halls, old neighborhoods that had held such poignant memories, when he or his friends had returned years later to relive those same feelings, the people in those areas had physically changed, radically so, or had moved away to greener pastures, usually out of state. Or the schools had been altered, radically so. Or the dance halls (chock full of love memories and might-have-been memories) had been razed to the ground in order to build a parking lot and a Kentucky Fried Chicken.

And it was not that the change had been for the worse. No! Rather, it was that something had simply been taken away, something terribly personal, that could not be shared with anyone else because no one could have understood what that particular spot on a warm May evening had meant to a young boy who is soon about to enter the world as a young man, full of eager excitement and boundless optimism. No two people have the same memories, or the same experience, and, so, each is unique.

And now Evans was being asked to agree--- not forced to, mind you, but asked to---to rip out the physical manifestation of a part of his life and, try as he might, he could not become completely callused over the transaction.

He got in his car and drove towards his aunt's house. He was supposed to meet Mister Vittorini there. He drove slowly since he had plenty of time and since he was still torn by indecision.

Driving down Douglas Avenue, on an impulse, he stopped opposite a nondescript museum. He had been there once before, years ago. If one did not read the small sign outside, anyone would think that this museum was just another two storied residence like the homes to the left and right of it.

He entered. It was quiet. Empty. Nothing razzle-dazzle. No Surround sound. No dinosaur animatronics. Quite simply, each large room, roped off with a thick, burgundy velvet cordon, contained the mundane home furnishings of a typical home a century or so ago. It was always nostalgic going through the place, even though he had never lived at that time, and this in itself was curious. Nevertheless, the furnishings looked homey.

Friendly. Welcoming. And it was also intellectually stimulating to see household objects that had since all but vanished, or transformed out of all recognition.

A smiling elderly woman came from the back of the house and welcomed him.

"I'm sorry. I didn't hear you come in. You're welcomed to look through the house."

"Thank you."

He strolled around, asking the name and the usefulness of certain items and she quietly named and explained.

At one point, Evans said, "It's a shame a lot of these things are no longer around."

"Yes, that's true," she agreed. "But you know what's interesting? Our own things that we grew up with are going down the same route: black and white television, pogo sticks, the hoola-hoop. I still have one of those old, huge, tape recorders; it's funny putting it next to a modern, tiny cassette recorder."

"Kids nowadays don't see any of the old films if they're in black and white. My kids refuse to see Laurel and Hardy, or Abbott and Costello films. I try to tell them that today's skateboard and video games may be tomorrow's Daniel Boone caps, or 3-D glasses, and they look at me like they don't even know what I'm talking about."

"It's a shame, really," he agreed.

"Yes, it's a shame with so many other things. Square dancing, for example, is disappearing. And that used to be so much fun! Banjo music has disappeared. And for that matter letter writing."

"Letter writing?" Evans frowned.

"Yes. Plain writing---I mean to friends and

relatives. It's a lost art. Now, all one has to do is pick up the phone and call."

"Ah . . . yeah. You're right! I hadn't stopped to think about it."

The lady just smiled. It was obvious that working here had given her a lot of time to think on this subject.

The man had begun to feel uneasy and felt that he had to leave, so he bid her farewell and left.

He stopped briefly at *Cero's*, the unsurpassed candy store, a family business of two generations, that he had patronized since childhood and splurged (his favorite item, white butter rolls, could throw a hummingbird into a diabetic coma). The owner mentioned that the new highway construction on Kellogg might put him out of business and Evans showed the proper amount of concern and then left for his destination.

As he drove, he began to curse himself for syrupy sweet sentimentality. He was practically wallowing in it! His aunt was dead. He needed a new start in life. The money was good. He was just being maudlin---that was a new word that he had picked up.

This was America. What was important was the future.

Nevertheless, when he got there, he suddenly realized that the house's destruction would not only affect him personally but probably scores of individuals as well. The property probably had a lot of emotional significance to others. It was almost a landmark.

It was a large, pretty Victorian house with gables and a wooden wraparound porch, the kind that you rarely see any more, going all the way around the house.

Mister Vittorini was there waiting for him, ready to buy the whole lot for four times what Evans could have otherwise sold it for. The sum being offered was nothing to sneeze at.

They shook hands, greeting each other, went into some small talk before Evans came to what was troubling him.

"See, now, Mister Vittorini, it's not that I'm trying to get more money for the property. I'm not. It's just that I'm not sure that it's the right thing to do! You see, there's a lot of feelings behind this old house."

"I understand. They don't make houses like this any more. It's usually a bunch of boxes stuck together that they call a house. Modular, they call it. I don't blame you. If I myself bought it instead of doing it for a company, I'd be half tempted to chuck the deal and move in it myself." He chuckled.

Now Evans began to feel anxious that the deal was slipping away. "It's not that I don't want to, see. It's like I said, I'm not entirely sure. It's such a fine old house."

"Mister Evans, I want you to do what you think is right. But let me tell you about a trip I made this summer to Rome, OK? You ever been to Rome?"

Evans shook his head.

"Well, it was my first trip there. I'm Italian-American, so I thought I'd go over and see what the place looked like. And Evans, let me tell you, that city is old. I mean *old! Unnecessarily* old."

"People live in buildings which are *ugly.* Cracked. Dilapidated. They are one or two, maybe four, centuries old. Musty. It'd be one thing if the buildings were pretty, but they give a new meaning to the word 'ugly.' Nobody tears down anything old to build something new. *Europe is old.* All of it. Not just the museums and the cathedrals, but people's homes. It's decrepit."

"I went to Belgium. I did the tourist bit. On one tour they took us to some place where little old ladies make lace that *nobody* wants, but the whole thing's paid by the government to keep it alive. They don't want that lace making skill to disappear. Well, it *should* disappear. It's obsolete. An anachronism."

"Well, here in this country we look towards the future," said the visionary.

"And I'll tell you another thing! This state needs to attract industries and businesses. There's no reason on Earth why we can't compete in the near future with New York or California!"

"But, wait, do we really want Wichita to be like New York City, or Los Angeles, or Chicago, or New Orleans with all the smog and crime and traffic jams?" Evans countered and Vittorini sobered up.

"No, of course not," he replied in a much calmer vein.

"I think that we've got it pretty good in this here state, though New Yorkers see us as hicks," Evans added. "They're rude jerks anyway, so who cares what they think?"

Regardless, Evans knew that the sale was certain. He was just postponing the inevitable and he knew it. So did Vittorini.

The developer's office was nearby.

An hour later, he was driving home in an exultant mood, periodically glancing at the check in one hand. He had trouble believing the amount and kept looking at the zeros to make sure that it was true and that the check was real. All doubts had vanished from his mind. Vittorini had been right. The past can have an unhealthy stranglehold on a person.

He bounded out of his car, feeling happy and making all sorts of plans in his mind for a bright new future. He felt like celebrating! He poured himself a brandy snifter filled to the rim with Amaretto and decided to put on some loud music---really loud. In his exuberance he accidentally broke the last 48 rpm record.

"No matter," he told himself. "It was old. Anyway, I can now replace all of my old records with brand new CDs. They're better. Don't know why I've held on to these vinyl records for so long." And he put in a compact disc into the player, turning up the volume so loud that it drowned everything else.

II

"I said it before, it's out of the question! It's not even up for discussion! Do you understand me?!" Enodesto screamed to his son as he banged his hand on the dinner table, palm down. Even palm down all the utensils and dishes clinked with one another.

This explosive outburst startled all of us at the dinner table. We had been invited to one of their dinners, which was a reciprocation for one of our dinners, which had been a reciprocation for one of their dinners, which . . . . Anyway, Octavio, my teenage son, had innocently enough, asked Enodesto's son, Ramon, how he was enjoying his part-time job of bar tendering.

12

"Great!" Ramon had replied. "I'm making a lot of money in tips alone and all the girls come over to flirt with me. I'm making so much money, I don't see why I have to stay in school, I think it'd make more sense to drop out of school and work full-time at the job."

That had precipitated Enodesto's outburst, which had made us jump up in our seats with forks in our hands.

"I said it before, it's out of the question! It's not even up for discussion! Do you understand me?"

"Enodesto, calm down!! Lower your voice!" Olivia screamed back at her husband.

Not knowing when to leave well enough alone, Ramon kept on arguing, thinking that perhaps with guests present, his father would be cowed.

"But you have to admit that it makes perfect sense! The IRS doesn't deduct my tips for income tax and I make quite a lot of money. The clientele is good, it's not a riff-raff bar."

"I said no, and I meant it, dammit!" he again pounded the table as he roared, livid with color. "No son of mine is going to be a high school dropout! You're not only going to finish high school, but you're going to college! I don't care what profession you choose, medicine, psychology, biology, mathematics, or astronomy, but you're going to go to college and become a professional! Your father is a professor of literature, your uncle is an engineer and your other uncle is a doctor, your aunts are teachers, your mother is a nurse and your grandfather was a historian. I'll be damned if you end up as a bartender for the rest of your life mixing stinking drinks to stinking drunks!!"

"I don't see anything wrong with being a bartender. I like mixing drinks, I'm very good at it," Ramon persisted, oblivious to the fact that his father had not become restrained at al by our presence and was in fact, red as a beet and the veins on his temples were throbbing.

I cut in, trying to mollify the situation. "It's not that your father's saying that there's anything wrong with being a bartender, it's that he's got higher hopes for you, Ramon. You're a smart boy and you have to admit that it doesn't take much brains to mix drinks---even if it is fun. Sure, now it's fun because it's something new and the girls are after you and it's a good club, but five years from now, it'll be just another dreary job, a dull routine with no challenge for you and you may end up in a sleazy bar with knife fights and who knows what else?"

"Besides, everyone that I've met that ever dropped out of school has later regretted it. Everyone. No exceptions."

"See? See?" said Enodesto, still agitated, "Listen to what this man says, he's a psychologist, a professional!"

I tried to go on. "Besides, your father's not being unreasonable. He's not telling you what profession you have to be in, just that you *be* a professional. Just the same as I've done with Octavio." Octavio was being quiet throughout all this, apparently cowed by having unknowingly triggered the storm.

"Besides," Olivia joined in, "you should maintain our family's tradition. We've all become professionals, your uncles and aunts included."

"But it means that I have to wait four more years to get a degree once I go to college! It's a waste of time when I could be earning money instead."

"There'll be time enough to work once you get your degree," Enodesto replied in a much calmer vein. "Believe me, there'll come a time when you'll ask yourself if that's all that you ever do. Besides, I'm not asking you to pay for the schooling, I'll pay for that and for the housing and the books and the food. I don't mind it at all! We don't need the money from your job, but you can keep the job is you get such a kick out of it and you can use the money as spending money for your dates and entertainment, as you originally planned."

"What is going on here," I amiably suggested to his father, "is that Ramon has absorbed the American work ethic that says that you're not really a man until you've gotten a steady fulltime job. But, do you know," I now looked at Ramon, "that I have a friend who is paying all the expenses for his son in Madrid, who is going full time to medical school, even though he is married and has children?"

"You've got to be joking!" my own son exclaimed with disbelief and disgust. I looked at him out of the corner of my eye, realizing how Americanized he looked.

The talk at dinner continued more pleasantly but I noticed that Ramon remained sullen since he had not found a single ally there, not even Octavio, who was going to the university that fall, as was Ramon.

It was a month and a half later that the dispute between father and son came to a head. I learned the details from my wife, who had called up Olivia to gossip about something else.

Apparently, what had happened was that

Ramon had been openly muttering both at work and at school about his disagreements with his father and his friends on both ends had been filling his ear with advice and suggestions. From them he learned that once he reached "the legal age," he could become independent; he could vote, he could legally open up a bank account, own property, he could take himself out of school, all without his parents' signature. One of the waitresses at work, barely containing herself with anticipation, had offered him an invitation to stay with her in her two-bedroom apartment and supposedly split the rent and utilities. Being ten years his senior and Ramon himself being a very handsome young man, she was licking her chops at the prospect of having him all to herself to weeks and months to come. She was most definitely looking forward with much eagerness at wearing him down to a nub and had pressed him to move out and "cut the umbilical cord," as she put it.

In Ramon's mind, all the cards were in his favor. He had a good job, a place to stay, legal status and could now get out from under his parents' thumb. Except that he forgot that while Americans are even-tempered and legalistic to a fault, his parents were not Americans.

So right after dinner, he told his parents everything that he had found out and announced that he was moving out that very same night. Having announced his apparent *fait accompli*, he turned around and marched right to his room to pack up his belongings. But while Olivia was being overtaken by grief, Enodesto lost all control of himself, kicked open Ramon's door and proceeded to beat the living daylights out of his son with his fists. He had Ramon pinned down on the floor, punching his bloody face in and screaming at the top of his voice when Olivia, herself screaming, tried to drag her husband away from the boy. Not being strong enough, she then interposed her body with that of her son and it was then that Enodesto had snapped out of it.

His face a bloody mess, they took Ramon to the hospital. The nose was definitely fractured and it was decided to operate in a few days in order to repair it.

This was essentially the gist of it. I am leaving out all the names that she called her husband, among which "savage," "animal" and "beast" kept recurring.

My wife told her that we would be stopping by the hospital to see Ramon and so we did, later on that afternoon.

Parking the car, we crossed the street and approached the hospital. In front of the entrance, looking the picture of remorse, was Enodesto, apparently out for a breath of fresh air, away from the hospital smells. We awkwardly greeted him, asked how Ramon was and in what room, but did not mention the reason for his being there. My wife and son went on up to the room while I stayed with our dejected friend.

"Not exactly the type of counseling that you'd recommend, is it?" he asked me with a wan smile. "Well, what do you think? Do you agree with my wife, that I'm a savage?"

"I stopped making judgments about people a long time ago," I responded and he looked away, disappointed at my noncommittal answer. What he thought or felt I did not know, though I certainly should have asked. I was feeling a little awkward, you know how it is when you're caught in a family squabble.

No, I did not usually recommend nose breaking as a form of counseling in situations such as that between Enodesto and his son. And yet . . . and yet . . . .

All that I have related happened a few years ago. Today, Octavio and Ramon are graduating from the university, Ramon doing so with a *summa cum laude* in chemistry, Octavio *cum laude* in psychology.

Enodesto's son has turned down a very lucrative offer from Dupont in order to go on and get his Master's degree prior to settling down to work.

They say that he is very good at mixing chemicals.

III

The pilot of the KLM airplane announced that they had passed the Cuban air space and they were now over international waters and would soon be arriving in Miami. At this, a spontaneous cheer went up in the passenger section with whistling, clapping and shouts of "Viva la Libertad! Viva Cuba Libre!"

Among the passengers was a scared ten-year-old boy, out of habit too scared to join in the general cheering for fear that his particular expression might be noticed by a member of the Communist secret police. Of course, at this point, this was an unrealistic fear, but it was a habitual one for which the outcome had been self-preservation for him and his family.

Incidentally, neither the pilots nor the passengers had been aware that a man had attempted to stow away in the section of the plane where the tires fold into the wing and had, instead, fallen to his death.

Since the boy did not have any family in the United States, the Catholic Church automatically had taken him under its wing (as it had done this with other children once before with the Hungarian refugees of 1956) and sought out a sponsor. It had done this with thousands of other Cuban children sent over in a scramble by their parents during the early sixties (for all their many faults, Cubans are very family oriented and love their children dearly, so the fear and desperation that would prompt a father and mother to frantically throw their children out of their own home *and* country and into another, unknown environment, with no idea when they would be reunited can only be imagined; two hundred unaccompanied children a week were at one point arriving at Miami).

The boy did not have to wait for long, Americans being a kindly and generous people, and Kansans being the friendliest of them all, a family was quickly found in Kansas who would gladly take care of the boy until his parents escaped from Castro's clutches and off he went to a place that neither he nor his parents had ever heard off, one month to the day of his having arrived in Miami.

The poor child deplaned in Kansas in mid-November in the midst of a cold front. At that time, passengers used to walk across the tarmac from the airplane to the airport building (a cold front from Canada through the Midwest is always accompanied by continuous Arctic wind which feels, at best, like a razor-sharp knife is vivisecting you). He had taken four steps away from the mobile stairs used for deplaning passengers (which was the custom in those days in all airports) and stopped, shivering. He had never encountered this kind of weather before in his life and it was as if his body had stopped its power of movement, or his mind its ability to think. All that he could do was stand, shivering, with tears down his narrowed eyes (from the wind) and his arms around his little chest, with its short sleeve shirt, cheeks bright pink with cold.

A passenger behind him saw him and took in the situation at once. He swiftly took off his own coat and wrapped it around the boy, ignoring the sharpness of the wind on his own body until the boy warmed up enough to walk the rest of the way into the warm building, at which time a priest took over, thanking him for his act of kindness.

The priest, thereupon, gave him a coat which was slightly large---but which was certainly better than too little---and introduced himself in Spanish as Father Diego. On the way from the airport in a station wagon, he asked him about his family and conditions in Cuba and informed him about the family with whom he would be staying outside a nearby town, called Hutchinson.

Once in the rectory, he called up the family to come over and he tried to make him feel as comfortable as possible, repeatedly reassuring him about his foster family and that he would visit him every other day.

Mister Hansen, the temporary "father," was a meat packer in Wichita and knew no Spanish. His wife did, but her high school Spanish was sorely tested by the Cuban boy's machine-gun style of Cuban Spanish. Once he was convinced to slow down, though, some communication was possible.

Part of his excitement had been at seeing Mrs. Hansen; with her fair skin, platinum hair and blue eyes, Osbaldo thought that she was the most beautiful woman that he had ever seen.

On his way to his new home, outside the city, he was struck by the flatness and treelessness of the landlocked prairie. And no sea coast! And no palm trees!

And the silence! The silence of the prairie was deafening. To a Cuban, *any* silence was unnerving.

It was all so different from the tropical island that was his home.

It was the first of many adjustments to make. And, in the months to come, if he missed the mameys, the guarapos, the flans and the churros (and he did), at least it was made up by being introduced to heavenly pancakes, banana splits, pizza and apple pies. And if he missed the lechon asado during the holidays, there was, of course, turkey in Christmas, Thanksgiving (which was just a few days away) and Easter. On the flip side, if he was grateful at not having to eat yucca, malanga or name, he was now faced with the dismal prospect of having to eat broccoli, beets and Brussels sprouts. Being a child, he adjusted quickly, though he often voiced being homesick and of missing his parents.

Kansas had an early snowfall that year. It snowed soon after Thanksgiving, small snowflakes slowly drifting down from a reddish, cloudy sky (and so quiet!) and he became very happy at his first snowfall, watching the snow fall with excited wonder, trying to catch the snowflakes in his hands, only to melt upon contact. He soon learned about snowballs, icicles and slush (especially snowball fights with Mister and Mrs. Hansen). He tried to explain to Mister Hansen that there was never any snow in Cuba, though he had seen it in films in the cinema and pictures in books and he had always thought that snow must look like the inside of a refrigerator's icebox. One thing that he noticed---and he noticed this for years thereafter---was that all Americans also became happy at seeing the first snowfall of the year.

He learned English like a sponge picks up water.

His situation with the Hansens became a permanent one four months later when his parents were arrested and executed by the Communist secret police. Their deaths were unnoticed by the yearly stampede of intellectual sympathizers from France, Germany, Canada, Mexico, Venezuela and even the United States, who traveled all that distance with their hyena grins to kiss the backside of the Lider Máximo and, if truth be told, had they known, they would have heartily approved, or, at best, been indifferent.

Someone who was not indifferent was Osbaldo. The task of informing him of his parents' deaths fell on Father Diego, for the Hansens developed an instant phobia of having to do so and flat out refused---after all, how *do* you tell a ten-year-old boy that his family has been wiped out? And what do you say afterwards? "Sorry kid, tough luck"? The priest did his painful duty and they all tried to console him as best that they could, which was, of course, inadequate.

With time, he became accustomed to his new life and he settled down into a routine. And with time, and quite unintentionally by anyone, Osbaldo slowly began to forget about the sea and the hyacinths and the hibiscus and the sea and mameys and about always talking in a very loud voice and the hurricanes and the sea and the mangos and the afternoon downpours and the palm trees and the afternoon siestas and the sea and even most of the Spanish (although Mrs. Hansen pushed him to retain his Spanish). It was unintentional. It simply seemed to erode from his memory.

The one thing that he always had trouble with was adjusting to, in summertime, the sun still being out at 9PM.

In order to understand this story, you must know Kansas.

Kansas is in the middle of the United States, a rectangularly shaped state, landlocked, just like Nebraska and the Dakotas. Its main feature is that of prairie, that is, an endlessly "sea" of flat, undulating terrain stretching all the way to the horizon, with little variation, except for the Eastern part of the state. When the pioneers first settled the area there were no trees, so in order to build fences for their cattle, they invented barbed wire. The only way that they built houses at first was with sod ("sod houses"), since there were neither trees, nor stones, nor bricks. For fuel, the pioneers used buffalo "chips."

The trees were slowly introduced later and you can always find them around human habitations, nowhere else. The trees provided color, shade from the blazing sun (especially in August!) and a break from the monotony of the landscape. Cut a tree down in Kansas, even now, for whatever reason, even if it is in your own property, and your otherwise kind and friendly neighbors will hate you and will not speak to you for months. This is not an exaggeration.

Then, there is the sun. During July and

especially August, there is a baking dry heat which can only be relieved by staying indoors with air conditioning, or in a swimming pool. There are certainly no beaches, although a few oversized mudholes claim to be so. On more than one occasion, it has rained in the middle of the day, and steam has risen from the pavement.

I have painted a harsh view of Kansas and it is really not my intention. Quite the contrary. I like Kansas. A lot. There is no pollution, little crime, few traffic jams, the people are decent and honest and helpful and you can go to the corner grocery store without fear for your life, yet the cities and towns offer a wide variety of cultural entertainment. You will not find nearly as many obscene, obnoxious, rude, loudmouthed, pompous, shallow, criminally-minded, self-important people as you will in Texas, California, New York, or Chicago. Kansas, with Nebraska, Iowa, the Dakotas (and Alberta and Saskatchewan in the Canadas) also feed the whole world with their farming. There is also industry---clean industry.

It may sound hard to believe, but the Midwest prairie has a beauty all of its own. It really does. It is a subdued, understated beauty. It is not the beauty of a Montana mountain range, or a Louisiana bayou, or a Yellowstone, where the majestic beauty of those places overwhelms you. Rather, it is a quiet, serene beauty, with absolute quiet, a blue sky and prairie grass (or wheat) moving back and forth in uniform waves to the breeze, an atmosphere that makes you want to either cook an apple pie, or rest on a hammock and watch the different clouds float by, or ride a horse at full gallop against the wind.

But there is no getting around the fact that

Kansas is mostly prairie and, in August the sun is hot, barbarously hot. But, even here, Kansas is not truly exceptional. If you want hot, if you want desolate, if you want arid, go to western Oklahoma or the panhandle of Texas!

Now, in order to understand this story and how a Cuban went momentarily insane for no apparent reason you must also know Cuba.

Cuba is an island in the Caribbean. The biggest one. And the prettiest. Columbus himself dubbed it, The Pearl of the Antilles. Like Hawaii, to speak of Cuba is to speak of beaches. Crystal clear water. White sand. Palm trees. Under the surface you will find a rich variety of colorful sea life. Also, vegetation. As with most land in the tropics, the vegetation is luxurious and ever-present, from palm trees to hyacinths to banyan trees to mango trees to sugar cane.

Unfortunately, there is also the bad part of Cuba, which is that for over three decades it has been ruled by a clique of psychopathic, megalomaniac killers, with a bearded, potbellied lunatic as the head psychopath. They have justified their harsh rule with a crackpot, reactionary Marxist doctrine which has devastated the country.

And this explains why so many Cubans fled an otherwise pleasant island. By boat, by plane, by truck, by raft they left. Some did not make it, needless to say. Others did. Those that did so scattered to the four winds.

Some of them found themselves in Kansas, of all places, and very happy and grateful they were, too, to be there!

No contrast could have been greater than Kansas and Cuba to any landscape artist or naturalist. It was a real study in contrasts. In Cuba, there was a profusion of vegetation. In Kansas, the only trees were those planted inside cities or farms and they were seen as providing a shelter from the blistering August sun and as a blessed windbreak during winter, when the Arctic winds blew down at top speed. In Cuba the beaches were pristine, with white sands and green water and palm tress. What passed for a "beach" in Kansas was really a huge water-filled mud hole (to which people actually paid admission) and whose sticky "shore" clung to your ankles. The Kansas weather was also . . . noticeable. The lightning storms were downright spooky. They were always seen in the distance, the clouds becoming momentarily illuminated and outlined, but without *any* sound and without *any* lightning bolts ripping the sky; like the terrestrial prairie, the lightning storms in the sky were quiet. Although he never could become totally used to the silence of the prairie (and on Sundays, this silence was even noticeable in the middle of a huge city like Wichita), he did become used to the Kansas weather to the point that he grew to keep an eye out for tornadoes on certain times of the year, just like in Cuba he would have kept an eye out for hurricanes during another part of the year.

Osbaldo Uballe grew up, went to school, went to college, got married.

One day, Osbaldo decided to attend a nationwide meeting of his profession, which was that of anthropology, these meetings occurring once a year to exchange information of developments and discoveries in the field. He made the necessary reservations and mailed the necessary payments.

The day before the meeting officially begun, he boarded the plane and in a number of hours found himself landing in the large, filthy city of San

Diego. He made the mistake of taking a taxi cab rather than the bus and so, was overcharged. He arrived at La Jolla, a surprisingly very pretty town on the outskirts of San Diego. The university at La Jolla was hosting the meeting this year.

The taxi dropped him off at the hotel where he had reservations and he registered.

"Is there a place nearby that serves good food?" he asked the receptionist as he filled out the registration card.

"Well, there's a restaurant two blocks from here, on your right-hand side, that I like," she answered. "They have live music, rather pleasant. It's a nice place. You can walk from here; you don't need a taxi."

"Thanks," Osbaldo said and dropped off his suitcase in his room prior to going to the restaurant, which he found without difficulty. It was indeed a nice restaurant, with a pleasant sounding four-piece orchestra. The walk had also been very, very pleasant, with lots of flowering greenery everywhere.

Right in the middle of dinner and without any warning, the band began to play *Quando Salí de Cuba (When I Left Cuba)*. He had not heard that song since he was a child.

The song is a very sentimental, very touching, song that, nowadays in particular, has a special poignancy to all Cubans when they hear it. When the tune began, Osbaldo felt as if he had been given a jolt of electricity. He had trouble swallowing and his eyes watered up. Without intending to, he released his utensils which made a clatter against his plate as they fell to the floor and made the occupants at the table next to him glance in his direction.

"Sir, are you all right?" asked the waiter with a concerned look in his face, afraid that a piece of food had gotten stuck in the customer's windpipe. When the customer did not answer, he repeated his query. "Are you OK?"

Osbaldo nodded and waved him away, embarrassed. He had no idea why the song should have such an effect an effect on him and at the same time he did.

The song finally ended and Osbaldo was able to resume eating. When he finished, he left a large tip to atone for what he thought was his earlier rudeness towards the waiter.

It was night time by now. He hailed a cab and gave the cabdriver an address. There was to be a social gathering that night, prior to business in the morning. The cab driver found the place, dropped him off and Osbaldo went in where he was immediately made welcome.

Before too long, he was "talking shop" with a number of colleagues. It turned out that von Borsig was carrying out some absorbing field research in Guatemala in one of the Mayan temples, while Nelson in the Yucatan was progressing well in his dig. Berns was confident that he was on the track of another Mayan Codex in El Salvador and Evans was searching for evidence of a Viking settlement in Newfoundland. Uballe's own work with the Kansa Indians paled by comparison, although one and all were politely interested, even asking questions and offering suggestions.

After several hours of conversation over varying topics, Osbaldo concluded that it promised to be a very good congress.

He stepped out for some fresh air, anthropologists being as prone as any other profession to the insidious habit of cigarette smoking. He breathed deeply of the night air, which was devoid of the pollution of San Diego proper and strolled around the grounds, enjoying the atmosphere. At one bush he plucked a huge hyacinth blossom, of which there were none in Kansas, smelled it and admired its beauty as he walked. He seemed to remember that he had seen such a flower once before and the smell tugged at his mind.

And then he heard it.

Faint, very faint, very, very faint, but he heard it. Unmistakable.

He stopped, frowning, concentrating on the direction of this faint, indistinct, yet unmistakable sound. A deep sound, almost rhythmic, it was like a siren song and he marched off in the direction where it seemed to be coming from, hesitating as to the direction at times, but determined to reach it, all the while his mind struggling with a long-forgotten memory. He walked in a straight line, past several residential streets, some of which had hyacinth bushes in their lawn and the sound very gradually increased with each footstep. Around that area, California is a bit hilly so he found himself traveling downwards, all thought of his colleagues gone from his mind, determined to reach the source of that sound, mesmerized by it, calling him.

He traveled onward. Then, he smelled it. Very faint, but again, unmistakable. He walked faster. He could hear it now, no mistake of it. And he knew what it was. He ran like a schoolboy. He reached a street that intersected the one that he was walking on and he could see that undeveloped land sloped downwards from the edge of the street to the source of the sound.

And there it was. He could see it. He could hear it. He could smell it.

The sea.

The smell of the sea. The sound of the breakers, the waves.

It seemed unreal, bizarre, surrealistic, because there was no daylight and so, no color, only the white of the waves' foam on black water.

He stood there for several minutes, stupefied, totally stupefied, his memory rekindled not with memories, but with sensations of long ago, buried deeply and now surfaced, and an overall feeling of unreality also struck him.

It had been so long ago.

He had . . . forgotten.

As he stood there gazing down, absorbing the sight, warm tears fell from the corner of his eyes.

Nobody can love the sea like an islander.

Osbaldo awkwardly climbed down the slope towards the beach. At the water's edge he inhaled deeply of the smell. The sound of the waves was all around him. There was a strong breeze.

A wave broke on the surface and at its utmost extension a thin, flat sheet of water momentarily touched his shoes. He grinned from ear to ear, so full of joy that one would think that he would have to burst with so much happiness in him.

He went in. He walked towards the waves as first his shoes and socks got wet, then his pants, then as the waves broke all around him, his shirt and tie, his hair, his glasses.

And throughout it all, he was laughing, laughing hysterically and at full volume. Uncaring.

A wave bowled him over and he got up, laughing. He waved his arms at the incoming waves for the sensation of breaking them up. Once, he almost lost his glasses. He was like a child who has just been introduced to the sea.

And, throughout, he laughed like a maniac.

(Xenophon relates in *Anabasis* how a large group Ancient Athenians, a maritime people, went off to arid Persia to fight as soldiers for a local general. Matters went wrong, and they had to retreat thousands of miles, with the enemy nipping at their heels. Finally, going over a rise, they saw the sea and, although still far from Athens, they broke ranks, and forgot discipline, laughing, dancing, crying, jumping up and down and shouting over and over, "The sea! The sea!")

Osbaldo continued this way for a long time, a very long time it seemed and he lost track of time, until he slowly began to calm down.

"I've got to come back here tomorrow in the daytime," he said eventually to no one in particular and with that huge smile still on his face.

Reluctantly, he turned and began to climb up the slope back to the street, every once in a while, looking back, to make sure that it was still there, that it would not go away.

Once above on the street he took a long last look at the bizarre black and white surf and then turned and began to retrace his steps back towards his colleagues.

He entered the room full of anthropologists.

"Uballe!" exclaimed von Borsig. "What in the world happened to you?" Others also looked at him with amused curiosity, or surprise.

Osbaldo looked at himself, suddenly self-conscious. His shoes and socks were wet and caked with sand. He had seaweed sticking out of one pocket. His wet hair was in disarray, his clothes were sporadically dark with water, his glasses had water spots. And he smelled of the sea.

"Oh." He said sheepishly. "I guess I went for a swim."

"Well . . . and did you have fun?" asked Nelson, smiling, finding Uballe's grin infectious.

"Yes, I did. I renewed my friendship with an old friend. A dear, old friend."

"Anybody we know?" asked Nelson, still amused and curious.

"The sea," he replied.

He slowly looked around the room looking for someone that he could share with what had happened to him, what it meant to him. He could not find any, of course, but even so, he did not feel one whit less happy. He returned his benign gaze to the two anthropologists who still viewed him with amusement in their eyes.

"Well, gentlemen, a very good night to you! I'll see you in the morning!"

And with that, he walked out into the darkness, without a doubt the happiest man, not just in that room, but in all of La Jolla.

IV

The restaurant had closed well over an hour ago. The customers had departed. So had the cooks, the waiters and waitresses and the busboys.

The only ones left were Lucinda, the hostess, and Mister Nelson, the owner and manager. Lucinda was a very tall, shapely brunette with long hair; she always wore a long one-piece cotton dress where the skirt reached the ankles and was so flexible that if she turned quickly, the bottom, with its bright patterns spread out in a roughly circular shape. Mister Nelson was a very thin man (he had been seriously sick once) with a Roman nose and brown/blonde hair, who used to claim that he was Italian although he could not speak five words of Italian and had been born in Topeka; one of his fingers had been bitten off years ago by a horse. This was the first restaurant that he had ever owned and was very proud of it and, consequently, kept a sharp eye out for quality.

They were in Mister Nelson's office, going over that night's receipts. After a while, all the tickets tallied with the money received. It had been a good night. Plenty of customers, plenty of compliments, plenty of good food and plenty of tips. The restaurant had been favorably reviewed (actually, raved would be more accurate) by the newspaper and television reviewers of restaurants.

"And not even a weekend," said Lucinda, quietly satisfied.

"Yeah, if business keeps up like this, I'll have to expand the restaurant."

"There wasn't even a mix-up in the orders, or anything."

Mister Nelson nodded. "That new boy is working out fine, he catches on quick."

"And he's cute, too," she retorted.

"Oh, *really?* I hadn't noticed," he said with a smile.

"Uh-huh," she smiled back. "And he's going to college."

"I see. Well, shall we call it a night?" he asked and they both got up. He stretched and carrying the money bag, which was to be dropped off at the local bank's night deposit, then walked out of the office and into the restaurant."

Lucinda stopped and sniffed the air.

"What's that?"

"Oh, no," Mister Nelson groaned with a sinking feeling. "It can't be."

They both quickly looked at the restaurant. There was some smoke, but no fire. The man ran across the dining room and into the kitchen.

The kitchen was on fire.

The fire extinguisher was on the other side of the kitchen. He was going to try to dash across and attempt to use it, but, instead, he had to get out of the kitchen, his lungs racked with coughing from the smoke, his eyes watering. He looked up and saw the girl talking on the telephone, a look of deep concentration on her face.

"Lucinda," he croaked, "get out. Get out!"

He himself got off his knees and stumbled towards her.

"The fire department will be here soon!" she announced.

"Here!" he said, thrusting the money bag at her, then grabbing a couple of expensive ornaments and handing them to her. "Take these out to my car. And-stay-outside!" He then whirled into his office.

The clear air in his office was refreshing. It partially cleared his mind and his lungs, though he still coughed.

But what to salvage? How bad was the fire going to be? Was it going to extend all the way here? Should he be saving something else in the dining room instead?

He came to, realizing that his hesitation was wasting precious moments and started grabbing things, anything of monetary or financial value and stuffing them in a large bag that was lying on the floor, in the corner. Documents, too.

He looked at the desk, wishing that he could carry it out. It had been a good luck present from his wife when he had opened up the restaurant.

He dashed out of the office. The smoke was worse. He saw Lucinda struggling with a case of expensive wine, angrily muttering that she wished that she had a man's muscles.

"I thought I told you to stay out!" he snapped.

"I heard you and I ignored you! All right?" she snapped right back. Outside, he saw that there was another case of wine that she had salvaged. The sirens were getting closer.

He dropped the bag by the two cases of wine and then, purposely hyperventilating first, and taking a deep breath, he went back in for one last time, deciding that she had had the right idea, the bar being on the opposite side of the kitchen, yet containing valuable wines. She followed him in and each grabbed almost a dozen bottles of expensive wine before exiting.

The firemen had arrived and were beginning to cover the building and unrolling the hoses. The revolving colored lights of the fire trucks were sweeping the area, giving the area a surreal appearance, as such lights usually do.

The restaurant was located in one of those streets that is neither fully commercial nor fully residential, but both. People began to peer outside their homes and, before too long, a crowd was gathering to see the spectacle. A crowd always gathers around to gawk at the scene of a crime, or accident, and this time was no exception.

The hostess and the manager had, in the meanwhile, taken what little they had salvaged, put it in the car so that the firemen would not trip over them and then moved the car a block away in order to provide extra space for the rushing firefighters.

Parking the car, Nelson ran back to the crowd that had formed a semicircle around the restaurant and the fire trucks. There were children there with their mothers, who were explaining to the little ones with a smile on the mothers' faces what the firemen were doing and pointing out the fire trucks and the hoses.

"Looks like the restaurant is being cooked," said one woman with a laugh.

"Yeah, medium well," a man guffawed.

"I hope that they don't put it out too soon, I want to see some fireworks.

Somebody called out, jokingly, "Hey, anybody bring marshmallows to roast?"

"No, but I brought hot dogs," someone else answered in the same vein.

At that moment, the roof of the kitchen either collapsed or a hole burned through. Either way, flames leaped up at that point now that there was a source of fresh oxygen and combustibles that had been smoldering flared up. The smell of burning drifted over.

"Oooh," the crowd uttered, appreciative of the conflagration. Some even clapped. One man yelled, "All right!" with enthusiasm in his voice.

Nelson knew at this point that the entire restaurant was a loss.

He had been so proud of that restaurant! When he had started, he had been warned that most new businesses fall within the first year. That restaurant had been around for six years, beating all the odds and all the pessimists.

It was like watching a dear old friend slowly

die.

A pillar of fire momentarily appeared.

"Wow," the crowd murmured approvingly.

"There goes the rest of the roof!" someone pointed out.

"I always said that it was a really 'hot' restaurant," a woman joked.

Someone, apparently drunk, began to sing very loudly "Smoke Gets in Your Eyes." Since he could carry a tune very well, a few in the crowd tore their eyes away from the fire to admire the singer. When he stopped after awhile, they resumed watching the fire.

The proprietor felt a hand on his shoulder. He turned around. It was Lucinda. She had tears streaming down her face.

"Oh, Mister Nelson, I'm sorry," she whispered in a broken voice. "I'm so sorry."

Nelson impulsively hugged her, hugged her tight as a sob escaped out of him.

The crowd cheered the fire on.

V

"Is not the Bible itself warning?" she asks. "Are not the words and deeds so vile that you did not stop to wonder?"
Stanley Shapiro, *Simon's Soul*

I travel by plane a lot, I would say about once very two weeks or so, on business, although I try to squeeze some pleasure into these trips. Like, if I am traveling to a city where a friend or a distant family member lives, I will schedule the layovers so that I will have enough time to meet with them, sometimes at the airport and sometimes at their home, if there is plenty of times between flights and it is not during rush hour. Oftentimes, though, I will also meet interesting fellow passengers and some of them I will even keep in touch with them afterwards. I have met a few ladies with whom I dated from time to time, if and when my flight schedule takes me back to their city.

Just as often, though, I will also meet, or be seated next to, someone really unpleasant, for example a loud, boorish Texan with a dark glob of chewing tobacco dribbling out of the corner of his mouth, a shrewish, ill tempered woman who is terrorizing or brutalizing her children, some pothead, a Third Word groupie on her way to some place in Latin America to fornicate with as many men as possible during her stay in order to expiate the colonization of the New World by Europeans, or a self-centered passenger who seems to think that the airline and its personnel revolve around him and should satisfy his every (ten minute) whim, to the detriment of his fellow passengers. Usually I forget them a few hours after we part company, or try to, anyway.

I have also met a few individuals that fall in between and are one of a kind, like the man who informed me that a person could go to a stockbroker and buy stocks in either the Democratic or the Republican Parties. Or the man who insisted that there were fifty-two states in the Union, while a nearby fellow traveler disputed this claim by pointing out that Canada was not yet a state.

I recently met a guy who really unnerved me.

I am still disturbed about some of the things that he said and they daily intrude upon my thoughts whenever I watch the news or come across an individual case of misfortune.

I was at the airport, watching the news on television in the waiting area, prior to my flight departing. An accident had occurred on a train and several people had been killed. The man seated next to me, watching the TV and rocking himself heel to toe, said, "Typical!"

"Mmm? What?" I asked him.

"That," he pointed to the carnage on the television. "Have you ever noticed that, invariably, in accidents, the people who die, for the most part, are valuable people? Decent people? Good people? And the ones who survive are the nasty ones or the worthless ones? Tattooed trash, brainless bimbos, the unremarkable human zero?"

"Oh . . . I don't know if that's true. I hadn't noticed that."

"I have. Keep your eyes open from here on out and you'll definitely notice a pattern. Almost like a law of nature. Like this accident here. A doctor and his family got killed; so did a vacationing engineer; so did some children. And you saw what some of the survivors were like: worthless."

"Well, who's to say who's worthless and who's not?"

"Me. You. Unless you have no standards of merit at all. Let me ask you. Do you know, personally, of an instance where someone praiseworthy died and a worthless person survived in his stead? Think. Go ahead. Take your time."

I did as he suggested, in both amusement and irritation. To my surprise I came up with three different incidents of people personally known to me who did, indeed, fit his curious assertion. But I felt that it was a coincidence and told him so after admitting knowing of a few cases.

"No coincidence!" he firmly asserted. "It simply supports my main point, which is, that God is evil."

"Say what? Come again?"

"God is evil. It's the only logical explanation."

I am not a religious person, by any stretch of the imagination, but this totally threw me.

"Now, wait a minute. You got it backwards. God is good."

"How do you know? How do you know for sure? Because someone told you so? But how many times have you prayed for something that you desperately wanted to happen and nothing happened? At one time, a religious person would have proclaimed himself to be a God-fearing man. Nowadays, that image is too harsh, so we say God is Love. We've made God more palatable. But, have you read the Bible? Have you, really? It's the exultation of mass murder, promoted by, or directed by, a deranged deity! The book of Job alone would convince any rational being that God is evil. But our thinking has been so twisted by centuries of brainwashing and terror that we use a pretzel logic to conclude that such acts prove the opposite, that God is good."

"W-Wait a minute-" I stuttered.

"And if you don't want to go back to ancient history, how about now? *If* God is a loving God, *and,* if you accept the unproven premise that He's all powerful, then how could He allow the killing fields of Cambodia by the Khmer Rouge to occur?

How could He allow the Serbs carry out their vicious, sadistic bloodbath in Bosnia? I'm sorry, but you can't have it both ways. Either He's Good or He's Evil. Me, I've concluded that He's evil and He's been enjoying our suffering for centuries. It's the only thing that makes sense."

"And here's something else: why is it that it's the nasty, callous, unprincipled and, in fact, *evil* people who seem to prosper in this world and seem to get the lucky breaks, yet the caring, sensitive, ethical and, indeed, benevolent ones are the ones who seem to be held back and never get any breaks?"

"Now, that's not always true. It's usually the other way around."

"I disagree."

"I was taught-" I began to object.

"Exactly," he interrupted.

I saw what he meant and hesitated.

"Now, I *know* you've seen this," the stranger continued. "Haven't you noticed that women stick to men who are abusive and treat their women like dirt, but if a man treats a girl like a queen, with love and respect, the women walk all over that type of man?"

"Well, yeah, but that's just women! It' s their nature: they're neurotic!" I objected.

"No! Same principle! In prison and jails, I've noticed that the most repulsive, evil convicts are visited by extremely beautiful women."

I thought for a minute. I saw a flaw in his system.

"But if God's truly evil, why aren't we all suffering? Eh? Why aren't we all wallowing in misery and disease and pain?"

He took his time to think about it.

"Probably for contrast," he slowly responded. "You can't fall sick if you aren't healthy. You can't feel, or rather the feeling of misfortune is intensified, if you were well off before. Or, if you see others well off. Envy. Yeah! Envy makes it hurt more and makes you yearn for it more."

"Contrast, huh," I nodded, "but I still can't accept your original premise."

"It's the only thing that makes sense," he said shrugging.

I was silent, trying to gather my thoughts together, but after a few seconds, he continued.

"And another thing: think about all the wars that have been waged in the name of God by the Muslims, the Jews and the Christians. Have you ever heard of a single war that was ever waged in the name of Satan? I haven't."

Well, yeah, that was true, but . . . . Something crossed my mind.

"I remember reading *The Bridge of San Luis Rey* in school-" I began.

Just then, the intercom announced the boarding of my flight and I took my leave of him, a bit too eagerly perhaps. The stranger was waiting for another flight. His words still annoyed me, though like I said, I am not religious.

Naturally, I never saw him again.

Yesterday, a neighbor of mine was involved in a car accident. His younger son, a healthy, athletic, beautiful boy with a natural aptitude for science and poetry, the apple of his eye, was killed when he was thrown through the windshield. His younger son lived. He is a juvenile delinquent who has been tormenting his family for nearly a year.

VI

Serena's hands trembled. She held a letter in her hand informing her that the short story that she had submitted to *Atlantic Monthly* had been accepted for publication. Her eyes were moist with tears and the words were blurred. Up to that moment none of her stories had been accepted for publication.

Her hands trembled from rage.

Her eyes were crying from frustration.

She had written many short stories depicting "the Cuban-American experience," as she liked to joke about it by indirectly alluding to "the African-American experience," the latter being much lauded by literary Establishment, particularly if it showered hate and condemnation on America or on white people.

The themes of the stories written by Serena were of Cuban families split apart and reunited, of persecution under a repressive Communist regime, of humorous cultural and linguistic misunderstandings of immigrants, of praise for a kind and generous American people.

All had been rejected.

As individual stories for magazines or in a compendium for a book.

The rejections had been impersonal form letters, but one editor (or editor's assistant), had once written her a note telling her that she could write well but that she was a Fascist, a racist and an anti-Semite. Shocked, she meticulously went over the particular story that she had submitted---word for word---again and again---but could not find any references to Jewish people, no matter how many times she reread her own story (what made this accusation particularly bizarre was that Serena was herself Jewish). And the only black character in the story was a one-line statement that one of the musicians in the band was black. And as for Fascist, well, the story was about a family of musicians fleeing Communist repression by taking to the high seas. Was hatred of Communism supposed to be Fascism? Apparently, to this reviewer at least, it was.

In spite of her failures, like Sisyphus she persevered. To her, every time that she finished a story it was an occasion for feeling pride.

She thought that giving birth to a child must feel the same way.

So why were her hands trembling with rage now that one of her stories had been finally accepted? And why was she crying with frustration?

Earlier, she had submitted yet another story to *Atlantic Monthly*. It had been rejected. This was during the time of the little boy who had been rescued at sea after his mother had drowned before his eyes in her attempt to bring him over to the United States. The Communist regime wanted him back. The boy's uncle had refused. The Cuban-American community in Miami had rallied around the uncle and the boy. An almost daily avalanche of racist vituperation was showered upon the boy's family and the whole Cuban-American community by almost every branch of the mass media. The curiously venomous, hysterical attacks upon the boy's family and all the Cuban-Americans was unrelenting. Nationwide, they were portrayed in stories and cartoons as Frito Bandito stereotypes, from *Time* magazine to the Chicago *Tribune* to the

Corpus Christi *Caller Times* to Ft. Lauderdale's newspaper. In yet another example of the bottomless hypocrisy for which they are so famous, the portrayals were blatantly racist, put out by those very same liberals who are forever crusading against racism---except for the Cuban-Americans, whom they despise. And, as everyone in America knows, the liberals in America have a stranglehold on the mass media. The attacks had been so blatant, so rancid that even some liberals had objected to the obvious racism---and that said something right there.

So, feeling the sting of the racist caricaturing and the boy's saga, in a bizarre leap of logic, Serena had taken the story that she had submitted before to the magazine, changed names, including her own, reworded and reworked a few lines and a few words and added three paragraphs with the result that the story now had a completely different slant. The story was now about a Cuban-American family who were vile and bigoted.

She sent it.

Atlantic Monthly loved it.

They wanted to publish it.

They were going to pay her for the story.

Hence, her anger and her frustration.

She knew then that, at this rate, she would *never* be published, no matter how good her stories, not unless she knuckled under and resigned herself to the invisible censorship and wrote clichés that were so loved by liberals.

And yet . . . she was tempted.

Yes, yes, she was tempted.

Oh, yes, she *was* tempted. She was tempted indeed. To see her name *in print*, finally, to have one of her stories *printed*, finally, even if it was a mutation, pabulum for leftist mediocrities, was a great temptation---for any unpublished author. Serena rationalized it. Yes, of course there must have been individuals like them, in fact, she herself had heard of cases like this, now that she thought about it. So what if she was not writing on her favorite themes? It was a start. Anyway, it might well lead on to others. She needed to get her foot in the door and if it meant catering to the Politically Correct fanatics at first, well, that was the prize to pay.

Serena became saddened as her rationalization petered out. It was a Faustian deal, she knew, pure and simple. Any other future stories would then have to be of the same caliber in order for them to be published, she knew that. She let the letter fall out of her hand, feeling infinitely sad.

VII

As a bartender, one of my favorite places to work in Wichita was the club atop the Bank of America building. You had a classier, more sophisticated clientele, but the building itself was impressive. When you went into the building, you were surprised. It was sudden, empty space for seven stories, with only a huge mobile sculpture of flat, red circles joined together, hanging above your head from the ceiling. Two whole walls were made of glass. And when you went inside, you went *down,* down some stairs, past a red circular sculpture (Wichita is really, really big on sculpture; sculptures are everywhere, it is a sculptor's dream city). It was really neat. And all the offices and businesses were along the wall all the way up those floors. The building was the opposite of claustrophobic. No doubt about it, it was impressive. And the club was on the top floor.

Most of the afternoon clientele were out-of-towners, people who had come to Wichita for business deals, particularly with the Coleman plant, or the aircraft companies Cessna, Learjet, or Boeing. Usually, they were Yankees from Ohio, New York, or Pennsylvania. The cleanliness of the city unnerved them.

They suffered from culture shock.

They were also hyperactive.

Especially the New Yorkers.

"Say, what's there to do in this town?" one of them would demand, usually in a hostile, accusatory tone.

"Anything that you want to do," I'd say.

"But what?! There's nothing!" This from a guy that had walked just a couple of street blocks to look around.

"Well, there's movies, there's clubs, there's a couple of plays in town, the art museum, it's supposed to be really good, shopping malls, Cowtown-"

"Cowtown?! What's that?"

"It's a collection of original houses and buildings from the Wild West days. You can stroll around; sometimes they have shows-"

"I don't believe it! What a hole to be stuck in!"

"I know what your problem is," I'd suggest, while pointing at him. "You're suffering from carbon monoxide deficiency. Too much oxygen. Clear sky---not enough smog. If you want to, you can go down to where I've got my car and for five bucks, I'll let you suck the exhaust fumes right out of the muffler."

But, you know, these guys from New York, or Philadelphia, or Chicago, or Boston, they were like those grotesque deep-sea fish that are brought up from those perpetually dark depths. When they come up closer to the surface, they cannot tolerate it and they explode. Now, these New Yorkers in Wichita were not hemmed in by canyons of concrete, particularly if they made a wrong turn and found themselves out in the open spaces, with fresh, clean air . . . and they got frightened. And Wichita is so clean! And so quiet! They found it intolerable.

They hid their fear behind hostility.

However, the waitresses and I had long ago decided not to take any guff from these self-important, condescending, loudmouthed Yankees, particularly the terminally rude New Yorkers, so we let them have it as soon as they started being obnoxious, which usually meant as soon as they opened their mouths, since most of them felt that being New Yorkers entitled them to insult our hometown, in which case we were expected to be grateful to them for their observations/insults and even laugh at their put downs, they were so sophisticated and worldly, don't you know.

At best, they were condescending. Blatantly so.

This particular waitress, by the way, her name was Brandy, had a head start of me in playing this sport. As a child living near Wellington, her family had been visited by out of state relatives. At one time, a twelve-year-old boy, a city boy from Boston, and her were walking down the road at a point that one of those containers of milk used in

48

dairy farms had spilled over onto the grass. Her city cousin pointed to the large white splotch on the grass asking what it was and without batting an eye, she answered him, "Oh, that's just a cow nest." He believed it, too.

"This town is hole!" repeated the sophisticated Yankee.

"If you're from New Joisey," another waitress joined in, "you probably miss the smell of refineries. If you want, I could fill up a container with gas and you could sniff the fumes."

"Nah, I know what it is," I told her. "He hasn't been mugged since he got here, but if you want me to, I could draw you a map to the black section of town. They hate white people. Wichita has the most racist blacks in the entire Midwest. We're very proud of that fact. Anyway, you're bound to be murdered if you set foot there---at the very least get assaulted."

"Now, if it's sexual perversions that you're interested in," Brandy continued, unrelenting, "I know the addresses of a couple of places that might accommodate you. By the way, are you a homosexual?"

And so on, back and forth. All in fun mind you.

But there was one time that it got really mean. And I was the culprit.

Before I tell you what happened, I have to explain a bizarre Kansas institution that we used to have at the time: the liquor card.

Kansas is a dry state. One of our former attorney generals, Vern Miller I think was his name, had had a very flamboyant style and he once boarded an airline flight and while it flew over Kansas, the waitresses---I mean, the stewardesses---

49

served mixed drinks to the passengers. So, he arrested them all as soon as the airplane landed in Kansas City. He had style, there is no denying. In another publicity ploy, he had arrested some little old ladies for playing Bingo in church, which he claimed was illegal gambling.

Anyway . . . Kansas was a dry state, but people still liked to drink. So, they invented the bizarre labyrinthic practice of "the liquor card." It's very frustrating (and that was the whole point, you see). It went like this: you plopped down 5, 10, 20 bucks for a liquor card; that allowed you to purchase your liquor. With mixed drinks, you then paid the setups with cash, thereby making it feel like you were paying twice. If you used up your supply of liquor purchased, then you had to buy another card, in order to continue drinking. Dumb? You bet! Even the natives hated it! Worse, when it came time to make fun of us by outsiders, the practice was indefensible, so we joined right in in condemning it and poking fun at it.

At any rate, right about the time of the famous obscenity trial against a pornography magazine from New York which was being printed in New York, but distributed in Kansas---I remember because the four out of town lawyers representing the magazine used to huddle every night in a dark corner discussing the trial and their strategies---a real scummy group, too, you felt like taking a shower anytime you went near them--- anyway, this one day this guy comes in. You could tell just from looking at him what kind of day he'd had, that everything had gone haywire. It was written all over his face. Still, that's no reason to be rude, or obnoxious. Or loud. Not in Kansas, anyway. Maybe in Chicago, or New York.

And as soon as he opened his mouth, sure enough, we knew he was a Yankee.

"Say, any way a man can get a drink around here!?" he yelled out as soon as he stepped into the bar.

"Of course. What would you-"

"Anything!! Just give me a drink!"

He made me angry right from the start. I didn't care that he was probably some guy from New Jersey, irritable from having withdrawal symptoms from not smelling all the refineries, or shock at the town's cleanliness and quiet, I was about to let him have it, in fact the waitresses and some of the regulars were smiling, expecting a snappy comeback when . . . all of a sudden . . . I had an inspiration.

I can only describe it as a wave of calmness washing over me.

A sadistic calmness.

"Now, sir, if you'd kindly sit down, I could perhaps accommodate you," I said in my most reasonable tone of voice. Brandy gave me an odd look.

He sat down. He spit out an obscenity.

"Now, sir, what would you like?" I smiled my brightest smile.

"A drink! I said I wanted a drink! You deaf or something?!"

"No, sir, it's just that we have a wide variety of drinks. Can you be more specific, sir?"

"Fine! A rum and coke! How's that? Think you can make that?"

"Excellent. Now, sir, do you have a liquor card with us?"

"A *what??*"

"A liquor card." I smiled. I blinked twice.

"And what is *that?!*" he yelled out.

The waitresses and the regulars were eyeing each other and you could see them silently asking themselves, "What is going *on* here?" It was so out of character for me.

The funny thing was that no matter what cuss words he yelled, no matter how often he interrupted, no matter how loud he yelled, I did not get angry. No, scratch that. I could not get angry. Really. I swear it! I literally could not get angry. It wasn't as if I was suppressing it. *I could not get angry*. And nothing was going to deter me from following the path that I had laid out.

Much, much later did I then realize the power behind the Christian saying of turning the other cheek.

" . . . so you put down a certain amount of money for the liquor-"

"I don't believe you people!"

"Yes, sir, I understand how you feel."

"Buddy, you can't *know* how I feel!"

"Well, sir, you may be right there. I can only imagine. This can be very frustrating," I said with a syrupy smile.

"Frustrating? It's more than frustrating. It's-" and he let loose with a volley of obscenities.

I didn't lose my smile.

"Be that as it may, sir, the procedure is as follows . . . ."

This went on for quite some time and everyone in the club was surreptitiously observing this bizarre spectacle. He was cussing me out. He was cussing out Kansas. He was cussing out all native Kansans. He was cussing out Wichita. It went in one ear and right out the other. I was the only person there smiling.

At one point you could almost see the light very slowly dawning in the man's head, that he was in a trap, but that he just couldn't stop himself from yelling out, cussing and, generally, being obnoxious. First, a suspicion, and then, a slow realization of what was going on, that I was allowing him to be as publicly obnoxious and rude as he wanted to be, that he was making a contemptible spectacle of himself, that by remaining invariably polite and courteous, I was deliberately setting up a sharp contrast whereby his behavior was, by contrast, appearing inexcusable and thoroughly contemptible to one and all, even to another New Yorker, regardless of the original reason for his irritation.

Ultimately, inevitably, he calmed down. He got quieter and quieter, then totally quiet.

He had some drinks.

He then bought drinks all around. Twice.

He apologized to the waitresses.

He apologized to the customers.

He apologized to the scumbag lawyers.

He apologized to me, over and over.

He felt lower than a worm. And although he started several conversations, you could see that his heart wasn't in it, that he didn't feel comfortable, that they were forced, that he had proven to the whole world just what an undisputed jackass he was, made worse precisely because nobody at all would allude to his performance, not even jokingly. Presently, he slunk off out of the premises.

He left me an enormous tip.

I was wiping down a bottle with a washcloth, smiling, when Brandy came over to me, frowning.

"I never imagined that you could be that

53

cruel," she muttered.

I just kept wiping the bottles, smiling.

VIII

The museum of art had received on loan from another museum in another country a very nice collection of Renoir paintings. They were on exhibit to the public and had been displayed for the better part of a month. The exhibit had, of course, been publicized, which publicity had resulted in a greater than average attendance. Although art lovers had attended faithfully, there had been also the curious, as well as those individuals who attend whatever is publicized, as well as those individuals who felt that they had to attend in order to maintain (in their own eyes as well as their acquaintances' eyes) the self-endowed title of Intellectual.

Among the curious had been Carlos Centeno, a tall, muscular man in his thirties with a prominent nose. He had gone the first weekend because, upon being exposed to the advertisements, and upon reflection, he had realized with embarrassment that he knew nothing about Renoir paintings, or for that matter, any kind of art and that constituted a gaping hole in his knowledge. Therefore, he decided that this would be a good opportunity to at least give it a try. He dragged along his recalcitrant wife who was in no way interested in art, nor, as was the case with many Cuban women, was she ashamed in the least bit about her total ignorance (they had long ceased to see eye to eye on many things).

The effect was unexpected, to say the least.

The paintings totally transformed him. He became completely, totally enraptured with them and would gaze at each one with awe and fascination. It was as if these particular masterpieces had awakened a dormant receptor that had heretofore been present all along, dormant, but to which he had been oblivious as to its existence. Each canvas struck a hidden chord in him. When his wife, bored, had nagged him sufficiently to induce him to leave for home, he did so reluctantly, but not without buying a book at the museum store on the life and artwork of Renoir. He read the whole book at one sitting, although it was way past midnight when he finished.

He returned the next day, Sunday, and was one of the first to walk in when the doors opened. And he was one of the last to leave.

Centeno returned every day thereafter without failing to marvel at the canvases. He would do so directly after work and stay on until closing time, which was about an hour afterwards. Sometimes he would take off early from work, sometimes not, after first calling his wife to let her know that he would be coming home late.

Whether it was a scene depicting a village or barges on the Seine, a crowd of people or a pastoral scene, the effect was the same: it was as if he was magnetized. Yet, their effect was nothing compared to the effect upon him by one particular masterpiece in the collection. It was one of Renoir's *Bathers*, showing a nude redheaded young woman.

By today's standards of what is beautiful, the model would be considered to be a bit too plump, but to Centeno she was the most beautiful woman that he had ever seen, either alive or in images. It would be no exaggeration whatsoever to state that he literally fell in love with the redheaded bather. No, not the painting, the *bather*. It was literally love at first sight. To many of us who have never before seen such an occurrence, it may sound bizarre but the same has indeed happened before to other unsuspecting viewers with other masterpieces of art and to both men and women.

Suffice it to say that Centeno was enthralled by *Bather* and would spend most of his time viewing it, going to other frames, then returning to it as if he was viewing it with a fresh perspective. She was exquisite.

As he gazed on it, he would wish, secretly, that he could somehow possess such a vision of loveliness. His five-year marriage had deteriorated in the usual pattern. He was still fond of his wife but she, for her part, had turned sometimes cold, sometimes distant, sometimes loving, sometimes hostile. He often wished for a return of that boundless love that had been present during the first year of married life. As he spent more time viewing *Bather*, the more this nostalgic yearning grew.

One day he decided, upon reflection, and feeling a bit guilty, that lately, this past week, he had ignored his wife and would, to make up for it, go home early and take her out to a restaurant, followed by dancing. She would like that.

Instead, he arrived home to find her naked in bed with another man.

Centeno went berserk. He seized a small wooden table by the leg and broke it over the man's skull. Still holding on to the table leg, he bludgeoned the potbellied man into senselessness and continued doing so, breaking all the man's ribs, his legs, jaw, nose, arms. Then, seeing his wife in the state that she was in, naked, covered with the man's sweat and hair, he lost what little self-control he had left and gave her the very same, equal, treatment that he had administered to him. When he was through, she was equally mangled and broken. Her face alone was a swollen, purplish mass, matted with blood that could still be recognized as supposing to be a face. Just before he left, he gave a parting kick to the groaning man.

He drove around the city for a long time, though he was not conscious of his surroundings or of the time passed. It was as if he was driving on automatic pilot.

He came to, parked at the museum's parking lot. Like a somnambulist, he got out of his car and entered the museum. The staff was surprised to see him there, coming in so late, it almost being closing time.

He walked around from painting to painting, pausing briefly before each. At most he felt a vestige of that elation that they had previously evoked in him. He now saw them as paintings, illusions, and not visions.

He came across *Bather*. The woman's hair was brilliantly red, her skin fair, her face childlike pretty in a decidedly woman's body and his previous yearning broke out once more, mixed with pain and anguish. He wished that he would be in possession of such a vision of loveliness and of love.

He felt hot, dizzy and perceived himself to be swaying back and forth.

He came to at the museum's entrance as several hands roughly manhandled him. The hands belonged to that of the staff, including the security guards, and they were separating him from his beloved *Bather,* wrenching them apart from each other.

IX

Eusebio quietly thanked another couple who came over to offer condolences in the death of his father. Quite a few individuals were present at the funeral, mostly his father's friends, although three of his own friends had stopped by to pay their respects, even though they had never met his father. He appreciated that gesture on their part. Everyone talked in hushed tones, as if afraid to wake up his father and they also moved slowly, carefully, as if afraid to break imaginary glassware strewn on the floor.

A few expressed a subdued sort of relief that if his father had to die, at least he had died in his sleep, painlessly. Others were awkward in their condolences. After all, what *can* you say to someone whose parent, or child, or spouse has died? No matter what you do say, it sounds so . . . empty. To both the speaker and the listener. But, at the same time, you want desperately to say something that may perhaps relieve the pain suffered by the surviving member.

Eusebio was attentive to all, glad to have his mind become busy with the details, rather than with his preoccupation with grief.

There was a pause in his role as "host" while the others either mingled about or talked with one another. Although not a veteran of burials of friends or relatives, he had to admit that the arrangements provided by the funeral home had been well prepared and with professional expertise. He also concluded that he preferred the funeral customs in America rather than those of Cuba, although the funeral director was himself a Cuban. Both his parents and he himself had been born on the island and, although they had lived most of their lives there, he had come over as a child. But even though he had never personally attended any Cuban funerals, his parents and their friends had occasionally related scandalous anecdotes of Cuban vigils. In order for the friends of the family to remain awake over the long vigil, they would sit at the back, telling one obscene joke after another (Irish wakes were supposed to be even worse, with drunkenness and even fist fights taking place, or so he had heard and somewhere else---was it Argentina?---orchestras were even hired for the guests to dance to while professional, paid, mourners shed bucketful of "tears" in their stead). No, American funerals were more . . . dignified.

Eusebio approached the casket and looked at his sleeping father and his previous preoccupation with grief resurfaced.

He felt none.

He was greatly troubled. He had discussed this with no one, although he had overheard "compliments" about his demeanor: "He's taking it so well, so manly." Yet, after the first ten minutes on being informed of his father's death, he had not grieved. He had been surprised, yes, actually shocked and there had been a stab of pain. But, oddly, he had not cried. And, after the initial few minutes, he had not felt grief. That was the strange thing. The only thing that he had felt was that there were many preparations to be made for his father's final resting place.

He had loved his father. Always had. And he

still did. Yet, he felt no grief. "I must be some kind of monster not to *feel* grief," he thought. "Even if I didn't cry, I should still *feel* grief. He certainly deserves even a few tears from me after all he did for me."

But no tears came to his eyes.

He wondered why this was so for the umpteenth time. Is it because I'm older? He thought. He could not say. Perhaps it's a physical defect in my makeup, he wondered. Maybe it's because I'm a man and I can't cry as easily as the women.

He now envied women, who could cry at the drop of a hat. They had tears for all occasions. They cried at weddings, they cried at funerals, they cried at birthings, they cried at graduations, they cried at birthdays, they cried at divorces, they cried at reconciliations with friends, they cried at pain, they cried at anniversaries, they cried at movies, they cried when abandoned by husbands, they cried when they abandoned husbands, they cried for grief, they cried for pain, they cried for joy, they cried for humiliations, they cried for pride, they cried for show, they cried for extortion, they cried for pity, they cried for sympathy, they cried for dramatics and, once in a while, they would cry for absolutely no reason at all. They were like saturated sponges, which only needed to be rubbed lightly for water to gush out.

And yet, he could not even conjure up even *one* teardrop as tribute with which to honor his father!

He stared at the grave where his father now lay buried. He had asked to be left alone after the services and his wished had been honored by all. They understood that he needed to be alone, or, rather, they thought that they understood.

Maybe it's because I've become Americanized and Americans are thought to be so cold by Latin American standards? But he knew better, he knew that Americans *were* emotional. They simply weren't hysterical and that important difference was where they were always misunderstood by foreigners.

Also, he knew from past experience that many of the "feelings" generously expressed by Latin Americans and Arabs were hypocrisy, pure and simple. He wanted no part of that.

He stared at the grave where his father lay buried. "Yes, I must be some kind of monster," he thought again.

He thought back at memories of his father, how he had taken him horseback riding in the country, in Cuba, with *bohios* and palm trees everywhere. He had taught him swimming and baseball. They had gone to the beach and played around with the starfish that they found there and with angry ghost crabs and blue crabs. One had pinched Eusebio's hand and, in a fury at his son's hurt, his father had stomped on the crab with his heel until the crab had completely disintegrated under his father's onslaught, then he had cradled his son to comfort him until he felt better again and could even joke about it.

He had tyrannically drilled him on his multiplication tables and had helped him with his homework at nights. They had eaten popcorn together while watching scary movies. He had urged his son on to better grades and on to college. He had bought him a car with which to date girls, a brand new, shiny, car and his social life and, more importantly his love life, had improved immensely as a result.

Nothing worked. Still, he did not cry. Instead, he became angry at himself.

Later, in his father's house, empty, empty of life, he went from room to room looking over the furnishings. There, in the corner was that guitar that his father bought a few years back when he had tried to learn how to play before he had realized that he was completely tone deaf. Over there were a pair of *maracas*. At least he could play *them!* That was his favorite chair; he could always be seen sitting there, usually reading the local newspaper or sometimes a few copies of *Diario de las Americas* that somebody had brought over from Miami for him. His small library. His reading glasses. His worn-out wallet with his credit cards. His calculator. A framed map of the Isle of Pines. Photo albums.

He opened up the albums and leafed through them. Photographs stared back at him. Numerous black and white photographs with jagged edges attached to black pages of odd texture showed his father, a younger man, with his mother or with him or with other relatives and friends. They were at the beach in that handful of snapshots with the sand and waves and palm trees and the *cabanas* Those were his Dad's wedding pictures. Pictures of the smiling family in their home. On birthdays. At the country. In the United States. Then, the color photographs with smooth edges replaced the black and white ones and they showed the changes in the happy family as the years passed. More birthdays. Thanksgiving. Trips. New friends. New relatives.

Eusebio finished the last album, closed it and waited a few seconds. Nothing. Absolutely no intense feelings. He-simply-could-not-cry!

"I must be some kind of monster," he concluded his head in disbelief and in sadness.

X

It was seven in the evening when the guests started to arrive. Being winter, it had started to become dark since five, but no one had wanted to have *Nochebuena*---Christmas Eve dinner, that early.

The first to arrive were Placido and his American wife, Samantha, with their children. They were greeted at the door by Placido's father as if they had not seen each other in months, although they lived in the same city, hugging and kissing everybody while shouting *"Feliz Navidad!"* and *"Felicidades!"*

Placido responded with a fluent *"Felicidades!"* while his two children and Samantha wished him *"Feliz Navidad!"* with a bit of an American accent. When the grandmother appeared from the kitchen the kids flew to her with hugs, yelling their greetings again.

Placido and Samantha made themselves at home right away while the kids, on their own initiative, disappeared into one of the rooms to play with the toys that were always ready and waiting for them at their grandparents' home.

The house interior was impeccable and the home was saturated with the delicious smell of *Nochebuena* dinner. Placido's stomach decided at that moment to growl loud enough to be heard by both Samantha and the old man. They both chuckled and teased him about it, while Placido made a face of embarrassment, whereupon the old

63

man opened up one of the two bottles of cider that he had once brought from Spain. The old woman declined for the time being since she was still cooking, so Samantha offered to help her. In the kitchen, every once in a while, the old woman would slip and call her *niña*, and she would laugh at her own silliness.

The men were about to sit down in the living room when the doorbell rang.

"That must be Nancy," the old man announced and it was. Placido's sister had arrived with her American husband, Harry, and their kids. *"Felicidades!"* and *"Feliz Navidad!"* were shouted out all over again, but there were no hugs: Harry and Nancy and their two kids were carrying plates wrapped in aluminum foil. Nancy had volunteered to make the fried plantains, both kinds, the red juicy *platanos maduros* and the yellow, dry *chatinos,* as well as the crisp, yellow banana chips, Nancy knowing how time consuming it can be to cook them, particularly in big quantities and her mother getting on in age.

It was Harry's turn to growl on smelling the food. He blushed while everyone else laughed.

Their kids disappeared to join their cousins at play and the grandfather but on the records of Benny More and Celia Cruz.

"I had the worst time keeping the kids away from the chips and the *maduros!"* Nancy complained in English as she unwrapped the plates. "They kept sneaking in, trying to sneak one. I had to whack their little hands with a spatula. You know how easy it is to get full on *maduros. "*

"She wouldn't even let me have one! Not even one!" Harry complained. "Grinch!" he called after her.

"Ay, chica, don't be like that," the old woman said to her daughter and took one of the plates to Harry. "Here, Harry, there's plenty," she said in heavily accented English. Harry grabbed two with a napkin and looked smug at his sympathy ploy having worked so well while Nancy just glared at him.

Placido served the *cidra* to the newcomers and Harry admired the Christmas tree.

Now, it was Antonio's turn to arrive, the last guest, also bringing a bottle of Bacardi rum for the Cuba libres. Antonio was the old man's brother, the uncle of Nancy and Placido. The *"Feliz Navidades!"* made the rounds once again.

They talked about this, that and the other for an hour, or so, and after a while the kids were called in to ask them if they thought that they might get presents from Santa Claus for being good that year and what presents did they want. Antonio, with his irritating sense of humor, and having downed quite a few Cuba libres in the meantime, insisted that all that they were going to get was a lump of coal and kept at it, reminding them of some of their acts of misbehavior, to such an extent that the younger ones started to really get worried and Antonio was loudly overruled and chided with cries of *"Isleño!"* by the grandparents and the children were reassured and sent back to play.

Everyone was enjoying the warm feeling of family and of well being which is the hallmark of Christmas celebrations. In addition, the Cubans, from Placido to Antonio, were also feeling nostalgic at previous *Nochebuenas* and the nostalgia was mixed in with a bit of sadness and homesickness at those *Nochebuenas* in Cuba that were no more, now that the Communists had outlawed Christmas, and also of family members left behind and how they were passing this special night, but these sad feelings were not allowed to surface and get out of control.

The women finally announced that the feast was ready. The children were served first and allowed to eat separately, while watching television, since *"The Grinch Who Stole Christmas,"* with the incomparable voice of Boris Karloff, was on. So, the portable trays were taken out and each child served. All the children in their broken Spanish objected to grandma serving them yucca, even though the grandmother pointed out that it was moist. The oldest blurted out, "Yucca-yeuch!" and Samantha glared at her son.

Now, the adults sat at the splendidly set table, which had been enlarged to accommodate the extra guests by inserting an extra board in the middle of the table.

It was the traditional Cuban *Nochebuena* dinner: lechon asado (roast pork), yucca, black beans with rice, fried plantains and for dessert, *turron*---several kinds---from Spain. It smelled delicious and no one had to be egged on at feasting.

"Remember how *Nochebuena* used to be in Cuba?" Antonio asked his brother in Spanish (the conversation flowing constantly back and forth between Spanish and English for the benefit of Harry and Samantha, with many of the sentences, unintentionally spoken in both languages). He now turned to them. "We used to roast a whole pig, from head to tail over a spit, just like a Hawaiian luau. The women loved to east the crispy skin, I don't know why."

Just then, the eldest boy came in with his plate, for seconds, and on hearing this, asked

Placido, "Dad, I thought you said that there wasn't any food in Cuba?"

"Uncle Antonio's talking about years ago, son. There used to be plenty of food. There isn't much food now, under the Communists," he explained softly.

The grandfather, angered, interjected. "Yes! They cancelled Christmas! Officially! Christmas can't be celebrated, by order of The Party!"

"And by order of the *Lider Máximo!*" added Nancy with sarcasm and bitterness in her voice.

"How can anybody cancel Christmas?" the boy asked, incredulously.

"There's some very evil people in the world, son, and they enjoy making others' lives as miserable as possible. That's all that they live for." The sadness was still in his voice. There was no anger in it.

Harry said, "I imagine that it's still being celebrated---under cover, probably."

"Oh, yeah," the grandfather said, "but they're lucky if they can find even a little bit of what we have here."

"Can't we send them food?" the boy asked.

"No, the Communists won't allow it," responded the grandmother. "We tried." She then served the boy seconds and he went back to his friends.

That brief little exchange dampened the mood. The grandfather then informed the gathering that he had been trying for days to call their relatives in Cuba, without success.

But, it's very hard to remain depressed, if not impossible, when eating excellent food and the mood improved once more.

Antonio began the perennial discussion.

Addressing himself to Samantha and Harry, "You Americans should really switch your celebration to *Nochebuena.* After all, Jesus was supposed to have been born at night. You need to switch."

Harry joined in in the yearly ritual. "He was born after midnight. That's why it's celebrated on the 25th."

"Then, why do we have *Nochebuena?*"

"Because you're all gluttons and can't wait?" Samantha hazard a guess.

"In anticipation," said Harry, diplomatically.

It went on and it did not mean anything. Antonio was simply being Antonio.

After dinner, they sat around, exhausted from eating, drinking coffee and talking some more, until it was time to leave. For once, the kids were eager to leave their grandparents home and go to sleep. The adults reaffirmed to meet at Placido and Samantha's house at three in the afternoon the next day.

As anticipated, the kids woke up bright and early on Christmas Day, very excited, and found Santa's presents under the tree. No coal. Soon, the floor was littered with wrapping paper and, once the opening frenzy was over, the children became quietly (or noisily) absorbed in their presents. Afterwards, the parents, as in every previous year, had that yearly surprise as to how quickly the unwrapping and the children's feeling of surprise and expectation dissipated, compared to how long it had taken for Christmas Day to finally get here.

Samantha and Placido exchanged presents.

"Merry Christmas, honey."

"Merry Christmas, darling." And they kissed. They kissed before opening them and they kissed afterwards. Then, Samantha disappeared to the kitchen, leaving him in the living room with a warm feeling of contentment. After a while, he got up to put on a record of traditional Christmas songs.

As anticipated, the grandparents arrived a little early later on that afternoon.

"Merry Christmas! Merry Christmas!" they called out, walking in, without even knocking.

"Merry Christmas!" Samantha called out.

"Merry Christmas!" Placido called out.

The kids rushed out to hug them, on hearing their voices, yelling, "Merry Christmas, *abuelo!* Merry Christmas, *abuela!"*

"Hey, hey, let me see. Let me see what Santa Claus brought you," and the kids scampered off to collect and show their presents.

The grandparents took advantage of the opportunity to hand Samantha and their son presents and for them to do the same with lots of "Merry Christmas!" This gift giving to adults was a custom that had taken time to take root with the elderly couple, but once started, they seemed to enjoy it more with each passing year.

The children came back, tottering, covered with presents, to show their grandparents, who made the appropriate noises of appreciation.

"Well, do you know? Santa Claus left you presents in our house, too! Go get them, they're in the back seat of *abuelo's* car!" And they rushed off towards the unlocked car.

Placido offered eggnog while his mother joined Samantha in the kitchen and the kids returned with their presents and unwrapped them in a whirl of action.

At three o'clock sharp, Nancy arrived, carrying a thick cheesecake that she had made, followed by Harry carrying a stack of presents, and

69

their children with some of the presents that Santa left them that they brought over in order to play with them and show their cousins.

"Merry Christmas!" yelled Nancy, echoed by Harry.

"Merry Christmas!" was the response.

The grandfather returned to the car and took out more presents from the trunk to distribute to the newcomers. At that point, Antonio arrived, late as usual, and gave him a hand.

It was a beautiful, bright day, with a clear blue sky. There was no sound at all, everyone being inside their homes and all businesses closed. The absolute quiet would have been unnerving, except that they had slowly gotten used to the Midwest silence.

After the presents and after the eggnog, the children were sent off with their Christmas dinner to watch "Home Alone" on the VCR, while the adults sat to eat at the table.

The turkey dominated the table from one end where Placido sat, followed by a bowlful of stuffing, gravy, sweet potatoes with toasted marshmallows on top and, for dessert, apple pie and cheesecake. Plácido always felt odd carving the turkey and placing the slices on the plates, but tradition was tradition and he carried it out.

"I'm glad that the holidays are over," announced Nancy. "After today, I'm going on a crash diet."

"Me, too," echoed Samantha.

"You do look a little hefty there, Nancy," said Antonio. Nancy shot him a dagger look while Harry chuckled silently, but not daring to say a word.

"You have to make allowances for

Antonio," said Placido. "Do you know what he said to me when I was a kid? You know how dachshunds look, how long they are? Well, one time we saw one waddling towards us and he told me, 'Psst, Placido, that's where they make hot dogs from, for those kinds of dogs, 'cause they're so long! That's why they're called "hot dogs."' I believed him too! I wouldn't eat a hot dog for a full year after that!" Antonio looked pleased with himself, remembering the incident.

"He's from Camaguey," complained the grandmother, "that's why he's that way."

"No!" disagreed Nancy. "He's that way because that's the way he is. What Camaguey!" she added with a gesture.

"Camagueyano!" the grandmother insisted, accusing Antonio in a teasing manner.

Placido spoke up again. "I'll tell you one thing that I'm definitely grateful for and that's that we don't have The Three Magi on top of Santa Claus. I don't think I could hold up. I want peace and quiet from this day on, for at least six months."

Nancy explained to her husband. "The Three Magi used to come on January 6 to leave toys for the kids in Cuba. I think it's a tradition in all Catholic countries. Anyway, because Cuba was so close to the US, we also had Santa Claus, so the kids got presents on December 25 and on January 6. On top of that, the Jewish kids had Hannuka, and they didn't get no stupid dreidel, so they *really* cleaned up with Hannuka, Christmas and The Magi. Of course, now with the Communists . . . ." She did not finish the sentence and just shrugged.

"Sad," Harry muttered.

"You usually picked a favorite one from among the Magi," Nancy went on. "Mine was

71

Balthazar."

"Any luck with the phone call to Cuba?" Antonio asked his brother and the latter shook his head.

The conversation went on through dinner and through dessert (pecan and apple pies, heated, with melting vanilla ice cream on top). Afterwards, they adjourned to the living room. Everyone, once again, had that same feeling of family and well being as had been present the night before, except that the feeling was now stronger in Harry and Samantha and memories of their previous Christmases came to mind.

After a little while, everyone began to leave. No matter how much you love your family, after one feast following another, you tend to overdose on family and you then just simply want to be alone, or with your immediate family, just like at this moment, nobody could have eaten another slice of turkey or *lechon asado.*

Harry said that they would probably take the kids to see a movie and Placido said that they might just do that too, later on tonight since, of the twenty some movies out at this time, there was actually one without the mandatory obscenities from Hollywood.

With coat in hand, everyone headed for the door.

"Merry Christmas, everyone!"

"Merry Christmas!"

"Merry Christmas!" yelled the kids.

The door was shut. Peace and quiet reigned again. Placido kissed Samantha on the cheek, then collapsed on his favorite chair.

"Until next year," he said.

"Merry Christmas, honey," she said.

"Feliz Navidad, mi amor," he answered

back.

XI

Estrella genuflected upon entering the church, rapidly crossing herself with the tips of her finger, wet with holy water from the fount nearby. She was in a hurry because her timetable had been set off by an unexpected visit from Linda, who simply would not take a hint and who finally left after more than an hour.

She went and sat on one of the pews. Several people were already there awaiting to use the confessional.

"I've heard he's very strict, very demanding," Estrella heard the woman in front of her whispering to her companion.

"Yes, and he's new! You'd expect him to try to be more accommodating, being a stranger and all, but no," the reply came back.

The list! The grocery list! She forgot the damned grocery list! Now she had to drive all the way back home, then drive all the way back to the store. It almost cut away the savings that she was going to make with the discount coupons that she had with her by wasting all that gasoline.

An elderly man came out of the confessional and joined four others that had been waiting for him and the group left. One of the women went inside the confessional.

Well, why go back for the list? She began to make a mental list of all the things that she needed. Let's see, ground meat, about two to three pounds, garlic, green peppers, onions, Spanish onions that is, olive oil, fruit, definitely fruit, she was all out of fruit, get all kinds, grapes, kiwi, apples. Also, some vegetables. A voice was raised in the confessional, but she did not pay attention to it. Salad dressing, a couple of T-bones, maybe, if they weren't too expensive, and should she get canned peaches or fresh peaches? If they even had fresh peaches.

The woman came out, joined her friend and they both scurried out. Estrella looked around. It seemed to be her turn, so she went in. She looked at her watch. Good! She might just make good enough time to confess, do the groceries and make it in time for her appointment at the hairdresser's.

She hurriedly crossed herself and mechanically recited, "Forgive me, Father, for I have sinned," and before the priest had even finished with his response, she launched into her confession. "I've been guilty of envy, my next door neighbor was given a brand new car by her husband and I secretly hoped that she'd have an accident and bang it up, I've been using cuss words whenever I get angry and I do it in public and in private both, I have no patience with some of my friends and snap at them if they don't hurry up and do whatever they're supposed to do, also my friend Linda came over today and I wasn't as hospitable as I should have been," flour, she thought suddenly, I must get flour. And sugar. I gotta make a bundt cake, "And the other day at the bank, the teller gave me twenty dollars over the amount of withdrawal and she didn't notice it, but I kept it and didn't give it back or said anything about it to her. My poor husband, I've been cross with him, I shouldn't . . ." and on she went. At last she ended. "That's all," she said after a pause. She glanced at her watch and nodded.

"That's it, huh?" the disembodied voice

answered back.

"Yes."

She waited.

"What are you waiting for?" the priest finally asked her.

What am I *waiting* for? "You're supposed to absolve me, give me absolution---you know. A couple of Hail Marys and I'll be on my way."

"Well, you're not going to get it from me!" the voice nearly screamed. "You expect to simply recite a list of sins, with absolutely no remorse whatsoever and then waltz out of here ready to do it all over again? Where do you think you are?!"

Estrella stared at the screen window, dumbfounded. This was unbelievable.

"Well, it's you job to give me absolution if I confess. Get on with it," she blurted out and immediately covered her mouth, embarrassed.

"Get on with it!?!" The scream nearly knocked down the walls of the confessional. "Do you think that you're in a grocery store?? Get on with it!? No! *You* get out! Yeah, you! Yes, you! Get out! Get out right now and don't come back until you're ready to truly confess, until you're sincerely ashamed of your sins and wish to turn over a new leaf. Don't come back with a recital. Now go! Get out!" Estrella hesitated in her bewilderment. "What are you waiting for?" asked the masculine voice. "Get-out-and-don't-return . . . until you're truly penitent. *Then* we'll see about absolution."

Estrella, cowed, exited the confessional. Her legs were weak. Gone was the hairdresser, the canned peaches, the olive oil and the flour from her mind. She sat down in an empty pew, weakly kneeled and prayed.

XII

Larry sat alone at a tiny table inside The Cotillion, scanning the faces there. He had gotten there about ten minutes before and it was taking some time to get used to the darkness of the club.

A waitress maneuvered through the cramped bodies and tables, having noticed his cleared table top. "What'll ya have, babe?" she asked him.

"Beer."

She made a note on her tray and wove and squeezed away to the bar.

As his eyesight got used to the darkness and he began to distinguish faces, his lungs likewise got used to the choking cigarette smoke. When he got home, from past experience, he knew that he would have to discard his clothes right into the dirty clothes basket to get rid of that putrid smell; they would be so saturated with the acrid smell that if he did not isolate and cover the clothes in a hamper or a plastic bag, the smell would spread and contaminate at least one room in his home with the sickening stench.

He tried to catch the eye of an attractive girl two tables down sitting with her girlfriends, but she pointedly ignored him.

The Cotillion was once again *the* club for the over-18 crowd. All of Larry's friends raved about it and would oftentimes mention that they had been at the Cotillion last night or two nights ago and had had a blast. They also bragged about how much they had puked afterwards (and they made it sound like they had broken a record in sports). Eventually, everyone felt that he had to let others know that he, to, had been to the Cotillion. Larry had been here before, usually with friends. Tonight, he had felt like company and doing something and so had come down. He had tried to get a hold of Sebastian or Leslie, but they hadn't been home. Maybe they would show up, later on.

The waitress brought him a beer and he paid and tipped her.

Larry tasted the beer and grimaced. God, how he hated the taste of beer! He forced a sip down, trying to convince himself that it wasn't so bad and that he would get used to it one of these days. His dislike of beer made him feel like an outsider, like he had a shameful secret. Although he would have much preferred a Coke or a 7-Up, it wouldn't do to just have a soda at the Cotillion. It just was not done. Besides, somebody might have noticed. At least the beer was cold.

Larry scanned the ever-shifting crowd again, this time surreptitiously. Everyone was trying exceedingly hard to try to be hip, thinking that everyone *else* was hip. A few even believed that they were truly hip.

Being unable to see through the surrounding facades, he always had the feeling that everyone was having a great time, but that he was just on the outskirts of this cool, ever-so-cool, group of good, fun-loving people; this had been particularly the case during the first few times that he had come when his senses had been bombarded; the sights, the sounds, the smells, the music had all made him excited him, made him happy, made him feel that he was part of an exciting, sensual, semi-secret world, with endless, unspoken promises of delights to come. It would still be many years before he would see the nightclub scene for what it really was.

He spotted Sebastian at the entrance, trying to adjust his eyes to the dim light before plunging in. His curly hair was outlined clearly by the light outside. The band was taking a long break, so it was darker than when they were on stage and the various multicolored spotlights switched on. He was joined by Leslie and after a few seconds, they went in.

They wove through the crowds, getting the feel for the place and now getting used to the dim lights. They spotted Larry and smiled and Larry waved them over.

"Hi, guy!" Sebastian said as he sat down.

"Where you been?" Leslie asked him.

"I went by your houses looking for you guys," Larry explained.

They laughed. "Well, *we* dropped by *your* house looking for *you!*" Sebastian said.

The waitress appeared out of nowhere, like a jinni. "What'll ya have?" she asked them.

Leslie glanced at the glass on the table. "Beer," he said and the waitress wandered off.

"How long you been here?" Sebastian asked.

"About . . . half an hour, I guess."

"You seen anybody you know?" Leslie asked him.

Larry pointed to a table opposite the dance floor. "There's Otto and Nancy." Otto was an exchange student from Germany. Both were drinking beer. They both knew that to Otto American beer was like water, whereas German beer was so strong one could use it as rocket fuel.

The waitress appeared with the drinks and

left after being paid.

Sebastian took a sip and hid the grimace of distaste.

Leslie took a gulp and tried to ignore the bitter taste.

Larry masked his feelings and took another swallow.

The three friends talked about Otto and Nancy, wondering if the relationship was getting serious enough that it was getting to the point of an engagement. Horrid thought. They all wanted to date her.

Sebastian suddenly grinned. "Hey! Look at Chucho over there," he pointed.

They spotted Chucho, a short, black-haired friend, who was trying to make his way to the bathroom, but somehow could not maneuver in a straight line and, so, was staggering from side to side, with an idiotic grin on his face, bumping into tables on the way. His eyes were half closed. The people at those tables that he bumped into were either amused or angry, depending on the amount of spillage from drinks. No doubt about it, Chucho liked his beer. The three friends grinned in amusement as he staggered out the door.

Larry glanced at the table where the attractive girl sat with her girlfriends and noticed that she now smiled back. She seemed to say something to one of her friends because the other looked over her shoulder to where Larry and his friends sat.

Now a change came over the crowd. The band members climbed on the stage and made themselves comfortable and adjusted their instruments. Larry thought that after they started playing, he would ask the girl to dance.

The three friends started at the sudden ear-splitting music coming out of the speakers, so loud that you could almost not hear the melody and you certainly could not talk with your friends. Each knew that it would take a few minutes to get used to and that afterwards, on leaving the club, their ears would be ringing and they would have some difficulty in hearing regular sounds. But, so what? They were there to have fun like the rest of the crowd. It was better than being alone.

XIII

From Topeka, Kansas, to Miami, Florida, there is no straight superhighway, or, for that matter, any other type of road. If one wishes to travel on this type of highway, then one must go due south on U. S. Highway 35 into the stinking wasteland known as Texas until it crosses U. S. Highway 10, then make a ninety degree turn due east to get out of Texas as quickly as possible, before something bad happens, towards Florida. But there is no such superhighway traveling the hypotenuse of this right triangle. And it was down this weaving hypotenuse of two-lane highways that the Nunez family was traveling on their way to a two-week vacation in Miami. Although speed is sacrificed by not taking the four-lane superhighway, there are many other compensations, including bypassing Texas and avoiding contact with its boorish inhabitants, always a bonus for the unwary. Additionally, and some would say foremost, it being a better scenery, particularly when traveling through small, quaint towns. They were passing through one just now.

"Look at that," remarked the elder Nunez to his wife. "That's one of the great things about this country! No matter where you go, or how small the village, it always has its paved roads, its post office building, its little city hall and its traffic lights. And everything is clean. Not like it was in Cuba. Out in the country, in the small towns, it was a pigsty. Just like a century or two ago," and he shook his head in disgust at the memory.

The family making the pilgrimage to its roots in Miami was the husband and wife, Conrado and Xiomara and their twelve-year-old Manolito.

The youngster had come to the States when he was eight, early on when it was still possible to send children out of the country before the Communists got their hands on them. His parents had followed months later.

The trip was a long one and conversation rose up and down, with long gaps in between and jumping from one topic to another. After one such gap, with his mind wandering as he drove, Conrado remembered a visit of a week ago and snorted. "I still can't believe that insurance agent," he said.

"Mmm?" she said, interrupted from her own thoughts and then she remembered. "Ah, yeah."

This was what had happened. An insurance agent, an acquaintance of his, had called up Nunez at work to offer him life insurance and he had agreed to meet the agent at home after work. The salesman gave him his sales pitch, showing him the advantages of switching policies. Everything was going smoothly; the customer was very receptive and had agreed to switch insurance companies. The agent, pleased, went on to suggest that he could also

81

include his wife and/or his son with their own life insurance policies, with Conrado as the beneficiary. And, as soon as he had said that, he realized that something was very wrong, for the elder Nunez was no longer smiling, but was, instead, tightlipped and frowning.

"What kind of a suggestion is that?"

The agent blinked in surprise.

"What kind of a man do you think I am?" Mrs. Nunez was also frowning, albeit not as deeply.

The agent stammered. "But, but, a lot of people have their whole family insured."

"No, sir! I'm not going to be insulted! I'm not an immoral man! No, sir! Do you think that I want to benefit from my wife's death? Or the death of my son? You're being very insulting, sir! Yes, sir, that's what you're being!" His arm was waving around in emphasis.

Not knowing when to leave well enough alone, the agent tried to explain, sinking deeper into the quicksand and continuing to prod the death taboo. "It's not for benefiting anybody, Mister Nunez. The money would be for the purpose of covering funeral expenses in the event-"

"I said no, and I mean no! So, don't talk to me anymore about this!"

"Very well," he meekly agreed, barely rescuing his sale.

Xiomara just shook her head, remembering the visit. They exchanged a few comments on the incident and the car became silent once more, each one left to his or her own daydreams.

Manolito stared out the window and, as they passed farmhouses, he saw poultry and wondered if once in Miami whether there would be any cockfights that he could go to since there were so many Cuban refugees there. Even in the capital of Havana, in wealthy suburbs, many children raised roosters in their back yard as pets in order to compete with the other kids. Manolito had fond memories of his red rooster that he had left behind; it was the champion of the block.

It should be said, however, that the boy had become thoroughly Americanized and had few memories of Cuba, although the ones he did have were strong ones. Like the one just now, as they passed a stand selling fireworks for the Fourth of July, which created a chain reaction of associations in his mind. They would be missing the Fourth of July parade back in Topeka, which would be no great loss. All "parades" in Kansas, indeed, the whole Midwest, from North Dakota to Texas were dismal, pathetic affairs. Regardless of the occasion, they were all unbelievably pathetic, consisting of a few noisy high school bands, interspersed with convertibles carrying schmucks waving at the crowd, with the parade ultimately petering out at the end. Sometimes they went to Wichita during the Fourth and it was just as dismal. No floats. No speeches. No raffles. No dances. No grand fireworks. It was pathetic. Parades were supposed to be emotionally cathartic, but these parades left everyone feeling empty and embarrassed.

On the other hand, carnivals in Cuba . . . now *there* was a parade! It was one of the few strong memories that Manolito had.

Of course, now with the joyless, fanatical Communists in power, full of hatred towards everything, the carnivals, like everything joyful in Cuba, had gone down the tubes.

For his part, Conrado was puzzling over a conversation that he had had with the mechanic at the gas station that he frequented a block away from their home in Topeka. He had taken his car to the shop for an oil change and a tune-up just prior to the trip. After many months of patronizing the station, Nunez had expected a "special price," that is, a reduced price, to be offered by the owner. None was forthcoming. Finally, this time, upon seeing the same amount as always for a tune up and oil change, he had asked outright for a "special price," not angrily, mind you, but definitely insisting. The owner looked at him blankly, not comprehending what on Earth he was alluding to. What was a "special price," anyway? What was that in reference to? He scratched his head in the American gesture of confusion and Nunez drove off, upset, after paying the bill, leaving the attendant wondering how in the world he had offended one of his regular customers.

As for Xiomara, she, too, was deep in thought, a little worried. Several years of living in Kansas had changed some of the habits among the Cubans living in the state, whether in Emporia, Wichita, Topeka, Newton, Manhattan or Kansas City. And she had to admit, deep down, that some of the changes had been for the best. For example, the old habit of dropping in on friends, unannounced, had been gradually abandoned; nobody really liked being surprised by people (even if they were good friends) who were under the assumption that the recipients of the visit would be ecstatic in seeing them again, irrespective of any plans that the victims themselves may have had.

Another habit that had slowly, and thankfully, gone by the wayside was that of insisting on paying for the whole tab whenever two or more friends got together in a restaurant. This had occurred, traditionally, even when two or more very large families had run up an enormous tab. The head of each family would insist that the other side was their guest and the grabbing back and forth of the check---with loud protestations and even the children making furtive grabs and bringing the check to their respective fathers---was always a lively episode. And a costly one. That custom had gratefully also faded away.

Nonetheless, Xiomara wondered if those customs still lived on in Miami.

*

The car slowly wove through the streets of Miami, as Conrado tried to follow the written directions that he had received from his cousin, Francisco. As they passed several streets, Manolito looked around. There was something odd about this place, he felt, but he couldn't put his finger on it.

They passed many stores with signs in Spanish rather than English. Several older women walked down the sidewalks carrying opened umbrellas as shields against the sun, even though it was not raining. This never happened in Kansas, *in Kansas,* not even in August.

A man noisily spat on the sidewalk and Manolito almost gagged.

The boy got the handwritten map from his father to help him out and read out the landmarks to look out for. He noticed that the address was 4772 and that the sevens were crossed.

They finally found the house and Francisco and Paula came out to meet them, noisily greeting them and hugging everyone, examining Manolito and loudly exclaiming how much he had grown. For his part, Manolito did not remember having ever met her.

Within minutes, they were inside sitting down drinking little cups of the strong Cuban coffee, loudly interrupting each other and talking about the other relatives who lived in New York. Paula and Xiomara mentioned several persons that they had known in the past. It seemed that both women came from the same town, Maguey Grande.

Before too long, Manolito began to get antsy, hearing them talk endlessly about people he did not know and had no interest in whatsoever and he just had to get out of there, so he went outside the house "to look around." Once outside, he felt calmer, less nervous. He could still hear them talking inside, even though he was standing all the way outside on the sidewalk. He frowned. Americans were quieter, more subdued, especially Kansans. By comparison, Cubans seemed to be in a perpetual state of hysterics. While the Latins' visage was always animated, many Kansans were stone faced; you could tell them that a tornado had carried off their homes and their kids and not a trace of emotion would cross their face (not even if you told them instead that the twister had only carried off his fat wife, to which you would expect at least a smile of relief).

But to get back to Miami . . ..

Manolito got tired of loitering around and began strolling down the street. Unlike Topeka or Wichita, Miami had sidewalks in residential streets, so he did not have to walk in the path of cars. He was grateful for that.

There seemed to be a couple of stores at the corner and he strolled over, yet became uneasy as he got closer, because of the noise in one of the stores; apparently, there was a stereo and the speakers were blaring. The teenage boy shook his head. It was Sunday. In any, every, city in Kansas it was so quiet on Sunday that you could hear a pin drop two blocks away. On those days the cities looked like one of those sci-fi flicks where the population has vanished into thin air.

He entered the small store and looked around. It was so different. Almost all of the products were alien to him. One wall was stacked with boxes of weird produce (including thick tree roots!) inside cardboard boxes, another wall had a counter with cut meats behind glass, but the butcher section was out in the open instead of behind closed doors. The little grocery store was shabby---not dirty, mind you, but indisputably shabby. The boy was not used to that. American stores were immaculate. You could practically eat off the floor. He got out of there and went into the next store.

This store was really strange. Eerie. It had dried up weeds for sale, along with a multitude of different candles and saints' statues. There were also those bizarre pictures of Jesus that he had seen before for sale in frames: they were those repulsive renditions showing Jesus as a blonde woman with a sparse beard. Manolito had no idea what this was all about, but he did know that he didn't want to have anything to do with it and exited.

At one spot, in one of the stores, he noticed that there were four older men gathered around a table playing dominoes with animation in their moves.

He avoided the store with the blaring music and strolled back to the house and went in.

"I was so worried for you guys," said Paula to his mother, "that something may have happened on the way. Imagine! I had a dream last night, I dreamed of a cup of coffee with clouds of milk in it!" Xiomara gasped. "I told Francisco this morning, didn't I?" Her husband just snorted contemptuously and resumed his conversation with Conrado.

Just then, their teenage daughter, Elena, came in, back from visiting her friends and was introduced all around. Manolito stifled a laugh; she was pretty and barely on this side of obesity. She had smooth round cheeks, seemingly about to pop. What had made Manolito almost break out with laughter was that in the moment that he saw her he had an irrepressible urge of sticking an apple into her mouth, thereby completing the picture of a cute little roast pig.

For her part, upon hearing him talk to her (in English, of course), Elena giggled.

"You talk funny," she told him in English.

"What?"

"You talk funny."

"Funny? How?"

"Like a hick. You got a hick accent. A Cuban with a hick accent." She giggled some more.

Manolito did not laugh, but was, instead, surprised to hear that he had an accent when he himself could not hear it (next day, and apart from their friends, his father would praise Elena's beauty to Manolo, implying that they should date, to the young boy's horror that his father would even think of matching him up to such a lard ball, not aware that to Cuban men, fat women are attractive).

With Elena home, it was decided to dine out and they all piled into one car, very crammed. As they drove off, they all proceeded to talk at the same time. Worse, they also switched on the radio and to Manolito's surprise, heard the disc jockey scream, yes, *scream,* nonstop (in days to come, he would come to know that this was not a bizarre, isolated case; Latin disc jockeys *screamed* at their audiences).

By the time that they finally got to the restaurant, Manolito was a nervous wreck.

But that was not the end of it.

Once in the restaurant, the waitresses (or even the customers) would yell out to each other across the booths. Even the older Nuñezes found this unnerving; like their son, they had gotten used to going to a nice, *quiet* restaurant in Kansas and speaking to each other in a soft voice instead of hearing everybody else's conversations and the waitresses' comments.

However, the food served helped to soothe everyone's nerves, not the least Manolito's, for the food was indeed outstanding. Cuban cuisine is one of the best kept secrets; few who sample it come away not hooked to it. The end of the meal saw a satisfied pair of families, whose two husbands now began to wrangle for the tab. Unlike previous endless friendly bickering, it was resolved surprisingly quickly by Nunez asserting, "All right. But next time, I get the tab." Manolito felt so full that he did not even mind the ride back with all the noise.

When they returned to the house and entered the porch, Paula screeched and yelled out, "A witch!" She pointed to the wall and Manolito's mother joined her. "Get it away! Get it away!" The boy looked at the spot where the women pointed, but all that he saw was a very, very large brown moth, really huge. Aside from its unusual size, it was just there, nothing else, and he realized, with an overwhelming feeling of embarrassment that it was indeed the large moth that the two women were hysterically referring to as . . . a . . . witch. Yes. A witch. A witch!

A witch!

The adult men laughingly brushed it off and the moth fluttered away, but not without passing by the women, who shrieked as it did so.

Manolito was glad that he was in Miami where none of his friends lived, otherwise he would have burrowed into the ground like a mole, out of sight, from sheer embarrassment.

Once inside, coffee was brewed and served. Then, with Paula's announcement that it was time for her *novela*, the women withdrew to an adjacent room where she switched on the radio to listen to an audio soap opera. She filled in the background for Xiomara's benefit, who for years in Kansas had been starved for a *telenovela*.

In the living room sat his father with Francisco. His father was telling his cousin about a friend of theirs in Wichita who worked for Cessna. He was ridiculing him because he was in the habit of saying to Nunez, by way of conversation, that "We're now going into overproduction" or "We're doing very good with overseas sales" and "We're looking into other types of designs." The use of the pronoun "we" was to them incomprehensible and they disdainfully interpreted it as an affectation. "As if he owned the company!"

It seemed to Manolito that his father and Francisco were missing an important lesson here, but he was too young to pinpoint what it was exactly and so, just got angry and he went outside.

*

By the third day, the boy was crawling up the walls and he was now constantly pestering his parents to go back home. He was on edge and restless and he told them that he was bored and homesick. What to his parents was a breath of fresh air to him had become a constant source of low-level irritation, all the worse for him in not being able to realize, exactly, what the problem was.

In fact, one afternoon, the two women came back from a visit to a santero and Manolo learned with horror that some witch doctor had waved a killed rooster by the neck around their heads several times while spitting in their faces . . . and that they had paid for that!

This is not to say that the whole time was spent in misery. Far from it! Being reacquainted with Cuban music (like Benny More, Celia Cruz and Gloria Estefan) was a delight. Listening to Three Skates daily on the radio had him doubled up with laughter, holding his sides, it hurt so much to laugh. He enjoyed playing *tute* and *brisca* with the playing cards from Spain, which were so different from *regular* cards. He also learned and thoroughly enjoyed playing dominos. Encountering a banyan tree one day sparked off nostalgic, long-buried memories. Likewise, going to the beach evoked an overwhelming, almost tearful reunion in the whole Nunez family, as if a long-lost brother had been found.

And then, there was the food. Apart from regular lunch and dinner, Manolito let himself go, continually snacking on forgotten fruits like guava, mamey, papaya and the diminutive Johnson bananas, sweets like *capuchinos* and *buñuelos,* drinks like Hatuey *malta, batido* and *guarapo.* And sandwiches like Midnights and Flying Saucers. At the rate that he was going, he would not be able to snicker at Elena much longer.

In between, however, he was intensely restless, nervous, like a migratory bird kept in a cage. It was as if a switch was turned on whenever his concentration was not on food, the beach, the music, *tute*, or Three Skates.

He pestered his parents so much that Conrado several times threatened to use the belt on him.

Even so, Conrado agreed to leave three days ahead of time. Truth to tell, the parents were also becoming homesick. So, they went on a shopping spree for supplies, the father buying bottles of anisette, records and books in Spanish, while the mother bought a huge number of yuccas, plantains, coffee, Hatuey *maltas, capuchinos* and Midnights and *Bustelo* coffee. Knowing that they were leaving soon only made Manolito that much more restless, so that he only finally calmed down when he was in the car on the way back.

When they finally got back to Kansas, to the small city of Topeka, he felt an enormous relief.

Naturally, none of the *maltas, capuchinos,* or Midnight sandwiches made it that far, the last one disappearing somewhere along Mississippi.

And the really odd thing was . . . as soon as he returned to Topeka--- that very same day in fact---the boy missed Miami and wanted very much to go back.

XIV

For the past couple of weeks, or so, Victor had been like a boy when Christmas is a few weeks away and is barely containing himself with eager anticipation. Deer season was imminent and he could hardly contain himself in conversation with others, volunteering details about his plans, or sometimes just plain daydreaming. He had rented a number of acres for three days in a part of the country where white tail deer frequented and such had been the demand that he had almost missed out on the rental. He would have it for three days straight at the very beginning of the season. A deer stand was included in the rental, nothing fancy. He disliked the deer stands that were so fancy that he referred to them as "penthouses." This stand was plain, a camouflaged stand on top of a tree.

During previous seasons he had failed to bag a deer, though he had sighted several. In spite of this failure, he had enjoyed himself enormously and had always come back next season, ever hopeful. Quite frankly, he had been contented simply with the silence and the solitude, in being alone with his thoughts, and not just because he had been away from the wife and kids---although that was enjoyable in of itself.

Today was the first day and he was driving towards the site along the country road in his pickup truck. Last night, although he had made careful preparations in packing, he had, however, overlooked to change the time for the alarm clock with the result that he had overslept by about two hours. Upon realizing his error, he had not become angry at himself, but had been, instead, amused by his silly oversight. Since the deer were usually actively feeding during sunrise and sunset, and he would arrive at the designated spot a couple of hours after sunrise, then it simply meant that he could look forward to simply enjoying Nature for most of the day.

Victor was leisurely driving his new truck down the country road, passing houses now and then, with his windows down, enjoying the brisk morning air. As he approached a house on his left, he saw a doe. It was simply eating by itself, with not a care in the world. What made the picture all the more appealing was that, apparently, it had jumped over a fence into the front yard of the house. Both the house and the deer were quite a ways from the road, on a slope.

Victor slowed down until he was parallel with the doe. He was very excited, yet held his breath absurdly fearing that the doe would hear him breathe, become skittish and run away. It did not run away, but munched on, oblivious to his presence. He slowly rolled down the window and, just as slowly, took his rifle and loaded it. He was surprised, on aiming, that, miraculously, the doe was still there and had not vanished. He sighted it. In seeing it, content and at peace with the world, he felt a twinge of hesitation and guilt. He suppressed it and gently squeezed the trigger.

The doe was killed.

Victor ran out of the truck, leaving his weapon behind and not even bothering to close the door behind him in his excitement at his first kill. He bounded over the fence and ran towards the collapsed animal.

Standing over it, he surveyed his victim. Yet, the mighty hunter did not feel unqualified pride, or even joy. For one thing, there was all that blood. And its once pretty head was now disfigured. And . . . what was that? Around its neck? It was a collar! It was a collar with a small bell!

The deer had been a pet.

The doe had not jumped over the fence from the wild. It had been raised there. The family living up there on the house had nursed it, raised it and taken care of it. That is why it had not been skittish. As long as it remained behind the fence it had been safe.

And Victor had killed it.

He broke out in a cold sweat and stared up at the house. Nothing stirred from it. His hands shook.

He broke into a run. He vaulted over the fence and got into his blood-red truck and screeched out of there.

Some time later, he stopped the pickup, turned it around and drove back the same way that the had come, towards home and away from the deer stand.

Passing the spot where he had made his kill, he could not help looking up the slope. He had told himself that he would not look, but he looked anyway. He wished that he had not. A blonde teenage girl was cradling the deer, its neck and what was left of its head was against her breast. Her blouse was stained with blood. She was crying and the look on her pained face was haunting.

He drove on home. His wife was surprised at seeing him return home so soon. He said nothing to her at first, but then found the strength to tell her what had happened and she tried to console him, to no avail.

The next day, he put an ad in the paper and within the week he had sold off all of his hunting equipment at a substantial loss. He did not care. He wanted no reminder. He never went hunting again.

But, every year during deer season, he keeps

seeing that girl crying and cradling her dead pet deer.

XV

"Mister Abelson?" the secretary stuck her head at the doorway of the Vice Principal's office. "I was able to reach the parents of Juan. They said that they'll be here shortly."

"Both of them?" he asked, a little surprised.

"Yes, sir. I got through to Mrs. Vallejo, but she doesn't speak English, but she did know, or at least she's memorized, enough words to tell me to call her husband at work. She had the phone number memorized. I got through to Doctor Vallejo-"

"Oh? He's a doctor?"

"Yes, sir, a dentist and he said that he'd be here shortly, with his wife."

"Good Lord, Margaret, didn't you tell him that it wasn't an emergency?"

"Yes, I did, but he said that he'd come over anyway, that he wasn't busy."

"All right, thank you." He sighed as she withdrew from the door. He did not want to inconvenience the parents on something that was relatively minor. Still, at the same time, he wished that more parents were as involved with their children as were Juan's parents. The children would probably benefit as much as the staff, directly or indirectly. But, nowadays, they just saw school as little better than a baby-sitting service.

The two boys, both eleven years of age, were waiting outside, all scratched up and bruised, still smarting from the fighting that they had been involved in. The Vice Principal was surprised that it was these two boys who had been involved. Among their other good qualities, they were both well-known as being very easy going and the best of friends.

He went to the door and called in one of the boys.

"John? Come in." He noticed that both boys were far apart from each other. The boy went in and the Vice Principal closed the door.

"Johnny" he said as he sat down, "care to tell me what happened?"

"Mister Abelson, we were just out at the rec yard, talking and he hauled off and punched me for some reason! I don't know why! I tried to ask him while sitting out there and he won't say anything to me." The boy was evidently perplexed.

"Well, something you said, perhaps. Did you insult him?"

"No, we were just making jokes."

"Aha. And what kind of jokes?"

"All kinds. Mostly knock-knock jokes. I wasn't making fun of him. Honest!"

"I thought you two were friends."

"We were! I don't know why he hit me."

"Mmm, go outside and sit down. And tell Juan to come in here."

The other boy came in, uncharacteristically surly.

"Well, Juan? What happened in the rec yard?"

"Nothing," he said, looking down.

"What do you mean, 'nothing'? Didn't you get into a fight?" The boy did not respond.

"Answer me."

"Yeah, I guess."

"Well, what started it?" The boy shrugged

his shoulders, still looking at the floor.

"I thought you two were friends."

Still that maddening silence.

So, the Vice Principal tried another tack.

"I contacted your parents and they're on their way." That did it. The boy looked up at him, all trace of surliness gone, replaced by a look of worry. Abelson could not help but smile, even though slightly. "Go wait outside," he said, almost adding "and stew."

In a little while, Juan's parents came in. The father looked angry, the mother concerned and Juan, well, Juan looked worried, only more so now that they were there.

"Doctor Vallejo? I'm Phillip Abelson, the Vice Principal," he greeted them, shaking their hands, "Mrs. Vallejo." They now both smiled at him. "Won't you come in into my office?"

"Thank you for coming," he said as the all sat down. "We're a little puzzled as to why-"

"-Excuse me, what?" Doctor Vallejo interrupted with a heavy accent in his voice.

"We're puzzled, ah, a little confused--- mystified."

"Ah, yes, *puzzled*," he said as if filing away that word for future reference.

"Yes, we're a little puzzled as to why Juan and John would get into a fight."

"Johnny *y Juanito pelearon?*" asked Mrs. Vallejo surprised. *"Un* 'fight'? *Pero son muy amigos."*

"Yes, they did get into a fight, in the recreation yard. One minute they were talking and in another they were fighting. It looks like Juan started the fight by hitting Johnny first. And it was a nasty fight, from what I heard. I wasn't there, so I don't know what triggered it."

"Excuse me, Mister Albelson, while I translate for my wife."

"Of course," he said and the Vallejos exchanged words. When they appeared finished, he went on. "Johnny doesn't know why it started and Juan will not say a word to me---which is very unlike him, he usually doesn't stop talking," he joked.

"Juan talks too much?" Doctor Vallejo said, scowling. "He interrupts teacher? Does not listen to her?"

Abelson saw his mistake. "No, no, that's not what I mean to say. I mean, that he's always talking with his friends or with a teacher."

"He talks too much."

"*Appropriately* so," he emphasized. "In a *good* way. We all enjoy listening to him, he's got a neat accent. Everybody likes to hear him speak. Believe me, he's fine on that point," he said reassuringly. "The other day, for example, I was told John told Juan that he was a real card. Juan was puzzled at that and he opened up his dictionary and read out loud the definition of a card: 'a stiff piece of paper.' The whole class got a kick out of that one," he chuckled. He looked up and realized that they were not laughing and it occurred to him that he was making things worse. "A 'card' is also a person who is humorous, has a sense of humor---is appreciated," he explained. Doctor Vallejo seemed to understand now and smiled.

"*Que dice?*" the mother asked, while the father once again translated at length.

"Excuse me, Mister Albelson, but my wife says something that is true. These two boys are good friends. Very good friends. Johnny comes over almost everyday or Juanito will pay him a visitation at his home. He come to eat in our house, our boy goes to eat at his house. They play all the time together. He comes to play in our house, our boy goes to play at his house. They are very good friends. Ever since we moved here four months ago."

"Where were you before, then?"

"What?"

"Where did you live before you came here?"

"Ah, in Miami. For eleven months, almost a year. Before then, you know, we were in Cuba."

"Castro took over, what, three years ago?"

"Yes. Horrible."

"We don't get too many Cubans here in Emporia," he smiled. He was aware that the Midwest had been settled primarily by Swedes, Germans, Czechs and, of course, the Indians."

"Well, what you say about the boys is true here in school as well. They're always together. They're the best of friends. In fact, they are two of our best students: excellent grades, they behave well, they're sociable, they have good manners, everybody likes them both." The father, visibly proud, spontaneously translated for the mother, who nodded as she listened, "which is why this is, like I said before, a bit puzzling. And since Juan won't say anything, I thought that perhaps you could get something out of him."

"Excuse me, what?"

"Get something out of him---find out why there was a fight."

"Ah, yes!" the father nodded vigorously, scowling. He would get something out of him all right, if he had to skin the boy to get it out.

"This school is very strict insofar as fighting

between students, very strict and since Juan did start the fight, I will have to punish him. Yet, at the same time, I'm very curious as to the whole thing. Has he been having problems at home?"

"No-o-o, no problems," the father responded, thinking.

"Well. Let's get him in here and see if you can find out anything," the Vice Principal said, getting up. He opened the door. "Juan, would you come in here?" The boy did so. It was apparent that the wait had frayed his nerves. "Your father wants to ask you something."

"Why did you fight?" Doctor Vallejo asked in English. The boy looked around, hesitating, so the father asked him in Spanish. "Quiero que me digas la verdad, que estoy muy bravo! ¿Por qué Uds se pelearon?"

The boy hesitated for a second, then he blurted out, "Porque el me tocó la cara!" and he scowled.

Both parents said "Ahhh," and pulled their heads up. They looked at each other, nodding.

"What? What?" asked Abelson.

"He says that the other boy touched his face," he said with a tone that indicated that this was a different matter altogether, now it made sense and was even justified.

The Vice Principal, frowning, went to the door and opened it. "John, come in here!" The other boy did so and the Vice Principal regained his seat. He looked at the two boys standing side by side for a second, then asked the one, "Johnny, why did you hit Juan?"

The boy's eyes opened wide. "But I didn't hit him!" he protested.

"He says that you did."

"I did not!"

The father asked his son, "El te dio en la cara, o te toco la cara?"

"Me toco la cara," he responded.

"Mister Abelson, Johnny did not hit Juanito in the face. He touched Juanito in the face."

Both the Vice Principal and the boy looked lost. Then, the adult had an inspiration as a thought popped into his head. Something that he remembered having read once, somewhere that in Thailand it was considered very insulting to touch a Thai on the head, also in Indonesia, and someone had told him that some Japanese men preferred their wives to give them a haircut rather than let some stranger touch their heads. But that was in Asia, not South America.

"Doctor Vallejo, in your culture, in your country, that is, is it considered bad manners if someone touches your face?"

"Oh, yes! Only a girl lets herself be touched on the cheek! If a boy touches another boy in the cheek, that means he's a girl, a, what is that word? I saw it the other day, ah, yes, he's a 'sissy,' a sissy, it means that he's a sissy, a girl. So, of course, Juan, he had to fight him." Both parents felt that their son was vindicated.

Vice Principal Abelson began to comprehend, but the other boy saw nothing but absurdity.

"But I didn't hit him!" Johnny finally blurted out.

"But you did touch him in the face, in the cheek?"

"Yes, I did. So what? I didn't hit him! I was telling him a joke and he didn't get it and I had to explain it to him and when he *finally* caught it, I said, 'Very good, Juan,' and patted him." He motioned the gesture in the air. "But I *didn't* hit him!"

The educator glanced at the parents and realized that they, too, did not understand. Neither did Juan. Nor did Johnny.

"Doctor Vallejo, Mrs. Vallejo, Juan, do you understand that in this country if a boy touches another boy in the face it doesn't mean anything?" They looked at him as if he was speaking another language. "You do realize that different countries have different customs?" The dentist and his son nodded. "And what is considered bad manners in one country may not be bad manners in another."

"Bad manners is bad manners. All over the world," the father said.

"Yes, that's true. But up to a point. But in certain other things, it doesn't mean the same here," he motioned with his hand a spot in the air, then moved it to another spot, "as it does here. Different languages, different weather, different laws, different customs." He looked at them. He still could not get through to them. It was as if they were deaf. Johnny too. "It's the same with language. For example, the United States and England both speak English, but we have some words in this country that we use every day without problem, but which in England are very bad words. Even though we both speak English."

"Yes. This is also true in Spanish, you know," the father said. "I understand. In Spain and Mejico they use the name for a, a, ah, yes---a sweet---that in my country is a very bad word, very bad. And in Cuba and in Spain the word for insect is a very bad word in Puerto Rico."

"Exactly! You see?"

"Ahhhh," Doctor Vallejo let out slowly. It all finally clicked. He turned to his wife and started explaining. The Vice Principal turned to Juan.

"Do you understand, Juan? John was not insulting you. Here, in this country, it doesn't mean anything if one boy touches another in the cheek."

"Yes . . . I think so. I think I understand."

Was it his imagination, the Vice Principal thought, or does Juan now look thoroughly embarrassed?

"It's just a custom in your country that means something bad. Do *you* understand, John?"

"Yeah . . . I guess so. It sounds kinda funny, though. I didn't know."

"Well, men, you still have classes. Are you ready to shake hands and be friends again?" Both boys nodded. "OK. Shake!" The boys turned around and shook hands.

"Well, now, usually whenever there's a fight, I have to paddle the participants," and saying this, he withdrew what seemed to the students a gigantic wooden paddle.

Their eyes got really big. They had heard of this paddle and of his wielding it. "But seeing as to how it was all a misunderstanding, that won't be necessary" and he began to replace it in the desk when he stopped in mid motion, "unless you two are going to start fighting again."

"Oh, no!"

"No! No!"

"OK, then, you're dismissed. Go to your classroom." The boys left, much relieved. He looked at the Vallejos. They were as amused as him. "Thank you both for coming, you helped to clear up the air."

"How you say? 'Clear up the air'?"

104

"Yes, you solved the 'mystery.'"

"Well, I'm glad that we could talk with you," Doctor Vallejo said, shaking hands. "Anytime, call us. For anything."

The wife touched him by the arm. *"Oye, chico, preguntale lo que paso antenoche con el bostezo. A lo mejor es la misma cosa."*

"Yes, that's a good question. Is yawning bad manners in this country?"

"Yawning? How do you mean? No, usually not. Why?"

"Two nights ago, we were on a visitation to a friend's home. I was tired and sleepy and I yawned many times and the man looked angry at me."

"Wait a minute. Was he talking to you?"

"Yes."

"Was he telling you a story?"

"Yes."

"Then, yes, he felt that you were being rude to him and that you were insulting him. If he was talking to you and you yawned, it meant---to him---that you were not interested in what he had to say."

"But that's not true. I was. I was just tired."

"It doesn't matter."

"Ah," said the husband. *"Si. Dice que si, que significaba ser maleducado."*

"Ya me lo supuse!" she responded, nodding vigorously.

"But only when someone is talking. Otherwise, it's OK."

"Dice que nada vez es cuando le ☐stuv hablando a uno. De otra manera esta bien, no significa nada," he translated.

"Thank you very much. I'm glad that we talked with you," Doctor Vallejo said.

"Thank you," she said also and she waved goodbye as they left.

The Vice Principal returned to his office, sat down and smiled. He stared at the wall for a full minute and then he sighed.

XVI

"Forgive me, Father, for I am going to sin."

The priest started, frowned, thinking he had misheard. "I'm sorry, but did you say that you are *going* to sin? As in future tense?"

"Yes, that's right."

The priest drew his head back, frowning deeper and looking hard at where the voice originated as if he could see through it with X-ray eyes and clearly see the face of the man speaking and the expression on that face. Although the vast majority of sins that he had been privy to in his career were relatively minor, he had occasionally had to deal with, and counsel, persons with mortal sins. But never in his entire career had anyone approached the confessional with intent to commit a sin in the near future. The first thing that crossed his mind, naturally, was that he was the subject of a practical joke.

"I've been thinking about what I am going to do on close to about two weeks, planning and debating with myself, you see. And today, I was walking by and I saw the Church and I had the urge to come in for just this purpose, to talk it over, here in the confessional booth where it'd be safe to do so."

"I'm almost afraid to ask you what it is that

you are planning to do. It must be serious if you have been thinking about it for two weeks." So far, he could not detect the slightest tone of humor in the voice which would be a giveaway that this whole scene was somebody's idea of a joke, but he would not rule out the possibility just yet.

"I'm going to kill someone."

"You don't want to do that," the father confessor said slowly. He realized that it sounded dumb. "You know---deep down---that you don't want to do that."

He had decided to play this through as a *bona fide* confession, just in case. A third possibility had intruded in his thoughts, namely, that this man might be mentally deranged and if that was the case, he would definitely have to take this seriously.

"Perhaps I should give you a little background so you can see where I'm coming from. A little over a year ago, an acquaintance of mine---I'll call him Pat---approached me with the aim of investing on the groundwork of a jazz club. He knew that I had money and was on the lookout for investments. It seemed like a good idea at the time and the location was good, available for leasing. 'Pat,' by the way, looks a little odd. One of his eyes is brown and the other one's green. Have you ever come across anyone like that?"

"No, I haven't."

"Neither had I before him. Closest was a Siberian husky with one blue and one brown eye. 'Pat' also had a purplish nose, like varicose veins. Quite a combination. But he's very talkative, very charming. Like all sociopaths. But I didn't realize it 'till later."

"Anyway, we set up the club and it went well. A nice place to come hear good music, dance a bit, have a few drinks---nothing immoral, you understand. One of the bartenders was a girl---I'll call her 'Vicky'---and we began dating before too long and she became my girlfriend."

"The club was barely breaking even. That's usually typical the first year as it tries to establish itself and build up a regular clientele. But I think that he had probably been skimming money all along."

"Then, eight months later, I was diagnosed with a heart condition, pretty serious too, though I'm relatively young."

"How old are you?"

"In my forties. Anyway, I had to have a bypass procedure. Fortunately, it was one of the new types of surgery that is much easier and less painful than before, or so I'm told. The point is, I spent some time in the hospital and when I came out, after a week of being at home and puttering around, I went on down to the club and found it closed. The furnishings were also pretty much gone."

"I made a bunch of phone calls. 'Pat' and 'Vicky' I couldn't get a hold of and I found out later that they had gone on a trip to Europe, blowing money left and right. The club had closed almost two weeks earlier, the furnishings sold and the bank account closed. I consulted both the police and an attorney and saw that he was untouchable from a legal standpoint. Frankly, I had been very stupid on a number of points and he had taken advantage of it. I couldn't sue him because he had almost no assets---none---on his name, that is. So, I was defrauded but I couldn't bring him to justice. He must have had a good laugh at my expense!"

"Did you ever confront him?" the priest

could see where this was heading.

"No, I didn't, though I did confront 'Vicky' when they came back. Typical woman, she wanted to get back together again with me, and told me that she had slept with 'Pat' just in order to go to Europe, since she had never been there. But I said no way, I didn't want her and for that matter by now neither did 'Pat.' By the way, she had visited me in the hospital for the first two days, then she vamoosed."

"Well, as you can imagine, I was *really* mad at this guy. Very resentful. I still am. And, to make a long story short, I've slowly made up my mind to kill 'Pat' in revenge for what he's done to me."

"Tell me, you're not planning on killing your ex-girlfriend too, are you?"

"Of course not! What an idea!"

"Forgive me for asking but, you see, I don't know what your state of mind is."

"The two are as different as night and day. There's no comparison."

"So, you admit that it's *revenge* that you're after, not justice."

"What is justice, father?"

"Earthly justice is carried out through a set of laws that have been passed and tested; divine justice belongs to God and is based solely on His judgment and there is no appeal."

"Justice is revenge and revenge is justice," he countered. "Revenge is what the whole legal system is based on. It's elementary."

"So, leave it to the legal system. As you say, that's what it's there for."

"But it's flawed. 'Pat' is an excellent example. And I firmly believe in the concept of justice."

"My son, Thou Shalt Not Kill is one of the most basic precepts of Christianity. It's a Commandment: Thou Shalt Not Kill. It doesn't get any simpler than that. Leave justice to God if you can't get justice here on Earth. What goes around comes around, as the saying goes. Besides, and more importantly, we're talking about your eternal soul---all eternity--- for just a few dollars. I don't have to tell you the obvious about Hell, do I?" Actually, he was intent on doing just that. Whether to reason with the man or "scare the Hell out of him," he was determined to dissuade him from a horrible mistake.

"Ah. Well. That's just it. I don't believe in God."

The father confessor was flabbergasted. He stared at the blurred image of the man. He wished that his vision was not impaired, thinking that if he could see the man clearly then he would better know his thoughts. Once again, he felt that he was the recipient of a practical joke---from an atheist. Nevertheless, he had to ask, "Then *why* are you here?"

"Good question. I . . . don't know how to explain it. I'm a Catholic, but I haven't been to services in years, not to mention confession. I have good memories of the church, from childhood. Every time that I pass by a Catholic church, I feel a little . . . warm inside. Silly."

The father nodded; it was common for people whose religious observances had lapsed to suddenly come back to the fold years later. On the other hand, it was just as likely that God had sent this man in here in an attempt to save his soul. This made him feel anxious with the responsibility.

"You must believe in God, deep down, my

son. Else, you wouldn't be here. You many not want to admit it out of pride, but you know it's true."

"Don't misunderstand me, father. It's not that I don't want to believe in God. I do. I desperately want to. But the whole idea's absurd. It doesn't make sense. Mind, I'm not one of those atheists that's belligerent and obnoxious. I'm a reluctant atheist. A sad atheist. It'd be so much better overall if there was really a benevolent God watching over all of us. But . . . there isn't."

"You couldn't be more wrong. The whole world-"

"I read the Bible a year ago," he interrupted. "First time I had ever read it. I came away shocked. The God of the Old Testament came across as a hateful, genocidal psychopath. The book seemed at times to even condone incest." The priest felt affronted, but suppressed it in order to keep the lines of communication open with this man. He wished that he could clearly see him. "The only redeeming feature of the Bible was its historical aspect. It's one of the few pre-Greek history books. Ancient Israel, being a theocratic state, incorporated its own political history as part of its theology."

"Anyway, I then read the Koran. A waste of time. It's repetitious, boring, banal, full of threats by a megalomaniacal deity. I then tried The Book of Mormon. I don't have to tell you what a crock *that* was." The priest realized that this man, at one point, and perhaps even now, had searched for a religious meaning in his life.

He offered the would-be murderer all the arguments that he was familiar with that had been given throughout the ages to support the existence of God, not once thinking why the arguments were

111

necessary. He was no Jesuit, but he certainly gave a good account of himself. Even so, his "pupil" made no headway. Realizing this, and not wanting to engage in a purely intellectual argument in regards to what, exactly, is justice, the priest approached the problems from a purely pragmatic angle.

"There is one thing you've overlooked in all of this and that is that you *will* get life in prison or capital punishment. And you don't want that. No matter how much you hate this 'Pat,' you *don't* want to end up in prison awaiting a lethal injection. I *know* you don't."

"I'm going to take precautions. I've planned-"

"Ach! Listen to yourself! You've taken 'precautions.' You make it sound like you're going to the beach and you're taking 'precautions' so you won't get sunburned. How many *criminals*" he emphasized the word to let him realize that he would become one, "have thought that they were going to get away with a crime by taking 'precautions'? The prisons are full of them!"

"I'm not a criminal, father, and I resent you calling me one."

"Granted. You're not a criminal. Now. But you *will* be if you carry through this demented project of yours. And you *will* be caught. To society you'll just be another criminal. An indication of this blindness that you don't seem to realize that you have is how much you've rationalized what's essentially an emotional and savage decision."

"Listen to me, father," There was a note of annoyance in his voice. "I will dye my hair. I will have a briefcase with my gun in it. I will go to his house at night to talk about a new project that I want him to be involved in---he already thinks I'm stupid and gullible, so he'll welcome me---besides, he's greedy. I'll open my briefcase to take out some papers and then I'll shoot him in the head. Right between the eyes."

"Listen to yourself! Listen to yourself! Let's put away for one second the moral arguments which are self-evident. Let's just deal with the details. You'll be the first suspect-"

"I'll have alibis. Already taken care of."

"You'll be seen!"

"Not at night."

"You don't know that. You're engaging in wishful thinking."

"Everything has been foreseen."

"You don't know that! Disraeli once said, 'The unexpected always happens.' Someone will hear the shots." He thought of another argument, Kant's categorical imperative.

"No, they won't. I'm going to put a balloon over the barrel which will serve as a silencer. It works. I've been practicing down at the gun range and the sound's muffled." The priest realized that the man had taken out his gun, which he was brandishing. A brightly colored object must have been the balloon of which he spoke.

The physical presence of the gun threw him completely off balance. He became stupefied by it. It was not fear, not for himself, anyway. It was the realization that the danger was very real, it was at hand, it was not an intellectual exercise; the murder could conceivably take place within a few hours. Up to this very moment, the argument had been almost hypothetical to him, something that the man was planning for a vague date sometime in the future. *This man was dead serious.*

All at once, he felt like he was not up to the

task. He sat there for several seconds, dazed and despondent at the enormity of what he was facing. One thing was to deal with and absolve past sins. Another was this. He felt like his mind had fogged up.

"He defrauded you," he finally spoke in a weak voice, "which makes him a criminal even though the law can't touch him. But if you murder him then you'll become an even bigger criminal, no matter how you justify it to yourself." His voice was returning to normal. "The man may be deserving of punishment, but if you take the law into your own hands, then the end result for you is going to be much worse than you've anticipated. Besides, there's the fact that if you do this stupid act, you're not going to recover your lost money. It's over."

The man was silent, apparently giving some thought to what the father confessor had said. He, too, said nothing in order to give him time to think

There was some rustling and a female voice spoke.

"Bless me, father, for I have sinned."

The man had left! While he had hesitated, he had left without a word or sound.

"Wait a moment, I'll be right back!" he told her and rushed out of the confessional. He looked up and down, but aside from two others waiting their turn, it was obvious that he had left. Nonetheless, he asked them.

"The man that came out! Where did he go?"

They pointed to the door and straight away he went there and opened the door. He was gone, of course. The man had blended into the anonymity of the crowd.

Slowly, depressed, he came back in. Had he convinced the would-be sinner? Had his words simply flowed over him like rainwater over a duck? Had the priest failed his God? Maybe not, maybe he had just left, convinced, thinking there was nothing more to be said. Maybe he would come back later. If he went away unconvinced, but troubled over the exchange of views, then it was still a minor victory and the doubts could take root and paralyze his murderous plan. He wished that he knew for certain. The uncertainty was deeply troubling him, more so than if he knew for certain that he had failed to save the man's soul.

He stepped back into the confessional troubled but ready to resume his duty.

He tried hard to concentrate.

XVII

"Why set up bonfires in the streets? Superfluous histrionics! Let's do it in some quiet corner, let's shove the books into the stove, the stove will keep us warm!"
Alexander Solzhenitsyn *Cancer Ward*

This event---this bizarre event---took place long before the term Politically Correct was coined and became widely known as a result of two front page articles that appeared simultaneously in two national news magazines. Not that the phenomenon itself was previously unknown! Quite the contrary! If anything, it was much more powerful and unquestioned then. It just simply did not have a name and so was not thereby identified as a phenomenon whenever it took place, which was daily. For many *decades*, certain political and social viewpoints simply were not allowed in print or to be broadcast in television and films unless distorted and caricatured beyond recognition, whereas their opposite views were widely propagated and nobly portrayed. And, in a local setting, if someone *did* voice views which were not Politically Correct, he/she would find himself verbally harassed in a vicious manner and would also find himself somehow not promoted to certain positions, or their contracts not renewed, or tenure denied, or their dissertations rejected or their books or articles remained unpublished (the irony of it all was that the two national magazines that originally broke the story had themselves for many years been guilty of just that practice; also, long after the stories were published and the term became well-known, the practice remained unabated). Undeterred, Politically Correct intellectuals (and they were always the power hungry intellectuals so well described by Eric Hoffer), being superbly organized and fanatically motivated, quietly or with much fanfare, continued to suppress articles, books, films broadcasts, lectures, meetings and even everyday language that they labeled "offensive," "sexist," "racist," "reactionary," "insensitive," "McCarthyism," in favor of those views euphemistically labeled "progressive," this being done through a wide-ranging arsenal of tried and true tactics. They were relentless and unforgiving. With single minded determination and unquestioned, unhesitating fanaticism, they would outlast and wear out their opponents and imposed total, mindless conformity. It was The Perfect

Censorship in that it was not official, it was not by any government agency or fiat.

In every corner of the globe, fanaticism convulsed the twentieth century with horrendous crimes not seen since the Thirty Years' War, back in the 1600s. Fanaticism had manifested itself in the twentieth century in every conceivably bizarre form, but nowhere was the doublethink aspect of fanaticism more evident and more ludicrous than in those fanatics found throughout Western Europe and North America who loudly, proudly, proclaimed themselves to be open minded and tolerant of all viewpoints on all subjects---and then set about stamping out "offensive" language and viewpoints, persecuting those people who disagreed with them and they did so without altering their belief that they were broadminded, receptive and tolerant.

But, as I said, at the time that this little incident occurred, the term Politically Correct had not yet come into being and, in fact, was not even recognized as existing, although it was, indeed, widespread and unquestioned.

Now, then.

There was at our university a group of students who got together at the student lounge on a regular basis. It was very informal and it had come about totally spontaneously, although Max had been the catalyst, Max being a silver-tongued devil and good looking to boot. There was always a constant nucleus of seven of us in the lounge with another eight drifting in and out between classes and, so, the group's overall composition in the lounge was any combination of the fifteen of us. It was mainly social, not just talking and joking between classes, but meeting in the evenings at least once a week for movies or a session of *Dungeons and Dragons.*

Yet, the character of our group was such that there were no deeply religious "members" because of the *D&D* game besides which we did not have much tolerance for fanaticism. As soon as a new (religious) member found out that we played *D&D*, they would proclaim it Satanic and insist that we sat around casting spells, probably stark naked, even though he (or she) had never seen, much less played, the game, or been in one of our gaming sessions. On one occasion, a student approached the group and without introductions by anyone within the group, enthusiastically urged us to attend an upcoming religious meeting. He took us by surprise. Halfway through, somewhat abashed, he apologized for his zeal, explaining that he was full of the Holy Spirit.

"Yep," said Max. "We can tell that you are really full of it, all right."

Likewise, there was not a single Marxist in our group, or to use the contemporary euphemism for protoCommunists, there were no "liberals," "radicals," "social activists," "progressive elements," "socially conscious persons," etc. Any that joined us soon fled when faced---usually for the first time in their entire social activist career---with a critically questioning audience and had to actually examine their premises or answer objections and questions in terms other than knee-jerk clichés. Foremost among the challengers was Max, or Maximiliano, who was a refugee from Cuba and his withering sarcasm on leftist sacred cows from Jane Fonda to Mao Tse Tung (or, as he like to spell it, Mousey Tongue) and his eloquent and vigorous defense of institutions and people that the Marxists loved to denigrate, left many a "progressive radical" shaken at the experience, leaving our group for the safety of the Sociology or the Political Science Departments where Joseph Stalin was still admired as a great statesman.

On one occasion, a guy who had joined us less than two weeks before, surprised us when he began to comment on the virtues of the Soviet Union from a propaganda television show that he had seen on NBC. Among its many virtues, he had been impressed that no one lacked employment, and thus "starved to death," with the implication that such was an everyday occurrence here. Karen, a Swiss girl, and a beauty, ripped into him. She pointed out to him that her Switzerland also guaranteed employment to its citizens and had not seen the need to resort to concentration camps, propaganda, a secret police, dictatorship and mass murder. And then she *really* tore into him, joined by the rest of us.

For some reason, we never saw him again.

One day during the middle of the Spring semester, Karen came into the lounge and sat down. She was visibly upset.

"What's up, tiger lily?" joked Carla. "You don't look so good."

"I've just had a strange talk with an instructor, two actually. I don't know, it's just, I don't know how to put it, it's a shock, I guess, I wouldn't have expected it from them. Not from them."

"One of them made a pass at you?"

"Oh, no, nothing like that!" She paused for a second, collecting her thoughts. She paused for a second, collecting her thoughts. "You know how I've mentioned my arguments with my history teacher, Doctor Ritter? That we always get into it

119

with disagreements about his politics and its role in the subject of history?"

"Yeah, I've had him before," voiced Sammy, a skinny redhead. "He's a Socialist. He's always trying to convert everybody, thinking that his classroom is the place for it, but he ain't a Commie."

Karen went on, ignoring the interruption. "Well, no matter how the arguments went, I always respected him, in spite of his putting his politics in the classroom, because he argued so well and with facts. I mean, he argued *intelligently,* even though he's a leftist, instead of the usual emotional slogans and clichés. I disagreed with him, but I respected him." She frowned, obviously bothered.

"So, what happened?" Max asked her with a malicious smile on his face, as if he already knew the answer to his own question and was amused at her naiveté.

"Don't look at me that way, Max!" she snapped at him.

"Like how?" he asked innocently.

"With that sarcastic look of yours!"

"OK, I'm sorry. You know how I am. I'll behave. So, tell us what happened."

"Anyway, I had just finished reading a couple of books that you recommended," she motioned to Sammy. "The ones by Ayn Rand-"

"Oh-oh," muttered Sammy.

"I can see it coming now," volunteered Carla.

"-and I asked him about the books, what he thought about them and all, and here I was, all ready to have one of our long-drawn-out arguments, exchanging points of view and facts and everything."

"And what happened?"

"He just cussed her out!" She sounded like she thought that she had imagined it. "He got very angry, real emotional---no; I mean he became *irrational*. No arguments, no facts, no anything, just pouring abuse. It was a shock. It was so uncharacteristic of him. It was like a mask had fallen off."

"I know what you mean," Sammy volunteered, nodding.

Max just smiled.

"So, I went to Doctor Mader in the Philosophy Department. I never knew his politics before and all I knew was that he had made me *think* in his classes. You know how rare that is in this college?"

"In *every* college," said Jim, who had been silent up to now.

"And I wanted to discuss her writings with somebody and she called herself a philosopher and if Dostoyevsky, who's a novelist, can be considered one, though he's a novelist, so could she."

"And . . . ?" prodded Jim.

"Yeah, Karen, cut to the chase," Max said.

"OK. The same thing happened. All right? It's not a big thing, I know. It's just that I respected these two professors and I even admired Doctor Mader, and yet they both reacted so *irrationally*, like they were illiterate and ignorant."

"You feel disillusioned," volunteered Carla, ever the psychology major.

"Boy, do I ever! I wouldn't have minded one bit if they had given me an argument why they didn't agree with the books, but their *reactions* were shocking to me."

"I had something similar happen with me,"

Jim said and he told us of a similar incident when he had suggested to a professor of literature to offer a class on Dos Passos. "The teacher freaked out on me, man. He started yelling about how Dos Passos was a Fascist and all, because he withdrew his support from the Republican side during the Spanish Civil War and all, and what gets me is, here's this guy who has a class where he's lecturing from *Soul On Ice* by Eldridge Cleaver, who's an admitted rapist and racist and the book is full of obscenities and racism and pornography and Communism."

After that, everybody had his or her own story as it applied to their own experiences in their own major field. As new friends joined the group, the conversation began again with fresh or rehashed stories.

"And what gets me," said a new arrival, "is that when you first arrive here, and at every university, they herd you into the auditorium and the Deans of every Department come and tell you how the university is a place for the free exchange of ideas and how this place will expand your mind! Ha! That's a laugh! There's more censorship and taboo subjects in this university than in a Baptist convention!"

Max suddenly sat up straight. He had a faraway look on his face. Everybody stopped talking a looked at him, expectantly.

"What is it, Maxy?" asked Carla. "You gonna tell us?"

"A book burning," he whispered. Then he leaned forward and started telling us his brainstorm. At first, the rest of them looked scandalized, then they began to mutter angrily.

"That's obscene," said Karen.

122

"Max, you can't possibly be serious," Sammy said.

"I'm not," Max replied. Then, he smiled as he slowly explained further while he doodled on a piece of paper an owl standing on a mirror, and then everyone broke into grins and began to make suggestions of their own.

Of course, this incident would not have occurred in the end but for three things. One was that demonstrations and political meetings by leftist students at that time, in the early Seventies, were a daily occurrence throughout the country. Second, the whole group was frankly and notoriously irreverent. One time they had attended a public speech in the campus and had surreptitiously put industrial strength soap in the nearby fountain. The resulting soap bubbles had distracted from the speech. Another time, they had decided to "get" a certain professor who was in the habit of seducing his students. For weeks, they put condoms around in his office, his mailbox, his doorknob, panty hoses in his car's antenna or license plate, pasted Playboy pinups on his office door and written graffiti in the departmental bathroom. This continued until his seductions were finally openly discussed and he was put on probation. And there were many other instances. In none, however, had we ever been identified as a group, certainly not an official group.

So when the student newspaper came out two weeks later with an article stating that a book burning was going to take place in the campus and it carried an interview with Max and Carla as the spokespersons for the group conducting the book burning, it was the latest in a long series of elaborate escapades. Naturally, the college was thrown in a turmoil---under the surface.

The whole prank was genius, really. In the interview with the student journalist, Max and Carla had come across as being serious and deadly earnest in regards to having a book burning. They adopted the leftist doctrine and spewed out the current buzzwords in explaining, quite patiently, that certain books were simply "unacceptable" and "offensive" in a college campus. Books which were blatantly "racist" and "reactionary" and "sexist" and had "right wing McCarthyist" plots, "had no place in a university campus" and would be consigned to the flames. The works of Alexander Solzhenitsyn, Mark Twain, Ernest Hemingway, Ludwig von Mises, Robert Ruark and Ayn Rand were given as examples. If anything, Max and Carla were bland in their statements and understated their case---on purpose. The budding journalist went away feeling that his leg was being pulled.

To be sure, there was indeed consternation in the campus and a lot of confusion. For decades, intellectuals had pointed to the book burnings by the Nazis and the Inquisition as instances of Neanderthal intolerance of opposing ideas by ignorant, evil, reactionary minds. So, everyone was conditioned against the idea of burning books. At the same time, these same intellectuals had for decades had an abhorrence to many books and ideas (which deep down they would have loved to burn, but could not since they saw in themselves as the personification of the Intellect) which if, they didn't burn publicly, they certainly aborted from publication, excluded from assignments and references, ignored, censored and simply pretended that they did not exist, thereby achieving the same practical ends more secretly and without the melodrama of a bonfire---thus, actually being much more effective in the end. So, on the one hand, they eagerly approved of these works' destruction, but they had a simultaneous ingrained abhorrence to book burning.

Clara, the psychology major, explained it in her terms. "See, it's like Pavlov's dogs. They've been classically conditioned to salivate in favor of statements and demonstrations against whatever is labeled 'right wing,' or 'sexist,' or 'racist,' like the books that we're going to burn and they've also been conditioned to growl at book burnings. And now both have been combined. It's a conflict of emotional reactions. They're having a predictable nervous reaction. It's called cognitive dissonance."

Max put it differently. "I just want to bring out their censorship out into the open, instead of pretending that it's not going on. This censorship is just one example in this country of That-Which-Must-Never-Be-Mentioned. This little parody that we're going to stage is just going to do the trick."

Between the appearance of the article and the date of the event, quite a few of the university professors and their student sycophants approached the two to voice their strong disapproval of their chosen tactic, although they embraced their goal of purging undesirable books from the university. Throughout, the group's members kept in character as "student activists," and, knowing just which buttons to push, accused their detractors with not being radical enough to their Cause, which stung their critics.

The big day arrived. A podium had been set up in front of the student lounge building in the spot where the usual demonstrations and political speeches took place. There was quite a crowd there, including the local self-proclaimed "student radicals," looking uncomfortable. There was also the student journalist who had interviewed Carla and Max and there was even also a real journalist from the city's newspaper.

Presently, the perpetrators arrived, grinning and carrying books. They took in the crowd with a glance and plunged in.

Max did the introduction, condemning McCarthyism and racism and everything else that the Left crusades against, reiterated his previously stated position that books promoting those views should not be tolerated in campus, and (here quite a few of the audience squirmed since they felt the same way though they disapproved of book burnings) although he approved of the tactics used up to now of not using these books in classes, never mentioning their existence, purging them from the both the university book store and the library, deleting them from references and not approving dissertations and theses on these works, he felt a more dramatic demonstration was in order. One last point that he wanted to make and that was that they had been lately criticized for utilizing a book burning to achieve these goals as not been congruent with tactics used by the left. He disagreed. There was historical precedent. The National German *Socialist Worker's* Party, i.e., the Nazis, had engaged in burning books and they had certainly been Socialist and against reactionaries. At this, several in the audience squirmed and looked like they were trying to jump out of their skin.

He had spoken out loud another facet of That-Which-Must-Never-Be-Spoken.

Carla then took the podium and was very brief. Holding up some books as she named them, she said, "In the field of philosophy, there is

Herbert Spencer's *Man and State,* William Graham Sumner's *What Social Classes Owe To Each Other,* Eric von Mises' *Human Action* and *Bureaucracy,* Eric Hoffer's *The True Believer* and *The Passionate State of Mind,* Ayn Rand's *The Virtue of Selfishness* and *For The New Intellectual.* Also, the works of John Dewey and Sidney Hook. She then got off the podium and gingerly stacked the books on the ground to one side.

Sammy gained the podium, his red hair shining in the sun, and was also brief and to the point. He also held up the books as he named them. "In the field of literature, the fictional novels *The Clansman, Gone with The Wind, She,* and *Something of Value* are racist and must burn. Mark Twain uses the "n-word" in *Life in The Mississippi* and *The Adventures of Huckleberry Finn.* So does Hemingway in *To Have and Have Not.* So does George Orwell in *Burmese Days* and Joseph Conrad in *The Nigger of the Narcissus.* So, of course, they all have to burn. Oh, and in the field of Anthropology, Coons is a racist and his books must burn as well."

It was Jim's turn and he took a bit more time overly condemning those novels that he had which had the audacity to criticize Communism and the peace loving Soviet Union and held up Leon Uris' *Topaz,* Richard Wright's *The Outsider,* Arthur Koestler's *Darkness at Noon, The Age of Innocence* and *The God That Failed,* Lin Yutang's *The Flight Of The Innocents,* George Orwell's *1984, Coming Up For Air,* and *Animal Farm,* Juan Maria Gironella's *The Cypresses Believe In God,* Gouzenko's *Fall Of A Titan,* Zamyatin's *We* and Solzhenitsyn's *The First Circle* and *Cancer Ward.*

Debra had only three books, *The Feminized*

Male, Sexual Suicide and *The Morning After*, which were all antifeminist in outlook (remember, this was before the days of Camille Paglia and Elizabeth Fox-Genovese), but in order to make up for the paucity of books, she contributed her brassiere to be burned along with her books.

Randy went for the nonfiction and added *The Case Against College, In the Clutches of the Cheka, The News Twisters* and *How CBS Tried to Kill a Book, The Wall of Shame, The Gulag Archipelago, The Bridge at Andau, A Question of Madness,* the writings of Arthur Jensen and *The Great Terror.* Randy then joined the others and whispered nervously, "He *is* going to be here, right? I don't want to lose those books." Clara reassured him.

Allan, the theater major, simply said, "*The Prime of Miss Jean Brodie,* Ibsen's *An Enemy of The People,* Shakespeare's *Titus Andronicus, Coriolanus* and *The Merchant of Venice,* George Bernard Shaw's *Major Barbara* and Sidney Kingsley's works."

Ira's turn. "Because of the anti-Semitism in these works, they should also burn:" *Jew Süss,* Sinclair Lewis' *Dodsworth,* Voltaire's *Candide,* Dickens' *Oliver Twist,* Hemingway's *The Sun Also Rises.*

Karen was last. "And, on general principle, we're going to add Edmonds' *Drums Along The Mohawk,* Taylor Caldwell's *The Devil's Advocate* and *Growing Up Tough,* Knut Hamsun's works, *Pan* and *Hunger* and *Giants Of The Earth,* Dostoyevsky's *Crime and Punishment, The Idiot* and *Demons,* and all the works of John Dos Passos, Giovanni D'Annunzio, Konrad Lorenz, Giovanni Guareschi, Ezra Pound, Rudyard Kipling and Drieu

La Rochelle," and she fixed her eyes on Doctor Ritter who was in the audience. Suddenly, Ritter straightened up his body and his mouth opened. He knew.

Max returned to the podium, frowning.

"I would like to add to the list the works of Robert Frost. That may sound strange to some of you, but the basis for my choice is a poem that he wrote, entitled, *The Case for Jefferson.* Since most of you have probably never heard of it, I would like to take the opportunity to recite it. You'll see what I mean:"

The Case for Jefferson

Harrison loves my country too,
But wants it all made over new.
He's Freudian Viennese by night.
By day he's Marxian Muscovite.
It isn't because he's Russian Jew.
He's Puritan Yankee through and through.
He dotes on Sunday pork and beans.
But his mind is hardly out of his teens:
With him the love of country means
Blowing it all to smithereens
And having it all made over new."

"Well! Let's get started, shall we?" He unwrapped a can of gasoline secretly containing water, amidst angry murmurs, whereupon a man quickly stepped from the crowd and approached Max. He was the Fire Marshall and he was putting a stop to the proceedings.

"But a month ago, there was a demonstration burning the American flag right here!" Max argued.

The Fire Marshall shrugged, frowning. "Unfortunately, nobody called us then."

Max nodded and returned to the podium.

"Sorry, folks. Show's over. Fire Marshall won't let us do it. It's a bit of an anticlimax, I know, but that's the way it goes sometimes." Some people applauded the Fire Marshall. Carla began distributing a list of the books that had been about to be "incinerated" with a warning at the top to avoid reading the books listed below, as they expressed dangerous views. The rest of the demonstrators got their books back and the crowd dispersed.

"Thanks. I didn't think you were going to be here after all," Max told the Fire Marshall. "I was beginning to get really worried." The Fire Marshall looked puzzled, then realized that it had been Max who had placed the telephone call to him.

The pranksters dispersed to the nearby Pizza Hut for pizza and beer, where they laughed over the whole episode. It was a good source of jokes for several weeks thereafter, until, one day, Karen dispelled the whole mood by making the observation, "You know what? Nothing's changed! They haven't changed one bit! It was all for nothing!"

And it was true.

XVIII

Benito Saucedo got up that Sunday morning and went into the bathroom to brush his teeth. In the mirror he saw himself: gray-haired, balding, potbellied, with a salt and pepper mustache. And he shrugged. After brushing his teeth, he picked up the newspaper laying at his doorstep and joined his wife for breakfast.

"Would you like something special today for breakfast?" she asked him in Spanish.

He thought for a moment. "Yeah! How about Eggs Benedict? I haven't had that in ages," he suggested with enthusiasm from anticipation.

"All right," she said and proceeded to get busy while he began to read the newspaper. After a few minutes, she groaned with disappointment in her voice.

He looked up at her. "What's the problem?" he asked her.

"I haven't got some of the ingredients. I'll have to get dressed and drive down to the store."

"Don't bother, then."

"But you want to."

"That's all right, don't go to any extra trouble. We'll just have it tomorrow," he said, knowing full well that there would be no Eggs Benedict tomorrow.

"Sure?"

"Sure. Just get me my *cafe con leche.*"

Benito had the traditional light Cuban breakfast of coffee with milk and a slice of toast while he read the newspaper, the same breakfast that he had had 364 times in the last year.

Halfway through the newspaper, the telephone rang. Since the telephone was closer to him, he answered it.

"I have a person to person collect call to Mister Benito Saucedo from Mirta," the nasal voice of the operator announced. "Do you accept the charges?"

"Yes, I accept," Benito said.

"Hi . . . Dad?"

"Yes, baby, it's me. How are you, hon?"

"Felicidades! Happy Father's Day!" She said it in both Spanish and English.

"Thank you. How are you? Never mind *you-
-*how's my granddaughter?" he joked. "That's what I really want to know."

"She's fine. She's just beginning to crawl."

"She is? Oh, good! Isn't that early for her age?"

"No, it's just about right."

"Well, how about sending me some pictures, then?"

"OK, I can do that. I'll send you some. Are you planning to do anything special today?"

"Oh, the kids are coming over later on about noon and we're all going to a Chinese restaurant that Ana Maria really likes and then we'll go see a movie."

"I'm glad. Is Mom there? Let me talk to her for a minute."

Benito handed the receiver to his wife. "Mirta wants to talk to you," he told her and he went to the living room to read his newspaper to the end, while they talked for the next twenty-five minutes. He sat down on his favorite recliner and happened to glance at the odd ornament resting on the coffee table. It was an arrangement sent by Mirta through one of the delivery agencies on last Mother's Day, which consisted of assorted dried sticks and seed pods. Admittedly, it had a sort of unusual symmetry to it, which was tolerable, but his wife liked it very much; apparently, her daughter knew her mother's taste, or maybe she had just asked her. He shrugged it off.

Once settled, he plunged back into reading

the news from Europe.

At about noon, Ana Maria showed up.

"Happy Father's Day," she announced as she bounced in, kissing him on the cheek and giving him a hug.

"Thanks, baby," he answered back and received the card that she handed him. He opened it and chuckled at its humorous Father's Day message. "Where's Adolfo?" he inquired of her husband, "isn't he coming along with us?"

"Oh, he told me to wish you a Happy Father's Day, but that he wouldn't be able to join us. He wanted to spend the day with his Dad."

"Of course, of course!" he agreed. How could he fault his son-in-law being an attentive son?

"Where's Mom?"

"In the bedroom, getting ready."

Just as she was about to go find her mother, her brother, Pedro, showed up. Like her, he did not bother to knock on the door, but simply opened the door and walked in, feeling right at home.

"Hi, Dad! *Felicidades!* Happy Father's Day!" he greeted the old man and they kissed each other and hugged.

"Thank you, son," the father said, as Pedro handed him a flat rectangular gift. Opening it, he praised the predictable striped tie that was contained in it. "Oh, very nice, very pretty. Thank you," and he showed it to his daughter before taking it out of the box and tying it around his neck, completing his wardrobe. He had been sitting around in his suit, tieless, waiting for his children to show up.

"What do you think about the news? Heard

133

what happened in Greece?" he asked Pedro, who sat down in the living room to discuss politics with his father while Ana Maria went to join her mother.

The women *finally* emerged, much to the heartfelt thanks of the half-starved men.

"About time!" Benito exclaimed.

"Hi, Mom!"

"Hi, son." She was wearing a solid lavender dress offset by the pearl necklace that Pedro and Ana Maria had jointly bought her last month. The pearls had a purplish tinge to them which blended well with her dress. The combination was attractive.

"Ready?" she asked them.

"Since about an hour ago!" the elder Saucedo growled with irritation and they exited from the house. "Are we all going in one car?" he asked, to no one in particular.

"I want to take my car along, Dad, that way I can take off straight off after the movie."

"Humph. You ought to take better care of it. At the rate you're going, it's going to fall apart soon," he groused, eyeing the Skylark.

"Aww, Dad, you're just grouchy 'cause you're hungry," Pedro complained.

"Hungry nothing! You take that car for granted! That was an expensive graduation present, let me tell you! It didn't cost me ten bucks, you know. I didn't use coupons from the newspaper."

"I'll meet you all at the restaurant," said a chagrined Pedro and he took refuge inside his car and sped off, leaving his Dad muttering behind. The two women smiled at each other as they got in the other car, the one that Saucedo would drive to the restaurant.

As their car backed up out of the driveway, Benito began to grouse at his daughter, though not as intensely as he had done with his son. She was, after all, his "baby."

"And what about *you?* Are you going to do anything with that degree in literature that you got? I put you through four years in college and all you did with was to get married." And so on. They all knew from experience that until he got some lunch in him, he would just be a bear.

At the restaurant, once he started eating, he felt much better and less irritable. He had wanted to eat Scheszhwan, but since none of the others could stomach the spicy cuisine, they opted for the bland Cantonese cuisine. So, they ordered moo goo gai pan, shrimp in lobster sauce and lots and lots of fried rice. After the appetizers and egg drop soup, he began to joke around.

"So, what are we going to see, *Mickey Mouse vs Godzilla?"*

"No, Dad, it's a Sean Connery movie, *The Hunt for Red October,"* the son responded.

"Is it any good?" he asked rhetorically. He relied on them for suggestions for going to movies.

"Oh, yeah! Sean Connery is my favorite actor."

"I know James Bond, but is the *movie* any good? What's it about? I'm sure you've seen the previews."

They discussed the movie's plot. It turned out that Pedro had also read the book, along with Tom Clancy's other books and he gave them just enough plot that to interest them, but not to spoil any suspense that the movie might have.

After a while, with the food having vanished, Pedro announced, "Well, we'd better be going if we're to make it in time." They started getting up. "I'll leave the tip," he said and flopped down a five-dollar bill while his father picked up the check and ambled towards the cash register to pay, trailed by the rest of the family. Then, they quickly scampered to their cars and drove to the movie theater, a few blocks away, by the shopping mall.

The movie turned out to be indeed every bit as good as Pedro had promised, and the father was very happy with having seen the movie. Of course, having Sean Connery in the film practically guaranteed it, though, in truth, in the past, he had been in some terrible "bombs."

"Glad you liked it," Pedro said.

"I did, I did, I really did. It was good!"

"Did you really have a good time, Dad?" his daughter asked him.

"Yes, I did, I sure did."

"Well. I'm going to go on, then," announced his son. "I've got a few errands to take care of." Pedro embraced his father again. "Happy Father's Day."

"Thanks, son."

They got in their cars and left the parking lot. Arriving at his home, Saucedo and the two women went into the house. Ana Maria went straight to the phone and called her home to see whether Adolfo had returned. He had, indeed, so she said her goodbyes and left.

Benito and his wife relaxed and began undressing, now that the kids were gone and put on more leisurely clothes, making small talk as they did so. He went into the walk-in closet. On one wall he had a tie rack originally designed to support no more than two dozen ties, but burdened with nearly three times that number, most of them presents from Christmas, birthdays and Father's Days. As he placed the latest one on the rack, he made a mental note to go through the ties one of these days and eliminate a few of them before the rack fell off the wall from the weight. He then closed the door to the closet and laid down on the bed to try to catch a *siesta*. His wife left him in the bedroom in order not to disturb him and softly closed the door behind her. After a few minutes, he was asleep, content.

XIX

As a teenager, Elmo had seen many films on Europe on television and the cinema. Whether they were documentaries, or fictional movies set in Europe, invariable there were attractive panoramas shown: a London with its Big Ben and Parliament, and the Tower of London, and London Bridge, its double decked red buses, its bobbies, its theaters, and its cheerful friendly people; a Munich with its double domed cathedral, its beer gardens, its Oktoberfest, its friendly people and its nearby castles; a Venice with its gondolas, its Murano glassware, its Piazza San Marco, its friendly people, its golden lion; a Barcelona, with its bullfights, its Güell Park, its Dali Museum and its friendly people; a Paris with its Eiffel Tower, its Montmartre, its Louvre, its Triumphal Arch, and its obnoxious people. Nor was he confined to just these cities. He longed to see Norwegian fjords, the ruins of Pompeii and Herculaneum, the Escorial, the forests of Germany, the misty Alps of Switzerland and Austria, the cities of Helsinki, Vilnius and Budapest, the region of Transylvania (home of Dracula), the green fields of Ireland, the Greek islands.

His family had no excess money with which to go to Europe, either as a family, or send him by himself, even if they had been so inclined.

Thus, he was doomed to a life of total, absolute boredom in Herington, Kansas.

To be sure, his parents wanted him to go to college. In Lawrence, Manhattan, Wichita, or Emporia.

All of them in Kansas.

"Close to home," his mother said. "So we can visit on the weekends."

Elmo gritted his teeth.

He had decided on an alternative.

He joined the Army. Right after graduating from high school.

He slowly came to this conclusion after watching on television two films, *Private Benjamin,* with Goldie Hawn, and *Stripes,* with Bill Murray.

Elmo knew that, because of NATO, the US Army stationed a huge portion of its army in Europe in order to deter Soviet expansionism in that continent. A bonus for many enlisted men, therefore, was that they got to travel, no, live, overseas.

And, as far as Elmo was concerned, that alone was worth it.

It was even worth getting caught up in a war later on, down the line.

So, he joined the US Army and was sent to

boot camp, where he was shorn of hair, made to get up before dawn, tracked miles of forest, rocks and muck, yelled at, given dismal food and clothes and was fatigued with endless exercise and drills.

After boot camp, *any* assignment was welcomed. Even Guam or Greenland. At least, going to those two remote places would be a change of pace. Besides, from Guam, he found out, one could hop a ride on a transport while on leave and go visit Japan, Korea, or Taiwan, or even the Philippines. And from Greenland, one could likewise visit Canada, Iceland, Scotland, or Norway.

Instead, for the next few years, until the end of his enlistment, Elmo was stationed at Ft. Riley, Kansas.

XX

"Where all are fools and all are knaves."
Swift

Then at all times he gibbers. Talk, talk, talk, talk. Heaven knows what it is all about; but certainly, four of them can talk for four regiments.
Stephen Crane, *Story of the Battle of San Juan Hill*

"Lo que le pasa a Uds. Es que tienen complejo de ser Cubano!"
"The problem with you is that you're

139

ashamed of being Cuban!" was the predictable reaction to Maximiliano's taunt.

It was a Cuban get-together at the home of the Munoz family. The get-togethers, or visits if you wish, seemed to occur on a certain schedule known only to the adults and which had an undercurrent of score keeping in the *colonia* of Cubans. As was usual in those cases, it was a family affair and the offsprings were dragged along, regardless of age, or, for that matter, interest. Although some of the teenagers would grumble, they would still come along with the 'old fogies' through a sort of duty which through the years had begun to wear very thin with the passage of time. If one of them did not show up, because of a pending exam or a date, or just plain refusal to come, adults at the gathering would casually ask of him, out of required politeness. The parents would afterwards report to the wayward son (or daughter) that "everyone" had been anxiously asking for him, with the unspoken threat that, in the next gathering, he *would* come along because "everyone" wanted to see him. Nonetheless, the attrition rate was climbing.

As was usual in those days, the talk *inevitably* revolved around politics and, significantly, all the adults spoke as if one mind. In those days, Cuban refugees lived and breathed politics---heated politics. There was seldom, if any disagreements. The gigantic strides of Communist conquests were noted and the lack of an adequate response by the Americans---if not hiding their heads under the sand altogether---was scorned (as with native-born Americans, they felt entitled to lambaste the government and/or people but became incensed if foreigners did likewise; another thing: it was always assumed that it was the Americans that had to do something, the idea of the British, or French, or Spaniards actively combating Communist aggression outside their borders never came into consideration).

The conversation had strayed onto other areas. At one point, Doctor Ybarra had mentioned that he had read a book stating that the first international underwater telephone cable, or something of the sort, had been tried in Cuba and he went on to bombastically proclaim, "Boy, I tell you, Cuba has always been on the forefront of progress. Makes one proud to be Cuban!" whereupon, his son, Maximiliano, had burst out with a loud, short snort of contempt.

His father, irritated, had turned on him and asked, "*Que pasa, chico?* You ashamed of being Cuban? Well, let me tell you that I'm very proud of being Cuban, so what do you say to that?"

"Just tell me one thing," his son retorted. "Just what *is* there to be proud of being Cuban, will you? 'Cause I, for one, don't see any reason at all. Do you?"

And sure enough . . . that did it.

There was an angry outburst coming out simultaneously out of all the older people. It was a typical Cuban discussion, loud, noisy, lots of gestures and inarticulate noises skillfully serving as arguments, some insults and absolutely no factual arguments, or facts, being presented. In Cuban mentality, at least at that time, if you waved your arms a lot and you made a lot of inarticulate noises and insulted the other person, and if you did so louder that the other person, then you had conclusively won the argument.

Nevertheless, Max stuck to his guns.

"Wait a minute! Go ahead and tell me: What

is there about Cuba to make one proud to be Cuban? Tell me! I want to know. I really do. After all, I'm Cuban and I, for one, don't see anything. It's like somebody from Paraguay or Nicaragua or even Honduras saying that he's proud of his country."

"Ach, chico! How can you compare us to the Mexicans, or the Honduran Indians?"

"Admit it! You're ashamed of being a Cuban! You've got an inferiority complex! Come on, admit it!" Mrs. Belen Munoz screamed.

"They're all like this, the younger generation; they're hopeless! Hopeless! They don't respect their Cubanness!"

"*Burro!*" his mother exclaimed, more to the point.

By now, he should have kept quiet, knowing that a rational, calm discussion was, as usual, out of the question, but not Max. Max had an uncanny gift of being able to detect an exposed nerve and then proceed to touch it. And touch it. And touch it. And prod it. And pinch it. In doing so, his guinea pig lost all rational, coherent thought and lashed out angrily and irrationally (and, significantly, it made no difference if his victim was Cuban, American, Swiss or English).

He was doing so now. He knew that by simply asking the question, he would send them spinning hysterically out of control.

"No! Is there one among you who can honestly point to anything in Cuban national history, in politics or government, that you can actually have any respect for?" The shift in emphasis was lost on his steaming victims, who grimaced with distaste at his arguments and asked to just change the topic or to go away. But Max, sadist that he was, was relentless.

142

"From where I'm sitting, Cuba's not worth dying for. I don't care what that noisy national anthem says. England, yes. Spain, yes. America, definitely. Germany, undoubtedly. But *Cuba?* It's like saying, Mexico is worth dying for! If all of Cuba, or Mexico, or Paraguay, or Honduras were to disappear from the map, nobody would care. I mean . . . what has Cuba ever contributed to world civilization?"

Mind you, throughout this they were interrupting him and attempting to shout him down.

"Look, let's just change the topic . . ." said Munoz.

"Oh, so none of you can tell me, eh?"

"'Cause there's just no convincing you! Either you are or you're not and you're not. So, let's just change the topic before the talk really gets ugly," and everyone else agreed, but in a bad humor.

Max slowly got up in disgust and left the room and Munoz's kids, Manolo and Cristina, who were his contemporaries, and two others, accompanied him, although (for once) they themselves had not participated in the heated argument. Irrelevant, though, since Max's contemporaries usually took part in other arguments against the older generation. As they left, they could hear their parents muttering about "these *pepillos* know nothing," "they should have lived longer in Cuba," and so on.

The five teenagers went outside the house, glad to be away from that atmosphere. "I'm so sick of them all!" Max exclaimed. "Sick! Sick! Sick!"

Manolo and Cristina nodded in agreement. Numerous times before they had all gotten into shouting matches with their parents, although tonight Max had carried the whole argument, or rather needling, by himself.

"They just can't seem to reason," said Cristina, shaking her head in wonder. "They couldn't even give you an argument."

"They just automatically went into the usual emotional hysterics," Manolo added. "They couldn't even come up with Carlos Finlay, Capablanca, Lecuona, Celia Cruz or the Heredia cousins. Unbelievable! They make you want to bang your head against a wall in frustration!"

"They wouldn't even mention music, or dancing," Max snorted again with disgust.

Cristina brushed her long hair away from her face. "You'd think that they'd *automatically* call up Marti's name, but no! What is *wrong* with them?"

"Marti!" Max exploded again, this time at her. "Marti! Marti! Marti! I've had it up to here with Jose Marti!" He drew an imaginary line at eye length.

"Marti's a good poet, chico," Manolo chided.

"I *know* he was a good poet. He was a great poet. But *everything* in Cuba is named after him. Even the kitchen sinks. I'm sick and tired of it. I'm surprised that we don't commemorate the first time that he picked his nose!"

"I don't know," Manolo said. "I think you were a little harsh on them, for once."

"Say what?"

"OK, think about it. When did Cuba first become independent? Around 1900, right? We haven't had the time to develop a good track record for literature, or science, or art. It's kind of unfair to compare us to England, or Spain, or America.

144

They've been around for centuries and you can see what they've accomplished."

"Man," he countered, "it's their reasoning---or rather, their lack of reasoning---ability that's got me ticked off. I mean, you're giving me a rational argument. OK. Fine. Great. They don't. All they do is wave their arms around like demented windmills, insult you and make a bunch of noises."

There was a pause as they all nodded in agreement. Inside, the older Cubans nodded in their own assessment of their sons and daughters.

"Besides, Manolo, you're wrong," he said after a while. "Germany and Italy didn't become unified, independent, countries until 1870 and look at all the culture and science that they've contributed. And then look at Cuba. A mere thirty years' difference can't account for that great a gap. No. It's the national character, I tell you. They worship Marti but they don't worship poetry. That's the difference. Otherwise, Heredia wouldn't have died in poverty. All the Cuban writers and poets have died in poverty. That's what the Cubans really think about them. They starve their writers and poets and scientists."

"No, Max, you're the one that's wrong. It *is* the time difference. Colombia and Argentina became independent before we did and they put that time to good use. Look at their literary track record."

"But, Manolo, you're giving me the very arguments I need to support my stand. It *is* the national character. Other countries that became independent at the same time as Argentina and Colombia, say Paraguay, or Ecuador, or Honduras have contributed diddly-squat. Zip. Nothing. Nada. It's as if they didn't exist. Same as with Cuba."

145

"And take a look at the scientific angle," Cristina suggested. "My God! It's even worse! Even though we had Carlos Finlay!"

Their discussion continued for a while.

"Have you ever noticed how Cuba's best literary minds have only been able to flourish in exile and never in their own country?" Max asked. "Marti, the Heredias, Arenal, Cabrera Infante. It's as if Cuba's cultural climate was only conducive to crass vulgarity."

And so on.

By the time that it was time to leave, everyone had cooled off enough for the two groups to approach each other without flying off at the handle, although nothing had been forgotten.

This dissension along generational lines was a long standing one, except that it had become more intolerant and aggressive lately on the part of the sons and daughters in the *colonia*, whereas previously it had been noted for its good-natured kidding. The last really big blowup had occurred at the New Year's Eve party given by the Villareals. They had been eating the traditional twelve grapes at midnight for good luck when Inez had voiced the ever-hopeful, "Next year, we'll be back in Cuba!" and had turned around to where the youths were and with an innocent, simpleton, face asked the rhetorical question, "Won't it be nice when we can all be back in Cuba?" not really expecting an answer, much less her son's response of, "What the *hell* for?"

Well, that did it.

All hell broke loose. Especially since they had just finished singing the Cuban national anthem.

All the adults were shocked by their sons

and daughters' matter of fact statements that they had no intention whatever of returning to Cuba to visit, much less to live in. Max even used the Cuban saying, "I haven't lost anything there" with an open sneer.

What none of the parents realized, however, was that, deep down, their offsprings really *did* secretly have every intention of visiting Cuba once Castro and his Communist butchers were overthrown. The defiance had been for its own sake, for shock value.

The "ringleader" (for lack of a better term) was Max, although in fairness it must be said right from the beginning that he did not set out to be such, it just happened. Now, by all accounts, Maximiliano was a silver-tongued devil. His good looks also did not hurt him none, either. To show you just how persuasive he could be, he had done what was rarely done in *el exilio* outside of Miami, which was to get his contemporaries, the young Cubans, to associate with each other on a regular basis and he had done so without consciously setting out to do so. We had all simply gravitated towards him. After a couple of phone calls from him inviting me (or, say, someone else) to come on over, *chico,* the guys were going out to see this new film and you can buy all our tickets, no, just kidding, come on over!

Now, you will ask, what is the big deal about this, it's very normal. That is true, except that young Cuban-Americans tended to avoid other Cuban-Americans as much as possible in the United States and instead strictly associated with American kids. It was almost a phobia. If one of us met someone else and we learned that he, or she, was Cuban, there was an initial brief burst of joy and friendship at meeting a kindred soul. We would ask the standard questions: when did you come over? Which city were you from? How long have you been in this town? (one thing, though: we never, ever, talked about the persecution we had suffered over there, we avoided recalling those awful times, they were too painful and if pressed by anyone we tended to be vague and general and changed the topic). And then we would get "ants in the pants" and could not wait to get away from each other and we would part ways, in an awkward manner, not even offering to stay in touch with one another. Why was this? Well, the fact was that all of the younger exile generation, from Florida to Nebraska had grown up deeply ambivalent about their Cubanness. As *individuals,* by the times that we were old enough to think for ourselves in late adolescence, each of us was actually kind of proud of our Cuban heritage, the music, the food, the dances and, when we actually stumbled across the names of a prominent Cuban like Jose Capablanca, Carlos Finlay or Ricky Ricardo. But, as a *group,* there was no cohesion whatever. None! And no desire for that cohesion either; in fact, each of us viewed with contempt and even loathing the idea of being with other Cubans. The constant asinine and ignorant pronouncements we heard from our parents and their friends on a daily basis often about things of which they themselves knew nothing about did not help any to exorcise this feeling. Then, to top it off, we would come across some dismal detail of Cuban history, or meet some Cuban politician in *el exilio* who was a ranting, raving, thieving mediocrity and that would further reinforce our feelings of alienation and disgust. With such people, no wonder the Communists were able to take over the country!

Max nullified and reversed this state, not only through his charm and sociability, but also because of his magnetic, razor sharp intellect. Looking back over the years, I am surprised that it was so evident during his adolescence. Like us, he had been starved for a glimpse of something good to say about being a Cuban and it had been he who had resurrected the names of Capablanca, Finlay, Lecuona and Heredia (that's all we had, by the way). He would then---very simply, and, in a very low-key manner---lend us an article or a book on any of them. We would, embarrassingly, borrow it, yet read it enthusiastically in private. Even better, sometimes, he would get a hold of their writings. And I do not want to give the impression that we were nascent chauvinists at this "ethnic pride," if you want to call it that. It was simply a very normal feeling that everyone has of pride in belonging to a group that acquires distinction through one of its members. We *all* feel that, whether you call it "school pride" or "patriotism." Hell, we Cubans in Kansas would also feel a small surge of pride whenever Kansas made the news or anybody famous, like Kirstie Alley, turned out to be from Kansas. And yet, what was paradoxical, and made no sense, was that the older generation, who *was* bombastically chauvinistic, had never read those works and most did not even know who Heredia or Finlay had been.

Along these very same lines, he was determined to uncover any writings, fiction or nonfiction, which was critical of Communism, which in those days were practically nonexistent, such was the absolute censorship power of the "fellow travelers" in America. People nowadays looking back at the Sixties and Seventies, and part of the Eighties will never realize, or appreciate, the almost total control of information that such Politically Correct people possessed; they were determined that *no* criticism of Communism or its leaders, *no* detrimental facts would be allowed to be shown in print, film or television. None! Under no circumstances! No way, no how! It amounted to an almost absolute censorship, the more insidious because it was never mentioned, much less acknowledged and the idea of censorship in a democratic society was an apparent paradox.* Millions of Americans lived through those decades without the realization that vital information was deliberately being withheld from them, which is not too surprising since much of them were clueless anyway. But, for Cuban refugees, who were constantly *craving* to learn more about the totalitarian terror that they had left behind, and expose it, the total absence of any critical material on Communism, the Soviet Union, or Castro, it was very noticeable. Any book encountered was like an oasis in a desert and it was a wonder at all that it had been published. And here is where Maximiliano further brought us together. He was obsessed with finding such books and had an uncanny ability to do so (think about it: if you do not know the title, or the author, of a book, and if it is not sold in a bookstore, how can you track it down?) He ferreted out a goodly number of them, which he then passed around, books like *Darkness at Noon, The God That Failed, Animal Farm, The Bridge at Andau, A Question of Madness, The Outsider, The Flight of the Innocents, The New Class, The True Believer, The Devil's Advocate* and *The Passionate State of Mind* and, of course, every time that one of

150

Solzhenitsyn's works was smuggled out and published in the West. This may not sound important to you, but to us, at that time of near-absolute censorship in America by the Left, and when we were starving for anything to read on the subject, to learn new, vital, facts, it was invigorating. And it took him years to find out that such books existed. Think of it, really think about it: if you do not know that something exists . . . how do you look for it? And remember something else: this was long *before* the advent of the internet and the computers, where anything can be found out through the worldwide web. It was this, more than anything else, that finally, and decisively, broke through the secret censorship.

More to the point: what had radically changed our attitude towards our elders towards one of open contempt had been sparked off in one of their get-togethers. During the Jimmy Carter years, yet another country had fallen under the Communist yoke with barely a shrug of concern in the West and some "social activists," "radicals," "socially responsible" groups---whatever the proto-Communists in America masqueraded themselves as at the time---praised the change in government by claiming The Poor were going to benefit from the change (as if *they* really gave a rat's tail about the poor!). And, sure enough, all this was being loudly discussed by the Cubans and in the middle of this Mendoza comes out with, "What these Americans need is a good, harsh dictatorship to put them back in the right track!"

"Exactly!"

"That's right! A military dictatorship's what they need!"

!

The rest of us, myself, Max, Manolo, Toni, Cristina and Isabela sat there stunned, blanched, our eyes popping out. I'm talking white---all the blood drained from our faces.

And then we jumped in.

I'm afraid that we, ourselves, behaved in a very Cuban fashion, shouting, interrupting, waving arms, insinuating (after all, they were adults) insults, being very emotional, very red in the face.

Hot? You bet we were hot! Even though we had heard this obscene proposal before, I'm ashamed to say.

"Have you ever come across such *imbeciles* in all your life?!" Isabela screamed to no one in particular when we were outside.

"What morons! Those geezers are such morons!" Toni chimed in (we were all speaking in English). He was the blonde of the group.

Cristina pointed out that, "They've been in this country, exposed to it, for what? Ten? Fifteen years? And they haven't changed one bit, not one damned bit! They're still the same as they were fifteen years ago!"

"Yeah! Why didn't they leave those stupid values behind? I mean, you can see what those values did for Cuba, can't you? If it wasn't for them, Fidel and his band of cutthroats probably wouldn't be in power."

"And it's for everything! You know what my mother did yesterday? She went to a *santero* to find out about her future, for Christ's sake! That ignorant witch killed a cat and waved it around on top of my mother's head. They're so damned embarrassing!" This from Manolo.

"No wonder Castro and his rats took over the country! With *that* in there, how could they *not* take over? The wonder is that they didn't do it sooner!"

Max had not said anything all this time and was frowning. He opened his mouth to speak and the words came out tentatively, unsure, not like his usually arrogant manner, and in complete contrast to everyone's mood there.

"What . . . if it's not just them?"

We all stopped and looked at him, wondering what he meant.

"What . . . if it's not just them?" he repeated. "What if it's not just . . . our relatives? What if they're typical of *all* Cubans their age? We're in Kansas, we don't really know. I think that they may be representative, that they really *are* typical." He moved around hesitatingly, his hand gesturing as if trying to capture some elusive thought. "I'm trying to put two and two together. I just read Hemingway's *To Have and Have Not* and it portrays Cuban students in the thirties. They. . . were irrational. Criminally irrational. They'd," he motioned towards the house, "be the right age." He arched his eyebrows. "So is Fidel and Raul and the others. And didn't they mention at other times that when Machado got overthrown, *their* generation, the students, ruled Cuba in the thirties and they couldn't decide which ideology to follow and that there were bands of student gangsters and terrorists operating out of the universities?"

"Get to the point, Max," Cristina urged.

"Maybe that was a crossroads in Cuban history . . . . Maybe, that . . . generation of '33 was always that way: irrational. Hysterical. Crooked. *Stupid.* Maybe the Great Depression also affected them. Didn't a politician of that time with a huge following make a two-hour speech, screaming in the

153

radio about nothing in particular and ended up by shooting himself on the air?" He paused and made a face. "The De-generation of '33. Has a nice ring to it, don't it?"

From that moment on, there was a palpable, yet subdued, element of hostility with us during the gatherings. Henceforth, our views of the older generation gelled; we saw all of their faults: ignorant, crooked, hypocritical, abysmally stupid, corrupt, ridiculously chauvinistic, two-faced, loud-mouthed, petty beyond belief, crudely insensitive to others' feelings and pathological liars. As if that was not enough, the women were unquestionably, contemptibly superstitious, shrieking loudmouths and who actually thought of themselves as being attractive by being animated lard containers with hips the size of a Volkswagen.

The invariable accusation, that we were ashamed of being Cubans, kept being hurled at us now more frequently, which was not true, not really, not deep down. We were just thoroughly disgusted and ashamed of them, of Cuban history, of Cuban politicians and just that whole corrupt "De-generation of '33."

Like, for instance, one day we found out that the early anti-Communist underground decided to strike back at the regime by . . .torching *El Encanto*, a department store (which the Communists hated and were going to nationalize). Now . . . what was *that* supposed to bring about? What was it supposed to prove? And how was it going to hurt the Communists?

That whole generation was so stupid.

And if that wasn't stupid enough, some Cuban exile organization in the United States, composed of persons as psychotic as the

Communists back in Cuba, decided to protest some decision or other of the American government by exploding a tiny explosive in the White House!

In the White House, for God's sake!

Jesus Christ!

How humiliating!

How embarrassing!

They were so stupid.

And it was not just in the abstract political sphere. Oh, no. Oh, no, no. It was present in everyday life.

Take, for example, Belen with her mustache. One day, Kansas being Kansas, a tornado was sighted hovering over part of the city, not yet touching ground and thus not leaving a wake of destruction behind (so actually, it was not a tornado proper but a funnel cloud). Air raid sirens wailed. Radio and television announced taking shelter in basements. Belen goes out the front door and, sure enough, it's right up there in the sky, no sound or anything! So what does the horse-manure-for-brains do? She stands at the doorway and rhythmically waves a kitchen knife in the cross pattern, repeating over and over and over again, "In the name of the Father, the Son and the Holy Ghost, Amen! In the name of the Father, the Son and the Holy Ghost, amen!" with her motions following her recitation. The funnel cloud never touched ground, a frequent occurrence, thank God, but horse-manure-for-brains Belen asserted that *el rabonube*, the cloud tail, had broken up because of her incantation.

They were so stupid.

Or take Inez, another mosquito brain, who looked like a five-foot-tall lard ball. It snowed one day and one of the neighbors' kids, an enterprising American lad, was shoveling snow away from all of the driveways for a small sum which he collected afterwards. Being conscientious, he also put rock salt on the pavement so that it would create friction when walking on it and thus nobody would slip and break an arm or a leg. Having finished his chore, the lad went up to the door to collect his money. Inez saw the salt on the ground, her eyes bugged out, she gave an air splitting shriek, which startled the boy into jumping a whole yard backwards, and began ranting and raving in Spanish at the top of her voice.

After several seconds of being rooted to the spot, the boy found his feet and ran away like a flash to hide behind a tree, emerging to look fascinated from behind the tree trunk at the sight of Inez as she continued to, with arms waving and hands pointing, scream Spanish curses on herself, her luck, the world, her future and the doom that was going to befall her and her home and why couldn't she have stayed in Florida where she had wanted to stay anyway and it was all the fault of that good for nothing husband of hers who should have been here to prevent this calamity and how is this going to be averted she's going to the church to light a candle for Santa Barbara and ask Her for Her help.

All this went on for a good fifteen minutes at full volume in Spanish with lots of fat arms waving; the American kid understood not a word and was spooked, but was rooted now to the spot in both fear and fascination and curiosity; what made it even more strange was that as she paced back and forth, she seemed to be arguing and trying to convince some unseen person in front of her. He could have easily stayed there another twenty minutes but her son, Hugo, happened to drive up and park at the curb. He got out of the car, quickly looked with an embarrassed expression around to see if anybody else in the street was watching the spectacle, saw only the kid and approached him, momentarily relieved, but now becoming furious with each passing second at having to be associated with his mother.

"Hey, kid! What's with her?" he motioned towards his mother.

"I don't know!" the kid blurted out in a bewildered tone. "She started screaming for no reason!" He pried his eyes away from the ranting, pacing apparition to ask Hugo, in all innocence, "Is she crazy?"

Hugo was taken aback by the simplicity of the question. Looking at his mother, whose sight he now loathed, the culmination of months of steadily increasing contempt, he shrugged. "Looks like it, don't it?" He strode up to the porch and faced her, sneering.

"*Oye!* Hey!" Inez came to, startled, as if Hugo had materialized in front of her out of thin air.

To end the story, the salt was swept away and put in a garbage can by Hugo and the kid was paid. At no time since that particular incident did the boy ever offer to shovel the snow away from that household after a snowfall, not even after a blizzard. And, anytime that he walked down the street and reached Inez's house, he crossed the street to the other side.

They were so stupid.

Then there was Lucinda who, on finding out from the doctor why her son was not yet speaking although he was five and a half, learned that he was mute. Once back at home she remembered that she had at one time repaired her radio which would not

157

talk, by banging on it, so she took her son and repeatedly slammed his head against the wall in order to fix him. "Speak! Come on, speak!" she yelled at him over his crying, as she kept on slamming his head against the wall, trying to repair him until the little boy died.

Lucinda was an extreme case, to be sure. But aside from her, these were not isolated, rare incidents. I wish they were. A fit of hysterics could be evoked in any Cuban woman in any day of the month, at any hour, simply by leaving a hat lying on top of a bed, or, by nervously rocking an empty rocking chair back and forth with one's foot, or, for that matter, if any one of them dreamed of coffee with a cloud of milk dissolving in it.

They were so stupid.

Nor was it just the women. Oh, no. No, no! The men themselves had also been blessed with more than the world's share of stubborn, unthinking stupidity.

My father, to begin with, made my life miserable for years in making me perform drills in handwriting to make it attractive. He used the famous Palmer technique as a guide and assured me over and over and over and over again that I would never amount to anything unless my handwriting improved. Now, I'm the first one to admit that American schools should have taught penmanship, since the handwriting of most American kids was atrocious and barely legible, but to make it such a dogmatic, Calvinistic obsession was absurd; four or five decades before, it might have made some sense since many legal and social documents required good, legible handwriting (and also, when letter writing between friends or relatives had not died out as an art form and been replaced by the telephone), but nowadays to attribute that much importance to elegant handwriting that he was attributing was nothing short of absurdity. After all, the United States was neither Japan, or China, or one of the Arabic countries, where calligraphy had become an art form. Nevertheless, his overbearing dogmatism on this subject continued for years. He would not budge. He could not be convinced. He would not even listen.

They were so stupid.

Then, there was the case of Fermin, with his bald spot and his little mustache (and *all* the Cubans of that generation had the same damned little mustache). One of his sons, Miguel, one of the most pleasant, most inoffensive individuals in the state of Kansas did not spot a Stop sign while driving. His car plowed into another, tragically killing the driver. Miguel himself was devastated with guilt and, on top of that, was arrested and released on bail. He faced prison. Fermin, in all innocence, many times started to drive down to see the judge and offer him a large sum of money so that the judge would be lenient. He thought he was in Latin America! He was only stopped by the desperate entreaties of Miguel, Isabela and myself, who assured him that it did not work like that in this country (certainly not in Kansas, maybe Philadelphia) and that he would, in fact, seal Miguel's doom and he himself would be thrown in jail in the bargain. Fortunately, Miguel was given probation, no doubt because he had not been intoxicated while driving and his conscience-stricken face spoke volumes (in this, he also benefited from the fact that the accident took place in Kansas and not Texas. In Texas, the philosophy is that everyone must be sent to prison, even if one is innocent, or rather, *especially* if one is innocent).

We all breathed a sigh of relief.

I could go on forever, though. Like, I could cite endless instances where they would lie for the sake of lying. It was a habit, an unbreakable habit. There was no ulterior gain in doing so and there was no loss of any kind by telling the truth. But, if there was a choice between telling a lie and telling the truth, with absolutely no consequences present for either choice, they would invariably opt to lie. Invariably. They could not . . . not lie.

They were so stupid.

And if they got into a disagreement . . . well! They possessed a steadfast inability---or refusal, it was hard to tell which---to see the other person's point of view.

The older generation of Cubans were undeniably stupid. I know that it sounds crude, but there is no other word for it.

They were so . . . stupid.

Oh, yes. And then, there were the *peleas,* the fights between families.

There would be a *pelea* between one family and another which would drag everyone else in and force them to take sides. Then, after months of petty viciousness, they would suddenly become reconciled in tearful reunions, all would go well for six or nine months and then another *pelea* would occur over some trivial, petty, yet "unforgivable" insult (sometimes imagined).

That spring we had one. It went this way. Blanco, one of those balding men who combed wisps of hair from his temple across his bald dome in a vain effort at mitigating his condition, secured a job for Fuentes where he worked; they had met, briefly, at a relative's house in Miami where Blanco had gone on vacation. Fuentes had called him up weeks later, inquiring of any positions being open, since they had the same professions and, indeed, there was an opening. Fuentes applied for the job, Blanco highly recommended him though, naturally, he had no idea as to his work habits. Within two weeks, Fuentes and his wife, Yolanda, had moved from Miami and he had started working, giving a good account of himself. Blanco also introduced him to all the Cuban families in the *colonia*.

The problem stemmed now in that, without actually verbalizing it, Blanco now expected Fuentes to be, if not his devoted servant, then at the very least his devoted friend. Aside from the round of get-togethers (which followed a crucial hierarchical-timetable protocol which was unfathomable to the uninitiated), Blanco and his wife, Ana, visited Fuentes and his wife, Yolanda, and expected those visits to be promptly reciprocated. There was some mysterious value attached to "being visited," and Ana would call up Yolanda to gently remind her, somewhat bitterly, or accusatory, that she had not done her duty, asking why had Ana not visited her "for so long" (really not that long; regardless, the fact was that Ana was one of those women who grated on everyone's nerves and, thus, was always on the short end of visits by all of the other women). To cap it off, Blanco and Ana had retained the irritating Cuban habit of dropping in on friends for a visit without any warning and their victims, bound by rigid rules of Cuban hospitality, had to cancel any plans to go out shopping, or relaxing, on that day, or go play baseball, and be forced to entertain the visitors after a hectic five minute whirlwind of straightening up the house and changing clothes or, if eating, setting down new places on the table for them and offer them a serving. The Cuban visitors, being congenitally insensitive, saw nothing wrong in the practice, even when it happened to them. To Fuentes and Yolanda, however, the American custom of telephoning ahead to see if their potential hosts were going to be busy and, if not, could they drop by, was the greatest thing since the invention of the automobile. After half a dozen drop-in visits they, finally and tactfully, requested that henceforth Blanco and Ana call ahead first, and although the latter agreed to do so, they afterwards sneered at Fuentes and Yolanda for putting on airs.

At work, relations between Blanco and Fuentes were deteriorating. At first, Blanco had been absurdly solicitous of Fuentes and now he wanted reciprocation, which was not forthcoming. On top of that, there were times when Fuentes disagreed with Blanco on work related matters.

Then, the straw that broke the camel's back came when Fuentes had a get-together without inviting Blanco and the news, naturally, filtered back (actually, on the second occasion, they found out about it ahead of time and spent the whole night calling up all of their friends to find out who had gone and who had not---not everyone else had been invited---their bitter reconnaissance being determined as to whether they answered the phone and engaged in conversation or nobody answered the telephone, which meant that they were at the party).

"This is a mortal insult!" proclaimed Blanco to his wife and Ana agreed, adding choice words of her own.

"Imagine!" she said. "She knew nobody when she came here! Nobody! She would have died of boredom for months all around in that house if it

162

hadn't been for me, you can ask anybody. Anybody! I took her out to go shopping, showed her which stores had bargains and which ones to avoid, even Inez said so that I was showing that miserable witch all the ins and outs because I've got a heart of gold that's what my problem is where my fault lies I'm too good and everyone takes advantage of me because that's the way I was brought up by my sainted mother may God bless her soul and Yolanda wearing those gloves of hers is not fit even to polish her shoes wearing those gloves of hers like she was an aristocrat I invited her to go everywhere with me showed her everything that worthless false friend even she admitted it one time the one time that she was honest and said the truth she said 'Ana,' she said, 'you know every nook and cranny of this town.' Yes that's what she said 'you know every nook and cranny of this town you know where to go for the best bargains' she said and she's a lazy homemaker too every time we went to visit I thought I was in a pigsty you'd think she'd find the time to dust the tables with all the times that she has free on her hand doing nothing but no her end tables have six months' worth of dust Belen said it the other day herself yeah she had noticed it but me every time I went over I thought I was going to stick to something and then they have the nerve to tell us to call ahead---what for---doesn't make a damn bit of difference whether she cleans up or not it still looks the same it still looks like pigs live in there."

"Yeah, that's a good one," her husband chimed in. "'Call ahead.' Yeah, 'call ahead!' The Count and Countess will now see you, it's a privilege, don't you see, for the Count and Countess to see you, after all I've done for that two-faced

163

hypocrite, he stabs me in the back. What infamy! What ingratitude! After all the sacrifices I've made, I moved mountains to get him perched up there in that job, it's a far better position than the one he had in Miami, let me tell you. Ask, just ask anybody, he's such a worthless individual, just look at his Christmas present, that rotten fruit he sent us, it could have been diseased for all he cared, every time that he parks that fancy car of his he takes up two spaces so nobody will scratch it, that shows you what kind of a person he is, right there, thinking he's better than anyone else and everyone else is a dummy, while in fact the person that's a dummy is him . . . ."

Just then, the phone rang. "If that's him, we're not going!" he shouted to his wife. "You want to have a party? Fine! Have it then! But I'm not going!" But it was not Fuentes. It was a kid selling magazine subscriptions by telephone.

Anyway.

At work, they stopped speaking to each other. After a tearful phone conversation, where Ana accused Yolanda, "You don't care about me! No! Not at all!" They, too, stopped seeing each other. And for the next six months, they intrigued with their mutual friends at isolating each other, holding get-togethers without inviting each other and tallying up who had come up to their party (allies) and who had not (false friends), with subsequent accusations and phone reconnaissance during those parties and taking note of who was driving down what street which led to either Blanco's house or Fuentes' home, all of it---all of that spent energy---being done for its own sake. Nobody had a goal in mind. It was just like the habit of lying for the sake of lying when telling the truth was just as good and at times even more obviously beneficial.

Inevitably, the petty, yet vicious, rift was mended. Perhaps it spent itself out and ran out of energy. A tearful reunion took place and the normal schedule of visits and parties was resumed, everyone acting as if nothing had happened.

Except for us. We---Manolo, Cristina, Maximiliano, Miguel, Toni, Hugo, Isabela---we were all sick to our stomach. All of us made a silent vow not to be like them. It was important for their generation to die out.

They were so stupid.

And it went on and on, until they finally died out.

*One of the many reasons why Ronald Reagan was so wildly popular is that he broke through the censorship by stating what everyone knew, but could not voice, and since he was a presidential candidate, it was impossible to not publicize his remarks: that Communism was evil, as evil as Nazism, that the Soviet empire was The Evil Empire. He tore through the veil of censorship by stating the obvious and the news media was *forced* to carry his message; they could not ignore it, or suppress it. The only alternative left was to bury Reagan under an avalanche of Politically Correct condemnation (that he was bringing back McCarthyism, that he was a right-wing nut) which he shrugged off like so many raindrops.

XXI

That is one of the great tragedies of revolutions: you have to suppress man in order to save him.
----Fidel Castro

I think our country sinks beneath the yoke. It weeps, it bleeds and each new day a gash is added to her wounds.
---William Shakespeare, *McBeth*

The plane landed in the tarmac and I was back in Cuba. True to character, it was still the last bastion of Communism (outside of Asia), just as it had been the last territory in the Americas that abolished slavery, just as it was the last Spanish colony in the Americas, finally becoming independent almost a century after the rest of the Spanish colonies. Kind of makes you wonder--- whether it'll be another one hundred years before we throw off the Communists (that would be *so* typical of us). When that finally happens, leftists everywhere---but especially in France, Germany, Mexico and the USA---will go into shocked mourning just like they went into catatonic mourning for a couple of years after the Evil Empire collapsed.

But, as usual, I'm digressing.

Everyone in the plane is what is nowadays called a Cuban-American, which means that you were born in Cuba but emigrated ("escaped" is the term that we use) to America. In order to return to visit our native country and see our family we have to pay hundreds of dollars to the regime. You see, the dictator and his sycophants see us as enemies, as traitors; we broke faith with the regime by not constantly praising The Revolution (always in capital letters), by not looking upon the psychotic Che's amputated hands brought back from Bolivia with the veneration due to a medieval relic, not viewing the old dictator with his yellow teeth and scraggly beard as our benefactor, not cheerfully starving to near death while Party members become bloated with food, not snarling at Americans as our enemies, or not reading only what the dictatorship wanted us to read (propaganda and more propaganda).

Before the Soviet Empire collapsed, there had been a somewhat similar arrangement with the Eastern bloc countries. Relatives in the West could bring over their relatives (only the "useless" people) from Romania or East Germany if they paid the governments a certain amount of money. In other words, a sort of slavery. The "social activists" and the liberal "progressive elements" in France, Italy, Britain, or Holland---much less those of West Germany---so hypersensitive about the plight of the oppressed somehow never developed a moral indignation over the open traffic in slavery.

Which goes to show that the most outstanding characteristic of leftists has always been a bottomless hypocrisy.

I'm digressing again.

I do that a lot.

You may have noticed.

So now we are standing before customs, waiting to have our bags scrutinized. The only real reason most of us are back here is to bring back supplies for our relatives in order to help them survive. But there's a catch. We cannot bring back food, the number one necessity---and see, here, Cuba is mostly agricultural! So we bring clothes. And medicine.

And there is a limit as to how much we can bring, which is one suitcase. The fat lady (and why are so many Cuban women so fat!?) next to me has three dresses, two hats and three panty hoses on and sweating profusely. Not a pretty sight. The extra clothing is perfectly visible and is allowed through customs since it is not in the suitcase. She, like most of the passengers, are scowling at the guards, who scowl back. They see each other as enemies, quite rightly so, and if they were all to be magically transported to another, safe, isolated, location, they would go for each others' throats.

I don't scowl. Waste of energy. Makes matters worse. Though, if magically transported, I too would join the fracas---with glee.

I am not expecting my relatives to pick me up, one of them is too sick and transportation this far out is out of the question for them, so I catch a dilapidated taxi. He lets me know right away that he expects to be paid with dollars---American dollars---and not the worthless Cuban peso. At one time, before Castro, the Cuban currency was on a par with the American dollar---that's saying something. It was a robust economy. Now, the Cuban peso, with its multicolored pictures of Communist revolutionaries is so worthless that it could be used for toilet paper. In fact, just before I took the taxi, I stopped by the ticket office of the government's currency exchange and I asked the girl, "I'd like to get some toilet paper, please."

"What?"

"Toilet paper, please," I show her my greenbacks.

"We don't have that here."

"I'm talking about the one-peso bills. Here's ten dollars."

She looks daggers at me but makes the exchange. For all of its vaunted revolutionary principles, the fact of the matter is that the regime and its minions are, like all gangsters, greedy for real money and won't let an opportunity pass by. It is a well-known secret that the regime is economically buoyed up by its most ardent enemies, the Cuban-Americans, who know this but can not control themselves. Like alcoholics.

As I had expected, the drive into and through Havana is depressing, just as it was the time I came before. Everything is dilapidated, the buildings crumbling, with not a drop of paint to be seen outside of official signs and the occasional government building. It is hard to believe now that once Havana was the liveliest, most colorful, most sensual spot in all of the Americas.

I ask the driver to go by the Malecon. El Morro is still there, symbol of the city like the Eiffel Tower and Big Ben are the icons of other, more famous, cities. I am glad to see the landmark again.

The taxi passes near the Peruvian embassy. By luck, before she died, my sister had been in the city when the fiasco occurred and thousands and thousands of people stampeded into the embassy grounds to seek political asylum. It must have been something to see. She did see part of the spectacle, from a distance, of course.

Then, we pass a billboard which depicts the dictator's face and a caption next to it. "Todo va bien. (Everything's going great)" and I burst out laughing.

We finally arrive at my aunt's house and I pay the taxi. I don't see her, but several people on both sides of the street look at my arrival with undisguised curiosity. No doubt she had told neighbors that I was coming. A couple of them, whom I had met before smile, call out and wave at me. I wave back and quickly duck into my aunt's apartment and knock on her door.

My other aunt opens the door.

"Pascual! You've arrived! Melina! Pascual's here!" she calls to my aunt who is unseen to me. We embrace and, of course, she begins asking me a hundred questions which I answer as we slowly go towards my other aunt's room.

Melina is in bed. Like my other aunt, Pilar, who has been taking care of her, she is thin from undernourishment, only more so. The weekly quota of food issued by the Communist regime is four pounds of rice, one pound of gnarly meat, two ounces of sugar.

That's *if* they can find the food.

The doctor had diagnosed Melina with beriberi, the illness which was eradicated in Third World countries seventy-five years ago. Beri-Beri has always been famously associated with Chinese coolies in rice fields. It is "simply" a vitamin deficiency and my aunt are wasting away. The doctor at the hospital could not give her vitamins; vitamins are reserved for Communist Party members and visiting tourists who come to praise the regime's "free medical care" as a model for their own countries.

And this is why I am here. I immediately open my suitcase and give her a multipurpose vitamin, the kind that are for sale at any local grocery store outside of Marxist countries

So why did they stay in Cuba? Well, for the same reason that so very many others did. Some, because they thought that the regime would not last and they waited too long until it was too late. Others stayed for the very same reason that so many people stay in their homes in spite of an order to evacuate from an incoming hurricane and later find themselves trapped, cursing their stupidity and wishing for others to come rescue them. And still others because they refuse to leave other relatives behind.

I pull over a couple of chairs from the other room for Pilar and myself and begin talking about everything. It is hot, so we also pull out three hand fans (air conditioning is a luxury in a Communist country reserved only for the homes of good Party members). At first, my Spanish is halting and they poke fun at me. I don't have much opportunity talking in Spanish where I live and I'm more comfortably speaking English---after all, I came over when I was thirteen. Pretty soon, though, the hesitation in my speech vanishes, it all comes back to me and I speak fluently.

There is a knock at the front door. Since I am closer to it and I already feel at home I go over to answer it. I open the door and it's the chairman of the neighborhood spy committee. His job is to spy on everyone in the neighborhood and stick his nose in everybody's business. He can do it with impunity, since the government set up the system in the very beginning. I met him before on a previous trip. A person to person representative of the regime and its firm supporter.

I slam the door on his face.

I return to the bedroom. When they ask me who it was and I tell them who knocked and what I did, they are angry with me. I realize that they are in the right and I was stupid: *I* will leave but *they* will have to stay here and put up with his petty harassment. Stupid, I'm getting really stupid. Stupid, stupid, stupid! Stupid!

Pilar goes to get him and they come back. He plants himself in the living room, visibly offended with me and asks me a number of questions. I answer with monosyllables or grunts. At some point, I realize that I'm tense and have been eyeing him, subconsciously thinking how I would physically attack him. The moment that I realize this, my animosity drains and I all of a sudden become verbose, even friendly, and this throws him for a loop. After a half hour of this he leaves, rather confused in my change in demeanor.

We return to the bedroom. Close on to dinner time, I suggest that Pilar and I go to a restaurant and we will bring Melina supper. The only restaurants available are the government owned "dollar restaurants." If you have dollars, then you can eat, courtesy of the Socialist government. If you cannot get dollars, well . . . .

And not just food. Clothes, vitamins, medicine, musical CDs, Japanese electronics, toilet paper.

A new type of underprivileged proletariat, courtesy of the Marxist people's government.

The only thing that works efficiently in this country are the instruments of repression.

During dinner I ask Pilar, for the umpteenth

time in so many years, why she and Melina have not come over to Miami. She mentions---again---her kids and grandkids, and Melina's. They can't leave them behind. But why not before? And why not one of them, then the rest will follow. Many did just that! But she can't say why, exactly. It's not that they have any sympathy for the regime. It's not that at all. Behind locked doors they will vehemently tell you---for hours---everything that is wrong with the decrepit regime.

I shake my head and continue eating. I guess that Melina and Pilar are like those people elsewhere that refuse to be evacuated whenever a natural calamity strikes and have to be forcefully evacuated. If they stay behind, and a force five hurricane hits and their home is crumbling around their ears, then they get on the phone and anxiously call for help. Like Melina. She wrote me asking me to save her life and I naturally complied. Had to. I loved my aunts.

We get a plate of food to go and suddenly realize that it is the most food that Melina has probably seen in a week and again I get angry again. Where are all the liberals that cry rivers of tears for The Poor? (somehow, they never seem to be interested in cases like my aunt, since it would mean criticizing Communism, and they go on to their next Crusade of the Week)

Once back, Pilar leaves Melina in my care while she goes back to her family. She leaves just before the lights flicker and go out momentarily.

"Say what?" I utter, looking up.

"The government shuts down power for many hours," she explains.

"My God, we're going back to the Middle Ages," I mumble in disbelief and sure enough, an hour after Pilar leaves, we're plunged into darkness.

I light a candle.

Melina and I pass the time in pleasant talk, reminiscing about old times and about family members. Gossip. Sometime around ten, for whatever reason, the lights come back on.

A claustrophobic feeling simply comes over me, totally irrational. I stand up.

"Aunt Melina, I need to go out for a walk," I tell her and she understands. I go out into the cool night air, thankful that it is not summertime. I walk around a few blocks before coming back.

The following day, Pilar comes back, bright and early, hoping that I will take her out for breakfast. I don't mind at all. Melina takes another multivitamin; she's already beginning to feel a bit better, she says, especially after we bring back breakfast for her.

Much later on, I actually manage to go to a beach outside a city on a taxi that was threatening to give up the ghost at any moment (whatever my original reason for coming here I have to go to one of the beaches; go to Cuba and not go to the beach? No way!). There are a few American cars on the road, all from the 50s, barely kept together by miraculous little acts of workmanship. It is kind of funny seeing them.

Cuba has great beaches. No question about that. That is one thing that the Communists have been unable to destroy and no matter what bastard's has been in power, the beaches will still be there. This beach is indeed beautiful, with a nice breeze and palm trees rustling from the wind. The water is warm and crystal clear. I love it!

But . . . wouldn't you know it.

After walking a while along the beach

towards a big hotel, a couple of men stop me and tell me I cannot go on. I snort with amusement.

"Oh, yeah? And why the hell not?"

The two creeps flash IDs. The secret police.

Of course.

Wouldn't you know it.

From what they tell me, but mostly from what other people I ask when I go back to the other side of the beach, a *de facto* apartheid exists, wherein Communist government prohibits Cubans from swimming in most Cuban beaches. They are reserved for foreign tourists, the type of tourists that at home joined frenzied demonstrations against South Africa's apartheid.

Oh, and it gets even better. The government at one time made it illegal for anyone to swim in the sea. In Cuba. An island. And this was actually enforced by the government's minions.

Only a Communist regime could come up with such a prohibition.

And only a leftist, a mindless, kneejerk liberal, could praise such a regime.

My earlier good mood is shattered, replaced with a mixture of nausea and anger. I hate feeling this way, I really do. I'm serious, I do. You think one likes feeling so angry? That's why I seldom make the trip here. The last time I felt this way was a year ago when I saw the film *Bitter Sugar;* I was glad that I had gone to see it, but still . . . .

A poem pops into my head, one by Armando Valladares, one that I have memorized because of the emotions felt.

They Have Not Been Able

They have not been able to

175

take away
The rain's song
Not yet
Not even in this cell
But perhaps they'll do it
tomorrow
That's why I want to enjoy it
now,
To listen to the drops
Drumming against
The boarded windows.
And suddenly it comes
Through I don't know what
crack
Through I don't know what
opening
That pungent odor
Of wet earth
And I inhale deeply
Filling myself to the brim
Because perhaps they will
also
Prohibit that tomorrow.

Tourism has become the main moneymaker for the regime. But tourists have to be kept away from the captive population. Hence, the apartheid. And, disproving their opponents' assertion that Communists were sterile and unimaginative in their thinking, they established government-run brothels. Just for foreign tourists. Like that repulsive-looking German over there with his fifty-pound belly hanging over his belt as if he was nine months pregnant; probably an editor from *Der Spiegel*. The irony, of course, is that for decades the Pavlovian dogs had pointed to the Castro regime as helping

The Poor as evidenced it having abolished prostitution (now, of course, those leftists are silent on the subject and have developed selective amnesia). I had often retorted that the Third Reich had likewise done away with prostitution but, predictably, the leftists blinked vacantly back at me with the Mongoloid expression that they adopt whenever present with facts that contradict their rosy view of totalitarian regimes. They are the kind of people who will only read Djilas, Koestler, or Solzhenitsyn at gunpoint; the only time that they had ever criticized the Marxist regime was when homosexuals, one of their sacred cows, began to be persecuted.

A lot of bad memories and feelings are coming back to me. I really hate feeling this bitter anger. Really. I honestly do. Usually, I'm a mild-mannered fellow. Hey, I'm a dentist. My life doesn't get blander than that. And I know what my friends would say now if they saw me. If they knew how I felt. They wouldn't like me right now and I can understand it. They would tell me that I'm getting too angry, too hateful, and they'd be right, it's true, it *is* true. But dammit! If you don't get angry because your relatives are *dying* from beriberi---beriberi, for God's sake!---and your countrywomen are being turned into whores by their own government, and your native country has been ruined, totally ruined, then what *will* you become angry about? And if you can't hate the bastards who've done this, and worse, much worse, much, much worse, the other group of scoundrels who praise these bastards as humanitarians, and *expect* you to believe it, who *will* you hate? My anger is exactly like the anger felt by the Holocaust survivors who learned of certain intellectuals dismissing the Holocaust as a myth.

By the time that I come back to Aunt Melina's home I've made up my mind and formed a resolution. I tell her.

"Aunt, I'm not coming back to Cuba again. Not until the Communists are out, anyway. I can't stand it anymore. It's too painful. It's sickening. You've gotten used to it; the change is too abrupt for me. One of these days I'm going to do something really stupid and put you guys and myself in a heap of trouble." I explain my feelings as best I can. "And from now on, if you or Pilar need anything at all, I'll arrange it with someone to send it to you. A friend of mine in Miami knows a couple of people who come down every other week."

Just then, Pilar arrives with her son, who is not working today and I explain it all over again. They all understand. But are saddened by it.

Eating at the "dollar restaurant" later on--- and bringing Aunt Melina food---alleviates their own feelings (it is hard to feel sad on a full stomach, a rarity in Cuba). During dinner I tell them about Cachao, Andy Garcia, Celia Cruz and Gloria Estefan; the regime has censored their existence, made them, in Orwell's words, "unpersons." They have never heard of them. Afterwards, I visit their home.

By the time that I am ready to leave for home, Melina is able to get up and walk for a few seconds before she has to lie back down, exhausted. She has a good supply of vitamins and if she runs out, I'll send her some more. Or anything else that they might need.

But I'm definitely not coming back.

It was an unpleasant airplane ride, with much turbulence. Anyway, once back at home, I went through all the rooms, experiencing that feeling that one gets when coming back from a long trip. I unpacked, then settled down to relax on my favorite chair with a mug of beer and watch some TV when, what should I see on the screen but The Human Slug, Michael Moore, gushing forth about how wonderful the Communist regime of Cuba is, since it provides its citizens with free medical service. More importantly, as far as he is concerned since he is a good liberal, the Cuba government hates his country and anyone that hates America is good enough for him.

Impulsively, without thinking, I throw the mug at the television, smashing the screen. Now I have to buy a new one.

XXII

The young couple moved into the house a day before the moving van arrived with their furniture and they cleaned all the rooms, though there was hardly any dirt or mess left by the previous occupants. They had bought the house from the previous owner, who had had to relocate because of his job. After a week, everything was in its place and all the empty boxes had been finally carried off by the garbage men.

While her husband, David, was at work, Daisy looked over her new house with the quiet pride of ownership, going from room to room, absorbing the look of each room. The twins were quietly watching *Sesame Street* on television, so Daisy decided to inspect the backyard. At one point, they had talked of putting in a small swimming pool or maybe a gazebo, or maybe both, but David was adamant against the pool until the girls were older and had become proficient swimmers. It occurred to her that a small flower garden (and maybe a vegetable garden to one side with tomatoes and okra) might be a good idea. At the very least, flowers could be grown all along the walls of the house and in front, a little area could be sectioned off with decorative bricks.

She looked out of the kitchen window at the backyard. There were two large orange trees towards the periphery of the yard, one straight back and the other on the right, both close to the mesh fence. There were oranges aplenty, both on the branches and on the ground and Daisy got a small basket in order to gather them in. She remembered what the precious owner, a Korean, had told them about the trees, that these oranges were bitter, but could be used just like lemons in cooking food, also that, years ago, he had had several branches grafted on from other trees bearing sweet oranges so each tree had both types.

She went out the back door with a basket and headed straight for the back tree. There was a house on either side of hers and two directly behind, all of them separated by the ubiquitous low aluminum mesh fence. She gathered the oranges and put a towel on top of them to distinguish them from the others and started walking towards the other tree. A dog had been barking at her in the neighbor's back yard and, as she approached, it became more agitated in its growling. The closer she got, the more vicious it seemed to become, no longer barking in a "woof-woof" voice, but actually snarling and slavering as it barked. She now saw that it was a huge dog and could, easily, if it decided to, clear the fence in one leap.

Daisy was nervous about the animal, though she began to gather the fruit, regardless. It snarled-barked unceasingly, hysterically. Moreover, any sudden movement on her part sent the dog into an increased frenzy, as it lunged at the fence. It was clear that it would have loved nothing better than to rip her throat to shreds. She tried talking to it to calm it down, to no effect. She remembered hearing somebody saying that bad dogs only acted that way behind fences, but became cowards once you crossed the fence. Maybe, but Daisy was not going to test that theory by crossing the fence. For one thing, the idea might not be applicable to all dogs and, for another, she had been hearing reports of vicious dogs, particularly pit bulls, jumping fences and attacking and even killing people, particularly children. Particularly children.

Some of the branches extended over the fence into her neighbor's yard and some of the oranges on the branches were within reach. She wearily reached for one and the dog lunged upwards for her arm, snapping its jaws in midair as Daisy quickly withdrew her arm. The fact that it had missed the opportunity to sink its teeth into her arm seemed to send it into another frenzy.

The oranges no longer seemed to be that attractive and she retreated back into the house, sending the dog into another hysterical frenzy at the prey that was eluding it.

Later that evening, when David came home, she told him, "I think we've got a problem: The Hound of the Baskervilles lives next door." She related what had occurred. "And what bothers me is having the girls playing in the backyard and the animal gets loose. That thing's big. And vicious."

"Are you sure you aren't exaggerating a little bit?"

She handed him the basket. "Go see for yourself. And what makes it worse is that the sweeter oranges are closest to the fence."

He went outside to gather more oranges. She could hear it beginning to act up and David attempting to make friends by talking to it and whistling to it, all to no avail. In fact, it seemed to make the dog angrier. A few minutes later, he came back with hardly a dozen oranges in the basket and an expression of disbelief in his face.

"Hey, you weren't kidding! That thing's vicious!"

"So, what do we do now? I'm really worried that it might get loose when I'm not looking and the twins are outside."

David leaned his back against the refrigerator, thinking. He grimaced. "It really hasn't done anything. That's the problem."

"The problem is that he might do something."

He sighed in frustration. "I'll go talk to them and see if anything can be done."

A few minutes later, he returned. "Nobody home and the lights are out. I'll try it again tomorrow." And with that, he refreshed himself with a shower and the topic was temporarily shelved.

It occurred to Daisy the next day that perhaps if the hound got used to seeing her on a regular basis, it would get used to her and be less aggressive, so she forced herself to collect oranges while talking and whistling to it, trying to make friends, all to no avail. The dog continued to lash out at her, going into sporadic, slavering frenzies. She tried it for a couple of days before her nerves gave out. Then, she marched next door and, before knocking, put on her best smile.

A middle-aged woman opened the door, a cigarette dangling from her mouth. She was frumpy, unsmiling and had curlers in her straw-like hair. She was like some sort of caricature right out of a cartoon. Daisy kept forcing a smile, hoping that her shock at the woman's appearance did not show through.

"Hi, I'm Daisy Toscano. From next door?" No response. "I hate to bother you, but would it be possible to restrain your dog? You see, I'm trying to pick the oranges from the tree and it keeps barking at me."

"It's a dog. It's supposed to bark."

"Well, yes, but, it's such a big dog that I'm afraid that it might jump the fence and come at me."

"Has it gone over the fence?"

"Well, no . . .."

"Has it bitten you"

"No, at least, not yet."

"Are you teasing the dog?"

"No! All I'm doing is picking fruit and it looks like it wants to have me for dinner."

"I don't see what the problem is. Elvis is a good dog. Now, if he had been in your yard, then I could see that there was a problem."

"My main worry is my little girls. I have two daughters and next to your Elvis is like their being next to a Siberian tiger."

"Well, just what is it that you want me to do, get rid of my own dog?"

"No, but could you just put him on a leash while he's loose in the back yard?"

"Put him on a leash while he's already fenced in the back yard. That's what you're saying." Her sarcasm dripped out of her mouth and Daisy felt absurd. "If Elvis had gone over the fence, you know, then I could see the point in that."

"That's what I'm trying to prevent: his going over the fence."

"Oh, stop wasting my time!" she exclaimed as she slammed the door on Daisy's face. Feeling angry and absurd at the same time, she stared at the door, debating what to do next, while the theme song from *Days of Our Lives* was heard. She looked at the mailbox at the names posted therein. Bubba and May Moore. That, plus the woman's accent and having glimpsed a wooden clock in the shape of the Lone Star State when the door was opened, replaced her anger with dismay.

"Oh, my God, they're Texans," she muttered.

She went home and awaited her husband's return, so she could break the news to him.

"Guess who the owners of Cujo are?" David arched his eyebrows in anticipation as she made a face. "Texans!"

"Oh, no," he groaned. "Are you sure?"

"Uh-huh, so there goes any chance of reasoning with them. Babe, I've been thinking. Let's get a fence, one of those wooden fences, real tall. We're going to need one, anyway, if we ever build a swimming pool." He started to stare off to one side, internally debating the matter until she gave him the clinching argument: "The twins."

That brought him back. "OK. Agreed. You want to take care of it, or shall I?"

"I'll get them to come over and give me some estimates while you're at work."

Next day, having called several numbers from the Yellow Pages and made appointments for them to come over, she looked around the back yard. The Moores had, in the meantime, put up a Beware of Dog sign next to the fence. It was obvious that the sign was just meant to diminish legal liability in case something should happen. That callousness was exactly what you would expect from Texans, she thought to herself.

The fence was built before the weekend rolled around. As the fence was built, Daisy made it a point that the orange tree's branches stayed in her own backyard by making the workmen pull them over and tying them to either the trunk or to the other branches.

At one point, their neighbors watched the construction and talked amongst themselves in their backyard. May had not improved her appearance one bit. Her husband, a middle-aged man, with a typical Texas potbelly big enough to make him look nine months pregnant, wore a cap and kept spitting out of his mouth a continuous spurt of black tobacco juice. Daisy was now doubly grateful for the fence, now that she would not have to be exposed to the sight of such crass neighbors.

Once the fence was up, they all felt secure in their privacy.

The whole incident faded like a bad memory.

Nothing much happened after that for weeks. Daisy made friends with the other next-door neighbor, a woman named Midge, who knew nothing about the Moores. Aside from noticing a lout who seemed to be the Moore's son and was yelled at as Josh, they kept their distance in their tobacco-spotted lawn and its inhabitants. Occasionally, very loud country music was heard coming over the fence, along with the smoke of bar-b-q. Elvis still barked whenever it heard anyone moving around on the other side of the fence, but the rabid snarl---and the potential danger---seemed gone.

One Saturday morning, a month or so after the fence had gone up, David and Daisy were breakfasting in the dining room while the girls watched the Saturday morning cartoons. Glancing out the window at the tall grass, she said, "You really need to cut the grass today, David."

He grimaced with distaste.

"OK, OK, I will."

"Today. You practically need a machete to get to the front door."

"All right! I said I would!"

If there was one household chore that David detested with an unbridled passion, it was mowing the yard. Whereas other homeowners weekly jumped at the chance of mowing the lawn if it grew a quarter of an inch, he let it grow until Daisy's nagging became more distasteful than the mowing. More than once he had suggested buying a lamb, or a goat, or even a Shetland pony. He was half serious in his suggestion.

Sighing with fatalistic resignation, he changed into old, smelly clothes from the hamper and went to the garage and took out the lawn mower. He wheeled it out to the garage to the front yard, where he would begin. He happened to glance at the front door where a note had been taped and he removed it and read it. It was brief.

Mow your lawn! The grass attracts snakes
and besides it looks bad. Yours is the only
one that looks this bad.

David reddened with anger and
embarrassment. It was true that the grass was tall,
but, so what? It was his yard and if he decided to
have bare dirt or jungle vines, it was his choice.
And whoever heard of grass attracting snakes?
Besides, he wasn't afraid of snakes, they were kind
of neat, really. He looked around at all the houses.
One guess at which one it had come from. He went
inside and showed it to Daisy.

"Betcha it came from them," he nodded
towards the Moore residence.

"It'd be just like them," she nodded in
agreement.

"And what's this about snakes?"

"Heck if I know, but there are a lot of
drainage ditches around the neighborhood."

"I feel like not cutting the grass, out of
spite."

"Oh, no, honey, it needs cutting."

"But, don't you see? They'll think that we're
cutting it because of the note. If I cut it now, it'll
only encourage their placing more notes in the
future."

He ended up cutting the crass.

The note exacerbated his ill mood at having
to do so. As expected also, the mower stalled
frequently from the bunched grass obstructing the
blades, which made it even more irritating. Thanks
to the sweat from the sun and the effort, itchy grass
particles clung all over him. Since he refused to
collect the mowed grass, there were concentric
squares and the air smelled of cut grass. But there

187

were no snakes. After taking a break, wherein he downed three glasses of iced tea, he proceeded to do the back yard. Then, he put up the mower and went directly to the shower, flushing the nasty particles down the toilet while in there.

Back in the dining room, his wife had another idea.

"Easter's in two weeks. I'd like to get two goslings for the girls. They're so cute."

"Are they hatched?"

"Yeah, I called a feeder store and they said that the eggs had just hatched. The goslings should be ready for Easter."

"Let's get them, then."

And so, they got the two goslings for the twins, who were delighted with them the first two days. They bought a plastic kiddie pool and filled it with water and the goslings were put in; they proceeded to swim and to constantly foul the water, so the girls were told not to get in the pool. The goslings gradually changed the color of their feathers and the tone of their voice. Throughout, they stayed in the backyard.

Then, one fine day, the Toscanos received a form letter from a city bureaucracy stating that it had received a complaint that the Toscanos were keeping farm animals, which was against city zone regulations and would have to do away with them, or be fined and the animals taken away, anyway.

"One guess!"

"Of all the nasty, petty . . .!"

"Why are they doing this?"

"'Cause they're Texans, that's why."

They both marched over to the Moore residence and knocked on the door. Bubba answered.

"What have you got against our geese? They ain't doing you no harm!" Daisy immediately demanded.

"Our geese are pets, they're not farm animals," said David.

"Those geese make a lot of racket. They're noisy and they never shut up."

"Noise? What about your dog? Every time we come out to our own backyard, your dog barks for hours on end!"

"That's beside the point! This neighborhood ain't a farm, though you people seem to think so. You act like you live in a barn." And saying this, he spit out a brown glob of tobacco juice onto the ground big enough to drown a sparrow, which made David retch.

Now the woman, May, joined in.

"You people need to mow your lawn. Don't you know it attracts snakes?"

"You're the only snakes we've seen: spiteful, mean, nasty Texas snakes. Why don't you mind your own business?"

"How can we mind our business when you live next to us and live like pigs?"

Josh then jumped in, offering to punch David in the nose and David calmly invited him to step out and do so and see just what would happen to him.

And so on.

Much, much later, after they had calmed down, which was not until four days later, David discussed the geese situation with his wife in a calm manner.

"The fact of the matter is, that the geese could be judged to be either a pet *or* a farm animal, it'd be a judgment call, but getting a legal ruling on it would cost us money, far beyond what the geese are worth, not to mention any fines that they might impose on us. And they'd probably take away the geese until there was a hearing, maybe. And, quite frankly . . . I'm getting tired of them birds."

"Me, too, and the girls have stopped playing with them."

"So, what do we do with them?"

"We could return them back to the farm where I got them from. I'm sure they'd have them back. And we could tell the girls that they're going back to their family, they'd like that. They'd also get to visit a farm."

"Let's do it." And they, the whole family, made a big expedition of it and the geese immediately blended in with the gaggle at the farm and the twins had a fun time.

When they returned home, they found a note taped on the door insisting that they cut the grass. David rolled his eyes in exasperation.

The situation escalated two weeks later when they returned home to find the dog in Daisy's flower border, having torn it up and now using it as a latrine. They chased the dog back---it had temporarily lost its ferocity---and the Moores came out to protect their Precious. Accusations and insults and warnings flew back and forth.

Two days later, Elvis was found dead in its own back yard. Daisy heard the accusations and the wailing coming over the fence. The word "poisoned" was used a lot. Midge thought that perhaps a rattler had come in from a drainage ditch.

David woke up one morning to find his car tires slashed.

If driving on the same street, the Moores would invariably swerve their car and almost hit them.

The police did nothing.

Late one night, Josh fumbled in the dark at the corner of the Toscano home. He had matches, a flashlight and three cans of gasoline. He was spreading the gasoline when he heard a "click" behind him and, turning around, saw the barrel of a .45 staring down at him.

"Lie down on the ground with your arms next to you, punk, and don't even sneeze, or you're dead. The police are on their way."

He had bought the revolver days before after much mutual agonizing with Daisy over the safety of the twins with such a deadly object around. However, the increased level of hostility and overt acts, plus the knowledge that their neighbors were psychotic Texans and, therefore, armed to the teeth, had ultimately made the purchase a necessity. At this moment, he was glad of the purchase. Yet, it took all his self-control from not pulling the trigger. They were at the part of the house which corresponded inside with his daughters' bedroom.

The police arrived and took away the whole Moore family. Josh was denied bond, but the parents were able to bond out of jail. Then, one day the following week, as Daisy and David debated on whether or not to move away, the question was resolved for them. Shots rang out next door and they called 911.

It turned out that Bubba had argued with May over something unrelated to the Toscanos. Angry, May had seized one of the four dozen guns that they kept and opened fire on Bubba. The police came and took her away. The never saw her or Josh again.

The Moore house was ultimately put up for

sale.

A nice family from Nebraska bought the house and moved in.

And David Toscano sold the gun.

XXIII

My friend, Casper, had a new hobby. It was photography. He was very enthusiastic about it, having bought a brand new 35mm camera with assorted lenses. He showed them to me and explained their uses and the possibilities for really neat images.

He had invited me to come along with him to the park and to the art museum, which is next to the park, and he wanted to take pictures there. So, I went along, since it was a beautiful spring day and a band was supposed to be playing, anyway, free to the public. He came by in his car and picked me up at my house.

We arrived and after an hour of crawling at a snail's pace along the crowded avenues of the park, we finally found a parking spot. We parked the car, got out and joined the festive crowd.

He immediately started taking pictures. With a telephoto lens, he could take photographs of people at some distance without their realizing that they were being photographed. So, he was everywhere, snapping pictures of the band playing, snapping pictures of the crowd, snapping pictures of the children playing or of adults with their children or with other adults, snapping pictures of motorboats on the river, snapping pictures of dogs that people had brought to the park, snapping pictures of flowers. You get the picture. Just click,

click, click, clicking away nonstop. Like a jack in the box. Click, click, click.

As for myself, I sat down on one of the benches, with the crowd and enjoyed the music, the crowd, the weather. Occasionally, I'd see Casper popping into view and then out again, busily aiming, focusing and then click. And then click again.

About an hour or two later, the band took a break and I went over to him. He was crouched, with knees bent, aiming his camera at somebody.

"That's a pretty good band, don't you think?"

"Huh? Oh, yeah, I guess."

"Haven't you been listening to it?"

"I guess I've been too busy to appreciate them."

"They played some good songs. How about you? Have you gotten some good shots?"

"Oh, yeah! Can't wait to get them developed! So far, I've shot about fifteen rolls."

"Good Lord! That'll cost you an arm and a leg!"

"Not really, I've got a friend that's got a dark room and he'll let me develop them for just the cost of the materials and I can get the rolls wholesale."

"Hey, look who's over there," I motioned to two beautiful girls in halter tops and shorts that we both knew from class at the college. "It's Sandy and Sylvia," and I waved to them. They recognized us and came over with big smiles.

"Hi! Enjoying the concert?" asked Sandy, the blonde one of the two. She was wearing her long hair in a cute pony tail. Sylvia was wearing her brunette hair short with the sides coming to a point, very nicely so. And boy, what a figure!

"Very!" I responded. "I like the way that they played those songs. Very original."

"That's what I was just telling her," said Sylvia, "that they've given the old songs a new twist."

"What'd you have there, Casper, a new camera?" asked Sandy.

"Yeah, it's less than a week old. I've been taking pictures."

"How about taking ours, Casper?" I asked him and he obliged with a couple of snapshots and then I insisted on switching places with him and he stood between the girls.

The band started tuning up again and I suggested that we grab a seat before they were all taken, except for my buddy who wanted to keep right on snapping pictures and even Sandy's urging did not budge him. So, the three of us sat, talking and enjoying the songs, while our shutterbug friend was frantically busy. Once in a while, Sandy would say to us that she wished that Casper would come join us.

Some time later on that afternoon, the four of us decided to stroll over to the art museum to enjoy a new exhibit. I was glad to see him pay attention and talk to Sandy, who reciprocated, in turn. Unfortunately, the idea occurred to him---and it was actually a pretty good idea---to bring the exhibit back home. In pictures, of course. So, he carefully went about photographing the sculptures and paintings. In the meantime, I got Sylvia off in a corner by myself and nuzzled her and asked her out on a date. When she agreed, I gave her a quick kiss and we rejoined the others.

Later, on our way back home in the car I

gave Casper some gentle advice.

"Idiot! Sandy was interested in you and you completely ignored her! She's pretty and she's nice and you ignored her! Idiot!"

"Really? I hadn't noticed she was interested."

"Of course not! You had your nose stuck in that telephoto lens and couldn't get it out! Idiot!"

He frowned, a bit troubled. "Maybe I should call her up."

"Do what you want. *I've* got a date with Sylvia for tomorrow night."

I wish that I could say that my buddy wised up in the weeks to come, but he did not. He became so absorbed in taking pictures that he would not even notice the very things that he took pictures of. Mind you, he did get some good pictures. It is just that in doing so, he missed savoring the moment. One day, after an afternoon spent in the public swimming pool, playing water tag with a couple of dozen friends of ours while he stayed outside the pool taking pictures, I tactfully brought it to his attention.

"Idiot! You didn't spend five minutes in the pool playing tag with us. You spent it all outside the pool! Idiot!"

"But I got some great pictures! You'll see, they'll turn out great!"

"I know they will! But the point is that you've been so busy photographing the things that you enjoy that you forget to enjoy them! Idiot!"

He pursed his lips, thinking. "Maybe you're right."

"I'm coming back tomorrow and if you show up, I'll push you into the pool, with or without the camera."

He complied the next day, but it was really no use. There was no change in him. He kept on overdoing it. And not only would he show me his photographs---which were good, I have to admit that---but he would also show me issues of National Geographic and point to samples of the quality of photography that he wanted to achieve some day. It was hard to find fault with such ambition, really.

About a month later, the four of us, Sandy and Sylvia that is, with myself and Casper, were together at the Civic Center waiting for the hour to roll around when we would go in to hear the symphony; half the fun was watching the little Belgian director in his colorful vest (he refused to wear a tux) practically go into a seizure while conducting (when he first got the position he had each member of the symphony audition; several refused and were instantly fired; that's when we knew he was going to be fun). The Civic Center, along with the new library and other architectural improvements downtown were the brainchild of the liberal members of the City Council (and funded by Richard Nixon's revenue sharing program) who had, thankfully, outvoted the one conservative council member who was a pathological liar and borderline psychotic. The Civic Center was shaped like a huge flying saucer with a blue top and a large metallic spider sculpture next to it (*really* neat looking) and as we paced around I was glad to see that Sandy and Casper were hitting it off great and he was not escaping into pictures with the camera that even now hung from his shoulder by the strap.

Now here I must digress momentarily and mention something.

In Kansas, we have a saying, "If you don't like the weather, wait five minutes and it'll change."

True enough. But what this does not tell you is that sometimes the weather is---odd. Sometimes at night, for example, the overcast sky will sporadically light up for hours, on and off, with lightning. Nothing unusual in that except that there is no sound and no lightning bolts; I believe they call it sheet lightning and I have never seen it anywhere else; the clouds simply . . . flicker. *Eerie.*

And then sometimes on a very hot summer day in August a brief rainfall will occur. Then stop. And *steam* will rise from the sidewalk. Definitely weird.

Well, on this day one of those freak weather manifestations occurred. Briefly.

"Oh, wow, look at that," muttered Sylvia.

"How strange," I whispered.

"I've seen it before," said Sandy in a referential tone. "It won't last long."

We had strolled around the "saucer" under its overhang and it had begun to rain, cooling the air. The clouds were dark blue-black and the day had darkened as a consequence. The four of us were just standing there, smelling the rain air, even if it had stopped raining. We then stepped out, looking around and strolling. Across the street there was an old landmark, the historical museum, castle-like, with a tall clock tower. The sun at this moment shone through---but just on this "castle." *And* it was not just sunlight, it was a bright, intensely *yellow* sunlight. This, in turn, made the green in the trees appear greener, while the rest of the area was darkish. It is impossible to describe it, the bizarre contrast, it was just weird looking.

I had an inspiration.

"Casper!" He snapped out of contemplating the mesmerizing phenomena. "Quick, take a picture before it goes," I suggested and he began focusing the camera. He looked up from the camera troubled, clicked a couple of times, stopped to look both at the spectacle and the camera, still with a troubled expression on his face. Finally, he spoke up.

"I don't think I can capture it," he admitted. "Not without it looking like it's a fake."

Sylvia put her hand on his arm. "Then enjoy it. It won't last long," she said and he visibly relaxed.

For the next two, maybe three minutes, we just stood there marveling at the odd colors and their intensity that Nature had briefly put together with the "castle" and its surroundings as her canvas. Then, it was gone. We felt privileged at having seen this eerie composition.

A couple of days later, Casper brought me the two pictures that he had taken. I could not read the expression on his face, other than he was not happy with the results.

The camera had, indeed, faithfully photographed the phenomena, except---it looked like a mistake, a clumsy error in lighting by amateurs, the kind that cheap cameras with clumsy operators make every day through blundering, except it was no blunder. The photograph *had* faithfully reproduced the meteorological chimera. Yet, the feeling in viewing the photograph was disappointment. It could never be truly captured in film. Even if it was acknowledged as being a faithful representation, it would still look like a mistake.

We did not say much in looking them over, but we both thought the same thing.

But the funny thing is, Caper has mellowed out since then. He still takes pictures. But he also stops to savor what he is photographing. And sometimes he even enjoys something without bothering with his camera at all.

XXIV

The director of the residential drug rehab center was putting the finishing touches on an evaluation that he had to write on a client for the court. The client, who was on probation for Possession of a Controlled Substance and had been placed at the center to complete the rehab program as part of his probation, had relapsed and used drugs. Sergio was not slanting the report either way; he was letting the facts speak for themselves and he was incorporating the client's counselor's assessment and recommendation without any modification. The judge would decide whether to send him to prison or let him slide.

He looked up at the figure standing at the doorway.

"Hey, hello, Megan."

"Hi, Sergio. This might be a little unpleasant," she said, handing him a typewritten sheet of paper. It was her resignation as counselor, effective in two weeks. Sergio's eyebrows arched in surprise. She had not given him any indication of being unhappy in her work.

"Come on in," he motioned. "Shut the door. Sit down." She did so. "How come, Megan? Are you going to another rehab agency?"

"Oh, no, it's nothing like that. I'm quitting the field altogether."

"Yeah? How come? I thought you enjoyed

your work. Don't tell me you've got Burn Out already! You've been in the field for only, what? Six years?"

"Seven. No . . . I was doing fine until about two months ago. Something crossed my mind two months ago and it's completely changed my outlook."

"Sergio, I mentioned it to you and to some of the other guys a couple of times."

"Refresh my memory. Please."

"It's simply that I've lost *all* respect and *all* sympathy towards addicts. I can't look on them without despising them."

"But that's what-"

"No, no, it's not what you think. I'm not being one of those people who don't understand the power of an addiction over an individual and think that all an addict has to do is 'just stop doing drugs,' that it's just a matter of will power. That's not me."

"Then what is it?"

"I told you then. All addicts nowadays are in their thirties and twenties and in their teens. How can they not know? Sergio, *how can they not know?* Sergio, you gotta be deaf, dumb and blind *not* to know about how addictive drugs can be! You've got to have been living *on the moon* not to know that if you use drugs, you're hooked! This has been known since, what? The Sixties? The Seventies? Back then! You gotta be stupid to know this and *still* go ahead and use drugs!"

"My Dad told me that in the Sixties liberals promoted using drugs to 'expand your minds' against a 'repressive government establishment.' I can understand," she was getting more agitated, "and I can sympathize with the old addicts. They didn't know. They were duped. They were

200

brainwashed. But *teenagers?* Nowadays? How can they *not* know?"

"It's like cigarettes. How can you *not* know, after all this time, after all this publicity, after all these articles in newspapers and magazines, after all these news stories on television? That if you smoke, you'll develop cancer. That it's a costly, nasty habit. That nicotine is one of the most addictive substances found in Nature. That it dulls your sense of smell and taste. Like I said, I can respect old timers who smoke. They didn't know! Hell, they even had *The Flintstones* promoting Winston cigarettes back in 1964. My Dad told me!"

"Look, Sergio, its simple: 'You take drugs. You become addicted to drugs. You destroy your life.' Now . . . *what* part of that don't you understand? Duh! Hel-lo-o?"

"All the more reason, Megan, to-"

"No, Sergio, I can't! I just can't anymore!"

"Are you sure? I hate to lose you, girl. You're good." He was trying to calm her agitation by speaking slowly.

"Thank you. But I don't think it's possible for me to just specialize in the old addicts," she smiled.

"No. Like you said, most are young people."

"Or, on alcoholics. Besides, they got AA for that. AA is good."

"You have no problems with treating alcoholics, then?" He was puzzled.

"No, of course not. It's a disease, an allergy, and a person doesn't know that he's one until he drinks and his peculiar biochemistry reacts that way and turns him into an alcoholic."

"Ah, yes, I see your point."

"I'll tell you another thing, Sergio and I

never thought I'd see the day that I'd say this. I can't blame the cigarette companies and the drug pushers for making money from these idiots. How can you have respect for them? It's like saying, 'Here, I'm stupid. Here's my money. *Make* me an addict." You remember that song?"

"Which one?"

"The one that says, 'Here's your sign for trying out a shark repellent and jumping in a pool full of sharks. The sign says, "I'm stupid."'" Remember that one?"

Well, Sergio tried to dissuade her, of course. No luck. And whatever her rationale, he put it down simply as another case of Burn Out.

A farewell party at work saw her off two weeks later.

For Sergio, the worst part was learning six months later that Megan had moved and had gone to work for Virginia Slims, the cigarette maker.

XXV

It is true that although Kansas is known for its prairie, it is nevertheless not uniform. The eastern part of Kansas (past Lawrence and Winfield) has rolling hills and many trees while to the west of those towns the rolling hills and trees abruptly disappear for the prairie whereas the western extreme of Kansas (past Dodge City) is downright arid. Regardless of the local contours, in the month of August, no matter in what part of the state one finds oneself in, he will be under the merciless, windless, relentless, dehydrating glare of the August sun. In August, there is no lifesaving breeze, least of all those raging Arctic gales coming down from Canada. And . . . there are no clouds.

And it was in the month of August that Max boarded a Greyhound bus that would take him, along with many other passengers to Denver, Colorado.

As before, the bus did not travel in a straight line but, instead, meandered through the various counties, dropping off or picking up passengers on the way. As Max's Cuban parents would jokingly say, it was a *lechero,* a milk wagon, stopping at every home to deliver the milk.

Regardless, Max had brought along a paperback novel, *The Spike,* that had been enthusiastically recommended by a friend, in order to read it on the way back to Denver and he was deep into it, occasionally glancing up at the chauffeur or the passengers, or looking out the window, particularly whenever they reached a bus stop at some town and, either someone boarded the bus or they got off, before resuming their zigzagged journey.

It was in the middle of the afternoon when the bus stopped in one town. Max looked up and saw that, in this instance, the bus driver stopped the bus, opened the door (which made its customary *psss* sound), got off, went around the front, reached in through the window and flipped a switch, which closed the bus's door with another *psss.* Then, the bus driver went back around and entered the small wooden building (either a makeshift bus station or a local store) that he had parked next to.

Within two minutes, it began to get warm. In two more minutes, it got hot. Max looked up from his book, frowning. Yes, it was hot in the whole bus and not just at his seat. He looked out, expecting the driver to come right back, but he did not. He looked forward to the front of the bus trying to detect a breeze from the air conditioning. No, there was no air conditioning coming through. Odd. He looked out the window again where it was glaringly white outside; the white paint of the station's facade and the dry white-gray dust of the graveled parking space seemed to accent the heat.

Max tried to resume his reading, but found that he could not concentrate because of the heat, so he laid the book down next to him. He frowned deeper and felt impatient, exasperated. Where *was* that driver? Why the devil was he taking so long?

The air also felt stuffy.

Maybe it was his imagination? He looked around at the others and saw that they, too, were sweating and had beads of perspiration on their foreheads and their upper lips.

Good Lord, Max thought, we're all cooking in here! Even so, nobody said a word, nobody muttered a word of protest, bearing the discomfort with typical American Stoicism and this made Max angrier.

"Just like sheep," he thought to himself as he fidgeted. He recalled a discussion with his relatives about the cattle-like characteristic of Americans when it came to following rules to a fault (written or unwritten) and not doing what was not expected of them, a characteristic that seemed to infuriate the anarchistic Cubans.

It got hotter.

When was that guy coming back? Why doesn't somebody do something? Or, at least, say something? It's obvious that the driver didn't realize the situation, or he'd be back.

Well, of course he's coming back. We've

got to be on the way, right? Just a few seconds more.

Jesus, it's hot! If this was a bus full of Cubans, we'd be screaming our heads off and rocking the bus! Christ, it's hot!

Max had a picture of himself going up to the front and getting out, then felt the inhibition of doing so as all of those eyes were on him and he got premature stage fright.

It got hotter. Everyone was now soaked in sweat.

"Oh, this is ridiculous!" he finally blurted out loud in disgust.

The young man got up and went to the front of the bus, meaning to get out. It was hot in the front, too.

Maybe he should honk the horn?

He looked at the panel by the window where the driver had reached in. There were several toggle switches and a couple of plastic covered push buttons.

Hoo, boy, which one to press? If he pressed the wrong one, the bus might just start moving, driverless, he told himself. He remembered hearing the sound of a click prior to the door opening and shutting, so that meant that it was one of the toggle switches. Besides, he had reached in through the left window and that was where the toggle switches were.

It was hot.

Arbitrarily, Antonio flipped the last toggle switch on the left and, with a *psss*, the door opened. He stepped out.

Great! It was definitely *much* cooler outside than inside, by at least fifteen degrees, even though he was standing in the full sunlight in the middle of

August. Oh, yeah! Definitely! That felt good. He had done the right thing.

He looked over his shoulder, expecting others to follow his lead and was surprised to find nobody behind him, preferring to remain in the bus sweltering, like good little sheep. Not even a peep. Amazing! If he related this event in another country *nobody* would believe him! It was incomprehensible!

He shrugged. Let them swelter. It would serve them right. Maybe the open door will get some air circulation going inside. No, there was no window open for the air to go through. Oh, well.

A few minutes later, the driver came out, still wearing sunglasses and on seeing him, snarled at him, "What are you doing out of the bus?"

"I got out 'cause it was hot," Max blandly responded and did not go back on the bus until he was sure that the driver entered first.

The bus driver, fuming, got in the bus and on his seat and for a moment stopped all motion as he realized just how hot it had gotten in the sealed-up bus. It was like an oven. Then, wordlessly, he got ready to go on as if nothing had happened.

Max moved down the aisle, past all the silent, sweating people with their drenched clothes and sat down on his seat. It was still hot and the air was very stuffy. But, in seconds, the bus was back on the road and the air conditioning had kicked in, restoring the temperature back to a very comfortable level.

Max forced himself to put the episode out of his mind in order to resume his reading, which he did. The plot of the book was so absorbing that he only thought about what had happened half a dozen times during the rest of the trip.

The bus reached Denver towards evening and Max and the other passengers disembarked. His relatives were there to pick him up.

XXVI

Oftentimes have I heard you speak of one who commits a wrong as though he were not one of you, but a stranger unto you and an intruder upon your world.
But as I say that even as the holy and the righteous cannot rise beyond the highest which is in each of you,
So the wicked and the weak cannot fall lower than the lowest which is in you also.
Kahlil Gibran, *The Prophet*

Four men sat inside a breezy porch, talking amongst themselves, on a warm Cuban night, the air strongly scented by honeysuckle. They were engaged in the Cuban national pastime of laughing at others' misfortunes. Since the events that they were discussing were ones that they coincidentally benefited from, there was quite a bit of gloating as well, since it dovetailed perfectly with the unstated precept by which all Cuban men and women lived by, which was, "Stab your fellow man in the back and laugh about it afterwards."

The four men were brothers and they, naturally, visited each other on a regular basis. Tonight, they met at Arsenio's home in Marianao, a Havana suburb. As was the custom, they sat apart from the women, who were talking about topics that could only possibly interest them. One of the brothers was Miguel, a farmer whose *finca* was near the border with Matanzas; he was not present in the frequent gatherings as often as the other brothers because of the distance. This time he had come to La Habana in order to go with his brothers to look over the display of brand-new farming equipment that the new revolutionary government was going to distribute to the farmers as part of The Agrarian Reform. It goes without saying that no one questioned how, or who, was paying for this beneficence.

They had returned an hour ago from the open-air exhibition. Although it had been much ballyhooed by the government and droves of people had gone to gawk at the various brand new tractors, mold boards, rakes, cultivators and disc plows, Miguel could tell that few of the passersby (city folk) were actually really enthusiastic by the display, being outside their field of interest. They had turned out just out of curiosity. Nonetheless, he himself had been impressed and was now anxiously anticipating the delivery.

The revolutionary government had also decreed, through The Agrarian Reform, that henceforth, farms would be restricted in size to thirty *caballerias* (a thousand acres). The idea had been around for many years, the implied argument being that no one should have too much land, but the real reasoning could more honestly have been voiced thusly: "Since I can't have that much, nobody else can." Needless to say that no one questioned by what right could a mob, or government, or committee, dictate to an individual how much land, or money, or cars, or clothes, or jewelry, or books, or neckties, that individual could own.

As a result of the decree, Miguel's neighbor, for example, Frank Martinez, would loose nearly half of his farm, the "excess" then being distributed to Those Less Fortunate. That Martinez and his family owned the land fair and square, that they had worked all their lives like plow horses from sunup to sundown, that they proudly loved their farm, that it was one of the most efficient, best run, farms in the region, that they had bought neglected and untilled land and had busted their backs turning said land into fruitful agricultural *caballerias,* and, more importantly, that they did not want to sell, was deliberately left unmentioned. Not that it would have made any difference. With a mixture of envy and greed, like circling vultures, Martinez's neighbors waited, wringing their hands in anticipation for the "redistribution of wealth" to occur, already making mental calculations as to how much of the booty they would each be able to grab.

Miguel was one of these neighbors. For years he had cultivated for bananas and tobacco in his ten caballerias, but it seemed that he was more proficient in harvesting tarantulas and bats than anything else. He was telling his brothers how much he expected to receive, what kind of land it was and his plans for that land, and as he did so, and his brothers offered suggestions, he could not help gloating over the anticipated acquisition.

"But isn't that stealing?" a small voice asked during a lull.

The men were stunned and a brief silence ensued.

The question had been asked, in all innocence, by Maximito, Esteban's ten-year-old son, who had been silently following the conversation throughout without saying a word, just listening and watching. The other children, as usual, had initially also followed the adults' conversation, but had earlier dispersed to play in the street and were now buying pirulí from a passing vendor. In his straightforward question and his staring eyes, little Max had stirred the broken, mutilated vestiges of what had once been a conscience within the adults. Because of this, he was instantly, momentarily disliked. Fortunately, his father came to the rescue of everyone.

"No, son, because, you see, the government is going to compensate the owner by buying up the excess land. So, he'll get money for his land. What a question!"

This was true, there would be compensation for the confiscated land. Little Max was relieved, being too small to see through this fatuous argument. The adults could have done so if they had given any further thought to Martinez's viewpoint, but likewise accepted the compensation explanation, satisfied at not having to dwell on an unpleasant topic and perhaps even revive and been forced to come to terms with their long-stunted conscience.

"Now, go play with the other kids, son."

"But I want to stay and listen."

"This is grownup talk. Go!" And little Max joined the other children and was soon happily busy playing ball with his cousins. The adults were relieved to see him go, although the gloating stayed subdued as a result of little Max's question.

Earlier in the year, a similar incident had occurred. The new revolutionary government had suddenly decreed that those families who lived in a rented home, or a rented apartment, now owned that dwelling and did not have to pay rent, since it was now theirs. This declaration greatly increased the popularity of the government. Since Esteban had been for years renting his home at a reasonable rent from a retired Polish woman living next door, he was overjoyed at the announcement and even became insolent towards her whenever they crossed paths. The Polish woman emigrated soon afterwards, having seen the handwriting on the wall, selling her own home in the process and damning all Cubans to hell in the process; she had had only one house to rent, having worked in painstaking frugality for over a decade in order to pay for her investment.

Soon, thereafter, the brothers had come together to visit and this was, naturally, a topic of conversation, or rather, gloating. Agustin, the third brother, had also been renting his home, so the amount of gloating can only be imagined.

At that time, little Max had, once again, with that untarnished sense of right and wrong that so many children all over the world are born with before their parents crush it out of existence with either scorn, cynicism, or justification, shattered the mood with his question, "But, Daddy, isn't that wrong?"

And, of course, there was nothing that one could have answered to that too innocent question, because it *was* wrong, it *was* unquestionably immoral, it *was* very wrong and this time there hadn't even been an anesthetic-like excuse of "compensation" because no compensation had even been contemplated anyway and the stark reality was there for all to see: that the drooling Cuban population, under the guise of politics, was taking turns in preying upon one another, tearing each other to pieces, without the slightest hesitation, or shame, on the part of those receiving a share of the spoils. In a certain sense, the fact that this victimizing of others who were better off was being done under the justification of an over glorified international political doctrine of rationalized cannibalism was merely . . . incidental.

So, the father had responded in the only way that an adult Cuban felt was appropriate.

"What a question! And what do you mean by interrupting the conversation of adults? You're just a child! What do you know? Go and play with the rest of the kids!"

So, he did. And it was a good thing that the boy had no idea of what buying items (cars, refrigerators, furniture, etc.) on the installment plan was all about, because the government then decreed that The People no longer had to make further payments on whatever items that they had bought on the installment plan and could go ahead and keep the items, said customers ending up with those items at a fraction of their cost.

Then, by the end of the year, the subsequent confiscation of American businesses, invariably described as "exploiting Yankee monopolies" and "colonialist footholds" were an accomplished fact and, of course, most of the country chuckled with approval. An abstract anti-Yankee feeling was a long-standing tradition of Cuban life and, in fact, of *all* Latin American political life, which to this day has been often utilized by dictators of the entire political spectrum, from the left and from the right, to either mask their illegal actions behind a show of hysterical chauvinism, or, in order to take attention away from their own crimes. From long practice, dictators throughout Latin America of the entire political spectrum knew that they could always count favorably on an otherwise pointless show of anti- "Yankee imperialism" gorillaesque breast beating. The Latin American masses---and *especially* the intellectuals---always responded automatically and favorably to this ploy, just like Pavlov's dogs salivated at the ring of a bell and with just as much mindlessness, the same mindlessness for which Latin Americans are so justifiably famous the world over.

*   *   *
*   *   *

The Communists desperately played for time. Each day, they consolidated their hold on the country that much more. On the one hand, they had to allay the fears of the Colossus of the North---only ninety miles away!---who was, after all, the primary opponent of Soviet expansionism and would, undoubtedly, invoke the Monroe Doctrine as soon as their suspicions were confirmed of The Revolution having turned Marxist. They would certainly not tolerate a Russian beachhead in the Americas! On the other hand, the Communists had to systematically, yet surreptitiously, pacify or liquidate those revolutionaries whose original ideal had been to get rid of the dictator Batista and his murderous henchmen, like the vicious Mansferrer, in order to reestablish a republic. The Communist clique had to replace them with their own Marxist henchmen, particularly in key positions, or turn as many of them into Communists as was possible.

Even more daunting, they had to downplay the obvious Communist makeup of many of their followers and their policies and continue to ride the wave of overwhelming enthusiastic support that had been present because of Batista's overthrow. It was a formidable, unenviable task. It was a real tight wire act.

Many of the original rebels who complained of Communists being placed in key positions, particularly of Communists who had not lifted a finger to overthrow Batista and who, in fact, had *supported* the dictator right up to the end, actually blamed Raul and the psychotic Che and assured themselves that as soon as Fidel learned of the problem, he would take the proper steps---unaware that he himself was the Prime Mover in the events taking place. When they finally came to the realization of how matters really stood at, it was too late. The Trojan Horse was inside the gates and its contents had discharged.

Baseball in Cuba, as in Japan, Santo Domingo and the United States, was a national mania. A glimpse of Fidel Castro's mentality occurred when, months after having seized power, he appeared in a Havana stadium as a batter for one of the national baseball teams and was struck out. He immediately declared that it took four outs to strike out a batter. The pitcher and the umpire, being nobody's fools, instantly agreed and the pitcher then pitched a ball which could have been hit by a teenager. The Cubans altogether missed the significance of what had happened and, instead, thought it was a funny, quirky episode. Castro was happy; he had proven his proficiency in baseball for the whole world to see and admire; at that time, no one knew that years prior he had traveled to

America to play in one of the national baseball teams and had been rejected, hence his rabid hatred of Americans. That particular incident should have right away sent up a red flag of warning and set people to thinking, but, as we all know, Cubans find thinking---accompanied by silence---to be a distasteful, painful activity and dutifully avoid it whenever possible.

The international Communist conspiracy rallied to their colleagues' defense. A torrent of articles, petitions, newscasts, films, demonstrations, documentaries, declarations by ad-hoc political--- and supposedly nonpolitical--- groups appeared praising the Cuban revolution, the newly acquired benefits to The People, and pointed to the grass roots support of The Revolution, and condemned American "paranoia," which was obviously based on "McCarthyism" and was going to end up sending Cuba into the arms of the Soviet Union if American pressure did not let up, and which demonstrated America's colonialist outlook towards its southern neighbors. Legions of proto-Communists, with their hyena grins, tripped over themselves in a stampede from all over the globe towards Cuba in a pilgrimage, all for the privilege of meeting the Maximum Leader and then groveling at his feet and also give The Revolution (always spoken in capital letters) their own particular seal of approval. Some, like C. W. Mills and Jean Paul Sartre even published tracts gushing their enthusiasm and lambasting the United States. They spoke not a word of Spanish. No matter.

*　　　*　　　*　　　*
　　*　　　*　　　*

Let us look closer at the brothers.

A short man, prematurely balding, Agustin was a civil servant whose specialty was sports, that is, the representation of Cuba in the international arena through sports, a position which, although unknown in the United States, is common in many countries. Such a position has many perks, foremost being paid travel to other countries. When Batista had been in power, he had been a fervent Batistiano and sang Batista's praises. Upon hearing of Batista's overthrow, he had been the first in his street block to sport the red and black armband with the yellow "26" in the middle of it. He genuinely welcomed and applauded the revolution and the anticipation of a return to democracy. At the present, he denounced "Yankee imperialism" and the counterrevolutionary "caterpillars" along with the best of them and could outshout anyone in the open-air mass meetings with the preferred slogan, *"Patria o Muerte! Venceremos!"*

Nor was this hypocrisy. On the contrary! Each time he had been sincere. He was simply an unconscious chameleon. Had the United States Marines landed instead of the American government adopting a pusillanimous policy towards Castro, I dare say that he would have been singing *Yankee Doodle* at the top of his lungs in the Malecon. Curiously, far from being seen as unreliable by the Party, his star was rising rapidly within his bureaucracy and was actually even being deemed as above suspicion and allowed to travel abroad without fear of defection, or espionage.

Arsenio, the eldest brother, was a high school principal. He had earlier been a teacher, but was now a principal in a new State school which had formerly been a school run by the Catholic church and had been confiscated by the State. Since the overthrow of Machado in the Thirties, he had been a closet Marxist; that decade had been a turbulent period in the nation when college students had actually, briefly, for all practical purposes, run the country and debates as to which ideology to follow (National Socialism, Fascism, Socialism, Communism, Anarchism, maybe something new and vague and purely Cuban) had never gained a consensus and public debates were oftentimes resolved with bullets. Many concepts in Marxist ideology had always appealed to him, both the stated ones and the implied, and he had promoted those ideas and debated them with his colleagues and his brothers, though he had never joined The Party. As such, he was what is known as a "fellow traveler." In recent months he had refrained from formally joining The Party and declaring himself a Marxist-Leninist at the request of The Party: the time was not ripe. Soon. Very soon. In the meantime, he continued to promote government proclamations and advocated vigilance in the schools and elsewhere for the safeguarding of The Revolution. Children were to extol the virtues of Fidel, Raul, Che, Russia, China and, of course, The Revolution itself, and they were to notify their teachers at once if they overheard their parents making any derogatory remarks on the new icons. In their turn, teachers were ordered to report any counterrevolutionary statement blurted out by any of their pupils. The G-2 would then "investigate" (if he had known just how many of his teachers risked their necks by *not* reporting such occurrences, he would have had a fit of apoplexy).

He personally conducted tours of visiting foreigners---sympathizers of The Revolution, of course---as they toured the "new, improved" educational system, so that they could return to their own countries and rave to one and all about the benefits to The People in Cuba. As they followed Arsenio with their perpetual hyena grins, they made mental notes of the proven benefits. And they did so uncritically, although usually and with all other topics in their own countries they were invariably cynical, sarcastic and suspicious. Had Arsenio casually informed them that, as a result of The Revolution and the new educational system, six year old children could easily carry out quadratic equations in their heads and recite *War and Peace* word for word, from beginning to end, and in the original Russian, the visitors would have uncritically accepted such claims and, what's more, would have returned to their respective countries and testified to such an achievement. And if any of them noticed the children toting submachine guns and being dressed and drilled in a decidedly militaristic fashion as potential cannon fodder for Fidel, Raul, Che and The Party against the "imminent" Yankee invasion, none ever commented on it---even though at home they were caustic in their stance against their own country's military--- especially if it belonged in NATO. They certainly did not condemn the fact that Cuba had, overnight, become the most militarized State in Latin America.

In his own block, Arsenio had formed one of the first "neighborhood committees" for safeguarding The Revolution, whose task it was to spy on his neighbors in that block, report conversations as well as comings and goings to the G-2, speculate as to any possible counterrevolutionary "caterpillars" infesting the block, organize "spontaneous" demonstrations and marches of contempt against the increasingly longer queue of those seeking a visa in order to emigrate, and assure attendance and support to the open air rallies where Fidel would hysterically rant and rave against the Americans, practically foaming at the mouth for four or five hours at a stretch, in Hitler-like fashion. He also had first pickings in looting any homes of their personal belongings deserted by emigrating "counterrevolutionaries" in his block and could even move in to the vacated homes if so desired (or move in a friend or relative) and if it was a step up in the quality of his domicile.

Needless to say, that he was intoxicated with all this new power that he wielded. He was living the dream of every 19th and 20th century intellectual.

The odd man out was Esteban. As the months passed, his disillusionment was steadily increasing. It was not that he objected *per se* to the anti-Americanism of the new government, nor to The Agrarian Reform, nor to the closure of the fifty-eight independent newspapers and magazines which were replaced by only one, nor to the persecution of the Catholic Church, nor even to the pro-Russian propaganda. Being Cuban, he could easily disregard others' persecution, suffering and deprivation. Rather, it was that he objected to the natural, inevitable byproducts of a decrepit Marxist economy, where guns, not butter, and where both quantity and quality of basic consumer goods had flown out the window. In other words, *he himself was being adversely affected.* Again: the detrimental end result of Marxism-Leninism was affecting *him and his family directly.* Suddenly, there was no soap, razor blades, or deodorant; no shirts, pants, shoes, dresses, belts; one had to line up for hours to get *one* can of condensed milk, or *one* can of coffee, or bonito, or pears, or rice, or milk (while chanting moronic pro-government slogans!); medical equipment, medicine and drugs had disappeared; nobody could find a television, radio, fan, record player, much less a car, for blood or money; bookstores became empty; decent entertainment became nonexistent; travel was restricted; all tools like flashlights, pliers, batteries, nails, hammers, resistors, gone; even *sugar, tobacco,* or *Bacardi rum* had vanished---in Cuba! In Cuba! He could not remember the last time that he had had a Cuba Libre, or his children a *guarapo* drink from sugar cane---in Cuba, for God's sake!

This was a novel experience. It had *never, ever* occurred before in Cuba. Not with Batista. Not with Machado. Not even during the Great Depression. It was unheard of!

So, this was Communism.

On the other hand, his brothers, in their enthusiasm, did not object to the adverse shortages because their rewards for unquestioned obedience outweighed any shortages that they had to endure and which would, "of course, be temporary."

And another thing: the politics likewise affected him directly---even though he had no interest in politics and certainly had no political ambitions. Heretofore, with the Machado and Batista dictatorships the government simply left you alone. True, they had been a national disgrace. They had looted the country. They were sadistic thugs. Yet, the implicit rule had always been that as long as you did not take any part in attempting to dislodge the regime, you had absolutely nothing to fear from the regime's killers. This was a rigidly enforced rule. Iron clad. But, if you planted bombs, hid a *cache* of weapons, hid conspirators in your home, well, then, all bets were off and you had to take the consequences. People began to mutter to their family that Batista may have been scum, no argument there, but at least you could eat, have food, go to a movie, or a bookstore, or a nightclub. Besides, if you did not mess with him, he really did not mess with you.

It then came as a shock that this new, *totalitarian* regime did not want to leave you alone, did not believe in privacy, that instead it saw nonparticipating neutrals with as big a fear and hate as the active "counterrevolutionaries." This new paranoid regime wanted your endorsement, your participation, your loyalty, your enthusiasm, your *soul.* So . . . all independent sources of information, education and entertainment were taken over and regimented for the purpose of ensuring that the whole country responded as with one mind, one voice, one mindless voice: endless adulation of The Revolution, Che, Fidel, Raul, Red China, the Soviet Union; everyone was equal; the Yankees were the Great Satan, the source of all evil, what the Jews had been to the Nazis; the rich had to be persecuted and robbed; militarism for the glory of The Party and The Revolution was noble. And so on, *ad nauseam.*

And it was this constant intrusion at work, at home (through the radio and television), at his neighborhood (with the Neighborhood Committees spy network), his children's school and the insistent demands for participation that both angered and intimidated Esteban and his family.

They-would-simply-not-leave-them-alone.

They even had to stifle their complaints

221

about the recurrent shortages. And since it was never certain whether the next-door neighbor, or the colleague at work, might be an informer, inhibition of speech became necessary. When one takes into account what the Cuban national character had been up to that time, which was to engage in endless verbal diarrhea (universally acknowledged, by the way), one can immediately sense that the situation was becoming intolerable.

The Communists had achieved what had hitherto no one had thought possible: they had made the Cubans finally shut up.

Which goes to show that every black cloud has a silver lining.

As for Esteban.

While Esteban suffered from this type of stress, his other brothers felt little, if any, discomfort. Agustin was busy wholeheartedly being a chameleon, while Arsenio endorsed everything that Esteban found intolerable. As to Miguel, he was too busy in the fields away from the capital to be bothered with much and, besides, the new cooperative was about to be formed soon.

Now, as to what Esteban did for a living. He worked as a physician, a doctor, in a hospital, making a modest, but comfortable, living, enjoying the respect that is everywhere accorded a physician (just as his brother, Arsenio, had with being a teacher).

*　　　　*　　　　*　　　　*
　　　*　　　　*　　　　*

At the present time, Esteban, Agustin and

Arsenio had returned to where Esteban lived in the Miramar suburb after having attended an exhibition of Soviet Russia's scientific exploits. It had attracted a large crowd because it included film clips of Gagarin, the first man in space and so, even "cowering counterrevolutionaries" had gone with curiosity and anticipation. The exhibition was a mixed success, however, because there had also been film clips of Leika, the first dog that had been shot out to space and another of a dog whose head had been amputated and successfully grafted onto another dog, now having two heads, and had lived for many hours. These two clips were a mistake and had caused subdued indignation since Cubans--- although having an innate talent---indeed, a gusto--- for tormenting helpless, inoffensive persons---they paradoxically hate to see animals abused and become very angry when they see an animal being cruelly mistreated (human beings, again, now, that is a different matter, that is Ok, that is enjoyable) . Inevitably, the exhibition had also shown film clips of the fiasco of the attempted space shots of American rockets humiliatingly exploding, toppling over, careening out of control, again and again.

Anyway, the brothers were now in Esteban's home and, as usual, there was the customary talk between them. However, lately there had been a noticeable change in the proceedings with Esteban on one side and Arsenio and Agustin on the other, arguing politics and ending in angry exchanges, though still within brotherly restraints. Up to now, it had been an opportunity for Esteban to blow off steam.

"*Y que?* So? What did you think of the whole exhibition, Esteban?" Arsenio prompted.

"It was good! But I wish that they had

223

shown more about the flight into space. How I would have loved to have seen that!"

"I wonder what it's like out there?" mused Agustin.

"Certainly different," said Esteban.

"Without doubt, a dangerous environment. Full of risks. Extremes of heat and cold. No air. Nothing."

"I can't even begin to imagine it," confessed Agustin.

"Nor I," said Esteban.

"A major achievement for the human race by the Soviets," Arsenio probed.

"Without doubt," Esteban agreed.

"So, wouldn't you agree now that the Russians, and Communism in general, are the wave of the future?"

"I just hope that humanity doesn't drown in this 'wave of the future,'" he retorted.

"There you go again! And what makes you say something so stupid? After what you've just seen?"

"Well, *chico,* when I hear Communists, I get the impression that they wouldn't have any hesitation at all in treating the whole human race like that poor Leika bitch and shoot it out to space just to see what it'd be like."

"So, what the hell does that mean? Now, you're talking just for the sake of talking."

"Nothing. I guess nothing. I just don't like that Communist mentality that everything and everyone is expendable. I was browsing last night through *Darkness at Noon,* one of the few copies left in the country; that Hungarian fellow practically says the same thing."

"Fellow should have been liquidated long

ago and all his books burned," murmured Arsenio.

"See? See? That's what I mean! That's just what I mean: 'Think like I do, or I'll kill you.' What kind of an attitude is that, Arsenio? It's not healthy! It's not normal!"

"It certainly wouldn't be healthy for the Hungarian," Agustin piped in.

"Yeah, well, it's that 'attitude,' as you call it, that made the Soviet Union what it is today-"

"I can't argue with that," Esteban muttered.

"-and that country's in the forefront of every human achievement. That's why I've decided to send Luisito to study there when he gets older."

"To Russia?"

"When did you decide that?" asked Agustin.

"A week ago."

"*Chico,* he'll freeze! Russia's in the North Pole. That's where Napoleon' army froze. And, besides, Luisito doesn't even speak Russian. And he certainly can't read and understand those chicken scratches that they make."

Castro was sending Cuban children to the Soviet Union in droves so they could be properly indoctrinated away from their parents and whether the parents wanted to, or not. Their numbers were reaching into the thousands. The Communists had also floated the idea of taking all the children away from their parents to be raised by the government in barracks. As an alternative, many desperate Cuban parents were sending their children to the United States, whether or not there was someone at the end to take care of them, and uncertain when, and if, they would ever see their children again, to the point that the numbers were 200 children a week. And those were the lucky ones

"Oh, he'll learn first. We'll have him learn

Russian first before he goes. But, like I was saying, Communism represents the progress of humanity."

Esteban blurted out an obscenity to indicate what he thought of that statement, then went on. *"Chico,* you're confusing Communism with Russia. The Chinks got Communism long ago and I don't hear of any space shots coming out of there. Nor the Koreans. Or the Poles. I don't know how it is in Russia, all I know is what I'm seeing right here with my own eyes and my eyes tell me that Communism is garbage! There's no food, no clothes, no cars-"

"Bourgeois desires," he sneered.

"Pah! It's bourgeois. So it's bourgeois. All right, call me 'bourgeois' and say I got 'bourgeois desires.' So what? Why can't life be comfortable and pleasant? Bourgeois! And is it 'bourgeois' to want to eat, or is starvation one of your Communist virtues?"

"This is temporary! Soon, the Russians will be helping us out and they'll be shipping you what you want so you'll be happy then!"

"Oh, so they're 'bourgeois' too, eh?" Esteban jeered and Arsenio boiled at having neatly fallen in the trap.

"And let me tell you something about that Russian foreign aid: I've had over fourteen cases of botulism in the hospital and each one has been caused by a can of that stinking Russian food! That never happened before! Have you opened one of their tins and smelled it? *Dios mio!* The food's spoiled! And *that's* what they're sending us? And have you seen their films? They make no sense! They're rubbish! The theaters are empty! Nowadays, you put on a film from Hollywood and there's a line going around the block four times over!" This was true and it was a sore point with the

Cuban Communists.

"At least we're no longer an American colony! You with your precious Hollywood, you don't seem to know what's really important! You can't see the big picture and realize what's truly important! You give up Gagarin's achievement for the chance to see a film with Marylin Monroe, or Sophia Loren!"

"Pah! Ah, *chico,* I don't know about being an American colony, but there was certainly plenty to eat! Nobody seemed to contract botulism, or were starving to death, and let me tell you something else, with all these pale faced Russians I see running around here, I wonder if *we're* not becoming a Russian colony!"

"You are a traitor! The Yankees controlled our economy, our foreign policy! We didn't even. . . ."

And so it went, each time getting more and more heated, arguing the only way Cubans argue, which is with a lot of screaming, arm waving, insults and making noises and faces when "responding" to an argument, with Agustin being less forceful.

But tonight, was somehow different. It was not the usual argument between the brothers. There was an underlying snarl to Arsenio's voice, an unspoken threat, particularly whenever Esteban would make one of his infuriatingly sarcastic comments. Agustin picked it up right away and was frowning at where the argument was going and the particular insults that Arsenio was using, while Esteban also felt it, but he was not conscious of it until the argument got so heated that Arsenio came right out with it.

"The Revolution can't afford to have traitors

227

like you in the rearguard sabotaging The Party! We can't have counterrevolutionaries like you hanging around, ready to welcome back the Americans! Wise up, or you'll end up liquidated---like Trotsky with a pickax through the skull! And it'll be good riddance, too!! You aren't just in the way! You're undermining The Revolution, the best thing that's happened to this country, with your seditious treason! The only way to shut you up is in front of a *paredon* firing squad!!"

The shouting ceased and the color drained from Esteban's face. Even Agustin, who had up to now agreed with everything that Arsenio had said, had blanched to the point that he looked like a Russian.

Finally, Esteban spoke and the calmness in his Cuban voice was eerie. "And would you pull the trigger . . . brother?"

"Don't 'brother' me! I'm a Marxist-Leninist and I don't go in for bourgeois sentimentalities! If you're going to call me anything, call me 'comrade.'"

Another pause in the argument.

Agustin then tried, awkwardly, to defuse the situation. He said to Esteban, "You said that it was the Russians and not Communism that was responsible for the advances, but it's not true. The East Germans have began training our athletes and I predict that before too long, we'll walk away from the Olympics with a handful of gold medals."

His mind still preoccupied, Esteban nevertheless calmly replied, "Germans. *Chico,* the Germans are not Germans for nothing. Anything they do, they do well. Always. East Germans, or West Germans, North Germans or South Germans."

Agustin nonetheless went on, describing the

training regimen, again trying to diffuse the tension.

Finally, it was time to leave and the visit broke up, Agustin and Esteban worried, while Arsenio fumed.

Immediately after they left the house, Esteban quietly asked his wife, "Did Kiki ever agree to put up the poster?"

"No," she replied, "he said that they were out of them, but he was lying, of course."

Esteban nodded.

Kiki, the head of the local Neighborhood Committee, had pasted one of those unbelievably asinine posters that Marxists are so fond of, extolling one moronic thing or another, in the garage door of every house where he felt the occupants were one hundred percent behind The Revolution. About three houses in the street did not have one and one of these was their home.

That night, Esteban came to the decision to go into *el exilio,* to leave the country. She agreed.

It took months of arduous and humiliating lining up for visas and passports and making the right contacts but, slowly, one by one, the members of the family left the country carrying just one suitcase of clothes, to be reunited at a later date. When the last family member left, Kiki had his favorite cousin move into the vacated, furnished home.

It was a very nice, very comfortable home, nicely furnished too. It even had two air conditioners. The new occupants had something new to be thankful to The Revolution for. Months later, they would meet a French intellectual to whom they would tell that The Revolution had given them a furnished home; the intellectual would assume that the home was created from nothing, out of thin air, by the regime and had he known whose home it originally was, he still would not have cared and would have still praised The Revolution, Communism, Fidel and his minions.

*   *   *   *
*   *   *

It was now in the open. Fidel Castro, in one of his five-hour megalomaniacal speeches, announced to the world that he was, and had always been, a Communist. By this time, the takeover had been successfully completed, against all odds.

And not only that, but the anticipated invasion at Giron Beach had been repulsed and the United States thoroughly humiliated. In one of the most incompetently carried out operations in the annals of military history, Cuban refugees had been openly recruited in Florida and trained in the jungles of Honduras by Americans (the Cubans had immediately begun to bicker amongst themselves, naturally). Everything that could possibly go wrong with a military operation went wrong. The American President---possibly the most overrated president in the history of the United States---had been half hearted in the effort.

Then, in 1965, two speeches opened the floodgates of refugees. Castro proclaimed that anyone who was not satisfied with The Revolution could leave the country. He had been urged to do so by his Russian colonial overseers who had profited from their lessons during the 1956 Hungarian Uprising: after the revolt, they had not sealed the borders into Austria and had thereby created a pressure valve. No more uprisings occurred in Hungary. After all, Cuba was an island and too far away for Russia to send in its famous tanks to crush any successful uprising.

The second speech came from the American President Johnson at the base of the Statue of Liberty as a response to Castro's speech: all Cuban refugees would be welcomed into the United States.

Like most dictators and all fanatics, Fidel Castro was unhinged and refused to accept what did not accord to his delusions and preconceptions. In short, he had believed in his own propaganda. The most that he expected to leave were a few hundred. When thousands scrambled to leave, he was infuriated and had to be persuaded from ordering his troops to machine gun the lot.

*   *   *   *
*   *

By this time, Esteban and his family had established themselves in their adoptive country. At first, it had been very hard because of the language barrier, the culture shock, the homesickness and the lack of a comparable job. But, they adjusted, always thinking that "next year" they would be back. Other Cuban families were encountered and they began to reach out to each other. Americans were very sympathetic and tried to help out, all but the American intellectuals, who desperately pined for a similar catastrophe to descend on their own country.

The doctor had not given up on his profession (unlike many other professionals who emigrated) and had worked his way up past the foreign language efficiency test, the residency and the unbelievable State Board Exams.

He had just passed the Florida Board and was celebrating in his Pensacola home with other Cuban doctors and their families. The phone rang and he answered it, a Cuba Libre in his hand.

"Esteban?" a voice asked. "It's Esteban? It's Miguel!"

"Miguel! Where the devil are you?" Telephone calls could not go out of Cuba, only incoming calls and it had been a long time since they had spoken. The family quickly crowded around the telephone and the others quieted down, also excited by the news.

"In Opa-Locka, some place called Opa-Locka, in La Florida."

"La Florida? You mean, you're here? It's Miguel! He's in Florida! When did you come over? God! What a surprise! I had no idea! When did you come over? Is Maria with you?"

"Two days ago, *chico*. Some people here tracked you down. We told them your name and what city you lived in and they found your telephone number."

"Listen! We're on our way down! When can you get out? I mean, where they got you?"

"We can leave any time. Soon as you get here, in fact."

"Ave Maria! What a surprise! We've got lots to talk about . . . !"

That afternoon, the whole family packed into the car and drove down to Opa-Locka.

Once there, amidst a profusion of hugs and kisses and "You look just the same!" and "My word, he's grown!" Miguel and Maria were crammed into the car and headed towards

Pensacola. Miguel recounted their passage out of Cuba. Then, the family began to reminisce and, for some reason, Maria recounted the time that she had climbed a tree to get some fruit at their finca and stumbled against a wasp nest and the wasps had covered her face.

Miguel recounted how bad things had become in Cuba, with all the shortages and the constant political meetings. But what really brought out his indignation was how he, for all practical purposes, had lost control of his *finca* once the cooperative finally got running and all sorts of interlopers stuck their noses in his business and he had to lend out his farming equipment, which was usually returned damaged, or unclean, and how he had been forced to allow others to live in his *finca* . . . ."

Throughout the trip, "little Max" (he was not so little anymore) just stared at them without saying much, unless he was addressed directly, much as he would stare at some curious insect. On several occasions, Miguel caught Maximito looking at him with that look that he had often seen in the boy's face, years back in Havana when the brothers used to get together and talk.

After all these years, that look still made him uncomfortable.

*   *   *   *
*   *   *

Meanwhile, very little changed in Cuba. Things just became more so.

After his secret, enforced hospitalization in a

mental hospital for paranoid hallucinations, Che Guevara left Cuba and invaded Bolivia with a tiny force of Cubans, attempting to take over that country. When the Bolivian peasants failed to idolize him and follow him, he brutalized them. Ultimately, hunted down and killed, his severed hands were secreted out of the country to Cuba, where Castro displayed them in a museum as medieval holy relics. Guevara's sayings urging death and destruction in every direction were posted throughout Cuba and his likeness was reproduced in billboards, airports, stamps, busts and whole sides of buildings. He was shown with flowing hair and Lenin-like Tartar eyes staring off into the distance dreamily envisioning whole countries aflame. That image was copied and adopted by legions of proto-Communists in the West from Sweden to America to Chile.

For a while, there was even hope in Havana that the United States (and for that matter, Italy, France and West Germany) would experience a similar Revolution. The activities of thousands of "peace activists" carrying Viet Cong flags and posters of Mao, Che and Ho were followed closely in Havana as they tried to shut down Chicago, Washington D. C. and other American cities. Bombs were set off by New Left (Communist) groups called the SDS, the Weathermen, the Yippies, the Black Panthers. Some of the wannabe "revolutionaries" even went to Cuba. The American mass media, for its part, lent itself one hundred percent behind the movement, helping to create a climate ripe for a leftist totalitarian takeover. Yet, somehow, inexplicably, The Revolution in the United States never materialized and the wannabes missed their rendezvous with history and faded into anonymity. The closest that they came was in the 1972 election with George McGovern when they hijacked the Democratic Party and its rank and file members, shocked at their tactics and their arrogance, deserted *en masse* and actively campaigned for the Republican Party.

Whereupon the wannabe revolutionaries did not simply disappear, but instead blended into the woodwork of universities and the mass media, where they would, for the next two decades voice their admiration for Cuba, Vietnam, the People's Republic of China and the Cultural Revolution and snarl about the rich being too rich and powerful in the United States, while simultaneously suppressing any views which were not Politically Correct, using a plethora of tried and true tactics.

But Cuba itself remained the same. Only more so.

*　　　*　　　*　　　*
*　　　*　　　*

Maximiliano, a young man now and attending college, opened the door at the request of his father, in answer to a persistent doorbell. Juan Garcia and his wife, Rosa, stood at the entrance. Max stifled a groan and a thought flashed through his head, "Ten years in this country and these idiots *still* haven't learned to call ahead, they just drop in!"

"Ah, hola!" he greeted them, forcing a smile of welcome.

The niceties of Cuban hospitality had to be observed.

"Hey, que pasa?" We were in the neighborhood and we thought that we'd drop by and see what you guys were up to."

"Come in," Max was forced to say. "Everyone's here. We just finished a late lunch," and he announced the visitors, who entered the den where the rest of the family was at, including Uncle Miguel and Aunt Maria. Additional chairs were brought out and conversation continued as if Juan and Rosa had been there from the start.

Max stayed with them for about a minute out of lethargy and then went to his room. He ordinarily took part in conversations now that he was an adult, but only if the topic interested him. He still made the others nervous, but this time with his relentlessly caustic comments and too truthful observations. In truth, he also had the same effect on those leftists that he mercilessly raked over the coals in college, completely unafraid of the repercussions. He puttered in his room and picked up a book that he had been unbelievably lucky to find, against all odds, entitled *Fall of a Titan* which he had almost finished (like all books---so very few books!---critical of Communism written in the 1950s and 1960s, it had been successfully relegated to oblivion, unread, uncited, unreferenced). He put it off for later and instead mused about possibly going to the shopping mall.

He went to the kitchen to get a Coca-Cola. Nothing of what drifted over from the den aroused his interest. He noticed on the kitchen counter a mailing from an exile political organization; in the flyer there were several pictures of the organization's officers and their fat wives in Europe, posing like tourists before famous landmarks. The bulletin stated how much lecturing about Cuba's problems the officers had undertaken while in Europe. There was no question whatsoever in Max's mind that all of their expenses---including their wives'---were being paid through the contributions of its members. All of their faces reflected that brazen shamelessness that is so typically Cuban.

Then, Max heard the faint hollow metal sound of the mailbox being closed and went to get the mail that the postman had just deposited. In reviewing the mail, he saw a small envelope of dismal quality with a stamp portraying the psychotic Che Guevara. In reading the return address, his eyebrows shot up. He opened the letter and read the contents.

He came into the house.

"Any mail?" asked his mother.

He handed the letter over to his father to whom it was addressed and said, "You're not going to believe this."

Esteban took the letter. "It's from Arsenio!" This caused a stir. He read it silently, then smiled. "He's coming! He's applying to emigrate!"

"No!" exclaimed his wife.

"When's he coming?" asked Maria.

"Just him or his wife?" Miguel inquired.

"Run out of victims, has he?" This from Max, with a smirk.

"Does he say when?"

"No, he doesn't know when it'll be, but he writes that he has made the decision for certain."

Max snorted. "I suppose he's expecting a welcoming applause."

"It's obvious that he can't say much, because he's afraid that the letter will be read. He's not going to put down his reason why."

"You know," said Maria, "I always thought that it'd be Agustin who'd come over first."

"Me too," Miguel agreed.

"You do?" Max quickly jumped in. "*I* don't. We've got a librarian in the college who was also a lifelong Communist and came over three years ago and he's always apologizing, or bragging, I can't tell which, about having been blind to 'reality' all these years as a Communist and how Communism is the pits. My guess is that the famous 'Party discipline' finally got to Arsenio."

They had no idea of what he was talking about.

But Esteban agreed with Maria. "I have to admit, I also thought that it'd be Agustin to be the one to get fed up."

"*Why?*" asked Max.

"Because deep down, he's a plain opportunist. Always has been."

"All the more reason why you're wrong!" he countered. "Don't you get it?"

Nobody did. They shook their heads and looked at each other, perplexed.

"Reason it out. Agustin is an opportunist, but Arsenio's a lifelong Communist intellectual thirsting for power, the pestilence of the twentieth century. All right, at first there's plenty of victims and lots of spoils, so all the cannibals benefit from the cannibalism, whether they are Communist, or not. It's all very Cuban. But, sooner or later, the victims run out. After all, there's just so many rich that you can feast off of. So, you fall on another group and devour them and redistribute the spoils. Now, of course, every once in a while, you have individuals who don't belong to the current group of victims that's being victimized at the moment and they either flee the country, or they get shot, and *their* goods get split up. Problem is, the quality of these goods is getting shabbier and shabbier as the years pass and as they get handed around, and the number of available victims gets fewer and fewer."

"Well, Arsenio is a good Party member and has to follow 'Party discipline,' which means mindless obedience and sacrifices for a future good. By now he's gotten jaded with his power, but the Party makes more and more demands of him. Basically, he's now just a flunky! A flunky who has run out of victims and of spoils."

"Agustin, on the other hand, makes frequent international trips with his sports teams. Buys a lot of first-class foreign goods: clothes, food, books, televisions, records, you name it. He's doing fine. *And,* his area of expertise has high priority with the regime because they want lots of medals from the Olympics because they think that that legitimizes their regime."

"It's not that the Communist countries are that interested in sports *per se.* They feel that an excellence in international sports mirrors the 'excellence' of their repressive, regimented society and eclipses its shortcomings---the lack of food, the lack of freedom, the lack of travel. And it's true. In a way, they're right. It works through a kind of 'desensitization' and you stop to think of them solely in terms of secret police and the Berlin Wall. Besides, they think that if their athletes beat the athletes from capitalist countries, that means that their political ideology is better. And that is why Agustin will always be in clover."

"Makes sense," his father said. He had never stopped to think about it in any depth. Come to think about it, he had never thought about it at all.

"And it fits with Arsenio coming over," said Miguel.

There was a pause, then Garcia spoke up. "What did you mean it was all very Cuban?" Miguel and Esteban quickly glanced at each other worriedly. They were used to Max's abrasive viewpoint, but Garcia had never been exposed to them. And Maximiliano could get so caustic when he got carried away in an argument.

"In a nutshell? That we deserve what we got," he acidly replied.

"What?"

"Just what I said: that we deserve *exactly* what we got."

"Well, explain that, I'm not a mind reader," he snapped back, already beginning to feel irritated, inexplicably so since Max had not been overly caustic. It was just that there was something about him . . . .

"Look, it's simple! We all keep referring to 'them' and 'the Communists.' All of us! But the truth is that the fault lies with *us*. It's really us, don't you see? *We* welcomed the revolution, *we* followed Fidel, *we* became anti-American, *we* did what we were told and *we* victimized others. Not 'them.' *Us*. But now we deny it and we've made ourselves forget that nasty little fact and we make out like we're the victims."

"Look, it's like this: the Germans, the Poles, the Hungarians, the Lithuanians---they had no choice! *They were invaded!* But we don't have that excuse. That's a luxury that we simply don't have."

"The famous Russian tanks went through Hungary and Czechoslovakia and Latvia and Poland. In those countries, their soldiers were slaughtered, their national monuments were blown up, their women were raped, their books were burnt in bonfires, their industries were dismantled and carted away to Russia and then the Russians told them, 'Congratulations! You have just been liberated by the Red Army!' But we don't have that excuse, that luxury. We did it ourselves---to ourselves! A Russian didn't put a gun to our heads and told us to chant, 'Cuba is! Yankee no!' We volunteered to do so. Be honest, now. Come on! And when we started to steal from each other and denounce each other to the regime, that was doing what came natural to us."

"No! There I can't agree with you!" Garcia finally put in. "When that *estúpido,* Batista, was overthrown, it wasn't to set up Communism! The original revolution was subverted. We were going to do away with the evils that plagued Cuba."

"Yes! Yes!" Max joined in, now becoming enthusiastic. "Absolutely! One hundred percent! I agree with you one hundred percent. The thing is that the original revolution was going to do away with those evils in Cuban society, but those perceived evils were only skin deep. They were going to cure the symptoms, but not the disease. The evils that were reflected in society were really the evils within the Cuban character---and there *is* such a thing as a national character. There is! *You* all talk about the American character all the time. Well, if you'll be honest with yourselves for five minutes and think back, you'll admit that when the Communists started their shenanigans, it dovetailed perfectly with our national character: the propensity to lie for the sake of lying, stealing from someone whenever the chance offered itself, taking advantage of those who were harmless and could not protect themselves, ridiculing others, not

241

respecting other people, incessantly talking badly about others. That is all part of the Cuban national character and that is why I say that we *deserve* what we got. We certainly can't blame anyone else. I mean . . . *who else is there to blame?"*

By now, everybody was interrupting and shouting, "Not true!" "No!" "You're exaggerating!" "You're just ashamed of being Cuban!" "It's not true!" "Where did you come up with such an idea?" He shouted right back and it was pandemonium.

At one point, after about fifteen minutes of chaos, he suddenly got quiet and calmly raised his hands, palm open, apparently asking for silence. After a while, he actually got it and he was finally able to speak in a normal voice.

"Let me ask you all one question, a simple question: who among you remember the Chinese in Cuba? I do, and I'm younger than all of you."

"OK. The *Chino manila.* So what?"

"Thank you. You just made my point. *Chino manila.* We showed no respect towards them, we stole from them, we ridiculed them to their faces, we never called each man by his name, just 'chino manila.' And to an Oriental, respect is everything! How they must be laughing at us now! Frankly? I'm ashamed of how we treated them, especially when I see how decently the Americans have treated us, with our thick accents and all. And if you *really* want proof of everything that I've said, take note that *none* of you feel any remorse whatsoever."

Strange to say, this last argument half convinced his listeners (only temporarily, of course) although they muttered that he had still exaggerated.

Nevertheless, he mercilessly went on. "And what about the times before Castro and the Communists? What about the corruption and thievery and the mutual victimization between neighbors? How are you going to blame that on Fidel? No. It's *us.*" Several heads were now nodding their heads in agreement. Two hours later they would forget everything.

Max gave a short laugh at a thought that popped into his head.

"And I'll tell you what else. I'm going to make a prediction. OK, you've got Arsenio and you've got that librarian jerk who was also an ex-Communist. One of these days the whole Communist Party, and the whole G-2 is going to come over and complain that conditions in Cuba are intolerable. Hell! We might even get Raul, or Fidel himself." He laughed again. "And if we ever overthrow them, *nobody* is going to admit that they were a collaborator. *Everybody will have been a victim.* Of 'them.'"

"Listen. I study history. When the Nazis occupied France, the French collaborated with them wholeheartedly and helped them against the British and in tracking down Jews for the gas chambers, but when the Americans kicked out the Nazis for them, not a single collaborator could be found. They all claimed to have been in . . . '*Le Resistance.*' So they attacked some poor women who had dated German soldiers, shaved their heads and used them as their scapegoats. Why? Because the French are pigs. They've always been pigs. Well, I predict it's going to be the same way in Cuba. Suddenly, nobody's going to admit to having been a collaborator---not even the Communists."

This drew a chuckle from everybody and several offered their own predictions along the same line.

"Look, it's simple," Max returned to his

theme. "If we don't admit it, how it all came about through our own fault and our role in it, nothing will ever change, even after Communism is overthrown. Nothing will have changed."

Several were nodding in agreement, saying, "Yeah, maybe he's got a point there." Two hours later they would forget everything.

Then, Esteban looked again at the letter and remarked, "I wish that I knew when he was coming. I suppose he can stay in the living room for a while, sleeping on the sofa bed."

"Eh? What? What did you say?" asked Max, wide-eyed.

His father repeated it.

Max spoke slowly.

"I can't believe you said that. I can't believe what I just heard with my own two ears. After all that he's done . . . ." He shook his head in disbelief.

"Well, *chico,* I don't care. He's still my brother."

"Bourgeois sentimentality," Max sneered and his father stiffened at the reminder.

Regardless, Arsenio was not able to leave for several years.

*   *   *   *
    *   *   *

And then, several years later, came the bizarre spectacle of the Peruvian embassy in Havana.

Castro, furious, since he had often stated that by that time most of those who could not stomach The Revolution had fled, proclaimed that whomsoever was not happy with the incalculable benefits that The Revolution had brought to the nation could leave the country, at which point a mass stampede took place towards the embassy. A police cordon was thrown around the embassy. Even so, over ten thousand people made it in to the point that there was standing room only in the embassy grounds.

The Maximum Leader was not a happy man.

The Peruvian ambassador protested over the conditions and, finally, the port of Mariel was chosen as the departure point for this new wave of refugees, over one hundred thousand, who henceforth became known among the Cuban-Americans in Miami as the *Marielitos.*

Upon arriving in Florida, it was immediately noted that they were different from the previous refugees. They were not as vociferously anti-Communist as their predecessors and, in fact, revealed little of themselves, partly, no doubt, due to an acquired decades-long habit of not saying anything incriminating in a totalitarian society which would have dire results. Many tried to keep a low profile, as if they did not want to be recognized.

There were also more blacks and more clue collar workers and more ex-Communists than ever before, people who had earlier seemed to have "benefited" from The Revolution and had themselves victimized others (quite a few of them were out and out criminals).

Among them were Arsenio and his family.

XXVII

When Mark learned of Herman's treachery, he was at first stunned in disbelief. There were many reasons inherent in this act of backstabbing that rendered Mark paralyzed, none the least of which was the sheer open blatancy of it all, with no attempt on Herman's side at hiding his actions at stealing Mark's ideas, nor in disguising Mark's plans with modifications of his own. Mark also wondered if Herman actually thought that he, Mark, was not going to challenge who had prior claim. Add to that the fact that Herman showed absolutely *no* change in the expression on his face, or in his speech whenever he now encountered Mark---as if nothing had happened! There was also no real, tangible gain from such a contemptible action, which made it all the more baffling. And, to top it all off, Mark wondered how anybody could possibly be so stupid, though Herman was definitely not stupid. In the former's mind, he could see the logic---if one was so unethically inclined---of stealing someone else's idea, or material property *if* one's position became much stronger and unassailable as a result, or, *if* the thief did not remain in constant contact with his victim and thereby remain open to either swift retaliation, or recriminations, or to constant guerrilla warfare. It made no sense at all. But then, it is often a fact that a rational, sensible person becomes paralyzed and befuddled before the irrational and the senseless.

Months ago, Mark had noticed an entangled practice within the small company in which he worked which had been going on for some time and which was resulting in needless expenditure. By studying the problem thoroughly and investigating other options, he found a solution which would unquestionably streamline the assembly of parts and, as a result, moderately cut costs and time with no expenditures by the company in implementing the reform. His coworker, Herman, had stopped by his office for some chit chat, as did many of his other coworkers from time to time. Mark had enthusiastically imparted what he had just concluded and Herman had been suitably impressed and encouraging. Right afterwards, he had gone directly to Mister Maddox's office and informally presented Mark's ideas as his own, offering many details in the process.

Mister Maddox, a very fair and wise man, one who---contrary to the practice of every business and/or every government bureaucrat---listened to his subordinates also liked to publicly give credit where credit was due, and he assembled the firm for a very brief meeting, wherein he presented Herman's ideas, which would be implemented in a day or two, praised his ingenuity and his initiative and encouraged everyone in a round of applause in honor of Herman. As everyone applauded, Mark stood rooted to the spot, stunned in disbelief. He had been typing up his report, which he was going to present to Mister Maddox, not fifteen minutes before.

The following morning, Mark told the secretary that he wanted to see Mister Maddox. Once in the office, Mark informed him of the true state of affairs and handed in his report. It was Maddox's turn to be stunned.

Maddox was the type of individual who disliked thinking badly of anyone. In his mind, wrong actions were more likely as not the product of a misunderstanding or a breakdown in communication between two parties or more which, when cleared up, the results were to everyone's satisfaction. This was his outlook on human relationships in life. It would be a mistake to say that he was naive. Rather, it was a matter of interpretation. The alternative, that evil and mendacity were very real phenomena, though reluctantly admitted as to their existence, in his mind they were not as prevalent as it was made out to be.

Upon recovering, it was this approach that he adopted.

"Is it possible that you both may have come up with the same idea independently of each other? It's been known to happen, you know."

"No, sir! When I discussed the plan with Herman it was obvious that he hadn't thought about it at all. It was totally new to him, although he was very receptive. Furthermore, he gave me no indication whatever that he had been working on the same project as I."

Maddox tried again.

"Well, could it be that perhaps you discussed it with him before---you know, casually---and he's been working on a solution ever since and he may have thought that your project hadn't become formal or definite, you know, that you two may have been brainstorming or may be just 'shooting the breeze' with each other."

Mark tried hard not to become impatient.

"Again, no, sir. I hadn't told *anyone* of this, until yesterday. I would have remembered for certain."

Maddox sighed. He decided to call Herman in to discuss the problem.

Herman blithely denied having talked to Mark about it at all! Mark, fuming yet subdued, tensely contradicted him and quietly accused him of lying and of plagiarism. Herman shrugged it off. Maddox suggested a compromise: to have another meeting and announced that Mark had also been working on the problem and come up with the same results as Herman, thereby being as equitable as possible. Herman politely declined, Mark tensely so, at which time Herman was sent back to work.

"Mark, I sympathize, but look at it from my point of view." Maddox then told him that there was nothing else that he could possibly do because of a lack of proof and that Herman had not received any financial compensation and went on to, nevertheless, thank Mark for all of his hard work.

"I understand your position, Mister Maddox. I do. Believe me, I do. Don't worry, I don't hold you to blame," he said and left. Maddox sighed. He now expected strife, the kind that, gone to extremes, can ruin the *elan* of a business.

Yet, it did not happen. Mark let it be known to others what had happened, but refrained to take the next logical step of forming a coalition of sympathizers against Herman, and thereby avoided what would automatically occur, an inevitable coalition of Herman's supporters. He knew how destructive such a civil war could be to any institution. Instead, he bided his time. Being forced to work in the same location, he knew that an opportunity to retaliate, to humiliate him would present itself (this was why, originally, he had asked himself how anybody could possibly be that stupid as to backstab someone with whom one is practically working with every day). His interaction with Herman, whenever unavoidable, were correct, though laconic.

As for Herman, he acted like absolutely nothing had happened at all and seemed at times perplexed over Mark's barely suppressed hostility. At times, he would even drop by his office whenever a group of employees congregated and join in the conversation, although others felt suddenly strained at the unexpected intrusion. This was no affectation on his part. The fact of the matter was that Herman was one of those individuals who will sue their next door neighbor over tripping over a garden hose, or cheat a fellow contestant in a race or contest, or even outright steal from another person, and then be genuinely surprised and uncomprehending---if not irritated---at the victim's sudden implacable hostility.

Anyhow, as someone once stated, all good things come to those who wait.

Mister Maddox invited his employees to the yearly company picnic at his spacious home. There would be a buffet, a swimming pool, a volleyball court, a bar, etc. Each year everyone, invariably, had a wonderful time, even the few habitual complainers.

Several guests had arrived early (in other words, on time). Among these were, independently, Mark and Herman. At Maddox's hospitable urgings, all were making themselves at home.

In one room, Mark was admiring an exquisite pewter chess set on an onyx chessboard, when Herman came up to him and looked the pieces over.

"You play?" he asked.

"Uh-huh," murmured Mark.

"You wanna play a game until everybody else gets here?"

Mark slowly looked up at him in disbelief, as if someone had just asked him if he would like a million dollars. He blinked at his would-be opponent three times.

[blink, blink, blink] "You . . ." [blink, blink, blink] "want to play a game of chess . . ." [blink, blink, blink] "with me?"

"Sure! Set 'em up!" and he cheerfully sat down in a chair.

"There *is* a God," affirmed Mark in a murmur.

"What?"

"Oh, nothing, nothing," and held out two fists. Herman tapped one and got black. Mark had white and would go first. He silently reaffirmed his belief in the existence of a benevolent and just deity. He came out with a pawn to king four, followed by queen's pawn four.

"You play often?"

"Oh . . . not as often as I used to," admitted Mark. It was true. He now only played with people whom he genuinely disliked, or with strangers, never with friends, not since he had discovered and become thoroughly addicted to a particular opening in chess.

Herman began developing a fool's mate, which made Mark chuckle and feel offended at the same time. No matter. This gave him the chance to develop his opening further without missing a beat while simultaneously blocking the fool's mate.

There. Foiled that little attempt. Now, what's next? There was a long pause and some fidgeting by Herman. Black now decided to bring out his knights and Mark smiled. He went ahead developing his position.

Herman looked at the board, frowning, for a long time. "What in the hell is that?"

"I call it The Cuban Pyramid Defense."

He looked up. "Capablanca?"

"No. It's all my own. One of my own ideas."

Herman stared at the board and fidgeted.

"Why 'Cuban Pyramid Defense'?"

"Why *not* Cuban Pyramid Defense?" And, of course, Herman had no answer to that.

At this point we should explain how Mark's position slowly developed. The king and queen's pawns were at four, defended by their respective bishops' pawns, giving it the appearance of a flattened pyramid. The rook's pawns had likewise moved to position four, supposedly to thwart the fool's mate but, in reality, to develop the pyramid further. The queen would move to position three, thereby reinforcing the king's pawn. On top of that, the knights could move into the interior of the pyramid, further reinforcing the position so that if the frontal pawns were taken the knights could replace them and, in doing so, automatically extend the reach of threatening (or, alternatively, replace the bishops' pawns if the latter moved up to position king and queen's position four after a pawn exchange at that site, again extending the range of control). To his delight, Herman allowed him to fully develop the pyramid to its utmost by being aimless. What made it worse for his opponent, it seemed that Mark had no intention of attacking him, which meant that Herman had to attack, which meant that a massive counterattack would ensue.

A few guests came over and began to examine the board. Two of them frowned. Herman fidgeted.

The music in the background began. The party was starting. Herman fidgeted once more. He wanted to get away, yet could not really do so. The music was distracting him and made it hard for him to concentrate. He retrieved his bishop which was obviously a stalling move, or more accurately, a wasted move, in order to get white to commit himself (Mark did not voice his opinion of players who waste a move that is useless, then retrieve that same piece back to its beginning).

White *apparently* refused to commit himself to an attack as the queen was brought up to reinforce the front line. Then, the knights behind the front line.

More guests were arriving and sounds drifted over of people enjoying themselves. Herman fidgeted, trying to find a way out of his impasse. He was so hemmed in! His bishops were paralyzed. White's pieces were so interconnected that a simple exchange of pieces would only worsen his own situation, bringing out white's big guns into excellent positions for an attack. He did the only thing that he could do, under the circumstances. He fidgeted.

Two of the spectators removed themselves, glancing at each other as they did so, making a face with their eyes. The tension was palpable.

Amy had been watching the players from the doorway.

"What's going on over there?" she nodded with her head to the two men in intense concentration. "It looks like sparks are flying."

"Don't go in there," one of the men joked. "It ain't safe."

By now, it will be obvious to the reader that Mark's so-called Cuban Pyramid Defense was really an exercise in frustration, to which the Chinese water torture would seem a relief by comparison. Add to this the fact that noises of merriment were drifting into the room calling them out to play and Herman's position becomes clearer.

To persons who have never played chess, the question will undoubtedly arise as to why, if he was under such stress, did Herman simply not get up and walk away from the chessboard. One simply does not walk away from a chess game. No one ever does. It can be argued that this is also true of all games, but it is particularly so with chess because of its unique characteristic: it is an extension of the male ego. Hence, the intense concentration of players, almost all of whom are male, by the way.

By now, it was apparent to the few remaining spectators, if not to Herman himself, that Mark was playing out a very sadistic cat and mouse, far beyond the game's stated object of simply winning. Black would not attack, would not commit himself, and was impatiently waiting for white to take off the strait jacket that white had neatly strapped on black and which, sooner or later, had to come off. White supposedly studied the board with as much concentration as black, ponder his move for the longest time as black waited impatiently, then make the move which black hoped would end the impasse, only to see that it had not changed one iota, since the rook's pawns had simply advanced one more and one more. Except that by scrutinizing the latest move, white's position had just become even more impregnable, while black's movements continued to be hemmed in. It was like a coiled spring that was being tensed more and more, with the concomitant dread of seeing it violently uncoil.

Meanwhile, the party continued. Sounds of people having fun drifted in.

In frustration, and against his better judgment, he committed himself. Mark looked at the board and smiled. It was time. He had gotten all the satisfaction that he was going to get out of this scenario.

Afterwards, they both rose and parted, each ritually complimenting the other.

"Good game."

"Good game."

Tight lipped and mentally fatigued, Herman joined the crowd in the back yard. He felt like he had wasted his time and, at the same time, was a bit dazed. Somehow, in some way that he could not tell, he also felt having been humiliated.

Amy strolled over to a smiling Mark, who was now emerging to the spacious back yard, where most of the party goers seemed to be at.

"Is it safe now?" she joked.

"Yes, it's safe," he joked back.

"Seriously, what was that all about?"

Mark chuckled silently, looking around at everyone enjoying themselves.

"Never mind, I'll tell you some other time. Come on, let's go play volleyball. Looks like another game's about to start and they're looking for players," he told Amy and led her to the volleyball court just as teams were about to form and a game about to begin.

He chose one team. Herman was in the other, opposite, team.

XXVIII

Lester Wallace had arrived early for his appointment in the Public Library to meet Timothy

Stein, the literary critic of the newspaper, which was housed in the imposing building a few streets down. He did not want to miss the appointment, wherein he was going to try to convince Mister Stein to review his novel, his first. Consequently, he resisted the strong impulse to lose himself among the bookcases and alcoves and nooks and crannies of the library in search of who knows what surprises, and, instead, stayed in the main lobby, near the entrance.

Aside from the importance of the newspaper itself, which crossed the state line, Stein himself was syndicated nationwide, a very unusual occurrence in a profession which firmly believes that only the opinions of journalists in New York, California and Washington D. C. are of any importance and both the Midwest and the South should be ignored as a whole. For his part, Stein influenced the reading tastes of many, many people, who depended on Timothy Stein to tell them what to read and what to think about books that they had not read.

At the present time, the library had one of its periodic exhibitions, this time on old maps and it was fascinating to watch the attraction that they had on men. Women barely glanced at them and kept on walking. Men were instantly sidetracked to them and stood in clumps, silently poring over the details. It was not the first time that Wallace had made the observation. Maps had an almost magnetic attraction for men: display a large map in a room and, invariably, men would be drawn to it, where they would stand before it, staring at it, mesmerized, scrutinizing it, as if the map was a narcotic from which they could not get enough of it. As Wallace mused on this observation---and resisted a temptation to be drawn towards them---he catalogued his observation along with other observations that he had made regarding the differences between the genders, for potentially future use in his next novel (yesterday he had become aware of the fact that women never whistle a tune to themselves).

He glanced out towards the glass door entrance and saw Stein walking towards the library. He recognized him. His photograph always accompanied his reviews, a trait that more and more syndicated journalists were insisting upon out of vanity. Stein's trim, dark beard added a distinguished touch to his reviews.

On his own initiative, Wallace had rung him up at the newspaper in order to convince the critic to review his novel in his column, feeling as he did, that not enough attention was being paid to it, among the thousands of new books being continually published. He had barely begun to explain his mission to Stein over the telephone when the latter cut him off---jovially---and suggested that he give him his sales pitch over lunch, whereupon they had agreed on a time and a place.

Wallace went outside to meet him.

"Mister Stein?" he approached him with hand outstretched.

"Mister Wallace?" he asked as he shook hands. "Call me Tim."

"Lester."

"How are you, Lester? Let's walk down the street to Giovanni's. Say, you do know that you're buying me lunch, don't you? That's why I picked an expensive restaurant. If not, we'll just grab a couple of hot dogs from that vendor over there."

"No, that's all right," Lester said. He couldn't help smiling at the man's brassy impudence.

It turned out that Stein had made reservations at Giovanni's, so they did not have to wait at all in order to get a table. Stein ordered the most expensive items in the menu.

After a few minutes of breaking the ice with small talk about the restaurant and the newspaper line of work, Lester plunged right in.

"Mister Stein---I mean Tim---I'd like very much for you to review my novel in your column."

"What's the plot? Very general, now, don't spoil it for me by telling me everything. I haven't had a chance to read it, yet. I've been swamped with a backlog of books to read."

Lester told him.

Stein made a face. "Mmm. It sounds interesting. Promising. It might even be good. But, you see, Lester, I'm inundated with books that publishers want me to review---favorably, of course. Just about every day, I receive one or two books by mail from publishing companies. I may even have received your book, for all I know, and it may be in one of those stacks. Then, sometimes, I just get fed up and clear out all the clutter and throw away the stacks of books---or give them away to friends or to the library---and start all over from scratch with the new books that I receive."

"Is it that bad?"

"Oh, yes!" He made another face. "The competition's intense, you see, and a review in my column guarantees additional sales. Automatically. And that's just for a mediocre review."

"I can see how that would be true."

"Are you also aware that this country is full

of idiots who can't discriminate quality and rely on 'experts' to tell them what to think? They like Charles Dickens and Anne Rice---equally. They love Kurt Vonnegut---and Stephen King. They see no difference. In fact, millions read a book simply because it's on The New York Times Bestseller List. It's a herd mentality."

"Yes, I know that's true."

"So, let me just come right out and ask you: why should I review *your* book? And, why should I review your book ahead of all the others?"

Lester thought for a moment.

"You mean, aside from the inherent attributes of my novel?"

"Yes. Exactly."

Lester thought again. He saw clearly where the conversation was drifting to.

"Well . . . I wouldn't want to offend you . . . with a bribe."

"Go right ahead. You can offend me. Try it. Go ahead and offend me."

Lester thought, then spoke.

"I'm not going to haggle or argue. I'm not good at it, so I'll just tell you right out that I can only offer you $3,000. That's all that I can personally afford and I don't know if I'm overpaying or underpaying. I'm new at this sort of thing."

"Three grands is about right for a fair review. I don't place books on The New York Times Bestseller List, so I can't expect too much more."

"So, how do we do this? Like I said, I'm new at this."

"OK. Tell you what. I'll read your book. Then, I'll write a review of it. Let's meet here a week from today, same time. I'll show you the review. You read it. You pay me half down then and the other half when it gets published. Sound fair to you?"

"Sure."

"Another thing, if I find that your book stinks, I won't write a review saying that it's good and you won't have to pay me anything."

"That's fair."

"Oh, and one more thing: of course, today's lunch is part of the fee. As is next week's lunch."

"You're something else, you know that?" he said, shaking his head and smiling.

Next week, they were back at the same table.

"Lester, I have to tell you, in all honesty, that I thoroughly enjoyed your book. I mean that. I'm not just being polite. I really did. "

"Thanks. Does that mean that you're not going to charge me?"

"Not a chance."

"Oh."

"But I did want you to know that. And . . . I think that you'll like my review." He handed over a sheaf of typewritten papers, whereupon Lester began to read eagerly, ignoring his food.

"Your foods' getting cold, Lester."

"Not hungry."

"Mind if I eat it, then?" he asked as he reached over, without waiting for his answer and helped himself.

The review was laudatory, indeed. Both the plot and the characterizations were praised as original and enough of the plot was given to tantalize the reader. It was a very good review.

Lester shook his head, frowning.

"No, this is not what I had in mind."

Timothy's fork stopped in midair.

"What?" He was plainly shocked, almost offended. "Are you kidding? I love that book! That's a great review you got there!"

"But, it's not what I want."

"And why on Earth not?"

"Because I want you to attack it."

"I will not! I loved that book! What are you, nuts?"

"Listen, Tim, I want you to make it a *controversial* book. Attack it as immoral; there are passages there that could be construed as such, right? Frankly, I thought you'd immediately pick up on that."

"Well, yes . . . I see where it could be. But, Lester, you've written a good novel. If I critique it, a lot of people won't read it."

"Wrong, Tim, if you critique it *on immoral grounds*, then everybody'll feel that they have to take a stand and discuss it among each other, in order to impress one another---and themselves---as to just how intellectual they are."

"Lester, listen to me. . . . If I pan it, it may not become controversial, it may not reach that level of intensity, it may just cut down on sales. Besides, I don't feel so good about criticizing such a good novel. Nowadays, they're few and far between and I enjoy it when I finally do come across one. Besides, has it ever occurred to you that it might just backfire on you? Remember what happened to that semipornographic film *The Last Temptation of Christ*? It got withdrawn from the movie theaters. Good riddance, by the way. It was awful!"

"Yeah, but I'm not attacking religion in my book and if the movie studios hadn't withdrawn it, it *might* have made a bundle. Look at the other side of the picture. Bookstores can't keep up with *The Bell Curve* ever since it was attacked by the knee jerk liberals, who didn't even bother to read the book out of fear that it might have made them think for themselves. The TV show, *Married with Children*, became one of the highest rated TV shows on, since it was condemned as anti-family. And a third-rate writer wrote *The Satanic Verses,* a boring, mediocre book, which became a bestseller. Why? Because that murderous psychotic, the Ayatollah Khomeini, put out a contract on the author for having written it. I tell you, I know what I'm talking about, Tim!"

"And *I'm* telling you that it can backfire on you! Your book may not become controversial at all! Sales may just die *because* of my panning and I don't want to be responsible for that! I *like* the book. This is a novel that deserves to live on and I don't want to be responsible for killing it."

"Not if you do it right."

"How so?"

"What's the one thing guaranteed to sell any product? Proven time and time again."

"Sex. Of course. So?"

"Right. Sex. Sex . . . sells. Critique my novel on immoral grounds and people will trample each other in their attempt to buy the book. You have to admit that some people could misconstrue what I've written. At least some parts. I hope so. In a way, I'm counting on it. A lot depends on how you put it across."

"Mmmm . . . all right. But I still say you're treading on thin ice."

"OK. And I won't blame you if I sink."

Next week, a revised review had Lester

Wallace happy.

"Not bad, not bad," he said, nodding appreciatively, as he perused the essay.

While condemning certain of the book's regrettable passages, in scandalized tones on moral grounds, while enthusiastically emphasizing the novel's other meritorious qualities, it managed to simultaneously eulogize and denounce the same novel.

"I'm truly impressed, Mister Stein. It's a superb balancing act."

"I'm very proud of that review, fella, and to tell you the truth, I can't wait to see what happens next with the sales of your book."

Lester handed the money over. "Worth every penny, in my opinion. Maybe you should take up writing novels."

"Nah, I'll leave that for my old age."

As Stein boorishly began to count the money, he muttered, "First time I've been paid to write a bad review. There's a first time for everything, I guess."

XXIX

Strickland tried to keep his mind focused on the purpose of his visit to his son's school, but the school counselor's nervous mannerisms and her off the wall comments and constant digressions made it difficult.

"Excuse me, but are you a social worker?" he suddenly interrupted her raving, knowing the answer as soon as the question left his lips.

"Yes, I am. Why?"

"Oh, just curious."

She resumed her irrational, tortuous labyrinth and Strickland wondered what it was about the field of Social Work that attracted so many neurotic, emotional unstable women.

His son, Andy, had put it more concise when his father has asked him, before the meeting, what she was like.

"She's nuts!" he had responded with a sneer.

Now, she was elaborating in a convoluted manner the reasons why the classes for intellectually gifted children, like Andy's, were going to be eliminated in order to reallocate those funds to amplify the classes for the hopelessly "remedial" children. As she described the latter in such tear-jerking, syrupy sweet terms, Strickland feared that she would dissolve in a sobbing puddle. He forcefully brought her back to reality.

"OK! Fine! You still haven't told me exactly *why* the gifted program is going to be phased out!"

"Oh. Well, it's simple. There are just not enough funds to go around. So, they're allocated to those with the greatest Need."

"The retards, eh?"

The counselor winced.

"Please don't use that term," she asked.

"I'm sorry if it offends, but you can understand my bitterness. My son, and others like him, may not reach his full intellectual potential because the gifted classes have been canceled in order to make way for paying instructors to teach, for four years, mentally retarded children to color inside a circle."

"But your child can always cope in society, whereas these other children may never be able to."

"If they may never be able to, then what's

the point of wasting limited resources on them, if you're not going to get practical results, anyway?"

The social worker was stunned at this pragmatic conundrum. One could almost hear the gears in her mind grind away in trying to overcome this thrown monkey wrench. Unfortunately, Strickland continued talking.

"Look, let me put it this way," he went on. "If there was some way, some method, some cure, to make these poor kids normal and it'd cost a million bucks apiece, I'd say, 'Go for it! Do it! It's worth every penny!' But, since nothing tangible's going to come out of it, anyway, then I see no point whatsoever in depriving gifted kids of their classes. Surely, you can see that."

"But gifted children don't have problems."

"Oh, I don't know. With so much mediocrity everywhere, they're practically drowning in it. They need islands of refuge."

"But, when they get to college, they can catch up."

"You kidding? Don't you know what it's like in college campuses anymore? Physics and Math Departments are being phased out and their funds reallocated to Minority Studies and Feminist Studies Departments. Everywhere, it's the glorification of the lowest common denominator: no one can be rich if there's poor, no one can be intelligent if there are retards, no one can be athletic if there are cripples. No wonder the Japanese are beating us in every field of endeavor!"

"Mister Strickland, I must ask you again not to use that word again. It's offensive."

"Huh! Fine! But, getting back to the topic at hand, I'm going to see what I can do to stop this."

There was a momentary look of triumph on

the social worker's face as the mask was cast off.

"Go ahead, but the legislature's on our side. The *federal* legislature. So's the media. It's mandated: we *must* provide adequate classes for the mentally challenged children. It's the law. If word gets out to the news media that these children are going to be deprived of their just rights, the news media would do a number on whoever tried."

"Show me these classes. Please."

The social worker's mask was back on as she led him down the school's corridors, past various classes in session. He was tuning out her verbal diarrhea, but, occasionally, some phrases filtered in.

"We're thinking of doing away with grades altogether; those who make poor grades suffer from such low self-esteem as a result! We'll give everyone equal grades."

And:

"There's a plan in the works of making regular and gifted students spend time with the mentally challenged during classes, helping them."

They got to one of the classrooms for the mentally challenged in an adjoining building. Not wanting to disturb, he looked around from the doorway. The walls were decorated with bright, primary colors and cartoons that one would find in a kindergarten, and not an ordinary, classroom of nine-year olds. Several children were seated in round tables. Most had their mouths open with vacant stares, one seemed to have a floppy neck. All had stupid expressions on their faces. All were trying to carry out tasks that they had tried to master numerous times before and which had been mastered by younger children the very first time. Strickland felt genuinely sorry for them. He also realized how impossible it would be to prevent what was going to happen, especially if the news cameras were brought in and the images manipulated just right.

They then traveled to a gifted class. Andy went in and took his place with the other boys and girls. All were absorbed in quiet, intense concentration in their investigations. All the pupils were the picture of physical perfection. Strickland observed a saltwater aquarium full of invertebrates, glass equipment for electrolysis, a map of the solar system on the wall, another of the world, several terrariums, microscopes, fossils, busts of Beethoven, Mozart, Handel, a world globe, an encyclopedia, thick tomes of *The Three Musketeers, She, Treasure Island, Uncle Silas, Swiss Family Robinson, Dracula, The Invisible Man, David Copperfield, White Fang, The Virginian* and many others, a model of the Space Shuttle, globes of Mars and the moon, photographs of Pasteur, Edison, Lincoln, Salk, Margaret Mead, a wall map of the Roman Empire, a bonsai tree by the window, a small telescope, a dissecting kit, various animal skeletons, a seashell collection, skeleton models of dinosaurs. One girl was fearlessly playing with a garter snake from the terrarium, several children were meticulously taking a radio apart into its components, two boys were looking at fungi under a microscope.

Occasionally, Andy, or one of his classmates, or even the teacher, glanced up at him. Strickland knew without a doubt that it was all his imagination, but, even so he could not help but read into their brief looks a silent appeal for help

XXX

Every villain is followed by a sophist with a sponge.
Lord Acton

Anatolio Silva and his teenage son, Jose Luis, were driving away from their neighborhood and towards downtown. Their destination was City Hall, where they were going to transfer the title of the car that they were driving. It had been bought the night before and although only two years old, they had gotten it for a very good price.

The car was a graduation present from Anatolio to his son, Jose Luis. He had graduated with excellent grades and had furthermore received a scholarship to attend the local university. The father was nearly bursting with pride.

"Isn't this country great?" asked the father rhetorically. Like most adult Cubans, he liked to talk endlessly. "Six years ago, we came to this country with the clothes on our back and now look at us! Remember how we couldn't find any cars in Cuba, they were all twenty-five year old junk heaps, thanks to the Communists. There wasn't a new one to be had. Not one! And the wrecks that were around, falling apart, the owners still held on to them. And now, we've got a brand-new car and you've got one to go to the university with." He was talking to his son in Spanish, as always.

"Watch the road," warned Jose Luis. If he got too emotional, his father had the habit of looking at the person that he was talking to while driving, thereby neglecting the traffic. The lad much preferred talking to Americans than to Cubans. That was the thing about Cubans, he thought, they seemed to be in a constant state of hysterics.

"I know what to do! I've driven longer than you have, you know!"

"I know."

"No matter how much we worked in Cuba, it was no use, it was all for the State, we couldn't buy anything---because there was nothing to buy! No cars, no radios, no books, no televisions, no clothes, no guitars, no movies, nothing but misery, thanks to Communism. A desert! That's what Cuba's become under those misbegotten Communists, a desert! And they, with their propaganda, the propaganda by cretins for cretins-"

"Dad, be careful of that car!"

"I see him, don't worry. Look at that, he doesn't even know how to drive. I can't believe that there's people to this day that are still taken in by the propaganda, it's a propaganda by cretins for cretins. If they only would go to Cuba and see the misery, the lack of food, of medicine, of everything! Everything except weapons! Weapons and propaganda! And look at the Berlin Wall! What kind of a government builds a wall to keep its own people prisoner? And if they try to leave, they shoot them down, like they were dogs. Can you believe that there are people that are Communists with the

Berlin Wall as testimony of what Communism is? If they only would go to Cuba and see with their own eyes. See the constant surveillance by the regime, the lack of food-"

"Dad. They go there and they come away praising Fidel."

"But why, Jose Luis, why? Are they blind?"

The son frowned, perplexed by the question, as if his father had suddenly, in the midst of his almost incoherent rambling, presented him with a crucial conundrum.

"I think . . . they're just . . . fanatical, I guess." He realized that his answer really answered nothing. "I don't know, I've been trying to figure it out myself. I do know that they hate this country, though, and for the most trivial of reasons. And some of them are Americans. They're Americans but they *hate* their own country; it's a point of pride with them to hate their own country. I think they're mentally sick, or something."

"And do you think that these Americans appreciate what they have?" his father continued. "No, not at all! They don't even know what they have. America is wasted on Americans! They don't know how bad things can get under a Communist regime---and they don't care! They're totally ignorant of conditions under the Communists. Not just in Cuba, but Poland, Hungary, China! And they don't seem to realize that the Communists are poised to pounce on this country, waiting for an opportunity, taking every chance to undermine this country and soften it-"

"Dad!! Red light!!" He frantically pounded the floor of the car for a brake that was not there.

Mister Silva slammed on the brakes, the tires screeched, but they avoided running the red light, entering the busy intersection and slamming into another car.

He was now quiet, feeling a bit sheepish. He turned on the radio and found some easy music, the type that his son called Lawrence Welk music. After a while, the son switched the station to rock and roll. The light finally turned green and they continued on their way along Kellog Street.

"Dad, don't get offended, but I'd like to get the car transferred to me in one piece. Please drive carefully."

"It is a nice car, isn't it? I got a good bargain. You like the color?"

"Yeah. I'll like it better once it's in my name."

The road now turned into a highway, converted years ago to alleviate traffic congestion. At the appropriate exit, they turned off the highway and navigated along the downtown streets until they found City Hall. They had difficulty finding a parking place, the parking lot being crowded. They finally found one, parked the car and went in.

What between finding the right office and waiting in the long lines and then waiting for the papers to be processed, it was over an hour before the teenager held the title to his car in his proud hands. His name on the title somehow seemed special.

"Dad, this time I think I'll drive back."

Their business transaction finished, they emerged out of the building.

"Looky there," said Jose Luis, motioning towards a crowd of people at some distance from the building.

"What's going on?" asked his father.

"I don't know. Let's walk over and find

out."

There was a crowd of about fifty people in a rough semicircle, some of whom they had seen inside and, like them, had strolled over out of curiosity. There were over a dozen journalists with oversized cameras clustered together, with as many policemen around the inner boundary of the semicircle.

The focus of the attention was on six wild-haired, leering individuals in the center of the crowd, one of whom was on top of a box making a shrill speech. They were the type of individuals, very common in the second part of the twentieth century, who studiously dressed in a manner for the express purpose of offending. They had not shaved for a couple of days, their hair was uncombed, their clothing was absurd or mismatched, with buttons and T-shirts prominently displaying hard-core obscene words or acts. One of the T-shirts displayed a picture of the psychotic Che Guevara. The expression on their faces was either openly sneering, or mocking as they looked the crowd over.

"What's going on, officer?" Jose Luis asked one of the policemen.

"Oh, it's those bums who won their court case to burn The Flag, thanks to the ACLU" he muttered with ill humor.

"You gotta be kidding!"

"No, I'm not," he said, making a face. The teenager now noticed that on the ground by the box was a can of lighter fluid and next to it a multicolored bundle.

"Excuse me," said the boy's father, frowning. "You say they want to burn the Flag? The American flag? This country's flag?" He was rapidly becoming indignant and as this happened, his accent became more pronounced.

The policeman nodded. "Afraid so."

"What are you going to do about it?" asked the boy, feeling a bit indignant himself.

"What do you mean, what am I going to do about it? If you're asking me if I'm going to stop it, the answer is no. I'm here to protect *them*." He motioned with his thumb to the agitators.

"He can't do anything," a woman that was next to them leaned over to explain. "That group recently went to court to challenge the state law banning the burning The Flag. The ACLU represented them in court and successfully argued that burning The Flag was an act of political expression, which was guaranteed by the freedom of speech guarantee. They've argued this in other states, with the same results."

"Excuse me," said Mister Silva. "What is ACLU? The university?"

"No," the woman smiled for the first time, but it was of brief duration. "It's the American Civil Liberties Union. It's a group of liberal lawyers who get together to legally represent subversive groups to make sure they can carry out their activities."

"They're a bunch of scum-sucking rats, is what they are!" interjected another man standing next to them. "These are the same characters---you may have read this in the 'papers a few months back---this Ukrainian family came over to the United States. The parents decided to return, they couldn't hack it over here. OK. No problem. It's a free country. But the teenage boy, he wanted to stay, he said that he didn't like the dictatorship in the Soviet Union and he was going to stay and they couldn't make him go back. So, the ACLU went to court to *force* to boy to go back so he could end up in a concentration camp or get shot!"

"No!" Mister Silva uttered. "This is true?"

"Yep, it sure is," replied the woman, with obvious distaste.

The rat faced speaker's voice squealed higher. He iterated a long list of grievances against America, wherein the words, "imperialist," "capitalist system," "corrupt," "racist," "Fascist," "repressive," "colonialist," and other leftist buzzwords came coming up again and again. There was a sort of schizoid unreality in diatribe, Jose Luis thought. He was shrieking that the American government oppressed the masses and was Fascist, yet, here he was being allowed, by a government court order, to burn the country's flag---which in almost every other nation he would have been imprisoned, if not shot and their act was being mass broadcasted by a gaggle of sympathetic journalists.

"Those are the ones that get me, though," said the policeman, pointing to the journalists. "Those guys give them publicity like they were heroes."

"I'll bet you something," said the other man, "if those reporters weren't here, neither would they," he motioned to the six inside the semicircle. The policeman nodded in agreement.

Jose Luis could not hear any more, his father's agitation was such that he was fluidly cursing the demonstrators in a jumble of both Spanish and English, since by now his English had become completely unmanageable.

The speaker apparently ended heaping his abuse, since he stepped down and, at a nod at his leering cohorts, two of them picked up the multicolored bundle and stretched it out revealing it to be The Stars and Stripes. With a mocking sneer at the crowd, the speaker picked up the can of lighter fluid and sprayed the fluid on the flag until it was saturated. He put the can down, away from the flag and took out a matchbox.

"No! I don't believe that these sheep are actually going to let this happen!" said the older Silva to his son in Spanish. "Such an insult to such a country! What a nation of sheep! So spineless! Who's worse, those pigs or these sheep?"

Jose Luis was himself becoming antsy. As much as he wanted the Americans to snap out of their lethargy and attack the would-be desecrators, he knew at the same time that they would not. They were too law abiding. They were legalistic to a fault. That was their weakness. Americans were law abiding to the point of absurdity. But, at the same time, they were also *so inexpressive.* Looking around at those faces, all he saw were silent looks of disapproval---that was all! For once, he wished that they were more Cuban-like in their emotions and less insipid.

The rat-faced leader lit a match and displayed the flame in a semicircle, ending back at the cluster of cameras.

"Nothing says that I have to stay here and watch," said the woman.

"Yeah, that's a good idea," said the man next to her and both began to leave.

That's it? thought Jose Luis. *That's all that they're going to do?*

The leader applied the match to the Stars and Stripes. It caught on fire and the flames began to rapidly consume it.

Jose Luis impulsively broke through the semicircle and bounded over to the grinning leader. He swung his right fist with all the anger that he felt and connected squarely with the leader's snout.

Almost at the same time, he was wrestled to the ground, lifted on his feet and taken out of the semicircle by two policemen who expertly pinioned his arms behind him until they hurt, all in a matter of seconds. He could hear words like "oppression," "Fascist attack," "violating our rights," being shrieked out far behind him.

The two policemen quickly segregated him far away from the crowd, near one of the patrol cars and handcuffed him. His agitated father had followed them. He was no longer infuriated, but was, instead, frighteningly concerned for his son. At first, they would not let him approach, but when it became apparent that there was not going to be a follow-up altercation, they relaxed enough to let him approach.

Americans have the tendency (at least outside the huge metropolitan cities) to think that once a foreigner sets foot on this country, buys a car, has a job and a place to stay, that he automatically becomes an American and thinks like an American, with an American's sense of values. The fact is, that if the resident alien is an adult, he has the same preconceptions, prejudices and habits that he had before, though they may be in occasional conflict with the new lifestyle. For example, policemen. People who have come from certain countries view policemen in one of two ways: either with distrust, cynicism and hatred, or, with automatic submissiveness. Mister Silva was now in a submissive mode.

"Excuse me," he timidly asked the policemen, "that is my son. What is going to happen?"

The two policemen looked around and saw

that no mob had formed and that no one else had followed and so, they visibly relaxed. One of the two was the officer they had talked to before and he was the one who answered.

"Well, I'm sorry to say that we'll have to take him downtown and he'll be charged with Disturbing the Peace, or possibly even Assault."

Mister Silva looked at his son. "I'll get a lawyer," he told him, but did not leave.

The four of them stood there for quite a few minutes, oddly enough, without saying anything. An eternity seemed to pass. Each one looked troubled, embarrassed.

Presently, one of the policemen addressed the boy in a low voice.

"Listen, kid, we have to arrest you, we have no choice in the matter. But, as far as I'm personally concerned, I want to thank you for what you did. I wish that I had had the guts to have done something like that, if I had been out of uniform, that is."

"Yeah," said the other one. "Same here, we gotta arrest *him* and we gotta protect *them.* Doesn't make any sense."

Jose Luis did not answer. All his concentration focused on the fact that he was going to jail. He had never gone to jail before. He looked glum.

Suddenly, his head snapped up and his back straightened. His expression changed completely. He knew it was a long shot, though.

"Let me understand this," he said. "There is a law against burning Old Glory, but they can do it since they are exercising their freedom of speech, which is guaranteed by the Bill of Rights. Is that it?"

"Yeah," one of the officers answered.

"The burning was not vocal, not speech, but it was still a form of expression, right?"

"OK. So?"

"Well, then, in my punching that flag-burner I was exercising *my* freedom of speech. I was expressing *my* political views, which were the opposite of his flag-burning. I was exercising *my* freedom of speech. Their action broke the law against burning the flag. My act may have broken the laws describing Assault or Disturbing the Peace, but it was done while expressing my political views."

"Therefore, I should not be arrested. Simple logic." He waited, expectantly.

Both officers chuckled and looked at the ground and said nothing.

"Sorry, kid, we're not the Supreme Court. But you did argue well your case," said one of the policemen. Jose Luis resigned himself to the inevitable.

Presently, after a couple of minutes, a large smile formed on the other officer and he nodded his head vigorously.

"Why not?"

"Huh?" said his partner, who now looked at him with a worried frown. The two looked at each other.

"Why *not?* "

"You can't possibly be serious!"

"Why *not?* " He paused. "Why not? It makes sense. It makes perfect sense!"

"Well, yeah, it makes sense, but the brass would have a fit!" he hissed at his partner.

"I'm going to let him go."

"Oh, no. You can't possibly be serious," he repeated. "Oh, no."

"I'm dead serious. I'm using my 'discretion,' aren't I? Isn't that what they're always telling us to do? You said so yourself: it makes sense. Why shouldn't we apply the same logic to him that we apply to *them?* Don't worry, I'll take the heat for it. I'm the one that released him, and I'll say you knew nothing of it."

"Man, the brass will have you for lunch!"

"Let them! What's the worst that they can they do to me? Fire me? OK. Big deal. Big-deal. Sometimes you gotta make a stand. Besides, this job doesn't pay that much, anyway, and the hours are killing my home life." He unlocked the handcuffs and put the away. The boy rubbed his wrists. Both father and son were relieved.

The officer who had freed them looked at Jose Luis and motioned with the fingers of his hand as if he was brushing something off that was bothering him.

"Go," he told them quietly.

The father and son scurried off, afraid that they might change their minds.

"And thanks again, kid," the officer muttered, but by then the Silvas were too far away to hear him.

XXXI

Ezra was eating some M & Ms when he saw the approaching car and knew right away that the driver was a stranger. In that tiny town with a population of less than 400, in the depopulated counties of western Kansas, everybody knows everybody, and everybody knows what kind of a

car, or truck, everyone else drives. So, when the
blonde fellow pulled up to Ezra's filling station, he
knew that he was not from this county, or any of the
adjoining counties, for that matter.

"Can I help ya?" he asked the driver.

"Yes-s-s. Cou'd you please fill up the gas
tank and check under the bonnet? The car seems to
be getting hot."

"Check under the what?"

"Sorry. Check under the hood." The man
had an unmistakable accent, the kind that is pleasant
to hear.

"Turn off the motor, please." The driver did
so and Ezra filled up the gas tank and, as he did so,
he wondered how he could get him to talk some
more.

"Anything in particular ya wanted me to
check?"

"Well, the temperature gauge indicated that
the engine was getting hot, so I was getting a bit
worried. I didn't wahn't to get strahnded on the
road."

"Say, you British, or something?" Ezra
finally asked.

"Yes, that's right. I'm British."

"What ya doing all the way out here? You
lost or something?"

The man chuckled.

"No. Ac-tually, I'm touring the Midwest. A
friend of mine back in London recommended it;
suggested I avoid the cities."

"Well, ya sure picked a fine place to get
away from the cities," he joked. "I'll check yar, ah .
. . bonnet, you called it, now."

After a minute or so, he came back to the
driver.

"Fella, the reason ya'r car's getting hot is because it's about ta give out on ya. Yar fan belt musta come off somewheres back."

"I say, I *did* hear a noise a few miles back, but I thought I had run over a tortoise or a rock."

"That was yar belt coming off."

"Well . . . can you fix it?"

"Sure thing! It'll take me awhile. Why doncha mosey on down to Annie's over yonder," he pointed to a cafe across the street a block away, "and gechaself a cupo coffee. It's about the only thing Annie cain't burn up. And stay away from her Beef Stroganoff; her gravey cain't disguise the fact that it's a road kill," he chuckled. "I'll call ya over when it's ready."

"All right, thanks. I'll leave the keys with you."

The stranger sauntered over, passing several closed-up stores. Everywhere he had gone in the Midwest, in all the small villages interspersed along the flat prairie, it seemed the same, that people were leaving the small villages for the cities and, as more and more people left, more and more stores closed up and churches and schools became emptier and emptier. The remaining people that he had talked with here and there had no idea how to stem the flow.

It was the same in Britain.

As he went into the cafeteria, he got the impression that they had been expecting him. There were three old men at a table, all of them wearing those ubiquitous caps, and two women behind the counter.

"Hi, what'll ya have?" one of the women asked him as he sat down on the stool.

"Coffee, please." She looked expectantly at

him, as if waiting for him to speak on, then, finally got him his cup of coffee.

"Where ya from?" she asked him.

"Britain. I'm on holiday."

"Oh, yeah? What holiday is it?"

"No, I mean, I'm on vacation."

"So whacha doing around these parts?"

"Traveling. A friend of mine recommended that I spend most of my time in the Midwest and avoid the big cities. He told me to just take a few days traveling on the small roads and avoid the superhighways. He said that that's where 'the real America' can be found."

"It ain't in New York City and that's a fact!" a crotchety old man chimed in. "New York ain't America!"

"I've been there. The people are cehrtainly . . . odd." He thought a mild agreement might be worthwhile.

"I'm Annie, by the way."

"Hello. I'm Trevor."

There was a clearing of throat by Annie's side.

"Oh, and this is Peggy."

"Hello."

"Howdy."

"So, are ya rambling somewhere special, Trevor, or jest rambling every which way?"

"I thought I'd go on to Topeka and see this Menninger Clinic and then stop by Coffeyville towards the south. I'm told that there's a little museum there where a gang of your outlaws tried to rob a bank during your Wild West days."

Peggy wrinkled her nose. "Ooooh, I just love his accent, don't you? It's so musical."

Trevor stopped, momentarily self-conscious.

"Oh, don't stop. Talk some more."

"Now see whacha done, Peggy! You've done and embarrassed the young feller," one of the old men chided her.

"What's it like, over in Merry Olde England?" Annie asked him, obviously trying to make him talk. He didn't mind. So, he spoke about the weather and its history and the difference between Wales and Scotland and England, and the Royal Family, and as he spoke, more people began to stagger in for a cup of coffee.

"Do y'all have TV in England?" Peggy suddenly asked him and he had to restrain himself from snapping at her. He had encountered this type of question at other times. The silly ignorance was not hostile or insulting, it was just . . . incredibly naive. Totally innocent. Oblivious. Yet, typical. As far as these people in the American Midwest were concerned, England, or Europe, was as far away as . . . Saturn. In fact, a Canadian cousin of his had been asked the very same question when she came over to the States to attend a university---and Canada was their neighbor! Americans' naive ignorance of other countries was simply unbelievable.

"Of course we have TV."

"Oh, yeah? What's it like?"

"Oh, same as yours. We have the BBC. A lot of cultural programs. Awfully boring. But we also steal your TV shows and adapt them to our taste."

"Oh, yeah? Like which ones?"

Truth to tell, he was really enjoying the rapt attention that he was getting from everyone in the diner, so he went on at length. A telephone rang and he continued speaking while Annie talked on the telephone, occasionally eyeing him. He was enjoying being the center of attention. Other Brits had told him, and he himself had noticed during his travel, that, away from the big cities, Americans went gaga over accents: English, Irish, German, Scottish, Cuban, Italian, you name it. They loved accents, with one or two exceptions. So, he continued expostulating. It was also obvious that these people hungered for novelty and news from the outside world, not news in the sense of political news, which they could get anytime from the telly, but more like everyday type of information. Gossip, if you will, and with a personal touch.

His coffee cup kept being refilled.

Ezra came into the crowded cafe and went over to him.

"Say, were ya in any big hurry to get to Topeka?" he asked the stranger.

"Well . . . no, not really. Why?"

"It looks like I might not get a belt for your radiator from Concordia 'til tomorrow morning. I don't stock it. Nobody in town does."

"Is it going to cost me a lot?"

"Oh, no! No, no! It just won't be in 'til tomorrow. And with this heat, ya can't take yar car out on the road. Now, if this was winter, that might be a working proposition. But in this heat . . . nah!"

"Mmm, well, if there's no avoiding it. And I'm not going by any schedule. Where's your closest hotel?"

"We don't have one," Peggy blurted out.

"Oh, no," Trevor muttered.

"We'd be happy to put ya up for the night," one of the old men volunteered. "We got a guest room in our house's never been used."

"I see. And how much would you want for my lodging?" he asked, expecting to be fleeced.

"You mean money? Ah!" He waved the motion away. "We'd be tickled pink to have ya."

"Nothing to do 'round here, though," said Peggy. "At night, we roll up the streets."

"Vittle's good," Ezra pointed out. "Leastways ya won't get food poisoning like ya wou'd if ya ate Annie's cooking."

"Ezra, you skunk!" She threw him a wet sponge.

So, Trevor spent the rest of the afternoon in town and, later, at Isaac's home with his wife Maud, and it seemed like everyone in town just happened to drop by and kept encouraging him to speak in subtle and not so subtle ways.

In truth, he certainly enjoyed being the center of attention.

Yet, there was one space of time when the others did most of the talking.

"Tell me about tornadoes. We don't have them in Britain. Have any of you eveh seen one?"

"Seen one? *Been* in one!"

"Ya kidding? This part of the country's called Tornado Alley!"

"I was living in Salina when one went over my house. Tore the roof plumb off-"

"It sounded like a freight train-"

"I've seen several start to come down from the clouds, but none of 'em ever touched ground, just went back up into the cloud-"

"Always hails when there's a tornado-"

"No, now that ain't true-"

"It sounded like a million bees swarming-"

"That tornado plucked the feathers off the chickens-"

"And they're so unpredictable! They do such weird things!"

285

"They always come *after* a storm-"

"One went across the street from our home, parallel to it and it'd go up and down, up and down, demolish one house, but sparing another-"

"A tornado doesn't *blow* yar house, mind you, it *explodes* a house! That's because of that there vacuum!"

"In Great Bend we found cows with nails and branches driven deep into them and one telephone pole had wheat stalks sticking inside the pole-"

"My wife was visiting her kinfolks in Medicine Lodge-"

"Tore the front door right outa my hand, but left me there without a scratch. Go figure it!"

"When the tornado hit Abilene, a mother hid in the stairs closet with the kids and felt the house shake. When it was over, she came out of the closet to find the whole house gone---clean plumb gone!--- 'cept the stairs and the closet. Even the pictures next to the closet were still hanging there."

"My sister was passing by Oberlin last year-"

They stayed up late that night.

The next day, in the morning, Trevor was invited to Church services after a hearty breakfast. On his return, his car was waiting for him. Ezra gave him the keys."

"And how much do I owe you?"

"Five dollars."

"That's it?"

"Uh-huh."

Trevor handed over a bill, then went over to say goodbye to Isaac and Maud.

"Thank you for your kind hospitality."

"Yar always welcomed, ya know that,

Trevor. Anytime ya go on another tour of yars to the Midwest, ya can spend the night with us again. Y'all always have a place."

"Thank you. You're too kind."

He was about to get in his car, when he turned around to face the mechanic.

"Ezra, I was not awahre of any dehlivery sehvices being open on a Sunday mohrning. Not in this part of the country. Not in Kansas."

Ezra stared at him and blinked thrice.

Then, he smiled.

"It was nice having ya, Trevor. And don't be a stranger. Feel free to come again. Ya'll always be welcomed. Ya gat friends here now."

He closed the door once the Englishman got in.

"Ya have a nice trip, fella."

XXXII

Our home was two street blocks away from a main intersection of streets. Like all intersections in America deserving of a traffic light, each of the four corners had either a filling station or a fast food restaurant. But one of them, the one that was catty-corner to the direction of our home, had a small strip mall containing a supermarket and several stores. Like most such places, it was pleasant to stroll around in, which I often did since it was a few minutes' walk from the house.

On this day, I had just walked in through the front door, carrying in my hand a small paper sack containing my purchase at the mall. My mother saw me come in and eyed the paper bag.

"What you got there?"

"A couple of paperback books," I said, taking them out of the bag to show her.

"Tch! Wasting your money again. When will you learn?"

"I like to read," I protested.

"As if you needed to read any more than you have to in school," she said loudly, shaking her head. She was very annoyed with my purchase. "Why don't you buy yourself something useful?"

"Well, it isn't as if I was going broke by buying books," I countered and went immediately to my room to read one of them and closed the door behind me. This time, it was a mystery and I soon lost myself in it.

After a couple of hours, she came into my room to tell me that dinner was ready, saw me reading and burst out with, "Fool! What good is it gonna do you to read so much?"

"Leave me alone, will ya?"

"Go ahead and waste your time, fool!"

"I did my homework already! What do you want? Why'd you come in?"

"To tell you dinner's ready," she said and went back to the dining room.

I went in and sat down, in a bad mood now, thanks to her nagging. In a small way, I had hoped that she objected for fear that I was neglecting my homework. She had been getting worse lately, really bad, nagging me that I was squandering my money on books, and when I switched to checking out library books which, naturally, didn't cost anything, she had still gotten on my case about all the time being wasted on reading. The thing that got me, though, is that she never had a suggestion of what else she wanted me to do with my time. No alternatives. None. Zip. When I got her cornered to offer an alternative, the best that she could come up with was "something productive with your time."

OK. Like what?

Anyway, it had gotten so bad that I had gone to waiting until she went to bed and I would read under the covers in my room with the aid of a flashlight.

She hated books. My mother hated seeing me read. And I think that she also hated to see me learn anything. I say this because when I was given a scholarship for college while still only in my junior year in high school, she threw a fit.

"You're such a fool! What do you want to go to more school for? Haven't you had enough by now? Do you know how long it's going to take you to get a degree? It's a waste of time! I've always said that you were such a fool!"

Whenever it got bad, I mean when it got so bad that I couldn't stand the sight of her, I'd walk over to my friend Eric's house. Now, *he* had a cool mom.

One day, I had an idea while walking home with another paperback in my hand and I went, instead, directly to Eric's house. Eric knew my problem and he was my best friend so I was pretty sure that he wouldn't mind, and when I asked him, he didn't. So that left his mom. I asked her right away.

"Mrs. Robinson, would it be all right if I sometimes came over just to read my books in peace and quiet?"

Her eyebrows shot up. "Do what?"

I repeated my question, then, at her prompting, ran down to her what my problem was. She thought that I was making it up, but Eric backed me up. He had been over to my house during some of the scenes with my mom.

"Sure!" she said, making a face at my situation. I don't think that at first she believed me. Later, when she saw me wrapped up with a book while Eric did his homework, she gradually accepted it.

I did this a few times and they were happy to have me over (by the way, me and Eric would also get together to do other things, like play video games).

One day, his mother interrupted my reading. "Carlos. Come over here for a minute, I want to talk to you." I sat opposite her across the table.

"I'm glad that you like to read books, but why do you read those types of books?"

"What kind?"

"Well . . . trash. I mean, if you're going to read, why don't you read some really good books?"

"Like what?"

"Like the classics?"

"Aww, they're boring!"

"Oh, yeah? Which ones have you read?"

She had me there.

I couldn't name a single one, but I was sure that they were boring 'cause they were old. But she insisted that I name her one, just one, and when I couldn't, I felt so *stupid.*

"Listen, the reason that they're called classics it that they're good and people never get tired of them. If they weren't good, they wouldn't keep publishing them and bookstores wouldn't stock them. The 'bestseller books,' on the other hand, go out of print eight months later and two years later, nobody can remember them, or their authors, but some of these classics have been around for a century or more and they're still entertaining people."

"Look, let's make a deal. I want you to read a couple of books that I choose for you. After you read them, if you think they were boring, I won't bother you again. Read anything you care to bring over. If you like them, then I'll get you some even more interesting, OK? Because, Carlos, you've got a good head on your shoulders and I hate to see you waste it. I want to steer you in the right direction. Is it a deal?"

"OK. Sure." Hey, why not? Besides, like I said, Mrs. Robinson was cool so maybe she knew something I didn't.

So she went to her library and handed me a book. It was called *Treasure Island,* by Robert Louis Stevenson.

Snea-ky.

Looking back, I can see that all her selections were brilliantly chosen. That was one smart lady. She knew *exactly* what it would take to entice a teenager into reading the great works of literature.

Hooked? You bet! I didn't just swallow the hook. I swallowed the bait, the hook, the weight, the leader, float, line, rod and tackle box!

"That was great!" I exclaimed handing it back a day or two later after having finished reading it.

"Here's another good one," she told me and handed me *The Invisible Man* by H. G. Wells. I finished it that same day (it was a thin book).

She followed it up with *Candide, Crime and Punishment, She, The Three Musketeers, The Count of Monte Cristo, The Lost World, Gulliver's Travels, The Hound of the Baskervilles, The War of*

291

the Worlds, Something of Value, The First Circle.

Hooked? Boy, was I ever hooked!

Like I said, she played me like a virtuoso with a violin. I put myself completely in her hands, though I would buy a book at the store from time to time (besides, she saved me money).

And now that she had me hooked, she would alternate "subtle" works and "direct" works: *The Prophet* followed by *The Gilded Age* and *Gone With The Wind, The House of Seven Gables* with *Catch-22, The Outsider* with *The Call of the Wild* and *The Pathfinder, The Little Prince* with *The Journey to the West.*

Yet, one of the things that I enjoyed as much as the reading of the books themselves were the discussions with Mrs. Robinson afterwards. I couldn't even think of my mother doing something like that (I had finally come to realize that my mother was unique, my mother was an idiot). Sometimes I'd argue that a particular book was confusing or not very good.

"I didn't like this one," I would say, handing back *The Strange Case of Dr. Jekyll and Mr. Hyde.*

"Really? Why not?" she'd inquire.

"I don't know, it left a lot out. I expected more . . . I don't know, details. It was just disappointing."

"Details. Blood and gore. Guts hanging out. That's what you were looking forward to, isn't it? Details of Mr. Hyde's depravity."

"Yeah, that's right. Sex and violence," I joked.

"OK. Now let me tell you why. Stevenson wrote this book during Victorian times. He couldn't give details of Mr. Hyde's depravity because he probably would have had difficulty publishing it.

But the *real* reason is that his wife wouldn't let him. She was a product of her times, a real Victorian lady, and she made Stevenson rewrite the story three times. The one you read is the last version that he rewrote and the only one that has come down to us. You see?"

"Yeah . . . I guess."

"Something else: the book expressed a terror that Victorians had: that the animal, bestial nature in each of us had to be controlled and chained and couldn't be let loose. Everyone had to pretend to be completely civilized and gentile. For example, a lot of Victorians were *terrified* of going insane and loosing control of themselves. In fact, one of the greatest condemnations in the British Empire was that one of their own had 'gone native' like the savage, bestial natives of Africa. You see now?"

"Yeah, I think I get it," I nodded.

"By the way, he got the idea for the story from a nightmare that he had." Then, as she handed me *Kim,* she suddenly asked me. "Carlos, don't you ever discuss your readings with your mother?"

I snorted. She got the hint.

"I see. Maybe you could get her to read one of these good books."

I looked at Mrs. Robinson like she had just lost her mind.

"Are you kidding? She won't touch a book! If she reads anything, it's *The National Inquirer.* That's when she's not watching the Spanish *telenovelas.*"

"The what?"

"The *telenovelas.* The melodramatic soap operas. It's a big thing with all the stupid women of Latin America. I'm told they're also exported to other countries."

"Oh. I see. Well. It was just an idea."

"Yeah, well, you can get that idea right out of your head," I replied, a bit rudely I realized later.

After *Kim*, she spurred my adolescent interest further by informing me that there were some great books with a little sex in them and began treating me to *The Decameron, Tom Jones, Brave New World, The Godfather, Roxanne,* and *Valley of the Dolls.* But she also introduced me to *Animal Farm, 1984, The Fountainhead, The Bridge at Andau, Rashomon.* I tell you, that was one cultured lady.

One day in the spring, Mrs. Robinson had a surprise for me. She gave me tickets to a play called *Antigone.* I had never gone to a play before and I certainly had never heard of *Antigone.*

"I can't take my girlfriend. Her parents won't let her go out on weeknights because of school." The tickets were for that Wednesday.

"Why don't you take your mother?"

"You're kidding, right?"

"No."

"What on Earth for?"

"Well, she might just like it. You never know. And it might make peace between the two of you. Besides, it's not a book, and I'm sure that she enjoys watching films and a play is just like a film, except it's live."

I thought about it and decided to give it a try. Besides, deep down I had to admit that I still had the hope that she could somehow transform herself into more like Mrs. Robinson.

So I did. I was half expecting her to decline, but she surprised me by saying that she would come along.

The play was at a junior college on the

nearby town of Winfield. I remember feeling excited in the theater (and out of place), waiting for the curtain to go up. I had never been in a theater before. It was different.

I loved it!!

After the play ended, I asked my mother, who, incidentally, spoke English fluently and could therefore follow the plot, "Well, what did you think of it?'

"I can't believe that you dragged me all the way out here to see this garbage."

It was at that point that I gave up all hope for my mother. She was a hopeless case, an ignoramus who enjoyed being one and preferred it if everyone around her was at the same dismal level of intelligence and culture as herself. And it was not just the fact that she was ignorant and stupid (they're both different, you know), it's that she was so aggressive about it. The Biblical phrase of casting pearls upon swine was tailor made for her.

And it was many years later, when my first novel was published that I dedicated the book with pleasure and gratitude to Mrs. Robinson.

My mother, on reading the dedication in the copy that I had mailed her, called me up by phone and cried out angrily, "What's wrong? Are you ashamed of your mother that you couldn't dedicate it to her?"

XXXIII

The sick in soul insist that it is humanity that is sick, and they are the surgeons to operate on it. They want to turn the world into a sickroom.

295

> **And once they get humanity strapped to the
> operating table, they operate on it with an ax.
> Eric Hoffer.** *The Passionate State of Mind*

"You know, I'm a great admirer of Fidel Castro," Pepe confided in Max when the latter told him that he had been born in Cuba (Pepe was from Mexico). Pepe was now sporting a grin, upon mentioning the Maximum Leader's name. It was not a mocking grin. On the contrary. That grin was almost a trademark, really, that hyena grin, for which the admirers of the Castro dictatorship automatically formed upon mentioning or coming into any kind of contact with the object of their adoration.

For his part, Max was reliving the feelings which he inevitably and uncontrollably experienced when a (previous) friend unexpectedly revealed his admiration for Cuba's totalitarian dictatorship: a deep feeling of betrayal, dismay, followed by a barely suppressed homicidal anger. He had experienced the humiliating situation many times since leaving his native country, as had countless other Cubans.

Max wanted to obliterate that hyena grin, smash it into little enamel pieces, along with the rest of Pepe's face.

*   *   *   *
     *   *   *

When the Cubans had fled after the Communists took over the island nation and began

296

perverting the original revolution against Batista, most fled to the United States, the historically traditional place of exile for political refugees being Miami and Tampa. Destitute, confused, disoriented, shocked, terrorized, all of them thought that their exile would be temporary, two or maybe four years at the most. They also thought that they had left the Communists behind them. They were wrong on both counts.

It was an uneven battle. In fact, there was no battle to speak of, just an endless succession of inconsequential propaganda skirmishes waged by individuals, with the Cuban exiles consistently coming out the worst. They were simply oblivious to many important details in the new culture, compounded by the Cubans' short-tempered, erratic actions and words, that is, *if* they were even noticed by their opponents. Usually, they were simply bypassed. Endless books, magazine articles, university lecturers, television programs and newscasts and even Hollywood movies cranked out the Communist Party line: The Revolution (always spoken in capital letters) had greatly improved the lives of the Cuban people, especially The Poor People, and now Americans needed to stop trying to undermine the new regime and just leave it alone (a much later variation on the overall theme would be that the health care in Cuba was far superior to that of America and therefore the regime should be praised for its humanitarian goals) to build up its military and to spread its "message" of Revolution to other countries.

This message was reiterated again and again and again and again, with no opportunity *whatsoever* given in the mass media in America and Europe to refute it, to the point that, inevitably, invariably, a Cuban refugee would be faced with that infuriating question that implied so much: "But didn't The Revolution really help The Poor People in Cuba?"

Which was like waving a red flag in front of a bull.

And this was what Max was now feeling.

Maximiliano had, like many other Cubans throughout the years, been confronted with that question. It spoke volumes of the effective, incremental, subtle brainwashing that was so pervasive at that time in both Europe and America and of which the inhabitants themselves were not even aware of. It had always, automatically, put him on the defensive.

The first time that he was confronted with this accusation, so unexpected it had been, that the teenager had simply stammered a denial, not really sure of himself, or of the person that he was talking with.

The man, noticing his accent, and asking its origin, as Americans are wont to do, Max had informed him that he was from Cuba.

"What was it like down there?" he followed up.

"Oh, terrible! There was no food, no entertainment, the secret police was everywhere, ready to spy on you and take you to a concentration camp. And propaganda all the time, in schools, in television, at work, everywhere."

"But, didn't The Revolution improve the lives of The Poor?"

And here the teenage Max was thrown off balance, not only by the question itself, which put him in the difficult position of having to prove the opposite, and what the question implied (that anything is justified and justifiable if it benefits The Poor, The Glorious Poor, The Sacred Poor), but by also hearing the buzzword "the poor." Like Pavlov's dogs, all types of leftists, from the Communists to the liberals, practically salivated at the sound of the words "The Poor." To Max, and to other Cubans, on the other hand, having heard those words so often used by the Communists to justify their crimes had the opposite effect and usually made him conclude that he was in the presence of one, which was *not* always necessarily the case.

"N-No, of, of course not," he replied, not sure himself, and repeated his litany of complaints against the dictatorship, barely noticing that his listener was now looking away to one side with a blank stare, thinking to himself that Max and his family must have been exploiting landowners who oppressed the peasants (and to Americans all farmers who are not American are peasants).

Through the years, Max continued to experience the same impasse. It was his naive belief that sooner or later, he would be able to get through to his interrogators and reach out to them and then they would be of one accord with him. After all, he reasoned, what sane man would willingly condone a proven totalitarian regime? He simply had to prove the regime's repressive qualities and they all would be in agreement. At that time, he had not yet come across the writings of Eric Hoffer, the longshoreman turned philosopher.

It was during his early university years that Max was able to surmount the impasse. He had just had another similar experience, this time in class, before the professor arrived: his accent was noted and queried upon, in a friendly manner by one of his classmates, he explained his origins, his country's political status was also questioned, he detailed his and his family's experiences and, then, the inevitable question was voiced. And, predictably, as soon as he replied in the negative, his interrogator began to adopt that blank stare and then to glance to the side, attempting now to edge away from the undesired response.

Afterwards, Max went to the student lounge where some of his friends occasionally congregated. Only Carla, the psychology major, was in their booth and he slumped down opposite her, in ill humor.

Carla looked up, smilingly, from her homework. "Problems, Maxy? You look . . . morose.

Max just growled and Carla wisely resumed her task, knowing that he would come around of his own accord. After a few minutes of sulking, he cooled down enough to speak.

"Carla . . . it's like this: I can't seem to make people understand, to realize, the oppression in Cuba. They ask me about conditions over there and when I tell them, they always ask me if The Poor People aren't better off now, as if all what I've told them hasn't registered, as if they hadn't heard what I had just said."

"You're falling into a trap, Maxy."

"What do you mean?"

"OK . . . . Let's say, for the sake of argument, that the revolution did benefit the poor . . . . . So what?"

"Huh?"

"So Castro may---or may not---have helped The Poor. So what? So . . . what!

Max was now sitting upright, frowning at her with a stare.

"Don't you see?" she went on. "So . . . what?"

He was still trying to weigh the implications of her statement. For her part, she was smiling at him; she felt that she could almost see the wheels in his brain whirring, desperately trying to solve the conundrum. She let him stew some more, then spoke up.

"Don't you see that even if it *is* true, it's irrelevant to the question of whether or not repression occurs in Cuba under Communism? *And* that the question of benefiting The Poor, The Glorious Poor, The Sacred Poor, is the justification for this repression?"

"The Poor are a fetish! Every major political crime of the twentieth century has been justified because it supposedly has somehow benefited The Poor! Whether it really did or did not is morally irrelevant. The Poor has become a sacred cow in whose name any act, no matter how criminal, is justified."

"You told me that you read *1984*. You remember that in one part, the hero goes to a working class section and tries to ask an old timer if, under the new totalitarian regime, have living conditions really improved for the proletariat as the Ministry of Truth proclaims---as if that justified the tyranny and cast absolution on all of their crimes!"

"And here's another little secret, Maxy, one you won't find in many history books, unless you dig hard, I mean *really* hard---my brother showed it to me: the Nazis did the very same thing, they justified their crimes under National Socialism because it helped The Poor. And here's where it gets even more complicated: The Poor really *did* benefit under the Nazis, who, by the way, were detested by the aristocracy. Yet, in the Soviet Union, under Stalin, millions of Poor People were worse off before, particularly during the years of the State-imposed famine in the Ukraine, Russia's breadbasket."

"But . . . whenever the leftists, by which I mean the liberals, the *other* Socialists and the Communists, talk about Hitler and the Nazis, they always talk about the Gestapo, the concentration camps and the repression . . . but they never talk about how The Poor benefited under the *Socialist Nazis*."

Carla sat back and smiled. "Interesting, hey?" Max nodded numbly, still trying to assimilate the new wealth of information which contradicted many of the values that he had subconsciously internalized.

"Have I blown your mind?" Max nodded again and his friend smiled. "Same happened to me. I'll lend you the books later. They're hard to find, for obvious reasons. For the leftists, it doesn't do to have this knowledge spread."

She toyed with her pen, smiling, giving her friend a few more seconds before springing her last surprise.

"I saved the best for last. Do you know what. . .? The Nazis outlawed prostitution in The Third Reich as being degrading to women."

Max started and stared at his friend. "That's . . . that's what they're always saying about the Communist revolution in Cuba, how wonderful it is because it's outlawed prostitution," he whispered.

"I know," she said with a smile.

"They're always bringing it up. Making it sound like prostitution existed only in Cuba. And as if there's no prostitution in New York or

Amsterdam or Berlin."

"I *know*. And the next time that they bring it up, tell them that the Nazis also did away with prostitution and see what they have to say to that."

The rest of that day Max spent in a daze, digesting and ruminating over the new information that she had overwhelmed him with. That evening he asked a lot of questions of his father. He was obtaining information apart from his own immediate experience. He was doing what people do when they first get out of a rut.

He saw Carla the next day and resumed their conversation.

"Well, it turns out that not only has Castro really built some public works like hospitals and schools, but so did the two previous dictators, Machado and Batista. Do you see the significance? *They all do it*. Batista even built a clock tower in some town so that the poor people could always tell what time it was; seems that he stole a watch in that town when he was penniless and got caught, so he had that clock tower built. And Machado had the National Highway built during the Depression. You see?"

"Uh-huh."

"Another point: in the 1930s, there was a revolution which got rid of Machado. They were going to right all the wrongs in Cuban society and make the necessary reforms, but for some reason, most of it got sidetracked. A decade or two later, Batista becomes dictator and the process starts all over again, except the feeling now is that '*now* we're going to get it right.' The revolution succeeds. Batista is kicked out. Problem is . . . some of the reforms are being implemented right away, particularly in the educational and medical fields while the other reforms---the political ones---are not. In fact, they're rapidly going the *opposite* way: *more* militarism, censorship, surveillance of the population, autocracy and illegality are increasing to an unprecedented level. Do you see the significance here?"

"Sure."

"No, you don't. What's the real significance?"

"That not all of the reforms took place."

"Wrong! The real significance here, in light of what we discussed yesterday, is that the original anti-Batista revolution was going to implement the various social reforms---for example, more schools and clinics in the rural areas---anyway!"

"The Communists simply took credit for it! Those desperately needed reforms were the next step and they *were* going to take place, with, *or without* resorting to the propaganda, the persecutions, the anti-American paranoia, the concentration camps, the destruction of the economy, the censorship, the militarism and the cult of personality. The trick that the Reds have pulled on everyone---everyone!---is that the two were interlinked, that you couldn't have one without the other!"

"Now . . . I see."

"And here's the clincher: Costa Rica." He paused for effect.

"What about Costa Rica?"

"Exactly. What about Costa Rica?"

"Are you going to tell me, or are we going to play Twenty Questions?" she snapped.

"Costa Rica is a unique country in Latin America. They have a superb educational and medical system, a constant democracy, a respect for the country's ecology, no corruption and no oppressive military. They were able to achieve this all by themselves---without resorting to a Marxist dictatorship. It's a model for the rest of Latin America."

"Yet, in spite of this, where are the hordes of intellectuals? Why haven't they publicized it and praised it? Where are all the books and articles and films on Costa Rica? When Castro took over, you had leftists from all over the world tripping over themselves in a mad stampede to get to Cuba and give the revolution their personal seal of approval and they all vied for the privilege of kissing Castro's backside."

"Were they really interested in Cuba? No. Were they really interested in the Cuban people? No. Were they interested in abstract values like reforms or democracy or justice? No. Otherwise, they would also have gone to Costa Rica and checked it out. All that the intellectuals *really* wanted was to worship Communist power and brutality. All that they wanted to do was to kneel at the altar of the red star full of human sacrifices in the hopes that, when they returned to The Left Bank in Paris, or Berkeley and Columbia, or Frankfurt in Germany, someday it'd be *their* turn."

Max now leaned back, resting against the seat's padded back. He took a long sip of his drink and set it down. He looked up at Carla with arched eyebrows. "So, tell me, shrink, after figuring all of that out, how come I still feel bad?"

"You feel bad?" she asked, surprised.

"Yep."

"But bad about what?"

Max arched his eyebrows a bit more. He made a face and gestured with his hand. "Well, I

305

guess that it's having to accept that---regardless of all of what I've just said---having to acknowledge that, yes, they did build a few schools and hospitals, that, even though the population of Cuba lives at barely a subsistence level, there are those hospitals or schools that the Communists can point to."

"So *what* if they did build a few buildings here and there? It's all window dressing!"

"I know! I know! I can't help it. You see, Carla, this isn't just an intellectual exercise for me. I experienced it. The terror, the persecution, the propaganda, all of it, I experienced it first hand! And, mind you, I was lucky---I got out. My life and my family's life and my friends' lives were completely uprooted. Cuba will never be the same again. It irks me to have to admit that they did carry out some public works-"

"Even if they were going to be carried out, anyway, by the nonCommunists?"

"Yes. Even so. Intellectually, I know it's of no significance, but emotionally, it irks me no end. You see . . . it's just that I automatically associate the building of schools and hospitals with people who are good---even if the schools are used for the purpose of indoctrination, brainwashing kids with their propaganda and, even if those hospitals don't even have aspirins or even clean sheets for the beds. Like I said, it's an emotional response."

"You associate the buildings of schools and hospitals with people who are good. Just like Pavlov's dogs, Max."

"Woof!" Max joked.

"Your problems, Maxy, is that you've fallen into another psychological trap, that a person, that is a famous person, is either entirely all good or pure evil."

"Come again?"

"I can explain it better with examples. Take the French poet Rimbaud. Great poet, lousy human being. Or Gandhi. Great philosopher and humanitarian---but don't look too closely, particularly at his private life, it'll make you cringe. Martin Luther King---great man, but he thoroughly plagiarized his dissertation. Robert Koch, a German doctor who discovered the tuberculosis bacteria--- among many others---yet, he refused to believe that Pasteur's vaccines worked, or that white blood cells attacked his bacteria. Or, better yet, Richard Wagner. My God, what a composer! What a genius! And what a rotten scumbag!"

"Now, take the other side of the coin. Take Hitler and Stalin. We all know what they did, what horrible crimes they committed. But, Stalin industrialized Russia, turned it from an agricultural state into an industrial state in only two decades. Hitler, personally was a charming, considerate individual and he also ended the starvation and the deprivation of the poor in Germany and did away with the absurd Versailles Treaty---by the way, did you know that his staunchest supporters were university students? Yeah! Another aspect of That Which Must Never Be Mentioned. Had he died even as late as 1941, he would still, today, be considered a great statesman by nearly everyone."

"The problem with most people, including you, Max, is that they cannot reconcile both aspects of a Wagner. Not emotionally, that is. So, they either accept him or reject him---totally."

"I can even offer you a contemporary example. We've just been through the Jimmy Carter administration. Jimmy Carter and his minions are the closest that anyone has come to destroying this country from the inside and, regardless of all that he's done to bring this country to its knees, you *have* to appreciate that he allocated huge tracts of land as national parks, *and,* that because of him, the Southerners are no longer seen as being all racists and they are even portrayed in the mass media in a good light instead of the usual stereotypical redneck that's been put forth for years."

"Hey! I got an even better example, Maxy, in my own field: Sigmund Freud! Perfect Example! Freud was a crackpot, pure and simple. That was one sick Jew. On top of that, he was a cocaine addict. His theories---if you can call them that---they really aren't---are pure rubbish, perverted rubbish at that. There is no data anywhere to support them and he didn't offer any either, it was just backed up by his own authority, it was one of the biggest bluffs---a con job---since Mesmer. Yet, some people still swear by him, religiously, and won't hear anything bad about him. Now, here's the kicker: the . . . anti-Freudians, if you will, in rejecting Freud's pseudoscience, have trouble accepting that old Sigy did actually discover some other, important, verifiable, confirmed, psychological phenomena, that of the defense mechanisms and the 'Freudian slips.' Everything else of his is garbage, though. Freud is the rarest of all creatures: a crackpot, overrated charlatan who *also,* paradoxically, did make a few verifiable discoveries! Yet, to some, he is accepted totally, completely, and they won't hear of any faults, and to others, they reject him *in toto*. Their emotions get in the way. You see?"

Max nodded slowly, frowning. He spoke slowly. "I understand what you've said, Carla, but I still feel bad." He made a face.

Carla smiled and shrugged.

"Mussolini made the trains run on time," she said and shrugged again. "And in Italy that's nothing to sneeze at, you know."

*   *   *   *
*   *   *

It was a month later, that in a nearby university run by the Quakers, an upcoming lecture was announced. As with most other similar announcements for lectures, it was a low-key announcement spread by tasteful cardboard signs put up in various places at both universities and a small notice in both the campus and the city newspapers. It was enough. The lecture was by an individual who had traveled to Red China and to Cuba and he would be reporting about what he had seen and learned.

To the uninitiated, it would appear to be simply a lecture, a travelogue. To those in the know, it was another gathering of protoCommunists, to praise the achievements of totalitarianism. How was this known? Simple. First, traveling to those proscribed countries was a defiance of the American government's proclamations since they were renegade countries, though it could still be done legally, albeit circuitously; the only ones who did so were sympathizers of the regimes---wannabe concentration camp commandants. Additionally, the subject matter alone was an indication of the lecturer's inclinations; if the subject of a lecture was Cuba, Red China, Vietnam, or the Soviet Union, its *raison d'être* was to invariably praise the regimes ruling there. The last tell-tale sign was that it was taking place in a university, a Quaker university at that. For over a decade, Quakers, whose motto was universal brotherhood, served as a superb front for goodwill propaganda gestures---trips, gifts, lecturers, etc.—and many Quaker organizations and Quaker individuals would visit those countries where any kind of religious observance was stamped out and persecuted, where freedom of speech was a thing of the past, where the slightest disagreement with the regime's officials resulted in a bullet in the back of the head, and deplore America's unreasonable and almost irrational hostility to those "people's democratic republics."

At any rate, when Max saw the poster advertising the lecture, he knew what the contents would be and the old familiar reactions of anger and bitterness welled up.

Ordinarily, whenever Cuban refugees encountered such displays of propaganda, they were not confrontational, not *en masse* anyway, but would instead slink away, muttering angrily. This time, Max decided that it would be different. He told his parents of the event and then began the arduous process of calling up all the other Cubans in the *colonia* to cajole them to attend.

The auditorium of the Quaker university was not even a quarter full. The lecturer's hyena grin while talking of the glories of Red China and Cuba was reflected by many in the audience (it almost seemed a trademark of theirs). Mixed in with them there were half a dozen persons who had attended out of genuine curiosity. Except in one section, where the temperature seemed to be a bit warmer, mutterings in Spanish were occasionally heard and angry visages were obvious.

The lecture ran the usual course. Conditions in Cuba and China were marvelous, simply marvelous. Under the enlightened revolutionary governments, the people's living conditions---particularly The Poor---had improved immeasurably. Everyone adored The Great Helmsman. Everyone adored The Maximum Leader. People helped each other. There was no longer cutthroat competition, no stabbing each other in the back for money, we could learn a lot from them. Everyone was guaranteed a free education, free medical care, free university tuition, housing and clothing were provided for by the government. No one went hungry. No one was unemployed. Oppressive landowner's estates had been confiscated by the government and subjected to equitable distribution, with the result that peasants now owned their own land and now had plenty to eat. So there was a lot to be said for Socialism. Everyone had been helpful towards him and had welcomed him everywhere he went. No one resented his being an American; they made an important distinction between him and the American government's policies. There was no need for hostility to occur between the American people and the Chinese and Cuban peoples. Could he bring back to the American people the message that the Cuban and Chinese peoples just wanted universal brotherhood and understanding. What was so bad about trying to get along together, anyway?

Not once did he mention the Cultural Revolution, which was still taking place.

At the end of the lecture, Max took the initiative in the question and answer period.

He stood up and asked, *Me puede Ud. Decir si Ud. Vio algunos casos de personas siendo secuestrado por la policia secreta cuando Ud. esstuvo paseando por la isla?"*

"What?" The lecturer blinked.

Max repeated the question and lecturer just looked on at him, rooted to the spot, confused. Finally, he said in English, "Do you mean to tell us that you profess to be an expert in Cuban affairs and you can't even answer a simple question in Spanish?" He paused for effect. "Well, maybe you could at least tell us how many provinces Cuba has---after all, that doesn't require any knowledge of Spanish, now does it?" Max was being smart. He was not challenging the lecturer on political and moral grounds, as would be expected from a Cuban refugee, but rather he was displaying the man's ignorance to one and all. Max knew that he was on safe grounds, knowing from past experience that such individuals were notoriously ignorant of anything other than the clichés and slogans of the subject matter. Sure enough, the lecturer just stammered while the audience rustled nervously.

"My God, do you even know the name of the secret police in Cuba?" The lecturer stammered weakly that he didn't think that Cuba had the need for secret police since it was a People's Government, but Max cut him off relentlessly, saying, "Good Lord, man, just what *do* you know? Do you know *anything* about the subject matter that you're lecturing us about? Listen, let me give you a piece of information that might come in useful some time: the capital of Cuba is Havana. Store that bit of information away somewhere, you might have need for it sometime." Max melodramatically snorted with contempt. "No wonder you're up there telling us what a wonderful place Cuba has become since the Castro dictatorship---you've demonstrated that you're totally ignorant of what the devil you're talking about!" And with that, he sat down.

Everyone was thunderstruck. Even the small group of Cuban exiles had not expected the attack to come from that direction. The hyena grins had vanished.

The other Cubans followed up, but their attack was not as powerfully oblique; rather, it was crude by comparison, limiting themselves to detailing how bad conditions were in Cuba and to accusations that the lecturer was really a Communist. Actually, this crude follow-up was counterproductive in that it helped the docent to recover, because it was the type of criticism that he was expecting---if any criticism came up at all in his tour (for example, on being accused of being a Communist, it was enough to utter the magic word, "McCarthyism," to magically cancel anything else that the individual had to say; and sure enough, the lecturer made use of this magic word when he was accused of being an agent for the Communists).

Many in the audience viewed the Cubans on the other side of the audience hall as drunken gate crashers to a party.

At the completion of the spectacle, Max started to leave, anxious to watch an imminent solar eclipse at noon, which, by coincidence. Had been announced earlier, when he found himself surrounded by a semicircle of the attendees to the lecture. Momentarily alarmed, he calmed down when he saw that they were not physically threatening, being merely intellectuals wanting to question him. However, it became immediately obvious that they were hostile and, curiously, had singled him out of the other Cubans, perhaps because of his age, perhaps because of what he had said, and/or perhaps because he had not sat with the other Cubans in a group.

The verbal duel ensued.

"Excuse me, but isn't it true that just before The Revolution, Cuba was essentially an American colony?" This charge coming from an American intellectual.

"I don't really think so," said Max. "that's just one of the propaganda myths that the Communists have passed around."

"But you're too young to know," said another. "How old were you at the time, ten, eleven?"

"You'd be surprised how much you know at that age, especially when it comes to something so traumatic. In your case, it's been so long since you were ten or eleven that you probably don't remember. But, in any case, keep in mind, and perhaps you don't know, that Cubans talk politics all the time, continually, even in their sleep. If Cuba was an American colony, I would have heard the complaints."

"But, face it, you were too little to know."

"OK. I tell you what: why don't you ask my father and his friends over there? Go ahead, they're right over there." None made a move to go. Obviously, they did not really want an answer.

"Cuba *was* an American colony," someone else asserted. "The Revolution ended that."

"OK! Fine! It was an American colony, if it'll make you happy! But you know what? Right now, at this moment, it's an undeniable fact that Cuba is a *Russian* colony. There are thousands of Russian troops in Cuba. There are economic treaties trying Cuba to Russia. It's got the Russian system of government. How come you're not upset with that situation, eh?"

"That's not important!" the man snapped.

Another intellectual instantly took up the slack. "But, didn't The Revolution better The Poor People in Cuba? Haven't their lives bettered as a result of Castro?"

"OK, maybe it has. So what?"

"Eh?"

"So *what?*" No one was prepared for that.

"Does that justify a dictatorship, concentration camps, persecution? *I* don't think so. *You* might, but I don't." He followed it up with his recent finding of Nazi philanthropy.

This exchange continued, then Max went on the offensive, firmly believing that since these people were apparently intellectuals, he could make them see reason by pointing out the regime's attacks against intellectuals and intellectuals' sacred cows. He did not speak of the shortage of food, of the persecution, or everyday items, or the propaganda. Instead, he pointed out the imprisoning or disappearance of people who exercised their freedom of speech, that independent newspapers had been closed down and the journalists had been jailed, that laws were ignored, that there were no elections, that books like *Animal Farm* and *1984* had been outlawed. While he talked, most of the persons avoided eye contact, looking to the side. When he finished, one of them countered with, why should The Revolution, with all of its benefits (of which he had only heard about but believed implicitly with the religious zealotry of a Muslim) be sacrificed just because he, Max, could not read a book or two?

And . . . then . . . it hit him.

Maximiliano felt at that moment like a veil

had lifted from his eyes, allowing him for the first time to see something that had been clearly in front of him all this time. It was like a revelation---the more unnerving because it had been so very obvious all these years.

He had been so stupid, so naive.

All these years, throughout all of the verbal confrontations, he had been under the firm assumption that he had to find a way, a common ground, to make the intellectual apologists of the Marxist regimes see reason. No sane human being could possibly defend such a blatantly repressive regime, he thought. All that one had to do was to demonstrate, *indisputably,* that such crimes did occur and then the apologists would see the mistake that they had made and automatically join the side of freedom and sanity.

Now, suddenly, he knew.

He had been so stupid, so naive.

He knew now that it made *no difference* what he said or showed them. Max realized, without the slightest doubt in his mind, that these individuals in front of him were nothing less than his deadly enemies. They were representative of that pestilence of the twentieth century that had caused so much suffering to millions: the power-hungry, bitter intellectual so full of hatred. There was no *rapprochement* possible, no *modus vivendi*, because ultimately, the only acceptable situation would be with them in total power, grinding their opponents' faces under their boots while self-righteously proclaiming their liberation of "the oppressed," just as it had been in Cuba, when former friends and colleagues had suddenly turned on their countrymen and delivered their island to the Soviet Union, reverting the nation's existence to a colonial status, with Fidel Castro as a satrap of the new empire.

It made no difference whatever what Max said to them, or what proof he offered them. As the old joke went, "I've made up my mind, don't confuse me with facts." They were fanatics. And they were power hungry.

When you stripped the Communists---for this was what they really were regardless of their camouflage---of all their pious sentimentalities, and their crocodile tears over peasants and workers and their pretentious "scientific" ideology, and their indignant condemnations (based on the same "bourgeois morality" that they sneered at when applied to *their* acts of oppression), when all was said and done and they were stripped of the above, in a sense, they were nothing more than agents of a foreign power that was attempting to absorb their own country and add it to its sizable collection of captive nations, at which time they would be rewarded with positions of power.

And . . . *they did not really care at all about The Poor. Otherwise, they would have been concerned about the impoverished people in Communist countries.*

All of this passed through Max's mind in a matter of seconds, during which he was stunned, the pack of hyenas now grinning again, thinking that they had scored an important point. He recovered and now tore viciously into them with his cutting sarcasm practically dripping from his words, having previously held most of it back for fearing of alienating them and thus preventing them from coming to a mutual understanding. It was not too long before his caustic observations and his cutting insults had dispersed them and left him in possession of the field, as it used to be called.

For the first time in years, Max felt good after such an exchange.

It was a watershed experience for him and he was to regret all the missed opportunities when, in a one-to-one situation, he had not (to use the Cuban phrase) "broken the face" of one of those grinning hyenas who proclaimed his admiration for the Castro dictatorship.

Later, ruminating on his insight while driving home, two disconnected pieces of information that he had read on different occasions merged neatly in his mind with what he had experienced. One was on Galileo after he had discovered Jupiter's moons. Learned intellectuals had gathered at his home one night to argue with him, in learned terms, why Jupiter should not have moons. They steadfastly refused to look through his telescope and settle the matter once and for all in their minds, thereby verifying his discovery. The other was from *The God That Failed* wherein Arthur Koestler, who had been a Marxist at the time, was touring the Soviet Union to bask in the accomplishments of the Bolshevik Revolution. The train that he had been on had stopped at the Ukraine, which Stalin had deliberately plunged into famine. Ukrainians had approached the train begging for food and holding up their skeletal children. It had not many any impression on him. None whatsoever. He had blithely looked over those famished faces with an idiotic blank mind. Max could almost picture in his mind a hyena grin on his face.

*   *   *   *

Two of Pepe's teeth went flying as Max's fist came crashing into Pepe's grin, having taken Pepe completely by surprise. Years of piled frustration and humiliation went behind that fist. The time for talking and patient explanation was past.

XXXIV

Even though it had not been raining hard, Lucius had not wanted to go out driving. Now the rain had stopped, so he told his wife, Eve, and his two children to get ready to go. In a few minutes, they were in the car on their way to the shopping mall, glad to get out of the stuffy house.

The sky directly overhead was black, but off to a little ways out there was a clear line of demarcation where the black cloud abruptly ended and a very bright sun shone, a very surrealistic scene, but not that unusual in this part of the country.

They heard a noise. It came closer, getting louder and louder and they looked around for a train or truck. At the very last moment, Lucius understood.

A tornado.

Somewhere, in the distance, they also heard the town siren beginning to wail.

And, suddenly, it was right there.

In front of them and to one side.

The funnel cloud had almost touched the

ground. The whirling wind was swirling up dirt and debris, lifting up to meet the funnel, until there was a continuous funnel.

And then, it came for them.

It all happened very quickly. The air became oppressive. The world became dark, blotted out. Everyone screamed. The car shook furiously. The noise was deafening, but Lucius could still hear his son, Arthur, scared out of his mind, screaming "We're gonna die!"

The nightmare continued. Grit, dirt, cold, deafening noise, whirlwind, the car shaking. They felt terror, pure terror. And insignificant. They kept screaming, the kind of animal scream that no one ever wants to feel.

Whether it was a minute later, or an hour later, they could not tell, but the nightmare receded.

Eve and Lucius looked at their two sons. They, too, were alive.

"You boys OK?" she managed to croak out. The terror-stricken boys just nodded, their eyes bugging out.

"Where are we? Are we in a ditch?" she asked him. The car was at an angle, with the hood tilting slightly upwards. The windows were covered with mud.

They looked out their windows. He looked down.

"Don't nobody move," he whispered. "Don't even move a *finger!"* Everyone froze at the intensity of his command.

"We're on the roof of the Palmer building and the car's right at the edge!
If we move the wrong way, we'll go over! Don't panic! Don't move!"

Eve just stared at him, her heart racing. They

said and did nothing for a few seconds. Then Lucius spoke slowly, carefully, with complete authority, as if too many words spoke would tilt the car over.

"Boys, do *exactly* as I say . . . . Just move your hands, slowly, just your hands. Don't reach over with your whole body and see if the doors unlock."

Both doors slowly clicked open. They were not jammed shut. Lucius sighed with relief.

"Listen of me. *If* I yell out, you guys jump out. Right away. And run away from the car. But, right now, for the moment, sit still.

"Eve, very . . . carefully, go over your seat to the back. Boys, don't lean forward to grab her as she comes over."

"What about you?"

"Shut up and do it, dear. Slowly," he said carefully.

In slow motion, the wife went over the seat. At one point, the car made a small noise as it settled, which almost made Lucius yell out to his boys, but it was a false alarm.

"OK . . . now lis-ten care-fully . . . . Both boys get out slow-ly. Then, go around the car and sit on the fender. *Don't* rock the fender. *Don't* push the fender down. Just sit on it and make sure that your clothes don't get caught in the fender. Make sure of that. It's important. You can go now."

"Eve . . .when they do it, you follow them . . . slowly."

"But, what about you?"

"Dear . . . please shut your trap . . . and do as I say," he enunciated carefully.

The two boys emerged out of the car in slow motion and did as their father had told them. Eve followed and at that point the weight differential was immediately felt. The car moved slightly.

Lucius gasped.

But Eve quickly sat on the fender and the balance was restored.

Lucius now began to dislodge himself from the steering wheel, where his hands seemed to have become welded to, edged towards Eve's seat, tried to turn himself around, with difficulty, being much bigger than his wife, ready to go slowly over the seat to the back of the car. His first fear was that any sudden movement or shift in weight would tilt the balance and send the car over the edge and then it is goodbye for certain. His second fear was that if the car did go over the edge, his family might try to hold on and go over as well.

He was now turned around. First, he raised one leg over the seat.

Then, his torso.

Then, his other leg.

Without straightening up, he slowly crawled out the door on all fours. Then, he stood up.

"Thank God. We made it," he said.

They all spoke at once.

"Dad, I was so scared!"

"Me, too, Dad!"

"Honey, you had me terrified!"

"We all were, guys! Wait, I want to see something."

There was a two feet decorative ledge around the rim of the roof, over which the car rested. He went to the edge of the roof, away from the car as if it would reach out and grab him, and looked down. It was four stories. Eve and the boys were also looking down. They backed away from the edge. Now, they looked at the car propped on the edge at the rim of the roof.

Lucius became aware of his arm. His right arm was shaking, uncontrollably shaking, all by itself, of its own volition, and he stared at it as if it was another entity, totally apart from him, like a fish or a bird, and his wife also stared, and his sons stared, and they all suddenly surged together in an embrace and sobbed uncontrollably, releasing their pent up fear and tension.

XXXV

Oliver had lived his entire life in New York City, among the concrete canyons where it is impossible to see the horizon. Many New Yorkers have never seen a tree in person, much less climbed one, but not so Oliver. Oliver not only had seen one, he had actually touched it. In this, he was unusual for a New Yorker. In that he was also not obnoxious he was, likewise, uncharacteristic for New Yorkers, who are themselves uncharacteristic of Americans, since Americans are almost always friendly, courteous and helpful.

Anyway, Oliver moved for business reasons to Wichita, Kansas---actually, the outskirts. At first, the clear skies, the clean streets and the friendly people temporarily threw him into culture shock, but he recovered nicely in no time at all.

He made friends just as quickly, principally from his work.

Now, it just so happened that these men were almost all avid hunters and hunting season was approaching. So, the conversation would, sooner or later, drift into deer stands, venison, ducks, etc. Anecdotes were exchanged (and repeated) about the one that got away, unexpected stumbling into game and confrontations with the occasional vicious boar. Obviously, Oliver felt a bit left out, though he listened with increasing interest until he decided that he had been missing out and he would give this hunting hobby a try. Subconsciously, he felt that it was part of being a man.

What triggered his decision, as odd as it may sound, was when he was driving around on a weekend and saw a sign pointing out where one could pick your own strawberries for a fair price. On an impulse, Oliver stopped and did so and felt that unique pleasure that city folks get when they, for the first time in their lives, pick their own fruit from a tree, or drink ice cold milk fresh from a farm for the first time (and he also felt a secret embarrassment as he bent over to pick the ripe strawberries lying close to the ground; he had always assumed that strawberries grew on trees).

So that did it. The next time that his friends gathered round the water cooler to trade "war stories," he was ready.

He asked questions.

Two days later, he had his rifle, his ammunition and his camouflage outfit.

That weekend, Oliver set out for a distant spot that had been recommended to him by his friends. He expected to spend the whole weekend hunting.

But luck was with him. As he was driving down the country road, he saw to one side of the road a big turkey with the characteristic red wattle. It was a big one, too. With his friends' stories fresh on his mind about suddenly, unexpectedly, coming across game and stories about the ones that got away, Oliver was determined to bag this one. He stopped the car, fumbled with the rifle and ammunition (at one point almost blowing a hole through the roof), steadied the rifle against the car window frame, took careful aim and---as his colleagues had repeated told him---slowly, not jerking, squeezed the trigger.

And he got him! He shot his first turkey!

On the first time of using a rifle!

With excitement, he ran over to the bird. It was a pretty big turkey.

Right then and there he canceled the rest of his hunting weekend. He put the bird in the car trunk and headed on home.

There, he plucked the feathers, decapitated the bird, disemboweled it and cleaned it. That was a really, really messy and smelly affair and Oliver was a bit resentful that his friends hadn't warned him about it. Actually, they had, come to think of it. They had complained about the taste and smell of game and had talked about the ways of suppressing that element of hunting. With those tips fresh on his mind, he went about doing so.

Before too long, he had marinated the bird and had put it in the oven.

After a few hours of cooking, he took it out of the oven, bursting with pride.

He let it cool and took a bite. Truth to tell, it tasted awful, but he forced it down. He could only take a few more bites and decided that farm raised turkeys were the best. The gamey taste was just too powerful.

Still and all . . . he was now officially a hunter.

On Monday, as soon as it was break time at work, Oliver began to regale his coworkers with what had transpired. They were enthusiastic and encouraging, then asked for details. Oliver did so, not noticing a furrowed forehead here and there. Someone asked him to describe the turkey in detail and as he did so their eyes got bigger and bigger, until one of his listeners whispered, "Oliver . . . that, that wasn't a turkey. You didn't shoot a turkey. You shot a vulture."

XXXVI

Attendance was light, but steady, at the art museum that day. It was good weather outside, which prompted people to go outdoors and some chose the art museum.

One of the visitors to the museum was a young man in his early twenties, idealistic, with his whole life ahead of him. At this moment, he was staring at his favorite painting in rapt admiration. He would look at it, observing the details, take a rest and walk over to look at other paintings or sculpture in other rooms and then come back to worship. He had done this, sporadically visiting the museum, for he was no painter, no artist. He did not study the brush strokes of the canvases and he could not tell you why painting A was superior to painting B, and he could barely distinguish some of the schools of painting and only if they were outstandingly obvious.

As absurd as it may sound, his introduction to art had come through a newspaper article of an interview with the actor Vincent Price, who, aside from being an art collector and connoisseur, was that rarest of Hollywood actor, namely, a good and decent man, and even more unusual, an intelligent one at that, who had praised the Wichita Art Museum as one of the most underrated art museums in the country when he had visited the city. Having read the article, the young man decided to visit the museum, out of sheer curiosity, which he had never done before, figuring there must be something to it to gain such praise (that it reinforced Wichitans' feelings that their city was highly underrated, if not unknown, by the rest of the country, was not a conscious thought on his part).

Now, whenever you come across a masterpiece---a true masterpiece--- you *instantly* know it. You just know it! The work *leaps out* at you like a crouching tiger and it just seizes you. You are mesmerized, entranced, and you just stand there---awed. And what's more, you do not have to be told by someone that it is a magnificent work of art---*you know it!* You know it, even without knowing who the artist was or when it was created. In fact, the artist's identity is, in a way, unimportant.

You will be waking down a corridor, mildly interested as you look at some paintings or sculpture when, out of the corner of your eye, you see something that arrests your progress.

So, he had gone, strolling along the halls and was frankly unimpressed.

And then, he saw it.

It was a small painting called *Mortality and Immortality.* It immediately struck a chord within him, not because of the brushstrokes or the technique or the medium, but because of its theme.

The painting showed, in somber tones, a

jawless skull amidst a violin, sheet music and heavy tomes. The overall veneer of yellow-brown for the whole painting was deliberately similar to the brittle pages of old, old books and sheet music and, for that matter, that of aged bones or of violins, thereby enhancing the theme. To him, it seemed to speak volumes, that, yes, we may be mortal, we may die, but our works---our great works---live on. Mozart, Galileo, Finlay, Poe, Beethoven, Chopin, Dickens, Cervantes, Kipling, Edison, Jenner, Unamono, they may all be dead and buried, but their works are very much alive and we will remember those persons *because* of their works. Often, he drew inspiration from it and had come out of the art museum with a springier step, ready to face the world again.

He came back to the room to view the painting.

He liked to look at the minute details. He was certain that the violin must be a Stradivarius, though he had never seen one and would not recognize one if shown to him and that the notes in the sheet music, barely discernible, were from a master, Vivaldi perhaps. Having absorbed the painting, he moved around the room, wondering how the creator of such a painting could then proceed to paint such other paintings which were insipid and uninspiring.

A couple drifted in and paused in front of *Mortality and Immortality.* The man was speaking to the woman and, at the first words, which had to do with the particular painting, he drifted over to them the better to hear, eager at having found a kindred soul.

"Ah, here it is! This is one of my favorite paintings in this museum. You see how the light has been handled by the artist, and the exquisite detail given to the objects. The overall somber mood adds to the work."

The young man behind those words nodded in silent agreement as they then stared at it for a full minute before the man proceeded.

"This work speaks to me. It says that no matter what you may try to do to make yourself appear superior, write a book, or play the violin, the end result is going to be the same, death, and you're just going to end up as food for worms. All else is vanity." They contemplated it a few seconds longer and then departed.

The young man stood there, motionless, in shock, as if the man who had spoken had slapped him for no reason whatsoever.

He could not believe what he had just heard.

He actually began to get angry at what he had overheard about "his painting." It was blasphemy, sacrilege. How could the man be so stupid as to say that? How dare he! And that bimbo that he was with, why didn't she speak up? And how could such a dismal interpretation be inspiring to anyone? It was completely contrary to what the artist had intended to portray!

He looked at the canvas and wondered how anybody could be so blind as to what was right in front of their eyes, plain as could be.

He felt indignant and, yes, even personally insulted, though he could not then have told you exactly why. He peered at it to see if the man's version was anywhere on the canvas, hidden, and finally relaxed, assured that it was not there, yet still feeling incensed.

A new determination seized him. By God, he'd straighten him out! He'd show him what's what! Politely, but firmly.

He strode out of the hall in search of the couple, proceeding down one hall and looking into rooms, but they were not there, so he retraced his steps and went the opposite way but by then he was too late and they had already left.

XXXVII

The three Cubans were in the strip mall. A friend of Max's father had flown in to Wichita on business and after concluding his affairs dropped by their home to say hello. After a couple of hours, Villareal, for that was the name of his father's friend---and Max noted how even though they had known each other for years they still called each other by their last names; in fact, he noted, not for the first time, how all the Cuban men of that same generation all sported that same little moustache--- asked them if there was a shopping mall nearby. He wanted to get his wife a trinket, a souvenir. So, they had decided to go together and Max tagged along for lack of anything better to do.

Having accomplished his mission, the three had then strolled around the long strip mall and had stopped at an ice cream shop. The men ordered ice cream while the teenager ordered a pastry and milk. Apparently, all three were in the mood for something sweet, yet his father's mood had just soured.

"These Americans are so stupid," he complained. "I ordered chocolate ice cream and she says 'what? what?' I say 'chocolate' and she keeps saying 'what? what?' Come on! If you serve chocolate ice cream and vanilla ice cream, it's not that hard to figure out!" His friend nodded in agreement.

Max studied his chocolate chip cookies and smiled. As usual, it simply did not occur to his father that the fault lay with him, that his accent was so thick and his mispronunciation was so bad that at times he was unintelligible to listeners.

Besides, there were three dozen flavors to choose from.

"Here's another example," Villarreal chimed in, grabbing Max's milk carton. "Look at this. It says 'open' with an arrow pointing. Of course you're going to open at the top. How are you going to open it, from the bottom?" He replaced the milk back and Max took it up and while the adults continued talking, he opened it where the arrow pointed, mentally noting that the other side---on the top---was doubly reinforced, as was the rest of the carton, except at the spot that the arrow pointed to.

"And do you know what I heard the other day---you won't believe it," his father said. "They have colleges for farmers! Americans have to go to a university to become a campesino, a peasant? Can you believe it?'

"I can't believe it."

Max could believe it. He had studied The Green Revolution.

And now the two adults were on a roll, in a tandem diatribe as to the stupidity of Americans, particularly in the realm of politics.

Max listened to them and got angrier and angrier. Finally, he spoke up, with his usual sarcasm.

"Yes, they're stupid alright. They're so stupid that they go to the moon and the bottom of the ocean and they split the atom and every year they come back with a sack full of Nobel Prizes. And soon . . . they'll find a cure for cancer."

"Ack, what do you know," his father responded with impeccable Cuban logic.

"But they have no common sense," said Villarreal.

"These teenagers don't know a thing. Come on, let's walk around some more." So they did, Max still steamed while the two men continued, amused at the son's irritation. Presently, they finished their stroll and, still talking, but on another topic, they doubled back to near where they had parked.

They stopped to look at a window display that they had previously overlooked and, by a strange coincidence, since Wichita does not have as many foreigners as other American cities, a couple of men with different accents were arguing and gesticulating in a most un-American manner near them. They were so wrapped up in their argument that they had not really noticed the three Cubans who were overhearing them as they spoke in English. Max guessed from their physical appearance and their accent that they were from somewhere by India, or Pakistan, but kept his counsel.

And such was the bizarre coincidence that they, too, were busy lambasting Americans over some political issue, or action, by the American government, calling it "a stupid idea."

Max's father rounded on them with an angry expression, "Hey, if you don't like it here, go back where you came from!"

"Yeah, be respectful of this country when you're here!" Villarreal added. "Who do you think you are?"

"This is none of your business. We were

talking here by ourselves. We not talking to you."

"Yeah, well, but we can hear you and you're insulting this country. If you don't like it here, then go back where you came from. This isn't Russia or China, no one's stopping you," said Villareal with a very thick accent.

All four of them, each with his own thick accent, argued some more until one of the foreigners, that is, one of the Pakistanis, or Indians, or Ceylonese, or whatever, decided that it would be better to leave and so the two foreigners walked away, leaving the other foreigners, the Cubans, behind them.

"Damn foreigners," Villarreal muttered.

"Yeah. Let's just get out of here. Those two made me hot. Let's go," and they set off for the car. Neither noticed a stupefied Max behind them, rooted to the spot, with his mouth hanging open.

XXXVIII

It was Clara who suggested a little sendoff for Fatima towards the very end of the spring semester. It was going to be a quick get together at the cafeteria of the Student Union, over pizza. Clara told everyone that it was going to be a brief affair since everyone had finals to cram for, projects to finish, and homework to hand in which should have been handed in weeks before. She also warned everyone to bring a gift, or there would be no pizza; she was afraid of being the only gift-giver, which would have been very embarrassing and she knew how cheap college students are.

Like almost all Saudi Arabian women, Fatima was unattractive, but was of a very nice disposition. She had joined---actually drifted into--- the loosely knit group of fellow students that met almost every lunch hour at the cafeteria to talk about movies, classes, professors, books, politics, you name it. Occasionally they would make plans and meet at a movie theater to watch a well-publicized film and they would talk about it at school for days, with others who had not come along. There was a core group---Clara was one--- while others came and went with the vagaries of college life. One time, spotting the dark-skinned girl, she had called her over when she saw Fatima at the cafeteria---they had classes together---and Fatima had joined them. And since she was from Saudi Arabia, she had been the object of curiosity, or rather, the country was the subject of curiosity, and she had had to satisfy everyone's curiosity and answer a lot of questions. At any rate, the girl was leaving at the end of the semester to finish her degree in the KSA, transferring her American college credits, since her father, a doctor, had just finished his residency.

Anyway, Clara, Fatima and three others were sitting in one of the booths, with chairs around it. One or two of the friends would come over, have a couple of slices of pizza, talk about final exams or something, wish Fatima a good trip while giving her a small gift---she'd be missed---and hurry off to the next final---it was not the best time for sentimental goodbyes---whereupon another of their friends would show up, stressed out from the sudden onslaught of finals and term papers.

Even so, everyone was enjoying the brief time that they spent together. Fatima, it goes without saying, enjoyed the gift-wrapped trinkets that her friends brought her: books, pretty stationary, a collage of pictures of all the friends together, a scarf, a board game.

And then . . . of course . . . there was Max. Max, whom one could always count to be . . ., well, to be Max.

Max handed her a small, wrapped box.

"Oh, thank you, Max!" said the unsuspecting girl and unwrapped it. It was a curious, unfeminine, yet in a way oddly attractive chain-like bracelet. With very large links. She put it on and showed it off to the rest of the company for their admiration.

"I would have brought a bigger one, but I didn't know the size of your ankles."

"Ankles?" asked Clara, frowning, correctly expecting something from out of left field, at the same time that her friend made the same query.

"Yes," said the imp. "You're going back to Saudi Arabia and you've told you that women are not allowed to drive cars, go anywhere at all without a male relative to accompany them, can't get married without permission, can't-"

"Ma-a-a-x," growled Clara in a very threatening tone and showing her teeth.

"It's OK, Clara," Fatima laid a hand on her friend's arm. She was not annoyed. Clara was annoyed. "We've had this argument before." She was not insulted at all; amused, actually.

And it was true. To Max's taunts about women being virtual slaves in KSA, she had countered by pointing out the rampant promiscuity and drug abuse in Western women.

Yet, for all of her arguments, she had silently admitted to herself that he was right. It is just that it rankled to have a foreigner point out the unjust shortcomings of her country. No matter how true they were.

But, as far as the sendoff, Max's little antic hardly caused a stir. It was quickly glossed over and after a while the friends parted for home.

At her home, Fatima told her parents about her last meeting with her friends and showed them the little trinkets. Naturally, she also included about Max's gesture and they frowned at the telling.

Yet, later that night, her parents, independent of each other, were thinking about their daughter back in the sandy kingdom and were ambivalent. They loved their daughter and had watcher her blossom in her freedom. And yet---

And yet, they did nothing.

And yet, they did not change their minds.

A year and a half later, Fatima was sleeping in the room of her college dormitory inside the KSA. She heard shouts and she woke up.

The place was on fire!

There was smoke in the corridor and all the girls were panicking. The way towards the exit was blocked by the fire.

The firemen arrived outside the dormitory and were about to risk entering the building in order to battle the fire, or rescue the trapped girls, when the universally hated religious police arrived at the scene and forbade them to do so. Such an action would be un-Islamic, they proclaimed. Haram! They were not the girls' relatives!

The firemen argued. It was no use. If the firemen did their duty, they would be arrested on the spot and either tortured or beheaded by the fanatics.

Then the firemen suggested placing the

ladder by one of the windows to let the girls escape that way, but this, too, was forbidden---haram!--- because a female could not leave a home or a building without a male relative.

The firemen and the bystanders pleaded and argued, but it was not use and the fire spread and spread quickly. Some of the girls died from smoke inhalation. Others burned alive, shrieking from the disfiguring pain.

The very last thing that Fatima saw as she passed away was the bracelet in her wrist that a friend of her had given her a, what seemed now, a very long time ago.

TABLE OF CONTENTS

www.ingramcontent.com/pod-product-compliance
Lightning Source LLC
Chambersburg PA
CBHW060419030726
47495CB00003B/646